AUTHOR'S CUT EDITION

The Fish The Fighters & The Song-Girl

JANET & CHRIS MORRIS

Perseid Press
Box 584, Centerville MA 02632

The Fish the Fighters and the Song-girl

A Perseid Press Original
First Perseid Press Kindle Edition, April 2012
First Perseid Press Trade Paperback Edition, April 2012
First Perseid Press Electronic Edition, April 2012

Cover and illustration art: Feuerbach: *Amazonenschlacht* (detail), 1873
Cover image © Perseid Press
Cover design: Roy Mauritsen
Book design by Chris Morris and Marie Pitrat

Kindle ISBN-13: 978-0-9851668-2-3
Paperback ISBN-13: 978-1-948602-53-2
Hard cover ISBN-13: 978-1-948602-52-5
Published in the United States of America

Related Works
by
Janet Morris and Chris Morris

Novels:

Tempus (1987), Janet Morris

Beyond Sanctuary (1985), (2012), Janet Morris

Beyond the Veil (1985), Janet Morris

Beyond Wizardwall (1986), Janet Morris

City at the Edge of Time (1988), Janet & Chris Morris

Tempus Unbound (1989), Janet & Chris Morris

Storm Seed (1990), Janet & Chris Morris

The Sacred Band (2010), Janet & Chris Morris

The Fish the Fighters & the Song-girl (2010) Janet & Chris Morris

Contents

Chapter 1: Speaketh Like Men	*1*
Chapter 2: The Fish the Fighters and the Song-girl	*7*
Chapter 3: Gods Take All	*85*
Chapter 4: What Women Do Best	*93*
Chapter 5: Shelter From the Storm	*137*
Chapter 6: Power Play	*143*
Chapter 7: Strangers in the Night	*195*
Chapter 8: Pillar of Fire	*199*
Chapter 9: Joining Forces	*239*
Chapter 10: Sanctuary is For Lovers	*245*
Chapter 11: Lemnian Deed	*291*
Chapter 12: Wake of the Riddler	*297*
Chapter 13: Ravener, Where Art Thou?	*343*
Chapter 14: Red Light, Love Light	*351*
Chapter15: When the Right Song is Sung	*377*

The Fish The Fighters & The Song-Girl

AUTHOR'S CUT EDITION

Chapter 1: Speaketh Like Men

Amid a nameless wilderness, Tempus and eleven of his cavalry clustered for warmth around their campfire, mounts tethered nearby. This Sacred Band cohort had left its last posting in Sanctuary by cloud-conveyance, headed for Physca to regroup.

And ended up elsewhere. Not even Tempus knew where, or why. Yet.

Lost? His Sacred Band of Stepsons served at the pleasure of Enlil, Lord Storm, god of the armies, who had his own supernal plans. Not lost, then: diverted for celestial purpose.

So they could be anywhere, anytime: Chaetae, Thrace or even Pelasgia. Forests and plains often look alike; empires expand and contract. "We'll know soon enough, when the storm god pleases," Tempus had told Nikodemos, and Niko told Critias the same, and Crit told the rest. Now everyone was uneasy, as warriors always will be when the gods take a hand.

Traveling by way of heaven's clouds, anything can happen. Enlil is a trickster god, and Tempus ever suspicious of his tutelary's motives. Whatever Enlil has in store, the god in his head remains silent, barely breathing, just an echo in his thoughts.

The night sky above is clear, sparkling with stars; uncanny—for the storm god of the armies brings rain and wind, thunder and lightning with him, always. Always, but not this time.

The squadron talks and laughs too much. Lovers and beloveds, partners and divine friends must show themselves brave and bold in the face of the unknown. These are his best Sacred Banders: Stealth, called Nikodemos, Tempus' rightman; Fox, called Critias, the Band's task force leader; and Crit's partner, Ace, called Straton; the rest, hand-picked heroes all.

Straton was poking at the fire with a long branch when a twig snapped in the brush, and then another. Fighters sought their bows, their shortswords, their cavalry lances, shrugged into their shields. Golden Lysis, horsekeeper, ran with spear in hand, full tilt toward their mounts.

Then the youngest of their party emerged from the undergrowth with an armful of wood and wild eyes:

"I saw something," said Arton, lips blue and teeth chattering. "Out there."

Cavalrymen grumbled, relieved that their own sentry, not an enemy, had roused them. Returning from the horse line, Lysis saw hawk-faced Arton, paused, and snorted softly.

First blooded at Chaeronea, Arton was a budding seer and Lysis' partner. These newly-paired Stepsons had begged to join the advance party, volunteering to tend horses and warriors' needs. Tempus had allowed it; seasoning was what the pair needed.

When none responded to him, Arton insisted: "Sirs, Commander, I need to tell you what I saw."

Now the Band fell silent. Straton rolled blue eyes. Critias pulled on his long, patrician nose: "So tell us, Arton."

"An apparition appeared to me. It spoke. It said, 'Here lie many kinds of creatures who speaketh like men. But be ye warned, adventurer—some are not like you at all. What's done and undone can swap places if the wrong song is sung.'" Arton peered around at the fighters listening, then continued: "This *thing* had the head and breasts of a woman, the body of a lioness, the wings of an eagle, and a serpent-headed tail. I thought it was posing me a riddle but before I could answer, it disappeared."

Pairs whispered to one another, exchanging knowing glances. Arton might be young, but his foresight was valued by the Band.

"'If the wrong song is sung'? No singing, then. I hate obscure warnings," decreed Straton, the Stepsons' interrogator.

"Riddles from a woman's lips, lion's body, eagle wings and a snake-headed tail: Arton saw a Greek sphinx. We would heed an omen like that, back in Thebes," said Simias, putting a protective arm around his curly-headed partner, Perses. The youthful poet Perses for once was speechless.

From the north and east, a sudden wind begins to blow; nothing ominous yet, just a low susurrus that rustles leaves and trills on Tempus' nerves.

"Do you think this warning is for men only?" asked brash Dikti, right-side partner of Breisis and one-half of the squadron's only female pair. "Arton said 'like men.' So are Breisis and I immune? exempt?"

"This riddle's for fools only," Breisis said sharply. "A vision, seen by a boy sentry in the woods at night, and warriors take it to heart? Is this the Unified Sacred Band or a school outing? Commander, you are called 'the Riddler.' What say you?"

"I say we are in country strange to us. Niko, what does your *maat* say?"

Maat: Niko's Bandaran mystery of balance and justice, whose secular adepts fight for order in a disordered world. Tempus looked at his rightman, lover of the Theban goddess, Harmony. The sky above Niko's head still sparkled with stars but an army of clouds was on the march, east to west.

Stealth called Nikodemos replied, "Commander, my *maat* says truth is found by striving every day. Arton saw something. I don't doubt him. Or that we're not where we'd thought to be. But I say go forward cautiously until we find our way. We've faced stranger than this with less concern, a hundred times. Maybe it's the stragglers' influence, some echo of Meridian, calling to its own…" Niko looked at Dikti and Breisis coldly: two stragglers, Lemnian-born mercenaries recruited by Critias after the war was won, their loyalties as yet untested.

"Is that what you sense, Niko? Residual strangeness in the proportion?" Tempus said, very low. "If so, well and good. Let it come."

Niko shifted slightly, feeling for his shield and bow beside him in the grass.

When the Sacred Band defeated the army of Meridian, they loosed unpredictable forces on an unsuspecting time and place: revenants and relics of empires lost and to be lost. So Tempus had ordered his cadre north, hoping the vanquished would follow; even brought Breisis and Dikti with his men to help lure other stragglers in their wake. Whatever awaited his Stepsons in the aftermath of the Great War, they'd face it squarely, but face it upcountry.

In open country, where ghosts were few and memories fewer still. Far away from too many women and witches and goddesses and compromises, Tempus' fighters would fare better. And Enlil had agreed. They would sortie to Physca, and from there to Lemuria where a broad strategy could be planned, repercussions evaluated. So what *was* this sojourn of Enlil's into a realm unknown, where the first being they'd met was inhuman?

"Stragglers, is it? Following us? We beat them last time. We'll beat them again," said Straton. "A little brisk skirmishing's just the thing to keep us on our toes. But first, Arton—and Lysis—dish out our dinner. Heroes need to eat."

"Yes, eat. No portents tonight," said sharp-tongued Dikti as Arton and Lysis began ladling a steaming stew. "Critias, Straton: give us a tale of stirring exploits, bold Stepsons, to raise everyone's mettle while our supper cools."

"Tell us a tale to raise more than mettle, Strat," Crit suggested with his sly, cynical smile, trying to improve the mood in the camp.

A pair who'd been with the Band from earliest days caught Niko's attention, iron-eyed and somber. Niko leaned a bit closer to Tempus and said under his breath, "Riddler, remember what Arton said."

Tempus merely nodded. Beside him, Nikodemos was strung tight as a bow now.

"A tale, as you command, Critias." Strat rubbed his bearded jaw. "What story, then? How about telling how we came to recruit our two ladies of the point and the edge? That's heroic in itself…" proposed Straton in his most rumbly, confidential voice, so the words mixed with the thunder coming near and nine fighters leaned forward to hear him…

Chapter 2: The Fish the Fighters and the Song-girl

What did they do that I cannot do, beloved warrior,
Your bold-tongued leaders who enflamed your fierce desire?
Now you are hot for fighting.
You long to throw yourself against the body of your enemy, not mine;
And pierce his flesh, not mine.
What did they say, your bold-tongued leaders,
That I cannot say to win your love?
How now shall I pray, when you have battle pounding in your blood
And your heart is hard like bronze?
Come back to me unbroken, unharmed.
You live to breathe war's fury.
I live for the sight of you returning,
Your fine skin covered in armor, your beautiful head covered in glory,
Your bright shield and your ash spear in your hand.
Come back to me.

*

After the battle for the land of dreams, the losers straggled by threes and fours and sixes toward an ochre-walled city. They were dazed and hurt and lost in a strange country, with no way home. Some once were warriors from Macedon and Mygdonia and Megara and farther realms. Some were deserters who'd thrown away their shields and run. Some, abandoned, wandered off when the war was done. Some were conscripts, helots and slaves who'd dressed the soldiers and milled their grain and served their pleasure. Some were dreamers from Meridian, waking from nightmares ages long; some were dead and resurrected to fight the dream lord's foredoomed war. All were hungry, desperate and confused.

"What poor citadel is this?" said one big fighter to another man as their group of six limped and stumbled from a hayfield onto a road leading to the city gates. "It's not anywhere I know."

"Who cares?" said a third fighter, a woman just as big and just as tall and just as armored.

"We will make our way here," said a smaller, stout woman who used a broken javelin as a walking stick. "Trust in me. All cities are alike. But hurry. We want to be in before dark."

Behind her, a girl in a maiden's short skirt sang quietly of a hero and love and glory.

Then the last man said, "Cavalry." He dropped to his knees and put his ear to the road. "Lots of them. Coming fast from the north. *Hide.*"

So they scrambled back into the ditch and threw themselves flat in the field to wait while the victors thundered by in proud ranks of four on their tall horses. All that time, the girl softly sang her ancient song, until the stout woman stopped her mouth with a horny hand.

*

"Stepson!" called Hakiem the taleteller to the mercenary astride a brown warhorse. "Have you a coin for an old man in exchange for a bit of news?" Late summer day in Sanctuary: sunlight dwindling; sea air muggy and pungent; dockside boards tacky with salt.

The helmeted rider slowly turned his head Hakiem's way, paused, then carefully urged his mount up close and halted with a hand on his shortsword's pommel. This was one of Tempus' new boys. Hakiem didn't know him.

"Tell me where to find a boat that fishes for kite-shaped rays," said the cavalryman, taking off his helmet, "and I'll make it worth your while, old man." A fighter most striking was this one, a youth just tempered by manhood, his words clipped and edged with sibilants from beyond Wizardwall's high peaks.

Down Wideway at the pier, boats were putting in early from a day's fishing, chased to port by thunderstorms riling up the sea out where the sky was purple and black. "Come closer, Stepson, and say what you will pay."

The soldier hooked his helmet on his saddle and dismounted. He had a kind eye for a killer, curly brown hair tied back, and a lithe body that whispered of Tempus' Sacred Band of Stepsons—paired lovers and brothers and friends who were keeping order in Sanctuary once again. Tempus and his fighters had come riding back to town, wild weather and wilder gods and goddesses nipping at their heels. War and death and sorcery howled like cyclones in their wake, and nothing was the same thereafter.

"I will pay what it's worth, for helping me find the kite-ray I need," said the tall warrior in the Band's summer panoply of linen and leather, iron and bronze. "That's all I want from you today, Grandfather. I am called Cassander. Who are you?"

"*I* am Hakiem." *Every*body knew Hakiem. "Cas*san*der…" said the storyteller, slowly sounding out the fighter's name. "Your commander, Tempus, values my news of men and gods." This Stepson was definitely new hereabouts—and bold in a quiet way. "And I know what boat you'll want, for such a fish. Let me warn you, though, fish come dear these days. First the drought and then the storms… food is scarce. But you wouldn't notice that, eating what the palace sends you."

Now that the Sacred Band was back in town, everything, including weather, was topsy-turvy. Drought had fled before tempests from the angry sea as two returning storm gods, Enlil and Vashanka, reminded mortals who was who in heaven. First too little rain, then too much, brought the same result: crops ruined in the fields and ochre-walled Sanctuary staring Famine in the face. Moreover, a foreign deity named Harmony (black-armored goddess of love in war) had come from a world away with the Band, settling in with her Thebans and her sunshine out at the Stepsons' barracks. Priests and even common folk had seen her, dispensing justice with a sword beside her faithful, walking among her fighters in a red-crested helm and lifting her dead up to heaven on pillars of balefire.

"Tell me where to find my kite-ray, Hakiem, and I'll be on my way. I'm late as it is." The soldier dug in his purse and handed Hakiem a copper without checking its value, his probing eyes dark as the swells behind him. "If you have a message for my commander, I'll take it." Just a hint of a jackal's grin.

Hakiem pointed out a boat, tacking shoreward. "Yonder boat, Stepson, for your bottom-dwelling ray. But be careful of those sailors. They'll have more than fish waiting for such as you." This Cassander was riding alone; Stepsons didn't, normally. Even Tempus' unpaired mercenaries patrolled by twos this season, while Sanctuary smarted under more law and order than it liked. Some Sacred Banders had been injured or killed in the streets and in the fighting north of town; perhaps this one had lost his partner.

"My thanks for the warning, Hakiem," said the fighter dryly, as if nothing docking here today could threaten him. Nevertheless he squinted around and over his shoulder, professionally cautious, a survivor of a war in which too many of his brethren had died this summer.

"It's our pleasure to serve Tempus' forces. Convey my sympathies to your commander for his casualties from the fighting."

On too many days, funerary pyres had blazed high behind barracks walls. Fires had razed first the Stepsons' stables and next the town's decrepit Mageguild. Then, not far north of Sanctuary, war broke out: Aškelon, ancient demiurge, and the Riddler, called Tempus, battled until corpses were piled high and buried where they fell.

"Any other message for my commander?" The boy was ready to be on his way, looking out to sea where the oncoming storm raced one last fishing boat to port. A wet wind, picking up, moaned in Hakiem's ears and blew white hair around his face.

"You can tell the Riddler exactly this: that dreams are running wild in the palace and in the streets. And though you all may think you're out of danger, you are not. Many say you Stepsons are too much help for our little city-state. Some complain your hand is too heavy on our town; your Theban brothers' ways, too foreign. And deeds from thoughts and dreams do spring."

Now that the war was over, out at the Stepson barracks nearly a hundred fighters had settled in, policing Sanctuary for the palace, training for none knew what. In war's wake, Sanctuary's mean streets got meaner: all the stranded remnants of Aškelon's vanquished army straggled into town, confused and hopeless, bloodlust and vengeance in their hearts. Meanwhile, everywhere in town, dreams were out of hand. Men will dream of high adventure and women of taming fickle hearts, ever. But these dreams were different. These dreams were coming true: dreams of power, dreams of glory, dreams of love and dreams of death, all stealing into sleeping hearts and turning restless heads. True dreams or false, in Sanctuary dreams were for interpreting by priests and seers; for heeding by superstitious seamen and oligarchs; for bringing to life, if you were of a certain esoteric bent or sorcerous mind.

"Can you speak more plainly, old man?" asked the Stepson, watching the black and red fishing boat ship its oars and glide in to dock, ropes and ladders ready at forecastle and stern.

"Tell Tempus to look close about him, at his boys and their more-than-mortal friends. Tell him the Theban goddess has a curse on her and so does his pet witch. So beware. Troubles are coming, trundling after them like bastard children."

"That's enough, old man." Skin around wide eyes crinkling, the fighter stepped one pace back, then two, his bristle-jawed face guarded. "Curse on the victors, is it? If envy is a curse, then you're right. I'll not take that message to the commander."

"Then take it to his boy, you know the one—the special one, Nikodemos. And you tell Tempus what I said about the dreams, Cassander. Some dreams shouldn't come true."

The Stepson swung up on his horse: "A good evening to you, too, storyteller." Then he turned his mount and headed down the pier toward the fishing boat with crewmen furling its sail.

*

When Tempus rode his Trôs horse down into the valley beyond the Stepsons' overlook, Nikodemos was easy to find, instructing two sweating trainees at his gravel pond. Niko saw him coming and left the youths, climbing the slope on foot.

"Something's not right, Commander," Niko said when he reached Tempus' gray horse.

"Imagine that." Thunderheads rolled in from the east, growling; their breath stirred Niko's hair, just growing out after the storm god's war.

"Commander, I'm not imagining this." Hazel eyes met his own and shocked him. Sunlight kissed Niko's cheek from the west, as if to remind Tempus that this partner of his was the newly immortalized avatar of Harmony, the Theban goddess of balance and justice. Overhead, the weather from west and east clashed in battle, spears of sunshine fighting off a phalanx of cloud.

"So?" Once these were feral fields where wild horses and deer grazed among the grass and heather and roses climbed the slopes. Then came the Battle of Meridian, its army manifesting out of place and time, here where so many now were buried: soldiers and revenants, ghosts and dreaming dead. If Critias, Tempus' executive officer, had given Tempus such a warning, detail would follow: what was wrong, and where, and how to fix it. But this was Stealth, called Nikodemos, a Bandaran-trained warrior-monk, chary of words, and the best of his Stepsons. "Enlightenment steers all things through all things, Niko. You say something's not right. What?"

"Look at the sky, Riddler. Can't you feel it too?"

He could feel it; he just didn't like it: unrest in heaven meant chaos on earth: they'd just fought a war to restore celestial balance. And succeeded. Some of his Sacred Band of Stepsons called it the Great War. Perhaps it was. Wars don't bring lasting peace, only lasting death. His fighters had brought death aplenty, destroying an age-old enemy, an entelechy of great power. In so doing, they'd upset a fundamental order: all that once was controlled by Aškelon, lord of dream and shadow, regent of the seventh sphere, was now free to maraud among the worlds of men and gods. And theomachy was Tempus' war, always.

Thunder growled again; louder, closer. The god in Tempus' head growled too, shoving him aside in his own skull, peering out from his eyes: Enlil, storm god of the armies, agreed with Niko.

Not now, Ravener, Tempus told the god. *Not yet. My fighters are still weary, well and truly spent in Your cause. They need to rest and grieve and heal. Are You bored so soon? Looking for some new havoc to wreak?*

Enlil didn't answer, unless his answer was the booming of the oncoming storm.

"Niko, tell me what you want me to do about warring weather and heavenly disputes. Or what your goddess wants you to do." This fighter was complicated, a hero just made, uncomfortable with the immortality that the Theban goddess had burned into him—a foreign goddess for a man who was a secular adept and revered only his mystery of *maat*, his discipline of mystic calm. Until *she* came and changed him. Tempus had been down Niko's path and lived through such pain as mortals never know, recovering flesh from every wound but never soul, century after century, war after war.

"Harmony hasn't come to me lately." Reticent. "She comes and goes as she pleases—you know that, Riddler." A silence lasted too long. Finally Niko added, "Let me show you what Arton did. Maybe that will explain." Young Arton was one of Niko's trainees, the prescient one, who fought first at the Battle of Chaeronea with Tempus' Sacred Band and then was wounded in the Battle of Meridian. Niko reached for the Trôs horse's bridle and the man-killing stallion allowed it with nary a snort nor a snap.

Tempus swung his right leg over the stud's neck, cavalry-style, sliding down, butt to horse: never expose your back to an enemy. Ingrained caution for a man whose body healed from every enemy wound. Though there was no enemy here today. The ground was damp beneath his unshod feet, as if the blood of the slain still soaked the turf.

Today the Unified Sacred Band was building a training camp in the valley, beyond Sanctuary's sway, over graves trying to sprout green grass among the brown as the wet summer died. Hammering and banter from Sacred Banders and Stepsons down the valley near the creek mixed with approaching thunder. Southeast, Tempus could see black clouds racing toward the walled city and the old Stepsons' barracks.

Without another word, Niko led him down the hillside to the dark Stepson, Arton, and Lysis, his golden Theban partner: both stripped to their waists, raking the Bandaran-style gravel pond.

"Tell the commander what you told me, Arton," Niko ordered.

"Sir, you said to tell you whenever I… have a vision. This is it, in the gravel, what I saw," said the hawk-faced Arton nervously. "Something's coming, Commander."

Shaking his head, Lysis stepped carefully out of the gravel pond, put down his rake and looked first at his feet, then to Niko for guidance. Lysis had saved Tempus' stallion once: the Thebans said their goddess had blessed this young Sacred

Bander with a special gift for horses. Eyes downcast, Lysis came up and took the Trôs' reins; the horse followed him meekly toward two geldings tied to a nearby tree with Niko's goddess-given stud.

Niko hunkered down and stared at Arton's design, then up at Tempus: Arton had driven the butt of his rake into the center of the pond and raked a pattern: not a spiral, but concentric circles, none touching another, as if he'd thrown a rock into still water.

"Or something's here," Niko said.

*

"No, a live one. Or two," said Cassander, looking down from atop his horse at the fishing boat's captain, swarthy and squat, chewing a cud and spitting brown juice on his deck near the black kite-ray the crew had thrown there. "If you catch me the spotted kind—and big, not like this dead juvenile—I will pay a third more."

The little boat rocked and thumped against the wharf as the chop worsened, tugging on its lines like a horse anxious to be away. Lightning stabbed from heaven into the sea; thunder cracked: Lord Storm's blessing for this enterprise, any Stepson would say.

Behind the fishing boat's captain, amid bins of fresh catch, crewmen clustered, sizing up the Sacred Bander: whispering together, smirking and elbowing their fellows, caressing filet knives on their hips.

"He doesn't want this one," the captain barked over his shoulder, toeing the black ray on the deck at his feet. "He wants only lively ones. Back to work. We'll catch him some for tomorrow." Watery eyes in a wind-burned face fixed on him. "And you'll leave a deposit, soldier?"

Not likely. "A live one, or two, I said. By tomorrow, sundown, or I don't want any at all. When it moves, I'll pay for it." Cassander clucked once, shifted; his horse backed up one step, then another.

The adolescent ray quivered. Cassander saw it.

The captain did: "Get me a fish sack."

Men went running to find a leather sack and fill it with brine, but the Stepson didn't stay his horse. He needed a fish that would live to reach the barracks.

"Take this one… and if it dies," the captain called after him, "I'll give you one extra tomorrow when you come to get your order. Half the price."

Cassander halted his mount. He couldn't resist the kite-ray but only a fool would get off a horse and step onto that deck, alone, with the storm blowing in and the dusk coming down like a blanket overhead. Not with a predatory crew waiting to rob him and gut him and throw him over the side.

"Bag it and have one of yours carry it over here, then. I'll bring a wagon tomorrow. And my own tanks." This half-dead kite-ray wasn't worth much trouble, but he would take what he could get. He was really late now.

*

"He's beautiful," the girl sighed from shadows. "Like a hero from a song." Then she chanted on a whisper, "Sing of angry blood on shining shields and men, fierce-hearted, who never yield, kissing death before dishonor. Sing the gods who curse them for their long-haired pride and blind their eyes with love's sweet mist, these heroes who dare battle on the hallowed plain of heaven…"

"Is he all that, now? I'm beautiful too, don't you think? I'm just as tall," the big fighting woman whispered back.

"Hush," ordered the short, stout woman and the other two did as they were bid. "Once we find lodging there'll be time for gawking and gathering what wild fruit ye may. Meanwhile, let's sing those fishermen a song or two and get us one of those fish. If that soldier wants one, others will. And you can be sure it's worth more than he's paying."

*

Long summer evening; storm overhead, soughing in his ears, keeping Gyskouras safe. The god Vashanka's lightning makes the heavens pulse with glory, luminous and deep. Although his god is with him, the Stepson he's meeting here is late.

Outside the Vulgar Unicorn, Kouras sits astride his blue roan in the rain and waits as the gusts grow fiercer. Where is Cassander? Something must have happened. In Sanctuary, all plans go awry. He shouldn't be surprised. But Kouras is the son of Vashanka, the storm god's own blood, and expects the godly Pillager to clear his way.

He slides off the roan and ties it to a post, hanging his helmet on his saddle. Then he goes indoors. Too many watch his every move. They know who he is: the Stepson proclaimed Vashanka's avatar earlier this summer in a ritual copulation witnessed by Sanctuary's ruling class.

Knowing the city's elite have seen you naked doesn't help when you're in the worst part of town.

Just say something. Anything. I dare you all. He steps up to the bar to order ale. Two move aside to make room. Conversation around him stops. He's accustomed to it now, but it still irks him. Thunder smacks its lips outside. Whenever he loses his temper, the skies open up. Lightning flares sky-wide.

He needs to get to the palace. He's certain now that he should have told Cassander to meet him there, not here.

Too late. This bar is infamous: sawdust on the floor to soak up the blood that's shed here nightly; rough men, slovenly women, unfriendly faces and the smell of garlic. They all cleave together, these regulars of despair. Any Stepson in this place, even the storm god's son, ought to have a partner beside him.

The barman comes up: "Well, young avatar of Vashanka, it's an honor to serve thee. What's thy pleasure? Or is there a problem? We're all aboveboard, here."

Kouras can smell the drugs, smoke wafting up from the cellar and the catacombs below. His skin crawls. He's been trained in Bandara's misty isles to sense what others feel. Hostility washes over him in waves: from a nearby table where six sit, soaked and soused; from down the bar to his left, where two youths his age and weight appraise him.

He said, "Ale," ignoring the taunting manner of this barkeep. *Make light of me and my god? I am Vashanka's true son and all Sanctuary knows it: every fool here has heard about the rite that night, when thunder rolled indoors and the pillager god came into me. So watch how you go, barkeep.*

The two on his left sidled away, flickers in the corner of his vision. His dagger leapt into his hand. They looked at him sidelong. Patrons gave back. He started cleaning his nails as he'd seen Critias, the Band's task force leader, do once. The two young roustabouts muttered, tossing their coins on the bar as they left. The sounds were too loud in a room gone quiet as a battlefield when the fighting has stopped.

His drink arrived as Cassander strode in, all helmeted Stepson and hurried, and paused just across the threshold, double-headed cavalry lance and shield in hand.

"Kouras, we need to go. Now."

"You got one?" Kouras took a swig of his ale, sheathed his knife, and dropped a copper on the bar. Not how he'd envisioned this evening.

"It won't live long," said Cassander.

Everyone turned to stare at the scale-armored cavalryman by the door.

Good. Let them wonder. Cassander looked as formidable as he was: a seasoned fighter, one of the best of the Band. Kouras swaggered a bit. Now there were two of them, enough to do for this whole room if trouble started.

But it didn't. Not in the Unicorn. Not until they got outside in the blowing rain and mounted their horses, saddles slick and reins slippery.

Cassander had a sack like a big wineskin dangling from his saddle. "Let's hurry, if you still want me to look at your palace girl. I have to get this kite-ray to Critias before it dies. It won't last long in this leaky sack."

"I need you to see her—"

The two young toughs from the bar came out of wet nowhere with three, then four friends Kouras hadn't noticed inside. None were armored. All were armed. Silent. Two went for his horse's head without a word, knives glittering in the wavering torchlight to either side of the Unicorn's door. One grabbed his leg, trying to drag him from his horse. The roan screamed and reared, the only sound until thunder roared again.

Kouras dropped his reins, telling the roan, "Kill," with a thrill that startled him as much as the lightning that struck then in their midst. Their adversaries staggered back, rubbing their eyes, slipping on wet cobbles, cursing in the names of foreign gods. He drew his curved shortsword with his right hand, then gathered a fistful of Bandaran throwing stars from his belt with his left. The smell of the lightning was heady. *Now, Father Vashanka, I need Thee, Thy power and Thy glory.*

The god's speed comes into him. The stormgod Vashanka rises up in him, raging in his skull, glaring through his eyes. Rain whirls around them. Throwing stars fly from his fingers. He'd have preferred to use his sword, but the targets are too near his horse's head. Kouras downs the two toughs trying to pull him from his saddle. He only dimly sees Cassander, masked by the squall, thrusting underhand with his spear at three attackers.

Kouras put his right leg into the roan as another foe came up on Cassander from behind.

Without turning, Cassander thrust backward with his lance. The lance was jerked from his grip, locked between this adversary's ribs as the man fell to the ground.

"Seek," Kouras told his horse. The roan lunged forward, nearly unseating him. He saw Cassander's sword flash up, then down. Sparks flew as iron grated on iron. Blood flowed black in the torchlight. Then the roan was on Cassander's right, barging and bumping into Cassander's mount, more swiftly than Kouras had thought a horse could move.

Kouras slashes at one attacker and his curved short-sword shivers, cutting through shoulder, muscle and bone, separating the man's arm from his trunk. Leaning low on his horse's neck, he hacks at a second man, swinging down and hard to the right, across his assailant's midsection. The man's mouth opens wide in a silent scream as he drops like a stone.

The thrust and slash of Cassander's shortsword in the rainy skirmish seem too slow to Kouras, whose hand is speeded by the god. Cassander's sword finally connects, slicing down from right to left, and the last foe drops without a whimper.

Lightning forked again; thunder clapped as if heaven beat its chest. When Kouras blinked the afterglow away, Cassander was staring at him, wiping his blade on his *chlamys*. Beyond, in the Unicorn's doorway, patrons jostled one another, chuckling nervously, making good on their bets, trying to get out of sight now that the show was over.

"Friends of yours, Kouras?"

One tough still rattled softly, covered in blood, not even trying to drag himself away. Cassander's lance stuck skyward out of his chest like a battle standard.

Kouras reminded himself that he couldn't dispatch the wounded; this wasn't a battleplain. They were here to keep the peace, or restore it.

"More likely friends of yours," Kouras said. "What now?"

"Watch the live one," Cassander said. As he guided his horse past the dying man, the Stepson paused. Leaning down, he pushed and jerked his two-headed lance free from flesh and bone. Then he rode over to the Unicorn's doorway and, ducking his head slightly, halfway into it.

Kouras watched carefully for any last missile to be thrown, any death's-door revenge, but the doomed man only coughed and wheezed; then the wheezing ceased.

"We'll send some Sacred Banders back to clean up this mess, if you can't," Cassander called out.

Someone inside the tavern answered, "No, no. We'll see to it."

Cassander backed up his horse three steps, then wheeled it round. "Now we go to the palace, Kouras—if you still need to go there."

He did. They did.

Riding up Processional Way toward the palace, Kouras could barely hear: his blood thumped in his ears, his pulse pounding so fast it seemed two hearts beat in his chest as one—his and the god's. *Thank You, Father. My heart and hand are Thine.*

Cassander didn't say another word to him until they entered the palace compound and second-watch sentries took their horses:

"You're quicker than I thought, Kouras." Sliding off his horse, Cassander slipped his lance through his shield's handholds, exchanged his shield and helmet for the sack tied to his pommel, then slung the sack over his shoulder. "Quicker than I've seen, except for the commander."

"A gift from the storm god." *Godspeed.* Tempus had it, every Stepson knew. Now Kouras had it, for certain, this gift of heaven. Cassander had seen it, firsthand. Soon the whole Band would hear of it. "From Vashanka."

"Can you get me one, too? A gift like that's worth a bowed head and bended knee." Cassander jogged beside Kouras up the stairs in the rain.

"It doesn't work like that," Kouras said. "It's in the blood." *And with that gift comes all Vashanka's ungovernable anger, blazing in your veins.*

"I should have known. Up *here*?" Cassander looked dubiously at the imposing palace entrance with its liveried guard as they climbed the final stairs.

"Just come this way," Kouras said. "Your sack is dripping a little."

All palace doors open before Kouras. He felt proud, bringing this accomplished Sacred Bander along. "Get Torch," Kouras told the guards stationed at the tall oak doors.

Then they were inside the palace proper, out of the god's rain, in the black and white stone foyer with its fragrant cedar beams, its paintings and gilt.

"Tell me about her… this girl we've come to see." Cassander fingered the sack and then lay it down as they waited for the priest. The fish inside shifted and flopped.

"She's pregnant, we hope. But she's not right. She's sick all the time. Her feet are swollen. And her legs. It's too soon for that, isn't it? I don't trust the healers here."

"She's not a horse. I can't stick my arm up her and feel around. And I can't tell much from what you're saying. Women aren't my normal victims." Crouched over the sack, Cassander grinned a feral grin and looked Kouras in the eye. "This little ray can't do anyone else much good, the shape he's in. If they get us a basin, we'll try him on her. I'll never get him to Critias before we lose the seawater. That scuffle took too long."

"Torchholder will—"

"—will what?" Vashanka's priest, Molin Torchholder, descended the last few stairs with a flurry of robes and a concerned scowl.

"Molin, can you send someone to get some more brine right away? And some sand? And some live bait? And to the Shambles Cross station to get the wagon Critias prepared? We came here instead. This is Cassander. He's going to look at Seriti. He's the Stepsons' healer."

Cassander got up, wiping his hand on his hip, slinging the sack over his shoulder. "Nothing so grand as that, Eminence. But I work on wounded men and horses when we have them. Know a few things."

"Come this way, Stepson. If Gyskouras wants you to look at Seriti, then do so with Vashanka's blessing. It's the storm god's child inside her, after all."

"I'll need two clean, large bowls filled with hot water; some wool bandage for the two of us, and one empty basin or tank big enough for this." Cassander poked the leather sack on his back. "Both of us need to wash up. We had a little tussle outside the Unicorn. If you're sending someone to Critias, better tell him that."

Not until then did Kouras realize how much blood had spattered him, or that he had a stinging slash on his arm and a slice on his leg, both dripping bright red, or that Cassander was bloody as well. Kouras' wounds would heal fast; they always did: gift of the god.

Torchholder bawled orders to his staff.

As they headed up the broad marble stair with Torch in the lead, Cassander said, "Now, this is the priestess from the ceremony? That's why you think it's the storm god's baby she's carrying, not Kouras'?"

"I don't *think.* I *know.* They're always sickly when they carry the god's child. It's a strain for a mortal." Torchholder's pasty face was set and sour. "She'll survive. Vashanka wants this child."

Up more stairs and down two halls and there she was, on a silken pallet, with circles under her beautiful eyes. Servants brought steaming bowls and set them beside her, put an empty basin at her feet, and scurried away when Torchholder banished them.

Somehow, with Cassander here, Kouras felt reassured. He recalled Cassander's gentle hands, tending him when he was wounded.

"Sit up, my lady, if you can," Cassander told the priestess. "We should be able to ease your pain and bring down the swelling in your legs, if you do as you're told."

She stared at Kouras with eyes like a wounded fawn, dark hair making her skin seem too white for the living.

Then Cassander washed and Kouras did too, while the wizard-eyed priest studied them from Seriti's bedside. The healer's sure fingers bandaged Kouras' wounds before wrapping his own. "Kouras, you need to leave me alone with her and take Torchholder with you."

"No, I want to help you. You need help treating her, don't you?"

"This is going to be disturbing for you and the priest." Nevertheless, both Kouras and Torch stayed.

Seriti whimpered and wept once Cassander poured the sandy seawater and the kite-ray into the basin and explained what he was going to do and what she must do, and what the fish would do.

Despite everything he'd seen and done in battle, Kouras found that the healer was right: helping Cassander keep Seriti's feet on the ray's back, no matter how she jerked and sobbed, was one of the hardest things Kouras had ever done.

Every time Seriti cried out, the storm god in his head growled like a guard dog.

*

"The gods gave us horses so we wouldn't have to fight on foot," Straton reminded Critias as they leaned on the training field's fence to watch the exercise under way. Crit's legs and back ached too much for him to take part today.

On the cool breeze at midday, infantry maneuver codes ring out from Theban pipes; cavalry whistles and catcalls answer back. Stepsons on horses against Thebans on foot: strength to strength; too good a contest for any fighter to resist. Both sides want to win today, drill or no drill. Cadre honor is on the line for Stepsons and Thebans both. Light cavalry archers, recurved bows ready (armed with practice flights tipped in leather and dye, not iron), grouse and sneer at the dressed infantry formation before them, waiting their turn to try breaching the Theban line.

Straton was Crit's right-side partner and the best friend he'd ever had. Crit knew Strat resented taking instruction from Theban newcomers to Tempus' Sacred Band, but this tutorial was good for everyone: strong feelings aired and rivalries harnessed for the betterment of all. Straton spoke for many veteran Stepsons when he said bluntly: "Hoplite tactics for breaking enemy lines are all well and good, but we're cavalry. If this is how Gorgias got his face smashed, rolling in under enemy shields, then no man of ours in his right mind will want to try it."

"You know it's exactly how he got that face, Strat." Critias touched his partner's arm. "But our Thebans need to show us what they know. They learn from us; we learn from them. The more expert in an enemy's tactics, the better to meet him and defeat him. Anyway, it's good seasoning for the horses, facing phalanxes." *Hoplites with nine-foot dorys and eighteen-foot sarissas: horses don't like charging walls of shields and long spears. We didn't fare so well against endless ranks of foot, last time. Next time, we'll do better.*

Before them on the training field, five ranks of six men each were crouched: Theban Sacred Banders in linen and leather, greaves and helmets; shields overlapping, leather-wrapped spearheads bristling through. Not a line long enough or deep enough for conclusive combat, but good for the purpose, here today.

At least the rain had stopped. Theban hoplites set their *dorys'* butt-spikes deeper into muddy ground. At the far end of the training field, a dozen Stepsons on foot with repeating crossbows stepped up to shoot volleys overhead, simulating a rain of deadlier bolts, while other fighters on foot and mounted waited to try their luck with spear or double-headed lance or sword and shield.

"Enemy, Crit? What enemy would that be?"

No one knew what the Riddler was preparing them for, but preparing they were.

"Any enemy. It's a training camp, by Tempus' decree. So we train."

Dark Gorgias shouted a Theban war cry and ran forward alone, demonstrating his technique. He somersaulted and rolled with his shield on his arm. *Not easy: Roll with your left shoulder in your shield and come up holding a drawn sword in your right hand without gashing yourself.*

Gorgias tumbled under the shields of Theban hoplites raised to protect against archers' arrows, coming up into a crouch, drawing his curved *kopis,* a single-edged shortsword, to hamstring and maim whom he could, howling a Theban curse. Then stopped just short of mayhem as one veteran Theban, Charon, slammed a shield down toward his helmeted head, made contact, and paused with a kissing noise.

No single defender against this rolling tactic could get a spear freed up or even move backward or sideways unless they all did, so tight were the Thebans grouped with their shields angled skyward, protecting against any flight of arrows showering down. Once one man or two fell or gave way, cavalry could smash the hoplite line wide open. In combat, arrows would be armor-piercing, iron-tipped, barbed and painted with poison; dropping a shield meant putting the man on your left at risk from flying missiles. Sometimes you had to chance it, to keep a worse fate at bay. This was clearly how Gorgias had gotten his face smashed once… or twice: one example of the tactics that had made the Sacred Band of Thebes ascendant for forty years… until the massacre at Chaeronea.

Gorgias ordered, "Shield up, Charon."

The leader of the Stepsons' Theban contingent obeyed his dark-skinned, dark-haired, dark-eyed trainer, who rolled backward out of striking distance and to his feet.

"Now let's try it with enough line-breakers on foot to do the job, horses behind, and one more volley of arrows to keep my girls honest," Gorgias proposed. No one disagreed.

"Somebody'll get hurt," Straton prophesied, laconic and correct.

"Better on the training field than the battlefield," Crit replied. "I know how you're looking forward to scuffling in the mud, but—"

A hand came down on Critias' shoulder, so large and strong Crit had no doubt whose it was.

"Riddler," Critias said to Tempus, their commander, as he turned; "and Stealth," to the commander's right-side partner, Nikodemos: a clean-limbed, balanced force who looked at Crit askance today and every day.

Tempus, called the Riddler: Straton's height but more massive, ancient and immortalized, favorite of the storm god Enlil. Crit's breath comes sneaking into his chest while those long, hooded eyes strip him to his soul once more. Tempus never takes you for granted: he weighs you every time he sees you, chooses you all over again.

"Crit. Strat. With us." No war names. No Sacred Band greeting. No explanation. With Niko heeling like a hunting dog, the commander sets off toward the new barracks wing where Stepsons keep their wounded. Behind them, men whoop and yell as the mock battle is well and truly joined.

Straton, helmet under his arm, falls in on Crit's right in the Riddler's wake, an unspoken question in his bleak blue Rankan eyes.

When they reach the infirmary with its white-doored treatment rooms, at last Crit thinks he understands: Cassander's wagon waits there, empty; the fish tanks must be inside. *So the Riddler knows.* Soon everybody would.

Tempus stopped, folding vast arms. The commander wasn't wearing boar's-tooth and leopard-skin today, only a *chiton* and his god-given sword: not dressed for combat.

"What's this I hear about you needing some nursing, Crit?" says Tempus, that little kill-smile dancing at the corners of his willful mouth. A question asked so softly—in front of Strat, in front of Niko. All recognize that gentle tone, reserved for the dying and his horses.

Cassander, you dog. No one needed to know, much less Tempus.

Beside the commander, Niko stood hipshot, angular face turned toward the exercise as if Tempus hadn't spoken, clearly wishing he were on the field today with his fighters and his big black horse. On the Riddler's right, Niko always seemed deceptively boyish: Stealth, called Nikodemos was Tempus' *hipparch*, second-in-command and deadliest of the Riddler's fighters, with the possible exception of Strat.

Straton's head snapped around and he stared. "Crit? You're hurt? Why didn't you say?"

"I've got some aches and pains, nothing serious. Left over from the battle." *Demons blast and chomp on you, Cassander.* "Hurts when I sit still too long. I've got too much sitting yet to do, with the construction here and at the Mageguild and at the overlook… But since you're here, Commander…"

Tempus has been hard to find, slipping from this world to Lemuria and back in the blink of a god's eye. Niko was preoccupied, finishing some Bandaran gravel pond for his trainees—*if* Crit had wanted to report to him: Crit didn't. Critias has everything else to manage, for nearly a hundred fighters and their grooms and servants: "There's something else…"

Now Niko's gaze, flat and empty, shifts from the exercise to Crit. "Is there anything we can do to help you heal?" says

Tempus' partner so tenderly that Crit wants to slap him backhanded. But he can't.

We?

"You and your Theban goddess, you mean? She helped Straton after the battle and I'm truly grateful." Niko would hold it over Crit's head forever, but even begging help from a foreign goddess had been worth a try—to save his partner. "As for my physical condition, Niko… no. There's nothing you or your goddess can do for me that I want done." *Keep your place: stay out of my affairs; you're the commander's rightman, not mine.*

Strat swore under his breath, knowing Crit and Niko, and the irresolvable differences between them.

"Riddler, my battle-soreness is immaterial," Crit continued. "We have a real problem, though: all those deserters from the Meridian war. 'Stragglers,' the locals call them." *Dreamers and dreaming dead, lots of them from neither here nor there with no chance of getting home again, lost in place and time—disoriented conscripts who awoke stranded and stumbling about the battlefield.* "Wandering in and out of Sanctuary… men—and women, too. From every place I know and some I've never heard of. Causing trouble in the city. And if they die, when they die, sometimes there are no bodies… other times, they show up in gangs, preying on the locals. Torchholder's boy Walegrin and his city guard are out of their depth…"

"Which isn't more than a hand's-breadth," Strat added.

Nobody even smiled.

Cassander appeared in the doorway, wiping bloody hands on a wet cloth. The smell of black hellebore, boiling down to a poison for painting blades and arrows, wafted around him and out the door. "Critias? Oh… Commander. Sorry to interrupt, but Crit was mentioning the stragglers… Kouras and

I had a little skirmish with what might have been a couple or six of them outside the Unicorn yesterday. No armor. No shields. No war cries. Crit said there were no bodies—"

"No corpses…" Strat said, before Cassander got into too much trouble, putting words in the mouth of Tempus' Sanctuary task force leader, "…when we sent Sacred Banders to the Unicorn to check. Nothing for the city guard to poke or prod. Too many attacks like this, on too many nights, unrequited. They're getting too brash. Soon enough there'll be real problems. I say we clean up these stragglers, before they bite us in the behind."

"What say you, Niko?" Tempus asked his partner.

"About the stragglers, Commander? Strat's right. Ghosts or dreamers they may be, but they kill like men. Fight them like men and they'll die like men. We proved that on the battleplain below the overlook."

"Come in, if you will, Critias. I'm ready for you," Cassander said.

They all trooped in, where Cassander had just finished setting a man's broken leg with a bone clamp: four leeches sucked the patient's blood to keep it from clotting below and above the clamp; his eyes were half-shut from drugs or pain. Another badly-bruised fighter with a swollen arm and leg was lying on his right side on a straw pallet, a tank of sand and water on the floor nearby. Overhead, slit-bellied poppies beaded with brown sap hung upside down from rafters next to bunches of lavender, yarrow, seaweed and cyclamen. A wooden rack for reseating dislocated bones sat, forbidding and empty, opposite the door.

Cassander leaned close to Crit and whispered, "Should I tell the commander about the taleteller?"

Finally, a semblance of tact and discipline from this healer. Five years with the Band, but only a year or two since his left-side leader had died; no new partner yet: Cassander was far too junior to be holding forth in such exalted company. But things were as they were.

"You'd better, now," Crit said, softer still. Tempus had gods' ears; he'd surely heard.

Change the subject. Too much fuss over Crit's aches and pains. Too much fuss over one of three-score brawls in Sanctuary's mean streets nightly. From outside, a wolf-call sounded, picked up by twenty throats: Stepson horse charging Theban shields on the training field.

Howsoever, now they had the Riddler's attention and even Stealth was curious. Niko fixed those distant, hazel eyes on the healer.

Cassander said, "Commander, Hakiem the taleteller said to tell you that dreams are running wild in Sanctuary and that some dreams shouldn't be allowed to come true. That's all. Sit here, Critias."

Storyteller's message curtly relayed, reduced to the bare minimum. Whatever nuance was lost, it couldn't be helped.

"Cass, I'm too busy for you right now," Crit said. "We'll do this some other time." *Not with the commander here, and Niko. Not with Strat watching.*

"Critias, sir… the last ray died before I got it to you. This one will too, if we don't use it right away." Cassander's bristly jaw squared.

"What else did Hakiem say?" Tempus asked, voice like gravel shifting.

Silence.

Everyone turned to Cassander, young and plain-spoken, who'd joined the Band in Mygdonia, just one more eager hero among so many.

Cassander scuffed his sandaled feet, then looked at the Riddler. "It's street talk."

On Tempus' right, Niko took one step forward, merely a whisper of a threat. Tempus put a restraining hand on his partner's arm.

"Tell me, Stepson." Tempus' full attention wasn't something to court on a whim. Cassander squinted into that gaze. Crit knew exactly how it felt, looking hell in the face.

"Commander, Hakiem said that if I couldn't tell you, I was to tell Nikodemos… so I was going to do that instead. When I saw him." Cassander had tended Niko's injuries more than once; the two were well acquainted.

"Tell him porking *what?"* Strat demanded. The badly-bruised patient shifted on his pallet, unabashedly trying to hear better.

Cassander stood taller: "That there's a curse on the Theban goddess and on your witch, Strat, and trouble's coming after them—or us—or both."

"That's all?" Niko asked. "The whole of it?"

Crit said, "Curses? The only curses here worth our time are the refugees from the dream lord's army."

Tempus said, "Cassander, curses are something we know how to handle. What else?" He swept a glance over Niko and then Crit before moving toward the door.

Cassander sighed deeply and headed for one of the two tanks on the floor. "Sir? Nothing else, from Hakiem." He turned to Crit: "Critias, please, sir. *Now.*"

"What else?" Tempus repeated from the doorway, nearly whispering.

"Commander? Just that our young Kouras is a pretty fair fighter. And knows the palace as if it were his home. I treated his priestess there…"

Tempus looked back once more at the healer. "Yes, he is." Then he strode away, Niko pacing him.

Cassander puffed out his cheeks and knelt down, poking in one of his two tanks, shaking his head.

Critias couldn't sympathize.

"Next time, Cass," Straton said, "you come to *us* with anything for the commander as soon as you get it. *We'll* decide what, when, how and where to tell him. And when you greet him, you show respect; you bow your head." Strat was angry, protective of Crit and the chain of command; as worried about Crit's attempt at a surreptitious visit to Cassander as about Cassander's encounter with the Riddler.

"Strat, this is nothing. I'm fine," Crit said.

"Sit here, sir."

Resigned, Critias sat where Cassander bade him and did as Cassander told him: unlaced his sandals and sprung off his greaves, then put his feet in the saltwater tank and the sand at the bottom.

"Straton, help him hold position. Critias… sir," added Cassander, "this is going to hurt at first, but then it won't. Put both feet on the fish in the sand, near its tail, and push—"

The soles of Crit's feet connected with something that burned and throbbed and thrilled through him. Pain in waves rushed up through his legs.

Strat was pressing Crit's left knee down, Cassander the right, when Crit realized he couldn't feel Strat's hands on him. Or Cassander's.

Dizziness. Crit's heart skipped a beat. Then another. Something hurt far away but close-by he felt nothing. So he said, "I can't feel my legs," very carefully.

"That's fine. That's good. Strat, let his leg go and steady his shoulder."

Good thing. Crit felt as if he might topple over.

He wanted to take his feet off the fish in the sand but he couldn't move them. Both his legs were paralyzed. A fear beyond anything he'd ever encountered on a battlefield gripped him, jogging a memory from long ago—about another pain, another paralysis, and Straton's witch, the fearsome necromant—but then that recollection slipped away. Now he was sitting here in his own barracks, numb from the hips down, unable to move his legs, and worried that he might fall over on his face.

"You can move now." Cassander's voice was determinedly neutral.

"No, I can't," said Critias, holding tight to his temper and his courage. If he could have moved, Cassander would be up against a wall by now and dead very soon thereafter.

"Cass…" Straton craned his neck. "Critias had better be pleased with your work."

Cassander nodded. "He will be, Straton. Critias, Strat and I will help you get your legs out of the tank. No need to kill that ray. He might have a little more life in him. When the numbness wears off, we may try again, depending on how you feel then—whether the pain comes back. The more you do this, the higher your tolerance for pain will get."

"I'd rather have the pain than this," Critias said. The Theban fighter with his leg in the bone clamp chuckled ruefully where he sat, propped against a whitewashed wall.

Together, the three of them got Crit's useless legs out of the tank.

If this paralysis did not ease, if Cassander was mistaken, Critias by now had several exotic punishments in mind for the Stepsons' healer, all of which would be extremely painful and take a very long time to kill him.

Straton sat with Crit, making careful small talk in the mercenary argot that most Thebans had not yet mastered, until the paralysis eased.

When it did, the pain Crit had been trying to ignore for so long went with it.

*

Niko caught up with Lysis in the barracks stables, where the young Sacred Bander was tending burns on Niko's black colt from the barn fire that had touched off the Great War. "Lysis, tell me your Theban legends about the goddess." The colt nickered, pricking its ears Niko's way.

Lysis was always forthcoming. The shadowy stall smelled of sweet straw and hay and horse and bacon grease from the salve he was rubbing into the colt's burns. His hand, glistening with unguent, stopped still on the colt's back. "*Hipparch,* there are many tales told in Thebes of the goddess Harmony. I don't know which to tell you." Said so softly. The youthful fighter looked away. "You should ask my father."

Lysis' father, Charon, was the Thebans' warrior-priest of Harmony but Lysis was Niko's trainee and, like himself, a favorite of their goddess.

"I'm giving you an order, Lysis. Tell me. What would make someone say she's cursed?"

"Cursed? Oh, the wedding…"

"Wedding?" Whatever Niko learned from father or son, Harmony would still be the same goddess who had remade him, body and soul, changed him forever. His mouth went dry. He recalled the Riddler's every caution in a rush of blood and heat he could feel in his face and in his hands, which wanted to spin the Theban around and pin him against the stall-boards.

Niko might have let things lie. But he hadn't: Harmony was gone from him on these lonely days. *She goes and comes as she pleases.* His heart pounded in his ears. Arms at his sides, he flexed his fingers, waiting for Lysis to explain.

"Sir… Zeus gave Kadmos, the founder of Thebes, our goddess Harmony to be his wife. Some of the gods were jealous. Mighty Athena and Hephaestos were the most wroth and made Kadmos two presents to give his bride: a deadly necklace and a robe dipped in crime, both of which brought ill fortune to Harmony's descendants, even after the gifts were enshrined at Delphi. When Kadmos left Thebes and was turned into a serpent, he tried to take Harmony and make her a serpent as well; but no matter how he hissed at her, her loyalty to Thebes was too strong. She came back to us and has always been the tutelary goddess of our Sacred Band. Is that what you want to know?"

Husband who turned into a serpent. Accursed children. Deadly necklace. Robe dipped in crime. He thanked Lysis and left the stables, climbing up to the modest altar of Harmony, next to Enlil's on the hilltop above the barracks.

Of course she'd had a life before him. Before their time together. He'd had a son, himself, who'd been killed horribly by a witch who stalked Niko, destroying all he loved. Then he'd left his royal wife, returned to the Band, never looked back… Which was worse? Harmony leaving a cursed robe and necklace to her descendants or Niko letting Roxane live long enough to kill his son? She'd had a husband; he, a wife. Now there was still a chance they could have each other.

If he were not a prideful fool.

He stood there on the hill while the sun set red amid purple clouds and the rain began, knowing what he had to do but not doing it. Tempus had cautioned him that he knew nothing about her, this foreign goddess, Harmony, who had stolen his heart and saved his life and resurrected him. Now he was different from his brothers of the Sacred Band.

The Thebans whispered about him, dropping their eyes worshipfully when he passed by. Aškelon of Meridian had warned him to beware hero-cults in his name, folk sacrificing horses at altars in his honor. He wanted none of that. He was a son of the armies, nothing more… or had been. Just a weapon of the god.

But he wanted that goddess. He wanted to feel her silky hair brush his skin, smell the sweetness of her, see the meadow of his rest-place in her wide amber eyes. He hadn't seen her since the commendation ceremony after the war. He hadn't wanted to see her, he admitted to himself. He was unworthy of such gifts as she'd bestowed on him. He didn't want eternity. Men weren't meant for immortality. One heart, one soul, one swing through life… so his mystery of *maat* had taught him. So he still believed.

But she had taken his heart and his soul and made more of them than a man should be.

Nowadays, even his own Stepsons were too careful around him. The Theban goddess had given him back his life… perhaps given him life everlasting. He needed to face what it meant, what she'd done; what he'd let her do—asked her to do. He healed like the Riddler now: every cut, every wound; flawlessly, with never a scar. And might always.

The rain swirled around him, spraying into his eyes. Then it was gone. And with it, finally, went his last, wild hope of resistance to it all: he was what she'd made of him. Tempus had accepted it, and loved him still. He must, and love himself once more.

He dropped to his knees before Harmony's altar and did what he knew he had to do if he ever wanted to see her again: he asked her to come to him. He hadn't asked her to come to him for so very long.

He spoke her name. He humbled himself before her, on his knees before that little pile of stones. He'd never gone to his knees for any man or god, except once when the dream lord had shamed him.

He knew she could see into his heart. She would see that he'd accepted her gifts, and all that went with them. He hoped it wasn't too late… that she wasn't angry with him. Ungratefulness wasn't fitting. He needed her the way he needed air to breathe.

In the soft dark night, a cool wind blew, caressing his face. He smelled a meadow, green grass… He held his breath.

Then she was there with him, right before him, standing on her altar stones. Still on his knees, he put his arms around her thighs and buried his head in the linen clothing her belly, smelling the meadow of her.

"Harmony, please forgive me. I'm a mortal fool. I've missed you so. Stay with me."

"I'm here, as you asked. You're neither mortal nor a fool, beloved. You needed time. You have all the time you need."

Now he could breathe again. He couldn't ask her about the curse, if there was one, or about anything else—not about her husband who'd become a serpent, or the evil necklace, or her family's robe dipped in crime. When he'd open his lips to speak, she'd stop them with her own. But it was enough, to feel her heartbeat next to his and let her long legs entwine him, and hold on to what he'd almost lost.

Whatever else she was, she was Harmony, daughter of Ares and Aphrodite: goddess of balance and celestial order; bringer of truth and justice; patron goddess of the Sacred Band of Thebes; and his divine lover. And he was… what?

Before the Battle of Meridian, Harmony had told Tempus, "Use him wisely. Few have been given such a weapon by the gods or Fates before."

Niko had no exalted aspirations. Whether he could truly be some such weapon was not his to know. The Riddler thought it so, and the cadre among the Stepsons had an inkling. But if there was something she wasn't telling him, if trouble came to her or curses from below or above, he was still Tempus' right-man, second in command of the Unified Sacred Band. He would protect her from all harm. It was what he did. It was what he knew. It was what he was.

*

Down beyond the White Foal Bridge later that evening, Straton tied his ghost horse outside the odd little house where his love, the necromant, made her home.

Ischade was waiting for him.

"Straton, what is it, what is it? Never fear… nothing can touch us here, no curses made for men, or by those once men, or those who would someday be men," Ischade soothed, a dark pool of deepest night among her silks and her spells and her madness, which brought the two of them back together time after delirious time.

Eyes so black, hair like spiders' webs but inky, skin softer than silk and a perfume he could never resist if his life depended on it. She let him put his big arms around her. So tiny was she, he never ceased wondering that such danger and such power could be contained in a package so delicate.

"What is it, Ischade? I'll tell you…" His voice echoes in that little space where time forgets itself, where everything is other than it seems; in this house, larger within than without and sometimes full of creatures who live a different sort of life than his. But tonight is his night, their night, and long planned. So he can say what he wants and ask her what he wants:

"…Critias called for a healer today. You know what he's like. He wouldn't, unless he's in dire need. And the Stepsons' healer brought a *fish* to cure him. I fear for Crit as I've not before, not in all our battles. Something's wrong… and not just with him. Sanctuary feels strange. Unfamiliar. You know how we fought, what we fought—what we won. You were with us. There on the battlefield. You saw the Theban goddess. She says the balance was restored. So what *is* this? Deserters wandering off the battleplain at the overlook, out of Meridian and into Sanctuary? Some not quite dead, but not really alive? Men, and women too—sleepers and dreamers? Ischade, my dreams are so unsettled…"

"Restless dead, my love, just released. Revenants. And dreamers, some of them caught for eons in Aškelon's domain." This ancient necromant has lived through millennia of men and gods and demons and worse. "On a trail blazed by the fated dead, all those Thebans whom the Riddler brought from Chaeronea. That path leads here, to Sanctuary. You know how high your commander reaches now. Vies with gods, he does. As for the balance, ask your Nikodemos: no balance stays restored forever. He and all his brothers of the misty isles, adepts of *maat,* dedicate their lives to restoring balance. Over and over again."

"So she lied, this Theban goddess? This Harmony, who has Niko's soul wrapped up?"

"She said the truth. You have heard the truth so little that when you do, you cannot believe your ears. The balance where the goddess lives, which matters to gods and demigods, has been restored. For how long? Only the Fates can say. Or powers greater than I. Other powers have other goals, other conflicts, and other needs. Powers such as the dream lord can and will upset celestial order. But Aškelon is gone now, and you and all your fighters paid the price. And pay it still. Some day another power may come to take his place. But not today. And your commander knows all this. So rest easy, Straton, here with me. Let fools kill fools and we will be the better for it. Dreams are unfettered? Well and good. Whose dreams will come true in Sanctuary? Do you care? Do I? If what the Riddler wants, and what you want, and even what your Critias wants, can be fulfilled, is that not enough for such as we? Here, now, with you and me, all is as it should be."

He pulled back from an embrace so heady he couldn't have said whether he was standing on his feet or lying in her bed or floating down the White Foal River, lost and dead. Her eyes in that white face seemed to swoop toward him, so close to his; he could feel her breath upon his cheek. "But, Ischade…"

"Straton, go you not against that goddess, Nikodemos' immortal lover. She'll protect her boy. She saved you once. Be careful. These imported troubles that the Riddler brought must play out. And catch yourself not up in warlords' schemes and mortal plans for glory, and all will be well for thee and me."

"And Critias? And the commander? And Niko?"

"And Critias," sighed Ischade, as if granting a wish or casting a spell. "And perhaps your Riddler. But Nikodemos… he is on another path than mortal men do tread. Be you cautious, Straton. And ride the horse I gave thee, back to me and forth to them, and back again. And all can still be well with us, if we do not seek to reach beyond our grasp."

"Ischade, you're wiser than even Tempus." *Older, for certain.* "What should I tell the commander?" When she 'thee'd' him this way, danger always lay in wait.

"Hope he asks you nothing. If he does, say you will ask of me any favor he so wishes. And leave it so. And let the fires burn low, for mortal striving. Your commander reaches for yonder stars and gods do eye him. And there are more Fates in the wide worlds of men than those whom he has aided. So confusion will reign once more in Sanctuary. What, dear Straton, is the difference, to you and me?"

Since he couldn't answer that, he lay back down atop her silks and velvets. There she clasped her hands behind his head and whispered of all they could do and all they could be together. She would protect him, as she could, and if she could, and even succor Critias, as he asked her.

More than that, this necromant, so wary, could not—or would not—promise.

*

Lightning thrust from the east of heaven to the west; the west of heaven parried, and the east then thrust again. Storm gods quarreled and rain poured down. Ever since the Sacred Band returned to Sanctuary, the weather had gone mad, so the Ilsigi locals said. Cassander found it hard to blame the weather on the Band's return. He was new to this city, just learning why the veterans so despised it. Gods fought in Sanctuary's heavens like dogs over bones.

Before first watch, under a scummy sky spitting rain, Cassander guided his brown warhorse toward Critias and the Shambles Cross station with all the care he could muster. Look up at the rooftops. Look down at the cobbles. Look around at the ramshackle hovels and the overhung alleys and the peddlers on murky streets. Look sharp through the gloom for the gleam of an iron point, a bronze edge.

Human debris was everywhere: refugees and conscripts from the armies of the dream lord, using spears for crutches and shortswords for currency; dreaming dead and dreamers, dazed and striking out at anyone and everyone better off than they. The 'Great War,' Stepsons were calling it, when Meridian manifested north of the barracks from a world away and the entelechy of the seventh sphere fought Tempus' Sacred Band with shades and revenants and so many souls ensorcelled for years beyond counting.

Every Sacred Band casualty of that war, horse and man, was Cassander's to heal and save. An impossible task, even with help from the Theban goddess and Straton's necromant. Winning can be worse than losing, when the fighting's done and men have too long to count the cost and wonder what comes next.

He'd lost too many. Nineteen was the death toll so far. Too many more at the barracks yet were crippled; too many fates uncertain: men healing from burns and cuts and broken bones, in need of nursing to stave off infection, amputation, or worse. In these sullen, sultry weeks of recovery, he had only one pair of Thebans helping him. Tempus' 3rd Commando had gone home to faraway Lemuria after the battle, taking their wounded with them.

Now Critias had summoned Cassander to the Stepsons' Shambles Cross station in one of Sanctuary's tumbledown slums, with no explanation why.

He tied his horse in the stable beneath Crit's hidey-hole and climbed the stairs, pausing on the landing. He'd been braver in the battle. Critias was the coldest and most demanding of the Stepsons, and displeased when the kite-ray numbed his legs. Making an enemy of Critias could end your tour with the Band abruptly.

As he climbed the final flight, Cassander's mouth went dry, his fingers cold on the wooden railing. Stealth, the Riddler's partner, might put in a good word, if one were needed: Cassander had treated Niko's wounds until the goddess

Harmony started working miracles, taking away his every cut and scar. No field surgeon could compete with that.

Straton, the Stepsons' interrogator, was waiting for him at the top of the stairs.

Not good.

"Ace, life to you." Words clicking off his dry tongue, Cassander called Strat by his war name, acknowledging danger close at hand.

Strat thrust open the door. "And to you, Stitch." Strat used Cassander's war name in return. "And everlasting glory." With a sweep of his big arm, Straton motioned him inside.

Metal shutters. One-board table. Creaking floor. Second room, door ajar. Cassander nearly drew his sword when the outer door thumped shut behind his back. Crit wasn't in here, but now Cassander was… and Straton was.

What is this? Everything else he'd promised to do tonight cascaded through his mind.

Strat said, "Go on through."

Cassander eased through the second door with Straton following close behind, making every floorboard squeak.

There was Crit, sitting on a sheepskin-covered pallet in a windowless room. One oil lamp burned: shadows played grotesquely on the cracked daub walls. The door behind Strat squealed shut.

Cassander's breathing was too loud. These two, among the Band's leadership, would go unquestioned if they'd decided to kill him despite Sacred Band oath or Stepson bond. He'd meant only to help…

Then he saw the pottery basin, took a deep sniff and smelled brine.

Crit said, "Again. Now."

Strat said, "And me, next."

Cassander said, "*Oh.* I thought—"

"You thought what?" Crit unlaced his sandals to put his feet into the tub.

"You didn't say it helped. You should have told me. I'd have put you on a routine…"

"I can find my own source of fish, Stepson. We do this here. For both of us. No one knows. Not the Riddler, not Stealth. Not anyone. Understood?"

"Understood," he said, moving to the basin where sea-water and sand hid a kite-ray from view. He knelt before Crit and stirred the sand. His fingers found the base of the ray's tail; he closed them and took the jolt. "Good one." The jolt trilled through him. His heartbeat leapt and steadied. Now he knew what to do, what they wanted. If he did it well, he'd live through this interview. "I need to check you, before we start. I'm going to get out my knife. I'll run the point up your foot, your leg, to where the pain is, and you're going to tell me what you feel, when you feel it. No blood, no cut, just a test."

Crit said, "This will raise our tolerance for pain?"

"Yes, but don't do it unless you still *have* pain… I need you to tell me the truth."

So began a negotiation with this fighter, so seasoned, so talented, and with his right-side partner—necessary with these two, who wouldn't, couldn't admit to weakness unless they were at death's door.

Halfway through Crit's treatment, the task force leader began asking about two men who'd been hurt in the last infantry exercise, and about stragglers on the streets. Cassander began to relax. Out at the barracks, when Crit had first realized he was paralyzed, Cassander had thought Critias was going to kill him on the spot, as soon as feeling returned to those legs again. But the kite-ray must have quieted the nerves around Crit's pelvis, where his horse had rolled on him, or they wouldn't be doing this now.

Strat helped Cassander get Crit's legs out of the basin. Then it was Straton's turn and Straton's left arm, poised above the brine.

"You need to be ready for the shock, Straton. It hurts, before it doesn't."

"By Enlil's long and warty wand, boy—just do it."

So he did and Strat didn't strangle him or gut him, merely grunted once when his left hand took the jolt.

"Normally I know what we're trying to heal… Where does it hurt?" Straton was among the Band's best fighters.

Critias spoke before Strat could answer: "You're treating the pregnant priestess tonight?"

These were Tempus' intelligence officers. Nothing escaped them. "Yes. Kouras asked me to see her again."

"You take orders from Kouras now? You're working at the palace when we have *how* many wounded and injured men and horses of our own?" Crit said. "And those two Thebans who got hurt in the exercise… Next time, ask me first."

Strat said nothing. His face was turning pale, sweat beading his upper lip.

"As you say, Critias, sir. Let go of the fish, Strat. *Straton!* Take your hand out," said Cassander. He'd never seen anyone keep contact with a ray so long. "And sit still until the feeling returns."

Strat lifted his left arm out with his right hand, staring at Cassander as he placed his left hand on his knee and poked at it curiously. "Tell him, Crit."

"Kouras wants to pair with you." Crit smiled his wispy, cynical smile. "Shoulder to shoulder, to the death with honor."

"What?"

"Think it over. He'll ask you. We'll allow it."

Strat scoffed.

Cassander said, before he could think, "He's the storm god's son. I'm a true Sacred Band fighter... he's not. He's a child. I had a complete pairbond with a brilliant older fighter. You know that. I need a rightman next, not... Kouras. Better you had offered me Lysis before he paired with Arton. That one, I could have made into a partner." *Are they teaching me a lesson, after all?* "Kouras doesn't need a partner, he needs an assistant. So do I... in the sickrooms."

"Just talk to him," Straton advised.

"He'll bring it up. Don't you broach it," Critias told him. "Let us know how it goes with Kouras tonight, when you're done. And you're right about one thing—we need you tending wounded, not getting wounded."

*

Rain poured from a roiling sky, dripping from lips and down woolen mantles in the dark where three stragglers hid behind piled crates, across from the Stepsons' Shambles safe house.

"See? I told you he'd come, girl," whispered the short, stout woman. "Where the kite-rays go, that Sacred Bander is soon to follow. Although I don't know what you see in him. Too slight, not meaty enough. Now, hush," she warned, "we don't want him to see you yet."

"He's got the meat she wants, doesn't he, little girl?" sneered the bigger woman.

"He's in my dreams," the young girl wistfully confessed.

"Dream lover, is it? Fighters like these... sack and pillage is their favorite sport. Why should they buy what they can get for free? But the songs you sing, that talent's scarce. Perhaps we'll sell you to him, not just rent you—make a pretty profit," came the big woman's husky chuckle from the dark, only half teasing. "Pay for your lodging—and both of ours. Get a spy in their midst, in the bargain. One way or another, you'll need to earn your keep."

The girl only hummed a love song, hoping against hope that the big woman was right and the wide-eyed fighter would want her and take her in his arms and make her dreams come true.

*

Kouras said, "So, Cass, I think we should pair."

Cassander said, "I'm flattered, but let's think this through. Are you offering me your backside, Kouras? As my *eromenos*, my right-side partner? Because that's how it would be. And if so, we should see how we fit first. I need to try you on for size. There are so many women in your life, a full Sacred Band pairbond might be more than you can handle." Cass looked him up and down, frank, appraising, challenging in a way that made Kouras uncomfortable, and was meant to do so.

They had just walked into the palace. "You think I'm too young? I'm sixteen. Alexander the Macedonian commanded cavalry at my age."

"A world away. With Philip's best generals close around to protect him. If he is your role model, you and I won't get along; I'm not that hungry for glory. I'm a son of the armies, a literate and loyal military professional, nothing more. No special gifts or royal blood. Honored to be one of this band. In training since I could drag a shield. I'd been in pairbond for years by the time I was your age, and stayed on my partner's right until he died, content to fight where and how he bid me."

"I am Vashanka's son. You've seen how fast I am, how I heal."

"I've seen that your partner is the god. He's not my god. Outside the Unicorn, you and your god nearly sliced me and my horse with that *kopis* of yours. It's a weapon for butchery, for a berserker. Maybe for you, since Vashanka is the berserker god, it makes sense. But think about it: curved, single-edged, wider toward the tip. Someday when it's muggy, or cold, that *kopis* will stick coming out of your scabbard. For power, you've got to slash on a full diagonal and control the arc of that single edge. What if the enemy's on your left, between our horses, coming in under your shield? You can't thrust with a *kopis* efficiently; it doesn't parry well; it slashes. It cuts through bone and severs. Hard to stop that swing on horseback once it's begun; hard to keep your balance. Shears, disembowels, amputates. Crude and unwieldy, but very scary. Better overhand. Hacking downward and across it's fine, but you can't develop the momentum you need to use it effectively on a horse like you can on the ground where you can get your whole body behind the swing—not without putting your horse and your partner at risk. I'm committed cavalry: I like a bow or lance for a little distance, and a double-edged *xiphos* in my hand for slash and thrust." He fingered his straight shortsword's pommel. "I have an extra *xiphos* scabbard stitched on my saddle, in case I lose this one. Maybe you should pair with a Theban. Hoplites like the *kopis.*"

Kouras didn't know where to look, what to say. His ears felt hot; his mouth was parched. He was prayerfully glad that no one lurked in the black-and-white marble foyer to overhear. "I'm Bandaran trained. There's no weapon I can't use. Any edge, any sword. Any spear: javelin, *dory, sarissa, xyston.* Throwing star, recurved bow, crossbow, sling, staff… whatever."

"The weapons I care about are here." Cassander pointed to his temple. Then to his heart. "And here." He looked hard at Kouras. "If so assigned, I'll ride on your left awhile and drill with you when I can. I've got wounded and injured to tend, men and horses. You need combat and seasoning, not pairbond. Not yet. Not until you think you can learn from a partner, take direction. I've fought so many battles I've lost count. I don't seek battle and I don't shy from it. I've patched up too many not to understand what bloodbath really means. You've fought… what, twice?"

Kouras forced himself to meet Cassander's eyes. "The Great War. Chaeronea and Meridian. I won a commendation there. And a few street skirmishes in Sanctuary, against the sniper." No one, not even Stealth, the Riddler's partner, had ever talked to Kouras this way.

"What's your war name?" Cassander asked him.

"I don't… have one, yet."

"Maybe Vashanka's son won't need one," said Cass with a flash of teeth. "But…"

Molin Torchholder came down the hall, rubbing bejeweled hands together, and the moment was lost.

"Ah, Cassander. Gyskouras. Seriti is prepared. And faring much better. We have acquired a ray and all is in readiness. Come this way." Robes swirling, Torchholder headed up the stairs.

Kouras and Cassander followed. Cass cursed under his breath and then said, "Eminence, you can't just use these rays without understanding… There's a right way and a wrong way, and too few fish to be had."

"Oh, I understand *all* of that. No one will be getting these kite-rays but the palace. I have prepared an edict. Any treatments from now on will be done here or in Vashanka's temple. This treatment is a gift from the Pillager, as is all lightning and thunder. And you, Cassander, are going to teach my priests how to properly administer the fish therapy."

Cassander bumped Kouras with his hip, murmuring, "If this is your doing…"

"It's not," Kouras whispered back. "Please, believe me."

But Cassander didn't.

Seriti's ankles were half the size they'd been when Kouras had last seen her, a great improvement. So great an improvement, Cassander insisted, that another treatment was an unnecessary risk. But Torch could not be dissuaded.

Finally, after too much argument, the Stepsons' healer crossed his arms. "Fine. I'm not treating her. Not until the commander gives permission. Your civil edict has no power over me. And if you overdo this treatment, you'll kill the baby. Is that what you want?"

Torchholder's eyes narrowed and he rebalanced his stance. This priest was once a warrior. His face suffused with rage. Then he said, "Gyskouras, I'll leave now. If you can prevail upon friend Stepson to do the bidding of the palace, his employer, then we'll forget about this. If not… other remedies will be sought." Torchholder flounced off, stiff-legged as a riled cat, and through the door, which he slammed.

Seriti began to weep softly, her pale hands covering her face.

Kouras could not remember anyone, even the commander, openly thwarting Torchholder. He would have intervened, but the god was aroused, ramping in his head and he didn't know why. Then he did: kite-rays in His temples… priests giving treatments…

"Cassander, do this for me. For Seriti."

"Kouras, I haven't even examined her yet. She may not need any more. Or she may have had too much. Everyone in Sanctuary seems to think they know more than I do about how and when to administer this therapy. So let them. I'm not taking the blame. If you leave the room, I'll look at her. Then I'm going back to the barracks."

"No, please. We're supposed to meet someone at Aphrodisia House…"

Seriti wept harder at the mention of Sanctuary's famous brothel.

"Your whore? I've heard about her. Now, *out.*"

So Kouras left. There, waiting outside the closed door, he found Torchholder.

But neither he nor Torch could get a word out of Cassander, when the healer came barging through, as to Seriti's condition or anything else.

Nor would Seriti tell them what had transpired, but would only hug herself, saying that Cassander had her solemn oath of silence and in future she would be treated by no one else.

Kouras was sure he had made the worst mistakes of his life this evening, but when he got to Aphrodisia House, Cass' big brown horse was there.

*

Enlil's chariot came clattering down a road of moonlit cloud, his mantle blackening the starry vault behind him. The wrath of the storm god whipped the world: four white horses with blood-red harness drew him; lightning from his chariot's wheels speared to ground within the city walls. Wind and rain followed in the storm god's wake, battering windows, rattling doors, putting summer to rout overnight. Cold blew into Sanctuary on a salt wind that turned the trees as red and amber as a goddess' eye by morning.

Tempus understood the wrath of the god—whose embodiment, at Enlil's whim, he sometimes was. And was on this day, golden with sunlight antithetical to his mood.

He had been summoned to the palace by Vashanka's priest. Tempus had won his war with Aškelon. Now the vacuum of peace lay oppressive on him. He sent back a message by courier telling Torchholder when and where at the barracks he could be found. There he waited, on the far side of the altar hill, for the high priest to arrive.

Before Torchholder made his appearance, other pilgrimages began. First Critias and Straton, their breath steaming, approached in bronze-bossed leathers.

"Commander, can we speak before the priest arrives?" Crit's quick glance took in Tempus' leopard-skin mantle and god-given sword. "It won't take long."

Tempus was sitting in the grass, some blades still blue-green, some already pale from the sudden frost. "Sit, Fox. And you, Ace." He needed to see if Crit could sit without a grunt or gasp of pain.

His executive officer folded into a squat without a hitch or a sound and Straton sat too, both watching him closely. Behind them, other Stepsons waited, clustered in a group, hoping to meet with him next: Charon and dark Gorgias, his Theban squadron leaders; and others behind them.

"Sir," Crit said, "we need to mount a foray, sweep up these stragglers in town. Everyone's ready, if you approve it. We think that's part of what Torchholder wants."

"Good. It's ours to do. We need the practice." Stragglers: detritus from the war. In his head Enlil stirred, rumbling, surging up in his flesh, thrilling his muscles, tingling his bones. *Is this what You want, Lord Storm? Vengeance upon the last of Your enemies? Then have at it, Ravener.* "I'll ride with you, Crit. We'll start planning tomorrow."

"Commander," said Strat, "our Thebans are peerless on the ground but they lack experience on horseback, riding down enemies. We need assurances that we don't have to take these stragglers alive." Straton wanted clear rules of engagement.

"No quarter, then. We root them out. Chase these deserters down and kill them. *If* they run. Some of them won't; they'll stand and fight. So be prepared. It won't be quick or easy. Is Niko done yet?"

"Still drilling pairs on horseback, with Sync. Sir, there's something else…" Crit's fine-featured Syrese face was carefully arranged.

There always was, when Critias came to him this way. "So? What else?"

"It's the fish… the rays. Cassander says the palace wants control of them: Torchholder issued an edict. Torch told Cass to teach his treatment to Vashanka's priests. Cass needs to talk to you about this, get guidance." Crit put his elbows on his knees, looking at Tempus squarely. "The rays helped me. We need to be able to use the fish as we choose on our own people. This is turning political."

"I'll handle it." In his head, Enlil snarled. Jealousy in heaven made for bloodshed on earth. Two storm gods, vying for position, for adherents. Surely the gods had more to do than fight over fish. *Enlil, tell me You don't care.* But wars had started over less, and empires fallen over even more foolish disputes, from time immemorial. A woman's kiss; a gift of earth and water; an invitation ignored: any pretext will do. Sometimes, none is needed. In his head, the god kept silent but came up, and up, and looked out of his eyes at his barracks and his men. Every hair on Tempus' body stood on end. "Crit, you stop by the mercenary hostel and see if the war's blown anyone useful in there."

Critias got up effortlessly; Straton, too. "Understood, Commander. We'll send Cassander to you now…?"

"Quickly, then. Alone."

The healer came before him bare-headed in a quilted tunic and woolen mantle. Critias and Straton stood nearby, clearly wishing they'd been asked to stay.

Cassander went down on one knee. *"Polemarch,"* he said, head bowed. The word meant 'warlord.' Enlil took note.

"'Commander' will do, as always. Sit, Stepson, and have your say."

Downcast eyes. Graceful fingers held a hand-sized terracotta jar stoppered with bitumen; two wires stuck out of the stopper. The healer said, "Critias told you about the palace's interest in the fish treatment, Commander? I didn't mean to start trouble..." Cassander waited for a response, got none, and continued: "These jars—I could show one of Torchholder's people how to make them. He wants me to teach his priests how to use the kite-rays. I'd prefer not. The priests can use jars like this, not the rays, on their congregation, which would leave the fish for us. The jar gives a weaker pulse, but strong enough for what the priesthood needs. More mystical, more miraculous. Less chance of harm from overuse. We'll make them with two types of stoppers; one plain-stoppered for storage, and ones like this, for treatment, with these wires protruding." He held out the jar, earnest, honest, troubled. "You just touch the copper wires to the skin..."

"You won't be teaching the palace how to use the rays. As for the jar, I don't need to try it. Leave it. Is that all?" So if he wanted a solution to the fish problem, he had one.

If.

Cassander scrambled to his feet, eyes still lowered. There was something else on this boy's mind.

So Tempus probed: "While you're here, how are our injured? Critias looks well-served."

"Our injured, sir? Coming along as fast as the gods allow. Critias, coming along as fast as he himself allows.

Commander… no one understands the need to use these rays under supervision," Cassander added in an exasperated rush. "Critias is only body-sore." Now he looked up. "These fish aren't toys. It would be better if the senior officers and the high-ranking civilians did as I advise. Kouras' priestess… they'll kill that baby, at the palace, trying to save it. They should leave her be. Someone should tell that to the priest, if we care about the storm god's child."

"We won't be treating anyone at the palace from now on," Tempus said. "Unless you have orders directly from me, don't provide Stepson services outside the Band."

Cassander sighed. "Thank you, Commander. Especially since Critias has me riding with Kouras…" He backed a step, then two, still waiting to be dismissed, but wanting to be, so badly.

Tempus let him go: a brave one, and canny, in a difficult position.

Next came his two senior Thebans. Charon was square-jawed, gray-haired, and a priest of the Theban goddess, Harmony. Beside him walked Gorgias, the Theban trainer with the smashed face, wanting to talk about weapons selection for mounted pursuit, and pairings. Both men had lost their partners: Charon's son had been given a new partner by Tempus; Gorgias' rightman had died in the war.

He finished with Gorgias, who saw life as black or white and usually chose black, and kept Charon with him a moment longer. "Charon, how do you feel about Kouras?"

"He fought beside me and my brothers, without being asked, at Meridian. He's fearless and skilled beyond his years." Charon was the best of the Thebans; his son, Lysis, was a credit to his skill at bringing young fighters along.

"Kouras needs a mentor, someone to make a man of him—someone not overawed."

"I would be honored to serve," said the Theban slowly, "should the occasion arise."

"Then it may." Behind Charon, waiting men rearranged themselves: someone was coming. "Before you go, Charon: is your goddess happy here? We have not seen her much lately."

"She is… Harmony. She goes and comes as she pleases. She comes here often. So it must please her to be here with us."

"And your flock?"

"Learning new ways, every day," Charon assured him.

Tempus dismissed the Theban, since the newcomer was Torchholder, enrobed and wearing curl-toed shoes and all the trappings of his high office, his Nisibisi-gray eyes smoldering. The priest huffed and puffed his way up to Tempus and said, "You sit here in the grass rather than come to the palace at my request?"

"Sit yourself, Torch. It's a beautiful day. I have something to tell you and something to show you." Enlil rattled his skull, growling, with the high priest of Vashanka so close at hand on Enlil's own ground, but the god spoke no word to him. Overhead, clouds raced across the sky, assaulting the sun.

"It is *I* who have something to show you, Riddler… and to tell you. And you had better tell *me* what I need to hear." With a grunt, the priest lowered himself to the grass opposite Tempus and pulled out a bi-fold of wood protecting a wax tablet. He handed it over.

Tempus read it and handed it back. "You're going into the fishing business? You have a navy now. If I had one, I'd be shipping in grain for winter, but you do as you see fit. By agreement, we are most specifically not involved with any naval operations."

"Don't play with me, Riddler. You know what this is about."

"Don't use my Stepsons without going through the proper chain of command. Don't browbeat or coerce my fighters. As for the fish: we'll take what we want, buy what we want, use what we want. Your edict has no force with me. We are in charge of peacekeeping and policing—tactics, techniques, and procedures are ours to determine. And we determine that we will offer you something that doesn't require our expertise for you to foist on a hapless populace."

He reached beside him in the grass and tossed the terracotta jar to Torchholder, who half-rose to catch it.

"What's this?" Torch demanded.

"Touch the ends of the wires to your wrist or your hand, a finger's breadth apart, and find out."

"Riddler, if this is…" Torchholder, touching the wires to his left hand, flinched and gasped; then looked up, disconcerted. "My hand is numb."

"Remove the wires," Tempus suggested.

The priest, trying not to look amazed, did so. He shook his limp hand, then rubbed it. "How long does it last? How often does one apply it? How do I get more?"

"You get more by agreeing to withdraw your edict in regard to the kite-rays. People always want what they're told they cannot have; we want the rays to remain unremarkable. We'll teach your people how to make the jars. You can make all you wish, an unending supply. You will have new revenue for the palace, of which we will require merely a nominal fee, say, twenty percent."

"Ten," haggled the priest.

"Fifteen percent, then—if you will, in gracious recompense for our generosity, stay out of my business, stop trying to control the kite-rays, and behave as an ally. Out of discord comes concord." Without haggling, Sanctuary's high-priest would never believe that the bargain was well struck.

"Ten percent. Yes, of course—if your people will teach only mine and keep silent about it." Greed and disappointment fought for control of Torchholder's pale, fleshy face. He'd come here prepared for an argument, ready to fan a dispute to open hostility to further his agenda. Now, there was benefit to be had through compromise. "Done?"

"Done."

Bargain duly consummated. But Torchholder wasn't satisfied: "Kouras' priestess is in need of regular treatment."

"Not according to our healer. But now her fate will be in your hands, since you'll have the jars. Your staff can treat her. What else?" Overhead, thunder rumbled; storm clouds swallowed up the sun.

"Else? Oh, else. Yes. You need to do something about these stragglers from your war. It wasn't even fought on our soil, but beyond our territorial limits, yet they're terrorizing my town."

"Your town terrorizes itself. These stragglers just broaden the selection of perpetrators and victims. But we will. I acknowledge our responsibility. Tell your city guard to stay out of Band skirmishes, except to provide any help Critias asks. And our military justice, not your civil code, applies."

"Now, you're not going to… Oh, so you are."

"We will clean up the mess, yes. All things out of strife are sprung." Tempus got to his feet. Torchholder did. "We're done here, Torch, unless you have another bone to pick, which I surely would advise against, since a storm is coming."

And it was.

*

In the common room of the mercenary hostel, walls dark as congealing blood still kept all secrets, quiet as the age-old weapons from bygone wars that hung there.

Critias was huddled at a corner table with two armored fighters tonight, the most likely of the sellswords gathered here. Strat came in, got a posset from the sideboard, and joined them. The two foreign mercenaries, sitting there in fine-bossed corselets, assessed Straton with game and calculating eyes.

"Strat, you look like you've seen a ghost," Crit said.

"Several, and more stragglers than I like." Straton frankly looked the fighters up and down. "I'm Ace, called Straton," he said. "Crit's rightman. Band tactician. Life to you both."

"And glory," said the first mercenary, short, moon-faced and throaty-voiced, with one elbow propped on the table. "I'm called Breisis. And I see what you are."

"Everlasting joy to you," said the second—a Sacred Band benediction for the dead. This fighter was big, broad and insouciant with dark hair glossy on a bullock's neck, leaning a chair back on two legs, one hand on a hip-slung dagger. "Call me Dikti."

Strat didn't answer.

"These two want to work," Crit told Strat.

"At what?" Strat asked.

Chair legs hit the ground. "Never mind," said Dikti, the younger fighter, and stood tall, kicking the chair away.

"Street cleaning," said Breisis, the elder, never blinking, reaching out and catching the younger's wrist in so practiced a motion that Crit knew this happened all the time with them. "Unless you think your leftman's in error, Ace, and you don't need any help who know the stragglers, your enemy's tactics and the lay of things hereabouts."

So now Strat understood that these were fighters from the other side of the war, and that they were women. Crit watched his partner's face closely and saw Strat think it through.

"Where'll they billet?"

"In town, wherever they choose. With one another. Infiltrating."

"You have your own mounts?"

"And every other little thing we need," assured the older fighter, whose hair was shorter than Strat's own.

"Then try your luck, if you've the stomachs for it."

"Our stomachs are just like yours," said the younger one, spinning her vacated chair and sitting on it backward, spread-legged and cocky. "Our arms as strong; our eyes as sharp. What's different is better."

Critias had found six male fighters but only these two women had flatly admitted to fighting against them in the Great War. He'd already put the others on the street: spies had limited utility and short life spans. For these two, this was the moment of testing: "So let's talk about strategy and tactics, and what you know of the stragglers here. Then, if we like what we hear, we'll put you to work for as long as you're able."

"Agreed," said Breisis, and Straton sucked in a deep breath as the short woman began to draw with her fingers in the wet-rings on the table.

The Riddler would be well pleased, if what these mercenary stragglers knew could tip the balance in favor of the Unified Sacred Band.

When they were nearly done, Cassander ambled in, casual and quiet in scale armor, pausing at the sideboard with a glance Crit's way, wanting to report but not willing to interrupt.

Crit motioned him over. "Cassander, meet Breisis and Dikti. Cassander heals our fighters and our horses."

"Surgery and cautery and herbs—no magic charms or prayers, but the occasional trick or two. Life to you, and everlasting glory, Strat, and to both of you, fighters. Sir," he said to Crit, "I saw your horse… just wanted to say the items are delivered, instructions given. They'll start offering services tomorrow. I have a private matter…"

"I'll walk you out," Crit said and, on the threshold: "What is it, Cass?"

Shadows from torches by the door made Cassander's eyes glitter. "Sir, Kouras says his priestess isn't doing well. The high priest is pressuring me to see her."

"Ignore him."

"Kouras is asking as well."

"Ignore him too. We, not you, will solve that problem. Be patient."

Cassander nodded. "I wasn't complaining. But thank you. And you? Are you improving?" Keen-eyed, concerned, careful. "Should I stop by Shambles later? One more treatment might be wise. I'm here all night tonight, on call. I have an errand at Aphrodisia House. I could see you afterward…"

"Come by at the start of fourth watch." *Good.* Crit felt better than he had in weeks but with the schedule he was keeping, any help was welcome.

*

A girl's lament spun upon the evening breeze in the alley outside the hostel, then stopped. "He was here," she whispered. "I saw him. He was in the room with both of you. What happened?"

"What happened is none of your affair," Breisis told her gruffly.

"But you said you'd ask him…"

"…if he wanted you. Yes, I remember. She's right, Breisis," Dikti said. "But we can't sell you to him now that we've an accommodation with his betters… Anyway, I quite fancy all this singing, these tales of heroes."

"You *promised.*"

"You keep silent and don't cry," Breisis intervened, "and we can still help you out, little one. Now, I did promise, so I'll make you a plan. You'll do just as I say, then we're quits. They'll be stalking stragglers, so this plot isn't entirely without risk. We'll find you a spot where Stepsons patrol and when he comes by, you'll beg his protection. He's a man; men do all for show. He won't be able to resist… a dangerous street, a pretty girl alone… If you play your part right, your Sacred Band boy will carry you away on that big brown horse and you'll never say a word to any Stepson that we helped you. But you need to understand that Sacred Banders don't tend to love women very long…"

"He'll love me. He'll want me. I saw it in a dream. He will."

In an errant moonbeam, the young girl's eyes seemed to glow like the eyes of something wild in the woods and soon enough she began once more to sing.

*

Simias tried to stop his rightman before young Perses spoke, but Perses was unruly whenever he was about to go to war.

"Menander was *there,* in the infirmary, having his broken leg set. He heard this blasphemy spoken by Cassander to Tempus and Nikodemos, Critias and Straton," Perses insisted too loudly. Glancing-eyed Perses nudged Simias with his shoulder; Simias took hold of the curly-haired poet as the Thebans waited for the sun to rise and Stepson grooms to bring their horses from the barracks stables. "Cassander said some Sanctuary fool calls our goddess accursed—and puts Blessed Harmony in the same category with a witch. *A witch!* We need to *do* something."

"Rumors and jealousy," Charon said patiently. Charon might not have been so patient if they were back in Thebes, or if fiery Perses weren't Simias' partner. Rank conferred privilege, even here, a world away from everything his Thebans had known and loved. "Ignore it. The goddess is with us. Thank her every day that you live to see a sunrise such as this one." Charon's face caught the first morning light; his eye-whites gleamed. As if on cue, the sky caught fire, cloud-bellies flaring red and gold in the coming dawn.

"Pay no heed to my Perses, warriors. The prospect of combat always makes him suspicious of everyone and everything," said Simias apologetically to the four other Thebans in their squadron. They'd ride today with Charon, the Theban warrior-priest, as his hand-picked personal guard: with Gorgias, the Theban trainer, dark and dour; with blond Agis, not much older than Perses; with Archias, Agis' partner and left-side leader here in this strange land where a demigod called the Riddler led a Sacred Band like no other.

Gorgias, never subtle, said, "Perses, this is life, not poetry—not some heroic tale. We've made friends among this Sacred Band of Stepsons. We're now part of the Unified Sacred Band to whom we swore our oaths. We'll not pick fights.

Our goddess decides the fates of us all. She doesn't need your protection."

"Trust not in Cassander. He's some northern fighter from Mygdonia—not one of us," said Archias, gruff and cold-hearted. "No one knows what his father was… a Macedonian, so I heard. He's not even a real doctor of men, but of horses.

So how can you put any faith in him, who serves under false pretenses?"

"See!" Perses said. "Gorgias knows I'm right. Archias knows. We should face down Cassander, make him take back what he said."

Charon said, "Perses, Gorgias knows no such thing. You're not helping, Gorgias. And Archias, Cassander healed you well enough, and the only part of you that's a horse is your ass. Let these stories fade away. Truth comes to him who is quiet and listens for it."

As Charon finished, the grooms began appearing with the swift-footed Stepson mounts, and there was no more time for posturing or nerves.

Charon said, "Time to pray, Thebans. We go now into battle. Must I remind you, remnants of our Sacred Band of Thebes, that we are all strangers here? In this mercenary band who saved us, none fight for their homeland, but only for Tempus. And our goddess approves of this *polemarch* and his warriors. She walks among us. She blesses us with her presence—our goddess comes to earth for us here, as she seldom did in Thebes. Now thank her that you live to fight on this day. May our swords be shining with victory and our heads covered in glory. Bow those heads and ask Harmony to guide our lances, our shields and our arrows as she sees fit."

Perses shivered when Simias let him go but, finally, kept silent while Charon intoned a benediction in the fire of the rising sun.

*

Moonlight kisses panoplies: lances with iron spear-heads at either end; crossbows and quarrels; bronze-bossed *linothoraxes* and jointed cuirasses; bronze helmets and shields; arm and ankle guards and decorated greaves. Clop of hooves, creak of harness, clink of metal among the ranks, fully armed tonight: Stepson heavy cavalry riding by fours and sixes down surly streets with crossbows and two spears each, hunting stragglers.

Tonight Cassander was seeing Sanctuary up closer than he liked: no watch goes unmanned, no stone unturned as Stepsons ride street to street, alley to alley, house to house to make their point. Urban raiding parties, shaking up the town. Families rousted, clutching one another outside their hovels, rubbing their eyes while babies cried. *Harbor no stragglers, w*as the message ringing loud and clear.

Red-haired, green-eyed Kouras rode on Cassander's right, sullenly silent. The storm god's son was angry not to be among the raiders. Muscled bronze cuirass, shield on his left arm, lance in hand: if a straggler war-party came their way, Kouras was ready. For any less, the storm god's son was overdressed tonight.

"To Aphrodisia House, Kouras." Cassander reined his horse to the west as another squadron went by, headed east. The Riddler himself on his gray Trôs horse led that hunting party with his partner, Nikodemos, beside him and four behind them: when the commander wore his leopard mantle, havoc rode on his left hand.

City guards blocked intersections, stopping folk at random. The two Stepsons urged their mounts on by, unchallenged, when Kouras waved his *kopis*.

"Put that damned *kopis* away." Cassander reached over his shoulder to get his recurved bow and five arrows from its case, a Scythian-style *gorytos.* Kouras, his crossbow hanging from his saddle, was peering hard into shadows, looking for stragglers. "Seek no trouble, Kouras. There are better targets than the two of us out here tonight. Just ride."

"I know you don't like the *kopis.* But Nikodemos says that the man, not what he carries, is the weapon of the god."

"I tended your Nikodemos' wounds after his battle with the wizard, boy," Cassander said, "until his goddess took a hand. For him, that's true. For you, son of Vashanka, and the other Bandarans, it may be true as well. It's not true for me. This Band is full of heroes made of sterner stuff than I. I'm just flesh and blood, and I hate patching myself up."

With a muttered curse, Kouras sheathed the *kopis* and hefted his lance. "What about my priestess?"

Cassander was ready. "The commander said treat none outside the Stepsons. Critias confirmed it. I can't, Kouras." He closed his calves on his horse's barrel; it began to trot.

"And if she dies?" Kouras' mount took up a collected canter on Cassander's right, more comfortable than a trot, but a waste of energy for a horse with a long night ahead.

"Then the high priest will be to blame." *She's too young for childbearing, no matter whose child it is.*

"She swears she'll let no one treat her but you." Kouras side-passed his mount until he was pushing Cassander's right leg with his left and his shield bumped Cassander's shoulder. "She's sure that only you can heal her. She had a dream about you."

He was about to tell Kouras that young girls commonly fix on anyone who seems powerful when another young girl came running out of an alley into their path:

"Stepsons, help me!"

"Keep going," Cassander said, but of course Kouras stopped.

In a heartbeat this girl was scrambling up behind the storm god's son, onto his horse.

Out from shadows came first three, then four more men on foot and Cassander was sorely tempted to leave Kouras to deal with them alone. Instead, he reached over and slapped Kouras' horse hard on the rump with his recurved bow. "Get out of here. Ride. Go. *Go.*"

The roan reared up. The girl slid off. Kouras cursed.

Now they had a tussle on their hands with seven men and a weeping girl in the middle of it. Kouras stabbed his lance down into darkness. It cracked and was lost in a moment as one foe grabbed the shaft and pulled, nearly unseating him. Kouras let go just before the rear head of the lance could slice open his palm.

"Get you busy, Kouras, you and your god." Cassander was nocking arrows, shooting into moving shadows, then sending his horse into the fray with his legs while he exchanged bow for sword. "I've got your back."

That he did, slashing at whatever launched itself his way or Kouras' but staying clear of the *kopis* and shield of the storm god's son, who was moving too fast to predict. Cassander thrust his sword into one attacker and felt meat and bone give way as hands grabbed at his legs and another man jumped for his horse's bridle. Someone else mewled while a throat rattled, somewhere. Otherwise the only sound was Kouras' crossbow, loosing bolts that whispered by Cassander's ears: one, two, three, four.

If one of those bolts hits my horse, god-child...

Then Kouras charged in front of him, yelling curses, brandishing his shield, a blur hacking about with his *kopis.* His roan whinnied and snorted and stomped.

Abruptly all fighting ceased. Cassander could hear his own breathing, his pulse in his ears; his horse was heaving loudly, shivering between his legs. No other sound remained but the girl's soft weeping amid the corpses—and Kouras' husky voice, consoling her and offering her his bloody shield-hand, helping her swing back up behind him.

This boy wanted so much to be a hero he'd be dead before twenty unless his father the god was very, very careful. Or more merciful than Cassander knew the gods to be.

The girl cooed and praised Kouras to the skies and Kouras made manly noises all the way to Aphrodisia House, while Cassander held his tongue and cleaned his blade and made sure he secured his bow in its shoulder-slung case.

By the time they'd stabled their horses out back, the girl had disappeared.

When they'd checked their horses for damages, found none, and climbed the brothel's front steps, the rescued girl was leaning against the door there. "Please, Stepsons," she said in a quavery voice. "Help me, please…" In the door-way's flaring torchlight, Cassander first noticed she was too bloody for splat-ter alone; next, that the blood seeping out around the hand at her belly was black.

"Bring her inside," he told Kouras before the young Step-son could ask. "I'll look at her." As soon as Kouras touched her, she collapsed against him.

Myrtis, the madam, saw the bloody girl in Kouras' arms and found them an empty downstairs room while patrons gawked and whispered.

They lay the girl down on a pallet there and Cassander cut away her clothes: her skirt's hem reached only to her knee, so this girl was yet a maiden. She had a long slash across her bel-ly, deeper in the middle—probably from that damned *kopis* of Kouras' or one just like it, although Cassander wouldn't say so.

Kouras fetched Cassander's kit from his horse while he cleaned the wound sufficiently to see why the blood was black and the girl was shaking. Then he gave her poppy by mouth for the pain before he packed the wound with herbs from his kit: kava and cannabis to anesthetize the site; seaweed, wood ashes, and salt to draw poison and disinfect; calendula to fight deep brewing sepsis; and yarrow to stanch the bleeding.

When he was done, her blood was still seeping too fast through the packing. She was small; the wound was deep. *Too deep. Too much rent and torn inside.*

"Who are you?" he asked, rocking back on his haunches.

"Nobody," she replied through pale lips.

"Everyone is somebody. You must have a name. How are you called? What were you doing out there?"

"I'm a song-girl, having a bad dream," she said. The poppy was doing its work. She reached out for his hand.

A song-girl. There were none in Sanctuary that he knew of. They followed armies, mostly, or plied their trade among sophisticates. So this girl was probably a straggler. "Kouras, get me some wine and some honey." He needed alcohol to prime his herbs and further clean the depths of the wound; he needed something sweet and gooey to stabilize his poultice and entice her humors to fight infection. She was wriggling around too much, touching herself, disturbing his work.

He looked up when no one answered. One of Myrtis' whores hovered there, pop-eyed. Kouras was nowhere to be seen. "Get Kouras. Get your mistress."

The prostitute scurried and then Kouras came back with a different, brown-haired, blue-eyed harlot and the madam in tow, bringing the wine and honey. By then Cassander had poured poppy-sap granules onto a broad leaf. "Take this and give it to her by mouth at the end of third watch, Myrtis." Myrtis took it and folded the leaf with practiced fingers.

The girl murmured softly, groping once more for his hand. He wasn't supposed to be treating anyone outside the Band, but this girl had asked the Stepsons for help and might have been wounded because of them—or by one of them.

If only I hadn't slapped the roan on the rump with that bow. If only Kouras hadn't laid about him with that kopis…

Portly Myrtis pursed purple lips and said, "What about your magic fish cure?"

"No such thing," he said. "No magic cure for this. Keep her quiet. That's all we can do."

He dripped alcohol onto the packed wound, then smeared the honey across her belly above the hairline, completing the poultice. Despite the drugs he'd given her, the song-girl mewed and writhed. With Kouras' help, he wrapped fine wool bandage around her hips and loins and knotted the ends as she slapped at him and pulled at her dressing. He didn't tie her hands: she was already too agitated; if he frightened her, things would only get worse.

"Girl," he said, leaning close to her face, "listen." Her eyes roved. "Be still and live, or pull at your wound this way and die. Your choice."

The girl tried to focus on him, then passed out.

If she lives, she'll never bear a child.

"Myrtis, I'll come back and sew her up or cauterize her, whichever's indicated, when the bleeding stops. But she'll need to stay here for two or three days. Reapply this poultice with alcohol and honey and rewrap her at every other change of watch." He put more herbs onto another leaf and fashioned it into a packet.

Myrtis didn't take it, just looked at him dubiously.

Kouras and his harlot were holding hands, whispering together. Then Kouras said, "We can take her to Shawme's house. She's the Stepsons' responsibility… *our* responsibility. If you hadn't hit my horse, she wouldn't have fallen off and none of this would have happened."

"She's not going anywhere in this condition. I hit your horse because I wanted to get us out of there, not stay to fight those stragglers with this girl up behind you, and I didn't want to argue with you about it. And I still don't." *Storm god's son or not, Kouras, you're a lodestone for trouble.*

Kouras said nothing but his face turned bright red.

"Kouras is right," Myrtis added quickly, rubbing her wattle. "She should go to Shawme's house. Or to your barracks where you can tend her yourself. She can't stay here. I can't treat an injury like hers. She's…"

Competition, from the streets. "Yes, she *can* stay here. And she will. You'll see to her personally, Myrtis. Critias will want to talk to her when she's well enough. You'll keep her here for me until I find a suitable place for her. I'll pay you for her care here."

Even if I could move her safely, I can't take a song-girl to the barracks. And Tempus himself had ordered him to treat none but the Band.

A song-girl. She was muttering in a tongue he hadn't heard for years.

"And your other companion for tonight, Cassander, the one you reserved?"

"I haven't time now. And I like this one better." Utter fabrication but good enough.

"Cassander, this is Shawme," said Kouras when they left the humming, incoherent song-girl with Myrtis. "Shawme, let me introduce Cassander."

"We've met before. Thank you for offering your house and your help, Shawme."

Shawme the prostitute said, "Will she live? The song-girl? And what's a song-girl?"

"She may live. She may not. Song-girls pleasure aristocratic officers on campaign, where I'm from." He wasn't going to tell them this girl was a straggler. But he must tell Crit.

"And that is…?"

"So far away it doesn't matter."

And it didn't, not since he'd joined the Sacred Band and Tempus' woman whisked them hither and yon in place and time.

*

Fighters dream of sack and pillage. Priests dream of wealth and power. Young girls dream of joy and old women dream of gods. Boys dream of pleasure; slaves dream of freedom. Teachers dream of famous names and witches dream of horrors only they can tame. Maybe Hakiem had been right: maybe things were different since the war. Maybe Sanctuary's dreams were out of control, but to Critias it seemed like any other day in this town worse than anywhere he'd ever been.

Certainly this 'song-girl' whom Cassander and Kouras had found was so full of drugs that she dreamed she was awake. Critias nor Straton could make any sense of a word she said.

Thereafter, with Straton by his side, Crit rode the sun up, crisscrossing Sanctuary, interrogating whomever his fighters caught in their net alive. They crossed paths with the healer and the storm god's son as dawn was turning to bright, light blue.

"That girl in Aphrodisia House is too drugged to tell us anything," Crit remarked when Cassander and Kouras came close. "You're sure she's a straggler?"

"I'm told that song-girls aren't customary hereabouts." Cassander's face was drawn. "What else would she be but a straggler? Her head will clear, if she lives. She can't be moved yet. I'll keep her at Aphrodisia House a few days. If you want to talk to her after that, we'll need another place for her, maybe at the Shambles station."

"Not at Shambles," Crit said.

"Then with those Lemnians of yours."

"Those *what?*" Strat asked.

"Breisis and Dikti, your two straggler man-killers: in one night, the Lemnian women murdered all their men for being unfaithful and lived on, manless, except for adventurers who reached their shores unknowing and did the needful. Meanwhile, we have something you two should see," Cassander said, his voice too snappish to be solely the result of a long night with Kouras on his right.

"Lead on." *Lemnians: straggler man-killers, lost in time and place: perfect.* "It's a new day, Stepsons, with a good night's work behind us." Crit urged his chestnut up beside Cassander's brown horse and Strat fell in on Kouras' left.

With Cassander leading the way, they turned into Promise Park where Critias saw a knot of Stepsons and Sanctuarites up ahead, before a tall tree with something hanging from a stout branch among golden leaves.

"What is it?" Crit asked.

"Stragglers," Cassander replied. "No one was here when we first found them."

"Well, they're here now," Strat said.

By then Critias could see two bodies, hanging upside down from the branch, a pool of blood below their heads.

Both men dangling there by the ankles had had their throats slit, their fingers cut off. They'd bled out, bound face to face, wrists tied together.

He and Strat dismounted; Cassander and Kouras followed. Sacred Banders and locals gave back before them. Cassander said, "I didn't want to disturb anything here until you saw them."

"You were right," Strat said.

Crit and Strat walked over and looked closely at the bodies and the blood pooled on the ground. *Not a pretty way to die.* It always surprised him, how much blood one body held. "An object lesson for any stragglers who might want to talk to us," Crit hazarded, hunkering down where the blood puddled thick.

"A warning: Stay away from stragglers," Straton proclaimed in his best battlefield voice for the benefit of the gathering crowd. Out of the corner of his eye, Crit saw Breisis and Dikti among the throng; unobtrusive, showing only the most casual interest.

"I wonder who'll get the fingers," Crit said. Here and there among the stragglers, little boxes would be sent, each containing a finger to remind selected folk to keep silent. "They're getting organized. Don't cut these men down until the Riddler and Stealth have seen this."

Walking past Breisis and Dikti without showing a flicker of recognition, Crit dispatched two pairs to find the commander. Only anonymity would keep those two female fighters safe long enough for them to prove their worth.

*

Tempus and Niko rode up to the hanging tree and halted their horses. Niko's black snorted disapprovingly and jigged in place, its tail clamped between its legs, its ears flattened at the smell of so much blood. Tempus' Trôs, seasoned warhorse, stood quiet, head raised, nostrils wide, a single muscle ticcing along its left flank.

This was a message from antiquity. Tempus had seen it countless times, but still it rankled.

"Niko, get Charon."

His partner obeyed without a word, casting only one backward look at him through flat and empty eyes. Niko had fought on Wizardwall and beyond; he knew what he saw: battle lines being drawn.

Now the god's pique made sense to Tempus, as Sanctuary's little troubles began to grow and spread. Well and good. Things here had been too quiet for his taste.

Before Niko returned with Charon, Tempus waved Crit and Strat to him and ordered them to bring him Cassander and Gyskouras.

When the healer and the storm god's boy came close, Tempus listened to their brief report and then said, "Cassander, you've done well, keeping Kouras on your right, but we need your full attention on our wounded."

Cassander inclined his head. "As you wish, Commander." Formal and controlled. On his left, Critias and Straton exchanged glances. To the healer's right, Kouras shifted in his saddle, at pains to seem impassive but flushing red.

Tempus heard horses coming up on his right; he didn't need to look around: Niko and Charon.

Vashanka's son met his eyes, ready for anything, braced, defiant. Tempus could see the god in him, blazing in his flesh. The youth kept silent, head high. Kouras was learning what it meant to be a Stepson.

Niko's horse jingled into place beside him. On Niko's right, Charon sat at ease: a fine mind and an experienced hand, taking everything in stride; a worthy example for anyone who must face the unknown.

Tempus let the silence stretch until these six were focused on him and nothing else. Some things deserve a measured pace. Beyond Cassander, the two bled-out stragglers reminded one and all that time is the only true wealth a man can claim: live to fight on other days; all else is folly.

"Gyskouras, we think it's time you had a permanent left-side leader, one familiar with your special nature. And the gods agree."

Kouras' head came up higher but he didn't look away.

Cassander peered around, then he too was still.

"Kouras, on this day, Charon—priest of Harmony and leader of our Thebans—has offered to become your left-side leader: to fight beside you, shoulder to shoulder; teach you all he knows about men and gods. Do you accept?"

"Accept? I am honored," Kouras said. "Life to you, Charon, and everlasting glory. And to us both. And to us all."

Charon rode forward and Niko flashed a signal to Kouras, who urged his mount out to meet the Theban warrior-priest. When the two clasped hands, Straton yowled the Stepson wolf call. Behind him, every other Sacred Bander within earshot howled back the same in unison.

Then Charon bawled the victory cry. Kouras did. Cassander did.

Tempus looked at Niko and Critias: it was done.

Afterward, Kouras rode up close to Niko and Cassander where they were talking softly.

"Life to you, Kouras," said Cassander to the storm god's son.

"Really?" said Kouras guardedly. "You mean it? You're not angry?"

"Really," Cassander said, as Niko rubbed his hand across his mouth to hide a grin.

Then Straton said, "You are truly blessed, Gyskouras," mimicking the Theban custom with a pious voice and a wink and everybody, even Charon, chuckled.

For it was true.

*

"Commander, please—a moment," Cassander said, summoning his courage when he got to Aphrodisia House and found the Riddler and Stealth there. "I need your help."

Niko turned around to face him and leaned back, elbows on the bar. Tempus merely stared at Cassander through hooded eyes and waited.

Cassander said, "I brought a badly-wounded girl here. She asked for Stepson aid and got struck in the middle of a skirmish Kouras and I had with stragglers during the raids. It's my fault she's hurt. I know I'm not supposed to treat wounded outside the Band...but if I don't, she'll die."

"Then see to her, Stepson," the commander said. "What else?"

"Myrtis doesn't want her here. If this girl lives until I can move her, I want to take her to the barracks where I can tend her better." Tempus almost never allowed women there, outside his own and Niko's goddess. *Almost* never. "Otherwise I have to come to town twice a day. I can't spare so much time away from my other duties. And when I'm here, I'm always dodging palace pressure to see to Molin's priestess."

Since the commander didn't immediately answer, Niko raised his eyes and said, "What kind of girl is this, Sacred Bander?"

"Maybe a straggler girl, or a song-girl from beyond Wizardwall, passing through. I don't know. She's incoherent. Young. A maiden." Cassander went cautiously. When Niko took an interest in women, except for his goddess, virgins were always his choice. If the song-girl caught Niko's eye, it might help things. But Cassander realized he didn't want that as soon as the words passed his lips.

Tempus stared at him thoughtfully; his kill-smile came and went. "If it matters so much to you that she live, then bring her to the barracks under your care until she's well."

"Thank you, Commander."

Niko said very quietly, "We have the Theban altar there." Searching eyes in a face carefully composed caught Cassander's and jolted him: mystic calm damming the gods' own wrath. "Perhaps the goddess will help her if you ask."

Cassander didn't want that, either. But he said, "Thank you, Stealth," and backed away, his heart pounding more than it had at any time during the raid or the tussle on the street.

Then he went to tend the song-girl, thinking that the taleteller had been right: in Sanctuary this season, dreams were coming true.

She was sleeping fitfully. She woke as he cut away her bandage. He wished she hadn't. Everything he was about to do to her would hurt.

Her face was pinched and pale from so much blood lost.

"Iatros?" Physician, it meant. "I was dreaming you were here… silly song-girl dreams…"

Myrtis is giving her too much poppy. "Not silly. True. You dreamed I'm here and here I am. Now be brave." As he pulled the bandage, sticky with honey and blood, off the wound, his mouth went dry. But the wound didn't stink: the poultice was doing its work.

"I've been lost for so long," she murmured. "So very long…"

"I know. But I've got you now."

While he tended her, she sang Sappho in a drifting voice, so sweet: "Some say an army of horsemen, some say an army of foot and some say a fleet of ships is the most beautiful sight on this black earth; but I say it is whatever you adore…"

When she sang in her lilting accent, Cassander realized how much he had missed these sounds, these songs. His fingers trembled as he worked upon her wound and she slipped into sleep, murmuring a song he didn't know but deeply understood: "Come stand with me, my love. Hold me and be bold by me. Where are you now? In this smoke of fury all around, my eyes sting till you come running, your rage unbounded. When we die, we die together."

*

"Cass, Strat and I were wondering about these fish. Can we use them to persuade some stragglers—those we took alive—to tell us what we want to know?" Crit asked the healer when Cassander dropped by the Shambles station to check on Crit's aches and pains.

The city guard had taken charge of the straggler corpses. The raid had yielded some likely informants and thinned the stragglers on the streets. The rest had gone to ground. A good result, all in all.

Cassander cocked his head, bristle-jawed face set. "I've never heard of using rays for interrogation, but… yes. Fish, or jars with a stronger pulse, as you wish. It should work."

It did work. Kite-rays loosened many tongues that day and that night and the next. And for days after that, Straton's interrogations were more fruitful and Sacred Band raids more useful, with Breisis and Dikti targeting the most likely stragglers.

The Riddler was pleased with the result, and Niko told Crit so.

In the palace and on the Avenue of Temples, Vashanka's priests applied the therapy jars to noble and common folk alike to chase their ills and empty their pockets.

Of Seriti, the pregnant priestess, Crit heard nary a word, even from the storm god's son: either the jars were helping her or the palace was keeping its business to itself.

Meanwhile, first in Aphrodisia House and then at the bar racks, Cassander's song-girl sang the songs the healer most wanted to hear.

Kouras was riding on Charon's right, which eased Crit's mind and improved Cassander's mood, though for days upon days thunder grumbled close at hand and lightning flashed from far to near and rain came pounding down.

The rain slowed the construction projects that Crit had under way at the barracks, at the gutted Mageguild, and below Abarsis' overlook, but didn't stop them. Crit loved making progress and he was succeeding at that—and at keeping Straton too busy to go sneaking off to see the necromant.

Considering that the Band was serving in Sanctuary, things were proceeding as well as could be expected.

Or maybe just a little bit better, despite the rain that poured down every day.

So when Tempus came in, dripping water from his leopard-skin mantle, and said, "We're leaving. Two days hence," Crit shouldn't have been surprised: things had been going too well.

But he was. "Commander?"

"Crit, staff an advance party: you and Strat, Niko, myself. We'll take eight more with us. Organize the rest to follow in a fortnight, or as soon as the wounded can travel. Leave no one behind. Put Charon and Sync in charge of forming up the balance of the force for the withdrawal." Then Tempus turned on his heel and stomped back out into the rain.

Withdrawal. No further orders. No explanation. Thus it always was, when you served the Riddler. Change was his lifeblood.

Since leaving Sanctuary meant leaving Strat's witch behind, Crit really didn't care about why, or where, or even how soon.

He'd done harder things at Tempus' bidding. And any place would be better than this one. What lies before is always better than what lies behind.

Chapter 3: Gods Take All

Far across the countryside rode the Sacred Band, seeing no one by day or night, until they came upon a hoary shrine with ancient plinth and pediment. And stopped, to make camp before sunset as the wind picked up. "Here is good enough," Tempus told Niko, and slid down from his gray Trôs horse, handing his partner his reins.

No city walls nor ruined town nor farm nor hovel could be seen, just twelve cavalrymen and their horses, pitching camp in a dell before an altar hill.

"As you say, Commander." Niko didn't like it here; dark hair lashed guarded eyes. He'd brought along a stone from the goddess Harmony's altar behind the old barracks: he palmed his belt-pouch where it lay.

So, despite a faint hope that going north would leave the Theban goddess behind, she was here in the heart of his rightman.

And before them stood an altar to an unnamed god.

What strange place was this? The wind smelled of salt but no sea could be seen. Autumn laced the air with daggers. Sunlight stabbed to earth in spears of amber and citron and rose, piercing cloudbanks in the heavens: down such a sky as this, the storm god might come rattling in his chariot.

But didn't.

Enlil had not deigned to join Tempus since they'd come here—wherever this place was.

Show yourself, Ravener. You brought us here, chose this ground. Explain Thyself.

Enlil gave him no sign, not even heavy breathing in his ear. The storm god of the armies seldom spoke to him on these eerie days. Instead Enlil lurked, silent, deep in his very bones and content with whatever game was in His bloody heart.

Other deities are here, though; restless, greedy; Tempus can feel them: theomachy is only a heartbeat away in these lands where other gods hold sway. The crumbling altar before him is proof of that. Everything is full of gods, fighters' hearts included.

Gods take all, in the end. You strive, you win, you lose and win again, and lose even the breath of life eventually. Fragile flesh is thrashed and shamed and always fails and falls away—unless, like Tempus and now Nikodemos, immortality is thrust upon you, burning away all but soul.

Then what difference does human striving make: mortal struggle, valor, pain? If you live, then live for the test of spirit, for the celebration of the heart. Live to fight on other days. Lose your beloveds, one by one. And remember. Exalt the kiss of friend and horse and wind and sun, which venality cannot cheapen nor stupidity belittle.

All things come into being out of Strife and Tempus is Strife's instrument. His Sacred Band, paired lovers and friends, fight across space and time for him: shoulder to shoulder, to the death, with honor. Unflinching, unwavering; committed, devoted in the sight of men and gods.

But now, here? Fight what? Honest battle would be a blessing. This abandoned landscape was too desolate to please any but horses.

While the cohort finished making camp Tempus climbed the hillock and the shrine's steps, then stood before the cyclopean red stone serving as an altar. Columns at four corners, paired pediments but no roof… he knew the style: Argive. And yet, the center stone was one huge block, older still, with a hewn top, angled so blood of ox or horse or man could pour down and into channels and from there back to the earth.

Then he knew whose altar this had been, once was, and now was again. Before Enlil's altar, he might bend his knee. Before his soldiers, he would not.

This altar had been usurped by other, later deities. Some folk believed that every stream, every mountain, every valley had its god who must be blandished and appeased. In those minds and in those lands, truth was as men and gods agreed.

So had warring gods put men to battle until none were left here? Until even the ruins were deserted?

Niko came up, barely a scuff of boots and whisper of greaves behind him; then beside him, as above his head black clouds fled the sun and blazing light spilled down.

"Niko, this was Enlil's shrine once—"

"I can feel it, Riddler," said his partner, and leaned forward to place the little white stone he'd carried north upon Enlil's altar, stained with blood from former times.

This was Harmony's stone, from her altar beside the storm god's, far behind and a world away: there was no going back there now, mayhap ever. Niko straightened up with a sigh:

"Perses wanted to recite a poem and asked Lysis to play his flute. Strat said no, they couldn't and Simias said yes, they could and Crit stepped in to solve it. So maybe you'd come down, to break the tension."

He didn't blame Niko for worrying about morale: *'What's done and undone can swap places, if the wrong song is sung'* the Greek sphinx had warned, or riddled, or cursed; warriors are a superstitious lot. 'No singing, then,' Straton had proclaimed days ago: one cure for that ill—but a divisive one.

"A moment, Niko; then I'll join you. And take your stone: your goddess and Enlil are where their faithful are, not chained to places such as these."

As for the greater curses dogging them—his own curse, the curse upon the Theban goddess, and curses wandering loose like refugees from the dream lord's war—these bothered him more.

So he tarries awhile at Enlil's altar, watching Niko descend the slope: balance and glory, humility enwrapping rage, perhaps forever; thinking that since he and Niko both are here, then the storm god of the armies and the Theban goddess of balance and justice are here as well.

Dusk overtakes him, his favorite time, when memory is lucent and hopes unbounded, when the world is full of whispered promise and anything can come to pass. In that dusk he bends his head to Enlil's altar and asks the storm god for a clearing of his path and of his heart.

And there he hears it, feels it: the breath of the god in his head, the warmth in his loins, the excitation in his soul. So he stays still, among the sounds of peepers and the coming dark, until the god rustles inside him, ramping in his skull—nothing daunting, but truly *there.*

Give me a sign, Ravener, why we tarry here. And for how long, in some fated nowhere only You could choose? Say what You have in Your mind. Or have done with this game and let us be on our way.

To that challenge, the god says not a word, but rasps against his bones and comes up in his eyes and looks, and looks; and chuckles. Or snarls.

Soon after, Tempus walked down the hill to join his fighters. Food was cooking over an open fire and Stepsons were passing a wineskin while, beyond, Arton and Lysis saw to the horses. And no one was singing or playing a pipe.

Possibly Enlil's dalliance with their fate was only whim, nothing more.

Strat lit torches and drove their butt-spikes into the ground, then looked up at the dark where a thin moon was rising.

Tempus looked up too, in time to see a shadow cross the crescent and disappear. Owl? Or something else? His fingers found his sword's hilt and grasped it.

Niko came to stand on his right. "Commander?"

"I saw, Niko."

Strat drove his last torch deep into the stony earth and joined them, his face screwed up. "What, do you think?"

Laughter rose from the seated pairs, giggles from the women lilting among the sounds of men. Simias called, "So where's tonight's tale, Straton?" The senior Theban was insouciant, placatory: morale problem solved, then.

Tempus said, "Strat, go tell them the tale they want—"

Then wings beat overhead, so close Tempus could feel the driven air upon his face.

Straton put up a forestalling hand, but Niko said, "It's fine, Strat. Go hold forth. We'll handle this."

With a doubtful look, Strat took one long stride. And paused.

Something glided to earth in the dark.

By then Tempus knew this was no owl hunting mice in the night.

Leaves shivered; branches bent; insects chittered; creatures unseen scurried and squeaked.

"Randal," Tempus called. "What took you so long?'

Out of the bushes rose a scrawny man, pulling on a cloak as he came their way. And sneezed. And rubbed his nose. Randal, the Band's sorcerer, was allergic to animal forms, especially when he became one; he'd flown here on eagle's wings to join them.

Niko strode forward and embraced the big-eared warrior-mage, then Straton crowded in to do the same.

"Commander," said Randal, formal but smirking. "Life to you, and everlasting glory. And to you, Nikodemos. And you, Straton. I was delayed by the… temper of the weather, out among the planes."

"No excuses, mageling," Straton growled, trying to hide his delight. "We're halfway to noplace and you're needed, Witchy-ears. A Stepson is expected to be where he's needed."

"We didn't know we'd need him for this, Strat," Niko said quietly, stepping back.

"We'll have questions after you're settled in, Randal," Tempus said. "Niko, have Lysis find Randal a suitable horse. He'll be with us awhile. And you, Strat—your audience awaits. Tell them a tale wherein Randal figures. Those Thebans and Lemnians still have much to learn of our cadre's history."

Straton started toward the bonfire alone and Tempus turned his attention back to the Stepsons' mage. Niko was already questioning Randal, who clearly wanted to go with Straton and warm himself by the fire: "…need to know where 'here' is. And why cloud-conveyance failed us."

Randal looks between Tempus and Niko and beyond, up to the altar of Enlil, and back. The mage's eyes glow as if with reflected firelight. "Niko, cloud-conveyance does not 'fail.' And you're south of Chaetae. Where else would you be? I've been in Lemuria too long; I've missed all this… The Riddler's sister sent me with a message to hurry your contingent home. Oh, Riddler… Commander, we're to accelerate our return to Lemuria. And I can't stay long."

"I know, Randal. But while you're here, lend a hand. Arton's had another vision…"

So they are, in general, where they are supposed to be: south of the Thracian border, trekking north to Physca: the storm god has not deserted them or played them foul.

Tempus' sister Cime has sent Randal looking for them as if the Band is a crew of deserters or a gang of truants: Cime always assumes the worst.

Straton begins telling the group by the fire a tale of Randal's exploits in olden times, while Niko questions his former partner about songs and inhuman creatures hereabouts.

Tempus is heartened that Randal is here. Had he not asked Enlil for a sign?

He sits among his fighters to hear Straton's story, although he'd rather be alone. Command makes demands. Too, he needs to give Randal and Niko time to bond: no longer paired, they are better friends than either will admit.

As Straton regales all with his tale, Tempus thinks he sees a lion, then an eagle, among the shadows and the trees. He doesn't pursue them or alert his troops: what will come will come…

Chapter 4: What Women Do Best

From a hunting blind of artfully-piled garbage guarded by a dozen fat, half-tamed rats, an Ilsig head, then another, and another, caught the moonlight as the death squad emerged from tunnels to go stalking Beysibs in the Maze.

They called their leader "Zip," when they called him anything at all. He didn't encourage familiarity; he'd always been a loner, a creature of the streets without family or friends. Even before the Beysib invaders had come and the waves of executions had begun, street urchins and Maze-dwellers had stayed clear of the knife-boy who was half Ilsig and half some race much paler; who hired out for copper to any enforcer in the Maze or disgruntled dealer in Downwind. And who, it was said, brought an eye or tongue or liver from every soul he murdered to an obscure and half-forgotten altar on the White Foal River's edge.

Even his death squad was afraid of him, Zip knew. That was fine with him. Every now and again, a member was captured by the Rankan oppressors or the Beysib oppressors: the less these idealists of revolution knew of him, the less they could reveal under torture or blandishment. He'd had a friend once, or at least a close acquaintance—an Ilsig thief called Hanse. This Hanse, with all his shining blades and his high-toned airs, had gone the way of everything in Sanctuary since the Beysibs' ships had docked: to oblivion, to hell in a basket.

Standing up straight for a moment in the moon-licked gloom to get his bearings, Zip heard laughter rounding a corner; saw a flash of pantaloon. He ducked back with a hiss and a signal to his group, who'd been trained by Nisibisi insurgents and knew this game as well as he.

The moonlight wasn't bright enough to tell the color of the Beysib males'—Zip didn't think of them as "men"—pantaloons, but he'd be willing to bet they were of claret velvet or shiny purple silk. Killing Beysibs was about as exciting as killing ants, and as fruitless: there were just too damned many of them.

The three coming toward his hunting party were drunk as Rankans and limp as any man might be who'd just come out of the Street of Red Lanterns empty of seed and purse.

He could almost see their fish-eyes bulging; he could hear their jewelry clank. For pussy-whipped sons of snake-women, these were loud and brash, taller than average, and with a better command of street-Rankene. From under their glittering, veil-draped hats, profanity worthy of the Rankan Hell Hounds cut the night.

There remained nearly the whole Street of Red Lanterns between the two parties. "Preposition," Zip breathed, and his two young squad members slipped away to find their places.

His death squads had done this every night since Harvest Moon. The only result Zip had seen was a second, then a third wave of Beysib ritual executions. But since those ceremonially slaughtered were hated Rankan overlords and Ilsigs who served the Rankans and the Bey, guilt wasn't keeping any of the revolutionaries up at night.

And you had to do something. Kadakithis had been a harsh ruler, but the Rankan barbarians were spoken of wistfully and with something bordering on affection now that the Beysib had come: a matriarchy complete with female mercenaries; distaff assassins; magicians more utterly ruthless than men could ever be.

The women warriors of the Beysib were enough to have brought Zip into the orb of the revolution—his manhood was something he'd fight to keep. More than a few exposed fishfolk titties would be needed to make him bow his head or renege on his heritage.

Right now, Zip was going to kill a couple of Beysib boytoys and lay their pertinent equipment on an obscure Foalside altar: maybe the river god within could be roused to action. Death knew that the Ilsig gods were out of their depth with these women—despots whose spittle was as venomous as the pet snakes they kept and the spells they spoke. The revolution could use the publicity and Zip could use the money their jewelry was going to bring once Marc melted it down.

Down the street came the Beysib boy-whores, laughing in deeper voices than Beysib men usually dared.

Zip could make out some words now: "—porking town down on its porking hands and knees with its butt in the air while those porking porkers pork it—"

Another voice cut in: "I've told you once, Gayle, to watch your mouth. Now I'm making it an order. Beysibs don't—God's balls!"

Without warning, and according to plan, Zip's two toughs jumped out from concealment as the three Beysibs passed them.

Zip readied his throwing knives. Once the Beysibs were herded his way, they were as good as dead. He widened his stance, feeling his pulse begin to pound.

But these Beysibs didn't run. From under their cloaks or out of their pantaloons, weapons suddenly appeared. Zip could hear the grate of metal as swords left their scabbards and the dismayed shouts from his toughs as they tried to engage swordsmen with rusty daggers and sharpened wooden sticks.

Zip had a wrist slingshot, his emergency weapon. He didn't mean to use it. He was still thinking to himself that he was better off not getting involved, that these weren't your average Beysibs (maybe not Beysibs at all) and that he didn't owe the death-squad members anything, when he found himself letting fly once, then again, with his wrist slingshot and making as much noise as he could while running pell-mell toward the fray.

One of his missiles found its target. With a yelp, a pantaloon'd figure went to its knees. Another turned his head, cursing like a soldier, and something whizzed past Zip's cheek. He felt warmth, wetness, and knew he'd been grazed.

Then he realized that neither of his squad members were still standing. He slowed to a walk, breathing heavily, trying to see if the two boys lying in the dirt were moving. He thought one was; the other seemed too still.

His adversaries, whoever they were, seemed to want to continue the argument. Parallel to one another, the two with the swords moved toward Zip. They split the street into defensible halves, far enough away from the buildings to avoid any more lurkers in doorways, and from one other to give each fighter room enough to handle anything that might come his way.

Neither spoke. They closed on him with businesslike economy and a certain eagerness that gave Zip enough time for second thoughts: these were professional tactics, put into practice by professionals. When times had been easier in

Sanctuary and an old warhorse named Tempus had formed a special-forces unit of Stepsons and then invited any Ilsigs who dared to train for a citizens' militia, Zip had taken the opportunity to learn all he could about the Rankan enemy. Zip had been taught "street control" by the same book as those now advancing down this particular street toward him.

Two to one against professionals, there was no chance that he could win.

He raised his hands as if in surrender.

The two soldiers-in-disguise growled low to one another in what might have been Court Rankene.

Before they could decide the obvious—to take him alive and spend the evening asking him questions painful, perhaps crippling, to answer—Zip did what he had to do: let fly with a palmed dagger and then a specially pronged slingshot missile.

Both of Zip's casts sped murderously true. Sped not into the probably-armored chests of the two big men with swords (whose companion was now on his feet and falling in behind them, perfectly and by-the-drill covering every move Zip's death squad made) but into the exposed neck and chest of Zip's own two men. No revolutionary could be captured alive.

Everyone in his death squad knew too much. They'd all signed suicide pacts in blood but, in this case, Zip had better help these two along. Rankan interrogation could be very nasty.

Then as the rear man yelled, "Get the bastard," and the two in front lunged toward him, Zip wheeled and dove for the tunnel entrance, down among the garbage and the rats. Pulling the cobble-faced cover into place behind him, Zip shot the stout interior bolt.

*

Two days later, Hakiem was sitting on a bench in Promise Park—not one of his accustomed haunts.

As a storyteller, Hakiem considered himself a neutral party in this war between Ranke and the Harka Bey for control of Sanctuary. In his innermost heart he couldn't help but take sides, though. And since his side was the side of the Ilsigi, whose land this once was and whose sorrow he now shared, he'd gotten just a *little* bit involved with helping the revolution.

This was nothing new for Hakiem: he'd been a *little* involved with Jubal the ex-slaver; a *little* involved with Prince/Governor Kadakithis' Hell Hounds... with everything, if truth be told, that concerned his beloved, benighted town.

He kept telling himself that there was a good story in whatever he shouldn't be getting involved in. The revolution, which might be the greatest story Sanctuary would ever offer him, was also the most dangerous. Already embroiled in it were Rankans and Ilsigs, fighting together (though some didn't know it and others wouldn't admit it) against the heinous matriarchy of the Beysibs.

But, Hakiem reminded himself as he waited for his contact to appear, he was an old man: he wouldn't have lived to be old if he were too foolish.

Yet Hakiem, who'd been safe on the sidelines, an observer and a certified neutral all his life, was beginning to feel the tug of revolutionary fervor himself. Politics, he well knew, was an old man's game: old men sent young men out to lose their lives for principles. He'd have to be careful not to become as deluded as those whom the Ilsigi populace fought: the Beysibs, the Rankans, the Nisibisi and all others wanting to put their stamp on his poor little sand-spit of a town.

Whoever had sent him a note which bade him come here (*'Hakiem, for the tale most worth telling this season, meet me at the bench under the parasol pine in Promise Park at mid-day, two days hence.'*) was willing to take outrageous chances: even in daylight, the Beysib discouraged public gatherings.

Two, these days, was a public gathering.

Still, this was the first time the rebels had tried to contact him, although it seemed to Hakiem that they should have realized they needed him sooner. Without rumor, without stirring stories of heroism and daring, without a vision of the revolution to come, no insurgency could succeed.

Two blond, bare-breasted Bey women went by, their bulging eyes downcast, demurely veiled. Beysib males pranced behind them, and behind those came Ilsig boys carrying sunshades.

When they'd gone, Hakiem took a deep breath. The tale-teller had no assurances that the revolutionaries had sent him that note: he'd made an assumption, one that might be false. Either of the fish-women with their trained serpents—now receding into the distance, their entourage behind—could have sent that note. But why would they?

Hakiem rubbed his face, bleary-eyed and weary: this final indignity of yet another foreign occupation heaped upon luckless Sanctuary was almost too much for him to bear. Daily, the rubble piles grew greater and the body count mounted. Orphans now outnumbered parented children. Child-gangs as deadly as the Nisibisi-sponsored death squads roamed the town at night when (everywhere but in the Maze, which was impossible to police) the Beysib curfew was in force.

Once, the town of Sanctuary had been dubbed the anus of Empire—but at least then it had been part of something comprehensible: the Rankan Empire, venal and vicious, was a creation of men and manpower, not of women and sorcery.

The Harka Bey and their sorceresses imposed a rule of supernatural terror upon Sanctuary that all priests—Ilsig and Rankan alike—agreed would soon bring down the wrath of the elder gods.

An Ilsigi priest, in his fiery sermons (held surreptitiously north of town in the Old Ruins), had warned that the gods might send Sanctuary to the bottom of the sea if the populace did not unite and oust the Bey.

Some had hoped Kadakithis might show his face there last night. No one in the city had seen the poor Prince/Governor up close since the takeover. Sometimes a personage who looked very like Kadakithis appeared at the high window in the Hall of Justice, but whispers said this was only a simulacrum of Kadakithis; that the Prince/Governor languished, all but dead, under the Beysa Shupansea's spell. Few beside Hakiem knew these rumors were not so far from the truth, though Kadakithis was held in thrall by love, not magic.

Things were so much worse now than they'd been when the Nisibisi witches had come down from the north, preaching Ilsig liberation and prophesying a great upheaval to come that if the most terrible Nisibisi witch—Roxane, Death's Queen—appeared now before Hakiem and demanded his soul in payment for the opportunity to tell a tale of Sanctuary's freedom, Hakiem would gladly have given it.

Things were so damned depressing, sometimes he wanted to cry.

When he wiped his eyes and took his old, gnarled hands away, a woman stood there before him.

He drew in a shocked breath and almost cowered: was it a witch? Was it dreaded Roxane, come back from the northern war? Roxane, who had all but destroyed the Stepsons and made undead slaves of her conquests? Had he just pacted with a witch? By the mechanism of a thought, just one errant thought? Surely, no one could lose their soul so easily, so offhandedly…

The woman was tall and broad-shouldered, with a firm chin and clear narrow eyes. Her hair was as black as a wizard's. Her clothes were nondescript but cut to facilitate easy movement: her tunic vented; her Ilsig leggings bloused at the knees and disappearing into calf-high, laced boots.

"Hakiem, are you? I'm Kama. Shall we walk?"

"Walk? I'm… waiting for someone—my apprentice," he lied lamely. Was this a Bey mercenary? He didn't know they covered their breasts or wore pants. Was he to be arrested? That would be a story—*'Inside a Beysib Interrogation Cell'*—if only he might live to tell it…

"Walk." The woman's voice was throaty when she chuckled. "It's safer, for this kind of meeting. And the someone you're waiting for, I hope, is me." She smiled, and there was something familiar about her eyes, as if an old acquaintance looked out of them. She extended her hand to him as if he were infirm, some frail woman to be helped to her feet.

Women were getting altogether out of hand in Sanctuary this season.

He brushed her hand aside and rose stiffly, hoping she wouldn't notice just how stiffly.

She was saying, "—your apprentice? That idea's not half-bad. I'd probably qualify, having won first prize at the last Festival of Man, wouldn't you think?"

"First prize? Festival of Man?" Hakiem repeated dumbly. "What did you say your name was?" The Festival of Man was held once every four years, far to the north. It was a festival for kings and armies, a matter of war games and athletic events, and included a poetry contest for historians of the field and tellers of heroic tales that every storyteller alive dreamed of winning. But even to attend you had to be sponsored by a king, a grateful army, a powerful lord. Who *was* this woman? She'd told him, but he was so melancholy and so depressed—*no, let's face it, fool: you're getting old!*—he couldn't recall what she'd said.

"Can I trust you, old man? Or am I safe because, though I told you my name once, you've already forgot?" Her mouth twisted in a sardonic little grin that definitely reminded him of someone else. But who?

Hakiem said carefully, "You can trust me if your heart is in the right place, Candy." That was what she'd said, he thought—or close enough to make her correct him.

She looked at her booted feet, scuffing up autumn dirt. When she raised her head, her gaze slapped at him: "I'm Kama, of the Rankan 3rd Commando. If *your* heart's in the right place, you'll put me in touch with the rebels. Otherwise," she shrugged, "you folks are going to have a lot of dead amateurs and a stillborn revolution."

"What? What are you talking about? Rebels? I know no rebels—"

"Wonderful. I like your spirit, old man. You're the ears of this town and, some say, the mouth. Tell whomever you *don't* know that I'll be at Marc's Junky Weapons Shop an hour before curfew and thereafter, tonight, to make sure we don't have another little problem like we had with the death squads on the Street of Red Lanterns two nights ago. If we're going to kick some Beysib pantaloons, we'll need every man we've got."

Hakiem had the distinct feeling that this Kama of the Rankan 3rd Commando had forgotten that she herself was a woman. "I can't promise anything," he said politically. "After all, I've only your word and—"

"Just do it, old man; save the talk for those who'll listen. And show up tonight, if you dare, to hear some tales you'll die from telling. Even if you don't, *I'll* be telling everyone I meet I'm your apprentice—so do try to remember my name."

She increased her pace, leaving him behind as if he were standing still.

Watching her draw away, Hakiem stopped trying to catch up. There were too many Bey around. If he wanted a story worth dying for, he could drop by Marc's.

He wasn't sure if he would, or sure that *not* going would save him from involvement by implication. But then, she—*Kama*—knew that. He'd been too daunted by her talk of the Festival of Man and her whole bearing to consider much of what she'd said.

Now he did, walking unseeingly Mazeward, toward the Vulgar Unicorn for the first of many drinks. The Rankan 3rd Commando were rangers with a very bad reputation. Ever since the real Stepsons had filled their ranks with locals and left town to fight the Wizard Wars in the north, there had been no force on the side of Empire worth rallying round. If the 3rd Commando was here, then the Empire hadn't given up on Sanctuary, all was not lost, and resistance was really possible.

Of course, given the stories about the 3rd's brutality and their provenance (they'd been formed by Tempus long ago to quash just such a revolt as might be brewing in Sanctuary), the cure for Sanctuary's Beysib ills might well be worse than the disease.

*

Straton wasn't at all sure this was going to work. He hadn't seen Ischade, the vampire woman who lived down by the White Foal River, since before the war for Wizardwall, when he'd been an on-duty Stepson with the whole cadre behind him and Critias beside him and the only troubles in

Sanctuary were sorcery and refractory death squads and the occasional assassination: all standard stuff.

Strat wished Crit was here, then slid off his horse before Ischade's oddly-shadowed house and, crossbow at the ready, tethered his big bay horse outside.

Crit would be along, one of these days. The whole unit was drifting in, a man here, a pair there. Along with Sync's 3rd Commando, they had a good chance of putting things to rights—if they could just figure out what 'rights' were. Sync thought they should put every Beysib in town on one big funerary pyre and give them to the gods, for starters.

Straton wasn't taking orders from Sync: with Crit still upcountry and Niko in transit with Tempus, Straton was in charge of the Stepsons, who wanted only to kill every idiot who'd made the unit designation "Stepson" a slur and a curse here while Tempus' Sacred Band had been warring beyond Wizardwall.

Kama had prevailed on Strat to try enlisting the vampire woman's aid. Kama was Tempus' daughter. Strat still respected her for that—not for anything she'd done or earned, merely for being his commander's progeny.

So he'd come back here, despite the fact that Ischade the vampire woman was more dangerous than a bedroom full of Harka Bey, to "invite" Ischade to the little party Sync and he were throwing at Marc's.

He'd probably have come anyway, Strat told himself: Ischade was dangerous enough to be interesting, the sort of woman you never forget once you look into her eyes. And he'd looked into them: deep, hellhole eyes that made him wonder what kind of death she offered her victims…

Nothing for it but to knock on the damn door and get it over with, then.

He tugged at his leather tunic and assayed the walk up to her threshold; as he did, the interior lights flickered and dimmed weirdly. The last time he'd been here, his eyesight had been bothering him. His eyes didn't bother him anymore, thanks to a benign spell cast during his northern sortie.

So he'd really see her, this time.

On her doorstep, he hesitated. Then he muttered a prayer that consigned his soul to the appropriate storm god should he die here, and knocked.

He heard movement within, then nothing.

He knocked again.

This time, the movement came closer and the lights in her front windows winked out.

"Ischade," he called out gruffly, a dagger in hand to pick the lock or slice its thong or pound upon the wooden door with all his might, "open up. It's—"

Her door seemed to disappear before him. Off balance, for he'd been about to thump on it hard with his dagger's hilt, he took a stumbling step forward.

"I know," said a velvet voice coming from a wraithlike face cowled in inky shadows, "who you are. I remember you. Have you tired of giving death? Or have you brought me another slave as a reunion gift?" Her eyes lifted up to his, her hood fell back, and yet, somehow, backlit in her doorway, her face was still in shadow.

Her eyes, however, were not.

Straton found himself forgetful of his purpose. He wasn't a womanizer; he wasn't an impressionable boy. Yet Ischade's gaze was like some drug which made the world recede until all he wanted to do was look at her, touch her, brave the danger of her, and do to her what he was nearly certain none of the sheep she'd fed upon had ever managed to do.

He said, "Invite me in."

She said, "I have a visitor, within."

He replied, "Get rid of him."

She smiled: "My thought exactly. You will wait here?"

He agreed: "Don't be long."

When her door closed, it was as if a bond had broken, a leash had snapped, a drug worn off.

He found that he was shivering, and it wasn't anywhere near as cold in autumnal Sanctuary as it had been on Wizardwall. Despite his shaking hands, sweat was beading on his upper lip. He wiped it and regretted shaving for this covert enterprise.

Either he was lucky, and she'd be sated by whatever meat she had in there so that he could talk to her, convince her, make some sort of deal with her; or he was walking into serious trouble, without Crit or any of his unit to get him out if he got in too deep.

About the time he was deciding that no one would ever think the worse of him if he just walked away from this one, left Ischade's stone unturned, and said she hadn't been at home, the door reopened and a delicate, white hand reached out to him: "Come in, Straton," said the vampire woman. "It's been a long time since one such as you has come to me."

*

Sync had saved the fabled crime-lord called Jubal for himself. The Sanctuary veterans he had on staff had warned him about the vicious squalor of Downwind, but he hadn't believed them.

Now he believed, but he believed more in his good right arm and the attractiveness of the offer he had to make.

This Jubal was black and stout as a gnarled tree, older than Sync had surmised by half, and sporting a fey blue hawk-mask that would have bothered Sync more if the sycophants around the ex-slaver weren't verifying Jubal's identity by every deferential move they made.

The head bootlicker here was named Saliman; the hovel was reasonably commodious once you got inside, but the band of pseudo-beggars ranged around it would give Sync a strenuous afternoon if he had to cut his way through them to escape.

Outside, beforehand, he'd unbridled his horse as a precaution: if Sync whistled, he was going to have twelve hundred Rankan pounds of iron hooves and snapping jaws crashing in here to back him up. 3rd Commando training told him he needed no more than that: one man, one horse, one holocaust on demand.

Sync wasn't a politician; he was a field commander. But he wasn't in this Downwind potty to fight; he was here to talk.

In a flourish of feathered robes, Jubal sat down on something very like a throne and said in a voice muffled through his mask, "Talk, mercenary."

Sync replied: "Get rid of the mask and your playmates and we'll talk. This parley is between us two, or not at all."

Jubal responded, "Then perhaps it's not at all. But then you've wasted our time, and we don't like that. Do we?"

Ten scruffy locals made threatening noises.

"Look here, slumlord, are you in the pay of the Beysibs? If not, let's get serious. I didn't come here to give your staff combat lessons. If they need them, I've got trainers in the 3rd Commando who specialize in making silk purses out of sow's ears."

Three of the ten were edging forward. Jubal stopped them with a raised hand. From under the mask came what might have been a rattling sigh. "Third Commando? Am I supposed to be impressed?"

Sync said, "I don't know what you're supposed to be, Jubal, in that cutesy feathered cape and mask. Is everybody in this town in drag?" He crossed his arms, thinking he should have sent a Sanctuary veteran to bring in this black man by the ear. He had to remind himself forcefully not to call Jubal a Wriggly to his face. It was a damned shame, having to join forces with an enemy you'd thoroughly beaten years ago—and on equal terms. The misfortunes of war were never ending.

"Not everybody," Jubal said, leaning forward.

The naked threat in Jubal's voice told Sync that he'd pushed just about as far as he could with this ex-gladiator-cum-slaver-cum-power player, so he changed tack: "That's comforting. Now, since you won't get rid of your bodyguards, even though it looks to me like you'd be safe enough defending yourself, I'm going to tell you why I'm here and we can have a democratic referendum on how much of a share in the profits your men here get, how much you keep, what everybody's got to do, and who else is—"

"All right," Jubal interrupted. "All right. Saliman, clear the room and make sure no one gets too curious."

"But my lord—" Saliman sputtered.

"*Do it*!"

Almost as if by magic, the muscle men disappeared.

"Now, what's on your mind, Stink?"

"You must have heard that the Third is operating independent of the Emperor—we're on our own."

"Yes?" Jubal purred.

"We're trying to put together a coalition to rid Sanctuary of the Harka Babies and install an interim ruler who suits us—make Sanctuary an independent state. I've got half an army with no place to call home."

"And you'd like to make your home in Sanctuary?"

"Remains to be seen. But if we try this, we'd like you to be a part of it—working with us. Nobody's going to take and hold Sanctuary without your active cooperation, we've heard."

"How do you know the Beysibs haven't heard that too?" Jubal asked cannily.

The old black was sharp, but Sync could feel that he was buying the deal—lock, stock, and misrepresentations. "Because they're having too much trouble, from too many unidentified quarters."

Jubal laughed. The laugh was amplified by his hawk-mask and boomed so loud in the small room that its curtains quivered. "That may be, that may be. But flattery won't get you everywhere—just somewhere. Now, let's hear the specifics." The ex-gladiator's arms came out from under his cloak and Sync could see purple scars that told one seasoned veteran of too many wars that he was looking at another.

Sync said honestly: "You can't believe I'd go into that here, with all those ears you've got. I want you to come to a little party we're having at Marc's Weapons Shop on the Street of Smiths this evening. Representatives of every faction my Long Recon people think useful will be there. I want to put them together—with your help, of course—in one well-coordinated, working unit."

"Intriguing." Jubal's hawkmask bobbed slowly. "And then what?"

"Then we're going to make this town what it ought to be, what it used to be, what it wants to be: a freehold, a safe haven where men like you and me don't have to kiss any pomaded pederasts' rings and women do what women do best."

Again, Jubal laughed. When he sobered, he raised his mask—not enough for Sync to see the face beneath; just enough to wipe his eyes. "You, me, and what army?"

"You, me, the Third Commando, and Tempus' original Stepsons. Plus, perhaps, the local death squads and revolutionaries, your odd mercenary, the downtrodden Ilsig populace, and the regular army garrison—the ranking officer over there is an old friend of mine. That enough manpower for you?"

"Might be, might be," Jubal chuckled.

"Then you'll come tonight?"

"I'll be there," Jubal agreed.

*

Marc's Weapons Shop had a trap door behind the counter, as well as a firing range out back, two display cases filled with blades, and two walls of high-torque crossbows.

Beneath, in the cellar, arcane and forbidden weaponry was kept: alchemical incendiaries; wrist slingshots such as Zip's; instruments of interrogation and of silent kill—poisons and persuaders.

It was early, before the scheduled evening meeting, and Zip and Marc were arguing, alone, while above Marc's blonde and nubile wife minded the store.

"You can't ask me to do this, Marc," Zip said from the corner in which he was hunched, bowstring-taut and feral, his eyes darting from shadow to shadow, looking for the trap he was sure would soon be sprung.

"I've got to ask you, boy, or watch you commit suicide: you can't fight this clutch of butt-banging warriors. You trained with Stepsons; you know that now they're drifting into town again, things are going to change. You stayed out of trouble when they were around last time. Now, you can't. They'll tan your hide and use it for a saddle blanket; your polished teeth'll decorate some warhorse's headstall. I don't want to see that happen."

"So you gave them my *name?* I trusted you. I got into this whole thing by accident. I don't want to be any rebel leader. I don't want to incite any riots or start any twelve-gods-damned revolutions. I just want to protect my own self. *Why* did you do this to me?"

"They're smart. They've had reconnaissance people in town for weeks—they *knew* about you already. If you aren't with them, that bunch assumes you're against them."

"Who? The Buggernauts? The Whoresons? Who cares?"

"You'll care, when they make you two inches taller before they make you six inches shorter—mercenaries are a very suspicious breed. I know Strat's Stepsons, and I trust them: they *have* to be trustworthy—trust is all they've got: trust of one another and the value of their word. Tempus will be along, Strat says, presently: that means the Storm God—if you still care about Vashanka—is coming home. I'm not good with words…" Marc rubbed his beard miserably; his round, brown eyes pleaded with the gutter-bred fighter jammed against the joint of two walls as if he were already at bay. "Please just stay and listen to their proposal: without you, the death squads will never give this alliance a chance."

"You're addled. Bewitched. Most of the death squad members got their start with Roxane, the Nisibisi witch. It's a trap: the Stepsons and the Third are looking for revenge. Roxane didn't exactly lose gracefully fighting the Stepsons. They lost men. Mercenaries never forget."

"You've got to stay… if not for yourself, for me. They've spotted you. They know you're using this place to rearm, to meet, to get in and out of the tunnels. If you don't pretend to join them, I'm having this conversation with a dead man—it's just a matter of days."

"Well, at least you're being honest now." Zip pushed himself up against the wall. He had a two-day growth of beard and looked a decade older than the years he'd lived. Erect, leaning back in his corner, he said despairingly, "I don't suppose it would do any good to make you promise not to reveal any more of our names?"

"On pain of death? Kill me now, then. And my wife. And everyone else who's helped you. I own, boy, I've seen a lot of action, too many wars to suit me, and I'm telling you: the only way to live through what's brewing in Sanctuary is to make a deal with the Third Commando."

"Just so long as it isn't the damn Rankan army—it isn't, you can promise me that, can't you? *Can't* you?"

Marc looked at his big-knuckled hands. The slit-eyed, scruffy youth before him had been orphaned in the Rankan takeover of Sanctuary. He didn't remember his parents and he'd grown up fast and hard, hating Rankans all the way. He'd had no connections, no advantages, no mentors. Marc had known Zip for years and never dared to get involved: Zip's kind died young and they died unpleasantly.

Now, for some reason known only to the gods, Marc *was* involved—it was a matter of pride, of gut resentment, of life and death.

"No, boy, I can't promise you that. But maybe *they* can. All *I* can promise is that if you don't show up, not me or my wife or this shop will be here in the morning: they'll level this place and bury us in it."

"Thanks for not pressuring me."

"You're welcome. Thanks for making my shop your favorite haunt."

"I give. Look, tell me who's going to be here."

With a sick feeling in his stomach, fingering an amulet of Irkalla in hopes that the goddess could keep this boy from diving through the open hole by his side into the tunnels and never coming up, Marc began to explain about the vampire woman, Ischade; the crime lord, Jubal; the Rankan 3rd Commando leader, Sync; the storyteller, Hakiem, and the acting garrison commander, Walegrin.

As he did, watching Zip's unbelieving eyes go icy and hostile, Marc couldn't even convince *himself* that tonight's meeting wasn't going to be a wholesale slaughter. Judging by the guest list, somebody could get rid of every trouble-maker in Sanctuary worth mentioning in one cleansing fire—Marc hoped to hell that "somebody" didn't turn out to be Strat.

The only element missing from the list of invited guests was a representative of black magic: some honcho from the mageguild or some Hazard-class enchanter who might be able to keep order through fear of mortal curse.

And if the Stepsons hadn't been allergic to magicians, they'd probably have invited one of them, too.

*

By the time Sync got to the meeting, the air was already blue with krrf smoke, the packed-clay floor spotted with wine dregs.

Kama was presiding, as best she could, over a crowd of thirty-five people who, under any other circumstances, would have been locked in mortal combat by now.

Hakiem the storyteller was the only person in the room who was unarmed, though Sync was well aware that the mouth was mightier than the sword in a situation like this. If things went badly, the rest could be let go, but Hakiem would have to die.

Walegrin, big, blond, and out of uniform, sat in the middle of a half-dozen plain-clothed officers who, by being invited here, would be sufficiently compromised that even if they weren't actively helpful, they wouldn't hinder Sync's progress.

Straton was sitting off by himself in a corner on a wine-keg with a woman who must be the vampire, Ischade, else they wouldn't have had that much space to themselves. It was a good thing Critias wasn't in town, or Strat never would have fetched the vampire woman. Sync had to stop himself from looking for signs of vampire-bite on Strat's neck.

The young guerrilla fighter with whom Sync, Gayle, and Strat had tangled on the Street of Red Lanterns—the one who'd killed his own men rather than let them be captured—had the other far corner; a mangy cur scratched fleas by his knee.

Sync nodded to Zip and threaded his way to him through the crowd: if there was one single element of this riffraff he needed, in order to secure his tactical advantage, it was this scruffy rebel leader called Zip, whose real name no one knew.

Reaching Zip, with all eyes on them, Sync held out his hand and said, "Last time, we forgot to introduce ourselves. I'm Sync. You're…?"

"'Zip' will do." Eyes narrowed, Zip shook Sync's hand.

"I'm glad you came, Zip. When this is over, I'll buy you a meal and we'll compare notes."

Sync turned and headed toward Kama at the table Marc had set up at the front of the room before Zip could ask him what kind of notes or decline his invitation.

Standing beside Kama, Sync waited for Jubal to settle down. Jubal was another one to whom this crowd gave extra room, though he'd come in late with only his first lieutenant: Jubal had been skulking outside in the shadows, waiting for Sync to arrive before entering.

"Now that we're all here..." Sync scanned the room, making sure that this was indeed the case; a particular pair of wolfish eyes in a furry face met his and he nodded as he continued, "I'd like to turn the meeting over to our resident expert on covert enterprise, secrecy, and wizardry, Randal, our own ex-Hazard, formerly of the Tysian mageguild."

Mutters broke out; men and women moved away from one another; necks craned, looking for the sorcerer in their midst.

From Ischade's corner, a musical laugh sounded. As all eyes turned to the necromant, the mangy cur, part wolf by the look of it, who'd been scratching fleas near Zip's knee, stretched, yawned, and got to its feet.

Then the dog, with a sneeze and a sniffle, wandered in seemingly haphazard fashion up to the table, where Kama knelt down, ready with the cloak she'd been wearing, and fastened it around the dog's neck.

In the back of the room, Zip rose to his feet without a sound; Marc the blade-monger put out a hand to stay him.

But no one noticed: the crowd's attention was on the dog in front of them, changing before their eyes into a man.

It was a smooth transition, smoother than Randal usually could manage. The Stepsons' allergy-prone sorcerer didn't even sneeze much.

When the mage rose to full man's height, the cloak and the smoke and the shadows thrown by flickering candles in that subterranean meeting room made him seem more imposing than he really was.

For the first time, Sync had that warm feeling in the pit of his stomach that he got whenever a strategy became reality.

Randal said, "Thank you, Commander."

Sync murmured, "You're welcome," and sat down.

"Good evening, gentlefolk," Randal began. "I bring you greetings from Tempus, and from all our friends on Wizardwall. The plight of Sanctuary since the Stepsons left it has come to our attention and, with your help, we're going to set about making things right here—by ousting the Beysibs and returning Sanctuary to its former… ah… glory."

There was a general mutter of agreement.

Randal smiled his boyish, winning smile. The redoubtable mage, his hair grown long enough to cover his prodigious ears and scrawny neck, was a born crowd pleaser. When he sneezed concussively and blamed it on his "lack of suitable garments" and the cold, the crowd bought it. They were so anxious to have the advantage of wizardly aid in fighting the Beysibs that if Randal had talked to them in the shape of a mule or a salamander, they would have listened respectfully, silently, gratefully.

It bothered Sync, just a little, that the credibility of honest fighters wasn't sufficient to satisfy this rabble, but a simple shape-change trick by a fey magician made everybody in the place feel like conquering heroes. He'd counted on that being the case. Still, it irked him: fighters tended to dislike sorcerers, class to class.

If there was one exception, one person not charmed and convinced by Randal's tricks (including the materialization of a topographical map of Sanctuary; a feast fit for the Beysibs in Kadakithis' palace; and "working capital" to the tune of five thousand gold pieces), it was Zip.

Marc knew it, and Sync knew it.

When the meeting was over, Marc delayed Zip's exit so that Sync could close in on the youth.

Sync detoured only long enough to ask Strat, in an undertone, "Still got your soul, buddy?" and receive a curt nod in reply before he took the rebel leader by the elbow and suggested they go to the Vulgar Unicorn for a "drink and whatever."

To Sync's relief, Zip agreed, saying: "If we're going to do this, we'd better do it right."

"What's 'right'?" Sync asked, not understanding.

"Right? With One-Thumb's help, soldier. Or are you afraid of Nisibisi magic? It's not like your little baby wizard's, up there." He indicated Randal disrespectfully.

"Magic? I'm afraid of *your* kind of magic—a knife in the back in the dead of night—not theirs," Sync quipped, wondering if this gutterpud wasn't smarter than he looked: no Stepson, no 3rd Commando, and especially no Rankan regular army officer, wanted anything to do with the Nisibisi witch-caste.

When Sync headed for the trapdoor with its stairs leading up into Marc's shop, Zip's hand closed hard on his arm: "Not that way, fool. You want to go to the Unicorn, we go through the tunnels. Smith Street's under curfew, even if the Maze isn't. And wherever you are these days, two men together rouse suspicion. Come on—that is, unless you're afraid of getting those nice boots wet."

Sync didn't know how Zip could find his way through that dank and slippery darkness. They slogged through sewage, then cleaner water up to their knees, in a phosphorescent green-dark counter-Maze no sane fighter would have entered without ropes, torches, chalk, and reinforcements.

Zip seemed right at home; his voice, at least, was relaxed, although Sync couldn't see his face and was concentrating on holding on to Zip's shoulder, as he'd been instructed, trying not to listen to the part of his brain that kept telling him he'd regret putting himself at the mercy of this sewer lord: Zip could lose him down here easily and Sync might never find his way out.

But the guerrilla either hadn't thought about treachery, or didn't intend any. Zip's tone was almost friendly when he asked, "Surely you don't expect this so-called alliance of yours to hold?" His last word echoed: *hold, old, ld, d.*

"No," Sync replied, "but before the Third starts warring, we like to introduce ourselves. Anyway, it's good form, and we might pick up a few allies, even if we can't assemble a coalition town-wide."

"In two weeks," Zip said with jocular bitterness, "there'll be twice as many factions fighting, thanks to you: army, death squads, revolutionary idealists, Beysib bitches, your rangers, fake Stepsons, real Stepsons… what's the point?"

"That's the point: it doesn't have to happen that way."

"If everyone lets you control it. The chance of that is about even with me marrying Roxane and becoming the reigning Nisibisi warlock."

Right about then, Sync began to wonder if Zip was really taking him to the Vulgar Unicorn. Even the mention of Roxane's name made his skin crawl. He'd had quite enough of wizard wars. That was one of the things Sanctuary had to offer as a winter billet: enough trouble to keep his men from going stale, with no uncounterable magic (just the Beysibs and the weakling sorcerers of Sanctuary's third-rate mage-guild) in a town that was a war-gamer's paradise.

"Roxane's that good a friend of yours, is she?" Sync took a shot in the dark.

"She's that much of a problem. You'll find out about her yourself, sooner or later. She's one very big reason why I can't hook up with you. Another is, I can't speak for everybody—hardly for anybody at all."

"Just the Nisibisi-trained and funded death squads?"

"That's right. Take a left turn here; we're going to start climbing stone steps: they're slippery; there's fifteen, then a landing, then ten more."

They climbed in the dark. Sync continued his interrogation: "I've heard that you control most of the territory in Downwind—that you've held it against the Beysibs and that at this point they've given up trying to take it back."

"'*Most* of the *territory*?' Three blocks? That's what I've got, all I can hold. We don't have drool in the way of arms, or fighters, or anything much but a little Nisibisi support. I'll show you my 'territory' sometime. You won't be impressed."

"I'll be the judge of that." Sync had lost count of the stairs. He tried to mount one and his foot thumped down hard through thin air: they'd made the first landing. Three strides, and they were climbing again. With a sinking feeling that had nothing to do with being underground and at the mercy of a boy guerrilla, Sync asked: "I'd like to meet her, sometime soon… this Roxane. Can you arrange it?"

"Life too dull for you? Just can't wait to lose your soul? Heard that undeads have more fun?"

"I'm serious."

"I wish I wasn't. If you promise me you won't consider it an act of war on my part, I'll hook you up tonight."

"Thanks, I'd appreciate it."

"We'll see about that. Maybe you won't be able to appreciate anything, afterward. Any next of kin you want me to notify? At least tell that baby mage of yours to avenge you?"

Sync chuckled, but he couldn't make it sound convincing. "Randal's going to be introducing himself to Sanctuary this evening. If Roxane's really here, he won't need to be notified. They've met before."

"Here we are. I'm just going to slide this bolt. Then we'll climb up, one at a time. I'll go first. And she's really here. Ask One-Thumb."

Sync heard the sound of wood grating, then saw a square of blinding light. Next, a dark silhouette appeared in its midst as Zip levered himself up.

Following Zip, Sync reflected that this wasn't as harmless an alibi as he'd expected. At least he'd be in public, drinking in the Unicorn, when as many of the hundred ruling Beysib women as had accepted an invitation to the opening of "Randal's Pleasure Palace" uptown were turned to wax statues in an exhibit of "Beysib Culture" which was the prime attraction of the mage's Beysib trap.

*

This Sync didn't understand what he was getting himself into, Zip knew. The trick was to let the crazy bastard have his way without Zip taking the blame for what became of the 3rd's commanding officer.

Zip hated officers, armies, authoritarian types. He also hated Roxane, when he dared. But not too often—she was more dangerous than three cadres of 3rd Commando and she had him by the jewels.

Roxane would appreciate Sync, all right, if Zip could deliver him. He didn't know why he felt reluctant to do so. Sync was just another murderer, and the worst kind: professional, efficient, charismatic in a Rankan sort of way. The less Rankans in Zip's world, the better. But still, if the Rankans got together and attacked the Beysibs, there'd be less Rankans for the Nisibisi sympathizers to deal with later. Right now, what was good for the Nisibisi-sponsored revolution was good for Zip.

So he took some chances, letting Sync see how Zip's sort got around in town without being noticed. He even showed Sync where you left your sewer-reeking clothes in One-Thumb's wine cellar and where you got fresh ones before you slunk up the back way and into the Unicorn crowd through the outhouse entrance as if you'd always been there.

One-Thumb wasn't behind the bar. He was probably upstairs with Roxane, or out at the estate. In which case, there'd be nothing Zip could do tonight: you didn't take people to One-Thumb's uninvited… not unless you wanted to end up as dog meat.

The waitress was one of Zip's people. Two hand signals he could only hope Sync didn't see brought Zip his answer: One-Thumb was in his office upstairs.

Since other things went on upstairs (a bit of whoring and drug-dealing), it was no problem for Zip to go on up, but the man beside him was attracting attention: Sync's sword was too service-scarred, his well-chosen and nondescript garb a little too well-chosen and nondescript, for the Unicorn denizens not to mark him as somebody trying *not* to look like a soldier.

So they didn't go upstairs right away. There were too many eyes on them and the place went too quiet when they entered. Instead, they settled down in a corner in the main bar room. That was another problem with the mercenaries: they couldn't stand having their backs exposed; if Sync could have handled a table in the middle of the room, the break in pattern would have relaxed the crowd and Zip wouldn't have felt like he was on display.

Asking Sync to sit with his back to the crowd was like asking a horse to fly. So they sat in a corner, at a table vacated warily by a couple of slit-purses who gave Zip dirty looks for consorting with the enemy, and pretended nonchalance until a serving wench came back with their ales and a message: One-Thumb would meet them out in back.

Just as they were finishing their draughts and checking their purses, Vashanka's own hell seemed to break loose outside.

The crowd surged toward the door, beyond which the sky was sheeting colored light, then back again as the dreaded Harka Bey—the Beysib mercenary women (assassins in full dress with their damn snakes on their arms)—shouldered their way inside, men-at-arms behind them, and backed everyone up against the walls.

"What the frog?" Zip breathed to Sync as the women (who could kill you by spitting on you, if rumor could be believed) started disarming everyone methodically, then binding their thumbs together behind their backs.

Ten Bey armed with crossbows took positions in the middle of the room.

Zip kept watch on them under his arms, which were still spread above his head like everyone else whose thumbs hadn't yet been bound. "Sync, now what?"

When Sync didn't respond, Zip whispered, "Well, Ranger, what now? If this roust is a result of Randal's little 'introduction,' we're standing in an execution coffle: Beysibs don't go after guilty parties; they just round up a bunch of folks at random and slaughter them in the morning. And they don't make it pretty."

Sync shrugged as well as a man can with his hands propped on the wall above his head and his feet spread-eagled: "I'm armed and dangerous. How about you?"

"Close enough, friend. I sure don't want my people seeing me led like a bull to the sacrificial slaughter. And if a woman kills you, your soul never finds its eternal rest."

"I didn't know that," Sync quipped.

"You know it now. Ready? Let's die with our privates intact—it ain't that much to ask."

"Ready," Sync breathed. "On the count of three, we break for the back door." He inclined his head to the right. "To make this work, we'll need a couple of those Beysib bitches as shields. So I'm going to start counting when they come to you: as soon as they touch you, grab an arm, jerk it in and spin her, get a choke hold on—"

"Silence!" pealed a deep but assuredly female voice, and the whole place froze.

Zip thought, at first, that it was a Beysib voice. Yet in its wake came no venomous bite, no snake's fangs, no crossbow bolt through his spine. And in the entire room, nobody so much as moved.

Sync's eyes met his enquiringly; Zip shook his head a tiny bit. Then, ducking his head, Zip glanced around his raised right arm to verify what his ears told him.

In this moment when his life might end, his hearing was preternaturally clear. Zip could hear a familiar tread on the stairs: the tap, tap, tap of Roxane's heels. He could hear the rustling of One-Thumb's muscular thighs as the barkeep descended the staircase beside the witch. Zip could even hear One-Thumb's heavy breathing, and Roxane's soft, low laughter.

Zip told himself he could hear these things so clearly because, throughout the Vulgar Unicorn, everyone else was still, frozen, motionless: everyone but him, and Sync, and the bartender and the witch.

The Beysibs stood with mouths agape and weapons at ready, but their eyes were glazed. Customers in mid-cower were entranced between blinks; tears glittered unshed in serving wenches' eyes.

Only Sync and Zip, of the entire ground-floor crowd, were unaffected by Roxane's spell.

And Sync was already pushing away from the wall, his sword drawn and a half-dozen Bandaran throwing-stars in his left hand. "Pork all! What's going *on* here? Who the pork is she? What's happening?"

Zip straightened up. "Thanks, Roxane. That could have been dicey." Her beauty didn't enthrall him as it once had—her sanguine skin and drowning-pool eyes couldn't tempt him. But he couldn't let Sync see that fear had replaced the lust he'd once felt for Roxane. Summoning all his bravado, he continued: "This here's Sync; he wanted to meet you, and One-Thumb too. He wants to join the revolution. Isn't that right. Sync?"

"Right. Right as rain." Sync was just a little bit intimidated, Zip thought. But Zip had seen Roxane spellbind a man before, and he knew that Sync wasn't immune: the ranger's eyes never left hers.

Well, Zip thought, he asked for it. Maybe we *will* be allies, after all.

Then Roxane came up, taking both their hands, saying: "Come, gentlemen. I don't want to hold this rabble entranced forever. One-Thumb and I will take you upstairs, and we'll let the slaughter recommence." Roxane licked her lips: she lived on fear, death, and suffering; she was probably having a feast on some psychic plane, just observing the Beysib about their vicious work.

For Sync and Zip, it was a lucky break: she wouldn't feel like teaching them any of her more difficult lessons, Zip was willing to bet—not tonight.

"Zip, my dear little monster, you've outdone yourself this evening." She caressed his face; above her shoulder, One-Thumb's eyes met his with what might have been sympathy.

"This?" Zip gestured around at the Bey and their hapless prey. "I didn't cause this. *He* did." Zip gestured to Sync. "He's got a mage on staff, and they worked up a little surprise for the Bey hierarchy, across town. This, I'll bet, is the Beysib reaction—or maybe just the beginning of it."

"It is, it is, indeed... just the beginning." Roxane was inebriated by whatever carnage her soul-sucking talents had been treated to, this evening. "A half-dozen, no less, of the high-ranking Bey bitches are dead, turned to waxen statues in a Tysian mage's museum." She smiled. "And these sheep"—her wave encompassed the room—"soon will be dying the slow and horrible death of Beysib retribution."

She caressed Sync's hand, the one with the throwing stars in it. Sync looked at her like a starving man at a laden feast-day table. "And," she continued, "since Zip assures me I've you and yours to thank, we'll have a long talk about our mutual future. I'm quite certain, Sync of the Rankan Third Commando, that we're going to have one. I may even give you Randal's life, a gesture of appreciation, an indication that we can and will work well together: an introductory gift from me to you."

As if from a dream, Sync roused: "Right. That's very good of you, my lady. I'm yours to command."

"I'm sure you are," Roxane agreed.

Zip knew Sync didn't realize how true what he'd said was likely to be. Not yet, he didn't.

"Would you mind," Sync asked Roxane as they moved among the frozen and the doomed, "if I slit these Beysibs' throats on our way out? It's as fair as the chance the Bey will give these innocents, if I don't." The big soldier's eyes sought Zip's.

Zip said, "It'll give the revolution credibility."

Roxane paused, pouted, then brightened: "Be my guests. Fillet fish-folk to your heart's content."

Behind her, One-Thumb muttered something about "the right slime for the job."

It didn't take long to slay the unknowing Beysibs. Zip helped Sync while the witch and One-Thumb looked on.

When they were done, they wrote the initials of Zip's 'Popular Front for the Liberation of Sanctuary' (PFLS) on the walls of the Vulgar Unicorn in Beysib blood.

By tomorrow, the PFLS's latest kills would be on everybody's lips and nobody would call them 'piffles' for at least a week.

Not bad, Zip thought to himself—not bad at all, for a start.

Then Roxane led the way up the Unicorn's stairs and through a door that had no right to open into the witching room of her Foalside hold, a lot farther than a few steps away from One-Thumb's bar in the Maze.

*

Three days had passed since the revolutionaries calling themselves the PFLS had slaughtered too many Beysibs in the Vulgar Unicorn.

Sanctuarites were finally daring to go abroad again, pale and haggard from fear and disgust. First the cutthroats and the drunkards, then the vendors and the whores returned to the streets. Then (when it was clear that no Beysib squadrons were waiting to swoop down and scoop them up) others ventured forth and the town returned to what had become normal: business as usual, with the occasional pitched battle on a street corner or sniper in some shanty's eaves.

Hakiem was down on Wideway, selling what tales he could on the dock. Pickings were slim because of his new apprentice, Kama, whose uncannily polished tale of the brave revolutionaries triumphing over the dreaded Harka Bey in the Unicorn drew endless crowds of thrill-seekers, while his own yarns of giant crabs and purple spiders weren't dangerous enough, or newsworthy enough, to compete, these days.

Hakiem told himself he didn't really have reason to be piqued: he'd been given money enough at the secret meeting beneath Marc's shop to cover twice what he might be losing.

And Kama, sensitive in her way, dutifully gave him half of all she made.

So Hakiem was watching, paring a bunion where he sat on a splintered keg while Kama pleased her listeners, when a dark youth, sporting a week-old beard and a black sweat-band tied around his head, eased toward Kama through the crowd.

It was Zip, and Hakiem wasn't the only one who marked him: Gayle, a foul-mouthed mercenary who'd joined the Stepsons in the north, was lounging between two pilings, as some Stepson always did when Kama was on the street.

Hakiem saw Kama pale as the scruffy, flat-faced Ilsig caught her eye. She lost her train of thought. Polished phrases turned to incoherent clauses, and she skipped to her story's ending so abruptly her gathered clients muttered among themselves.

"That's all, townsfolk … all for today. I've got to leave you—nature calls. And since you haven't had your money's worth, this telling's on the house." Kama jumped down from the crates on which she'd sat, ignoring the rebel leader and heading straight for Hakiem, her hand nervously pulling hair back from her brow.

The youth followed. And so, at professional stalking distance, did the Stepson, Gayle.

"Hakiem," Kama whispered, "is he still there? Is he coming?"

"*He*? They're *both* coming, girl. And what of it? That's no way to build a reputation, cutting out half your story and giving refunds before anybody asks…"

"You don't understand… Sync's gone missing. The last we saw of him, he was with that gutter-slime, the one from the meeting—Zip." As she spoke, Kama was tearing open her gearbag, in which metal clanked: this woman never went far from her squadron without her cache of arms.

Up behind her, while she bent over her sack, came Zip, who grabbed her with a crooked elbow around her throat and pulled her back against some bales of cloth before Hakiem could shout a warning or Gayle the Stepson, lurking at an appropriate distance, could intercede in her behalf.

"Don't move, lady," Zip said harshly through gritted teeth. "Just call off your watchdog."

Kama gagged and struggled.

Gayle took a half-dozen running strides; then halted, frowning, sword drawn but the other fist upon his hip.

Zip did something to Kama that made her writhe, then stand up very straight.

"Tell him," he said, "to back off. I just want to give your bedmates a message. *Tell him*!"

"Gayle!" Kama's voice was thick, guttural; her chin, in the crook of Zip's muscular arm, quivered. "You heard him. Stand down."

The Stepson, uttering a stream of profanity built around a single word, hunkered down, his sword across his knees.

"That's better," Zip grated. "Now, listen close. You too, tale-spinner: Roxane's got Sync. Sync asked me to set up a meeting, and I did that. But what happened after—that's no fault of mine. It might not be too late to save his soul, if any of you care."

"Where?" Kama croaked. "Where has she got him?"

"Down by the White Foal—she's got a place there, south of Ischade's. The vets will know where it is. But you tell 'em I told you that it's *not* my fault. And that if they don't get to him fast, it'll be too late. Hit the place in the daytime. There's no undeads around then, just some watchmen and a few snakes. Understand, lady?"

Again, he tightened his arm and Kama's head snapped back. Then he pushed her away and, jumping high, grabbed the rope on the bales behind him. Zip swung up and over and was gone, as far as Hakiem could tell.

Hakiem reached Kama first, coughing and trembling on the dockside. He was trying to get her up, while she shrugged off his aid and struggled to catch her breath, when he realized that the Stepson Gayle wasn't helping him.

Hakiem looked around just in time to see Gayle vault the bales after Zip, throwing-stars in hand, and let fly.

Kama saw it too, and screamed brokenly: "No! Gayle, no! He's trying to help us!"

"Pork help!" Gayle called back, just before he disappeared. "I hit him. He won't get far—and if he does, the porker's done for, anyhow." Then Gayle too disappeared.

"Done for?" Hakiem repeated dumbly. "What does he mean, Kama?"

"The stars." Kama got to her knees, her lips puffy, her expression unreadable. When she saw that Hakiem didn't understand, she added: "Gayle's throwing stars are what the Bandarans call 'blossoms.' They're painted with poison." And, hands on her knees, bent over, she retched.

Hakiem was still digesting all of this when Kama straightened up, took a handful of sharp-edged metal from her bag, and started climbing the bales, following Gayle.

"Where are you going, woman? What about the message?"

"Message?" Kama looked down at him from atop the bales. "Oh. Message. You take it. Tell Strat. He'll know what to do."

"But…"

"Don't 'but' me, old man. That boy's dead if I can't rein in Gayle and get to Zip in time. We don't kill those who help us."

Like a doused flame, she was gone.

*

Strat would rather have been anywhere else than in the brush surrounding Roxane's Foalside haunt. He'd had prior experience with the Nisibisi witch called 'Death's Queen.'

If he hadn't known that Hakiem was trustworthy, that Kama had disappeared, chasing after the street tough who'd brought the message (and that the success of the Stepson/3rd Commando mission into Sanctuary hinged on proving that Roxane couldn't send them running with their tails between their legs), he'd have passed on this particular frontal assault.

As things stood, he had no choice.

And he had a good chance of succeeding. He'd asked Ischade to come along: Ischade had her own bones to pick with Roxane. Strat had requisitioned enough incendiaries from Marc's illicit store to send all of Sanctuary up in flames. And his men knew how to use them. The trick was getting Sync out of there before firing up the witchy-roast.

Randal, their Tysian wizard, was sneaking around in mongoose form, right now, taking care of Roxane's snakes and reconnoitering the premises.

When they saw a hawk fly over, right to left, they'd light the horseshoe-shaped fire they'd prepared and rush the place: twenty mounted fighters ought to be able to do the job.

The horses were hooded, their blinkers soaked with soda water. The men had bladders of it on their saddles, to wet bandanas if the smoke got too thick.

Ischade was still beside him, in a meditative pose, whatever magic she was going to field unrevealed.

She just waited, tiny and delicate and too pale in the light of day, her claret robe pulled tight about her.

"You can still walk away from this," Strat assured her with a gallantry he didn't truly feel. "It's not your fight."

"Is it not? It's yours, then?" Up rose Ischade and suddenly she was terrifying: not small any longer; not the petite, sensual creature he'd brought here.

Her eyes were hellish and growing so large he thought he might be sucked inside them. He recalled their first encounter, long ago, on a dark slum street, when he'd been with Crit and they'd seen those eyes floating over a teenage corpse.

Strat found he couldn't answer; he just shook his head.

The power that was Ischade bared its teeth at him, the kill-fervor there as sharp as any Stepson's or any night-mad wolf's. "I'll bring you your man. All of this"—Ischade spread a robed arm, and it was as if night split the day—"that you do is unnecessary. Roxane owes me a person, and more. Wait here, you, and soon you'll see."

"Sure thing, Ischade." Strat found himself squatting down, digging in the sod with his brush-cutting knife. "I'll be right here."

He must have blinked or looked away. The next he knew, she was gone and a hawk's baby-cry resounded overhead; his men set their fires and ran for their horses.

Vaulting up on his bay, he wondered if Ischade was right: if he needn't risk all this manpower; if magic (hers and Randal's) alone could win the day.

He didn't like to think that way; he was used to letting Crit do his tactical thinking for him: in times like this, a man who was half a Sacred Band pair sorely missed his partner.

And so, thinking more about who was absent than who was present, he urged his horse into a lope and sought the fire gate, not realizing until a shape hovered in midair beside him that Randal, on a cloud-effigy of a horse, had drawn alongside.

"In her witching room, Sync is!" Randal shouted, his face white beneath its blanket of freckles. "And he's yet salvageable, if we can get him out. But it won't be easy—he's totally entranced. I couldn't rouse him in my mongoose form. I'll seek my power globe now and do my best. Fare well, Straton! May the Writ protect us all!"

And Randal's nonhorse thundered away on unhooves.

Craziest damn way to run a war. Strat had come back to Sanctuary to get away from just this sort of thing.

The firewall around him, hot and snapping, gave matters the immediacy of battle, the plain-and-simple truth of life and death.

The fire was a little out of control and his horse had to leap hot flames. Within, sod was beginning to smoke and combust. Sparks flew. Men yelled and squirted water on themselves and their mounts as they let flaming arrows fly and urged skittish horses toward Roxane's front door.

Strat's plan was to ride roughshod right into Roxane's house, snatch Sync, and get out before she could bewitch them.

It wasn't a plan such as his partner Critias might have made. Strat was aware that he might rescue one soldier only to lose another—or others—to Roxane. But he had to do something.

Just as he'd finally convinced his horse of this, and was ready to lead his regrouped Stepsons up Roxane's smoking stairs, an apparition appeared in the doorway: Ischade stood there with Sync, his arm over her shoulder, and they walked calmly out onto the veranda and down the steps, onto a lawn spurting sparks and young flames.

Men whooped and raced toward her. Beside her, Sync looked around calmly, his brow knitted as if a slightly amusing problem had him distracted.

Strat, wondering if he was dreaming, if it could really be this easy, got there first. With Ischade's help he pulled Sync up behind him on his horse.

The fire was loud and hot, and the horses and men milling around them made talk nearly impossible. But Strat bellowed to the man next to him: "Put her up before you. Let's get out of here!"

The Stepson's mouth formed the word: "Who?"

Strat looked back down. Ischade was gone.

So he gave the signal to end the sack and, with Sync holding tight to his waist, aimed his sweating horse at a narrowing portal in the flames.

*

In the thick of Downwind, it was nearly dusk, but the flames from the southeast made a second sunset which wouldn't die.

Zip was in a twilight all his own, stumbling from sewer to alley to dunghill, one hand against his bleeding side, nearly doubled over from the pain.

He'd been stabbed before, beaten often, starved and fevered in the course of his life, but never so close to death as this.

He'd pulled the barbed missile out; he didn't understand why it hurt worse now, not less.

He was sick to his stomach and only intermittently did he recall his determination to get home. Home to his own safe haven, or home to Mama Becho's where someone would tend him, home to… anywhere where he could lie down, where the Beysibs or the Stepsons or the 3rd Commando or the army wouldn't find him.

He was sweating and he was thirsty and he was nauseated. A red film before his eyes made it hard to tell which corner he was on.

If he was lost in Downwind, he was nearly dead, for he knew these streets like he knew the tunnels, the sewers… The sewers! If he could find a bolt-hole, he could curl up in one; Zip didn't want to die in public. That thought, and that alone, kept him on his feet long enough for him to stumble into Ratfall, where people knew him.

He heard his name called. He was down on his knees by then, with his head between them. The only thing he could do was lie down before he passed out.

When he woke he was under blankets. A cool cloth was being laid upon his brow.

When he could, he reached up and grabbed a hand there. He held tight to someone's wrist.

He opened his eyes. A face swam, unrecognizable, above him. A voice from that direction said, "Don't try to talk. The worst is over. You'll be all right if you'll drink this."

Something was pushed between his lips: hard like clay or metal; it grated on his teeth. Then his head was raised by another's will and liquid spilled down his throat.

He choked, sputtered; then remembered how to swallow. When he couldn't swallow more, someone wiped his lips and then his chin.

"Good. Good boy," he heard. Then he slept a sleep in which his side burned and flamed and he kept trying to put out the fire, but its flames kept starting up from ashes, and his body walked away from him, leaving him invisible and lonely on a deserted Downwind street.

When he woke again, he smelled something: chicken.

He opened his eyes and the room didn't spin. He tried to sit up, and then it did.

Voices mumbled just beyond earshot. A form bent over him. Long black hair brushed his cheek.

"That's a good one. Here you go: drink this," said a blurry face.

He drank and well-being surged through him. His vision cleared and he saw whose face it was: the lady fighter, Kama of the 3rd Commando, was tending him.

Behind her, the soldier-mage Randal craned his swanlike neck and rubbed his hands.

"Better. You're right, Kama," said the mage judiciously, and then: "I'll leave you. If you need me, I'll be right outside."

As the door closed and he was alone with his enemy, Zip tried to push himself up on his arms. He didn't have the strength. He wanted to run but he couldn't even raise his head. He'd heard all about Straton's skill at interrogation. He'd have been better off dead in the street than being alive and at the mercy of such as these.

Kama sat on the bed next to him and took his hand.

He tensed, thinking: *Now it will begin. Torture. Drugs. They've saved me from one death to offer me another.*

She said, "I've wanted to do this ever since I first saw you." Leaning close, she kissed him on the lips.

When she sat up straight, she smiled.

He didn't have the energy to ask her what she had in mind for him or what the kiss was meant to mean; he couldn't find his voice.

But she said, "It was a mistake. Gayle didn't understand what you were trying to do. We're all sorry. You just relax and get better. We'll take care of you. *I'll* take care of you. If you can hear me, blink."

Zip blinked. If Kama of the 3rd Commando wanted to take care of him, he wasn't in any condition to argue.

Chapter 5: Shelter From the Storm

Now the weather takes a turn. Now the gods spat and split the sky asunder with their warring while the world pulses and quakes. Now storms rule in heaven, buffeting Tempus' Sacred Band, soaking hill and dell and forest; changing fields into swamps and sluicing scree down slopes. Mud is everywhere, oozing in waves and bubbling. Cavalrymen don't like uncertain footing; riders grouse and give their mounts free rein.

Wet winds skirl loud enough to wake the dead. Soldiers pull their whipping *chlamys* tight about them; horses snort and neigh. The heavens rant and rave. Thunder deafens. Everywhere are blinding bolts that snap the trees while tempest soaks the world.

So they halt. And they huddle leeward of a rocky outcrop, scant shelter from the storm. While they wait, Perses spies a cave there, big enough and deep enough to hold the horsemen and their mounts. Shelter is where you find it; they file inside. The wind moans loud without and the rain pounds hard beyond and it takes four men to build a fire, but they manage.

Randal's veins show blue beneath his skin yet he is steadfast; the Lemnian women cuddle beneath a sodden blanket; Lysis and Arton nurse the fire, which belches smoke and cracks and spits sparks as kindling dries and flares. Without a word, Niko strips off his wet panoply and cloak, props them near the fire, grabs a torch and sorties deeper into the cave half-naked, two longtime Stepsons flanking him, spears in hand.

A blessing from their tutelary god is this storm, or any other, every Stepson knows. For days they've trekked. Even Randal calls it odd, how long and how far they've gone with no sight of men. But Tempus has seen the altar of Enlil and felt the god inside him: his path is clear.

If this route takes them through Mygdonia or Macedonia or ancient Thrace, does it really matter? Chaetae and Physca and so many other towns laid waste, ravaged, conquered and reconquered by empires that claim them under different men with different names and different goals. He's long since lost interest in who rules where. Living from empire to empire, war to war, he's learned that fools rule and blood sheds, everywhere.

Randal had found the Band, wherever and whenever the storm god had thrust them this time. So would his rear-guard contingent, with the leaders he'd left behind to guide them. The gods move Tempus where they will; his fighters move with him, as the gods allow.

The cave walls themselves seem to flicker in the firelight; Stepsons and Thebans seek the flames and hunker down. Straton says, "Someone else, not me, tell a tale tonight. Critias? Or Randal? Who's next?"

Crit craned his neck and looked where Niko and one of the senior pairs had gone exploring. "I'll do it—get it over with." Annoyance and mischief fought in Crit's normally impassive face. "But only until Niko comes back… he'll not like recalling what happened when an emperor friend of the Riddler's came south to us on behalf of the Slaughter Priest's ghost."

But before Crit could begin, a muffled call rang out from deep inside the cave.

Stepsons dove for arms and armor; the Thebans and the Lemnian women jerked upright; Arton and Lysis came running, leaving the cave mouth unguarded.

"Stay," Tempus commanded. "Crit, tell your story. Straton, with me."

So into the cave's depths he went, with Strat on his right, his shortsword in one hand and the god high in him, nearly overwhelming him, hungry for slaughter, ready for strife.

He barely needed Straton: Enlil was with him now, pounding in his heart, scalding in his blood. Or so he thought until he saw Niko and the Sacred Band pair, spears holding monsters at bay: a giant and a sphinx of sorts.

"Hold," he said, hoping he was not too late. "Put up your spears, Stepsons."

Inside his head, no god ranted now, or snarled, or proposed a single act of war. Intimidated, Lord Storm? Or driven off?

No answer from Enlil, here in the domain of unfamiliar gods.

The woman-headed lion's wings were spread, her serpent tail lashing. The huge man beside her had three heads, then two, then one, then three again; he was thewed like the gods themselves. Icons of antiquity: Tempus knew this deic son of Ares from myths: ancient and formidable: "Thrax," Tempus said familiarly, though he'd never thought to meet this legend in the flesh, "what brings the founder of Thrace and an oracle here, now? We're merely passing through."

Once, Thrace ruled here. But surely not today.

The godly giant settled upon a single head, a single face, and grunted. "Who are you, intruder in my house?"

The lioness rubbed her beautiful lips with one golden paw. "Yes, who are you, adventurer?"

"Thrax, Oracle," he said to the giant and the sphinx, "I am Tempus, called the Riddler, the Black, favorite of the storm god. You, Oracle, introduced yourself to one of my fighters some time back; these others are his brothers."

"You have us at a disadvantage, all can plainly see: coming into our cave uninvited, with spears and warriors and foreign gods. You see us rightly, so you have the Sight. What else have you got?"

"Niko, to me."

Niko knew that tone; with a hand sign, he bade his men retreat until they flanked Tempus and Straton. Now the cave was crowded where they stood. Niko said, "Commander, let me…"

"No, Niko." Don't start a fight we may not want to finish. Or be able to.

"Demigod," the sphinx accused Tempus.

"So? Sometimes. Pawn of heaven, more often," Tempus rejoined. "What do you want?"

"Leave matters here undisturbed: the gods have intentions," said Thrax, the giant.

"Gods always have intentions. We'll leave when the rain abates. Be patient," said Tempus.

On his right, Niko shifted and angled closer, protective, putting his body between Tempus and Thrax, plainly wishing he'd brought his shield, ready to test his goddess-given gifts against these foes. Straton, too, closed ranks, thinking a fight was coming.

It wasn't, if Tempus could avoid it. Not with these two powers.

"Then," said the winged lioness through her pouty woman's lips, "stay the night here, you who are called the Riddler. If you dare."

Not good, but good enough. Retreat sometimes takes more courage than combat.

"Agreed," he said, and began backing away, very carefully, hands at his sides, never threatening.

"Commander," Niko whispered. "How can we stay here now…?"

"We can, Niko. We will."

After that, his rightman, and Straton, and the two Stepsons kept silent, retracing their steps along the tunnel, until they emerged into the cave where their fire and their fellows waited.

Then Tempus said, very low, "Not one word of this to our fighters—not yet. We have an agreement with the owners of this place. Let the Band eat. Let them drink. Let Critias finish his story…

"And then?" Niko wanted to know.

"Then we will see what Enlil has in his mind."

Chapter 6: Power Play

Tempus, a mercenary general in the service of Ranke's new emperor, was knee-deep in the bloody purges marking the first winter of Theron's accession to the Rankan throne when the sky above the walled city began to weep black tears.

By the time dawn should have broken, ashen clouds massed to the very vault of heaven so that not even the Sun God's sharpest rays could pierce the arrayed armies of the night. The city of Ranke, once the brightest jewel of the Rankan empire, shuddered in the dark, her ochre walls stained dusky from the storm's black and ugly might.

Thunder growled; winds yowled. Black hail pelted Theron's palace, shattering windows and pounding doors. On temple streets and cultured byways it bounced, sharp as diamonds and large as heads, bringing impious priests to their knees and cheap nobles to charity in slick streets covered with greasy slush freezing to ice as black, some said, as their emperor Theron's heart.

For all knew that Theron had come to power in a coup instigated by the armies. He was a creature of blood, a wild beast of the battlefield. And the proof of this was in the allies who had brought him to the Imperial palace: Nisibisi witches, demons of the black beyond, devils of horrid aspect. Even the feared near-immortals of the blood cults such as Aškelon, lord of dreams, and his brother-in-law, Tempus, demigod and favorite son of Vashanka, the Rankan war god (to name but two) had lent their strength to Theron's cause.

Did not Tempus still labor at his gory task of purging the disloyal—all who had been influential in Abakithis' court? Did not women still wake to empty beds and find pouches made of human skin and filled with thirty gold soldats (the Rankan price for one human life) nailed to their boudoir doors?

Did not those few remaining adherents of Abakithis, former emperor of Ranke (now deceased, unavenged, much cursed in his uneasy grave), still scuttle even through the deadly, knife-sharp hail with bulging pockets to the mercenaries' guildhall to leave their fortunes at the desk with scrawled notes saying, "For Tempus, to distribute as he wills, from the admiring and loyal family of So-and-so," while servants spirited noble wives and children out back ways and slum-yard gates in beggars' guise?

Thus it was whispered, as the storm raged unabated into its second day, that Theron and his creature Tempus were to blame for this black blizzard straight from hell.

These very words were whispered by a woman to Critias, Tempus' first officer and finest covert actor, who had infiltrated the noble strata of the imperial city.

And Crit, with a wry twitch of lips that drew down his patrician nose and a rake of his sword-hand through dark, feathery hair, replied to the governor's wife he was bedding: "No one gives a contract for a sunrise, m'lady. No *man,* that is. Theron is no more than that. When gods throw tantrums, even Tempus listens."

Crit had fought in the Wizard Wars up north and this woman knew it. His guise was that of a disaffected officer who had renounced his commission after Abakithis' assassination at the Festival of Man and now, like so many others of the old guard, scrambled from allegiance to allegiance in search of safety. So the governor's wife ran a finger along his jaw and smiled commiseratingly as she said, "You men of the armies… all alike. I suppose you're telling me that this is good? This storm, this hail black as hell? That it's a sign we poor women cannot read?"

Thinking of his personal prognosticators (bits of hair and silver and bone and luck nestled in the pouch dangling from his belt that, with the rest of his clothes, lay in a heap at the foot of another man's bed), Crit replied in Court Rankene, "When the Storm God returns to the armies, wars can be won—not just fought interminably. Without Him, we've just been marking time. If He's angry, He'll let us know on what account. And I'd bet it won't be on Theron's—or Tempus'. One's a general whom the soldiers chose exactly because the god had abandoned us during Abakithis' reign; the other is…"

It wasn't the woman's hand, reaching low, which made him pause. She wanted Crit's protection; information was what he'd sought here in return. And gotten what he'd come for, and more from this one—all a Rankan lady had to give. So he thought (in a moment of unaccustomed tenderness for one who would likely entertain, on his account, the crowds who'd throng the execution stands when the weather broke) to explain to her about Tempus. About what and who the man Crit had sworn to serve was, and was not.

He settled for "…Tempus is what Father Enlil, Lord Storm to the armies, wills. And cursed more than Ranke and all her enemies put together. By gods and men, by magic and mages. If there's hell to pay because of Theron's reign, you can rest assured it's Tempus who'll suffer in all our steads."

The Rankan woman, from the look on her face and the hunger on her lips, had lost interest in the subject. But Crit had not. When he left her, he marked her door with a sign for the palace police without even a second thought to her fine body behind it that would soon be lifeless.

The sky was still black as a witch's crotch and the wind was chorusing its judgment song in a many-throated voice Crit had heard occasionally on the battlefield whenever Tempus' non-human allies took a hand in this skirmish or that—choraling the way it used to when wizard weather blew in Sanctuary, where Crit's partner and his brothers of the Sacred Band were now, down at the empire's most foul and egregious southern-most appurtenance.

By the time Crit had retrieved his horse, his fingers were playing with the luck charms in his belt-pouch. Normally, he'd have pulled them out, squatted down, shaken and thrown them in the straw for guidance.

But the storm was guidance enough: he didn't need to ask a question whose answer he wouldn't like. If his partner Strat had been on his right tonight, he'd have bet his friend any odds that, when the weather broke, Tempus would come rousting Crit without so much as an explanation and they'd be heading south to Sanctuary where the Sacred Band was quartered for the winter.

Not that he didn't want to see Strat: he did. Not that he wasn't happy that the storm god Vashanka, berserker god of the armies, lord of Sack and Pillage, of Bloodlust and Fury and Death's Gate, was manifest: he was. What he'd told the Rankan bitch was true: you couldn't win a war without your god. But Vashanka, the Rankan storm god, had deserted the Stepsons, Crit's unit, in their need. So the unit had taken up with another, perhaps greater, god: Father Enlil.

And the black, roiling clouds above, the voices which spoke thunder over the fighter's head, were telling a man who didn't like gods much better than magic and who was first officer to a demigod who meddled with both, that Vashanka might not be too pleased with the fickle men who once had slaughtered in His name and now did so in another's.

Things were so damned complicated whenever Tempus was involved. Grabbing a tuft of mane, Crit swung up on his warhorse and reined it around so hard it half-reared and then, finding itself headed toward the mercenaries' guild and its own stall, safety and comfort in the storm, fairly bolted through the treacherous, slushy streets of Ranke.

Despite the darkened ways and chancy footing, Crit let the young horse run, trusting pedestrians, should there be any, to scatter and armed patrols to recognize him for who and what he was. The horse had a right to comfort, where it could find some. Crit couldn't think of a thing that would do the same for him, now that the gods had dropped one shoe and all he could do was wait until Tempus dropped the other.

*

The storm didn't exactly break, but on the fourth day it mellowed.

By then, Theron and Tempus had summoned Brachis, High Priest of the Variously Named War-Gods of Imperial Ranke, and concocted a likely story for the populace.

Executions, held in abeyance for the first three days of the storm, were resumed. "More purges, obviously, Your Majesty," Brachis had suggested, unctuous to the point of insult, managing by his exaggerated servility to mean the opposite of what he said, "will appease the hungry gods."

Thereupon Theron, old and as gray as the shadows in this newly acquired but not yet conquered palace full of politicians and whores, gave Brachis a stare fully as black as the raging sky outside and said, "Right, priest. Let's have a dozen of your worst enemies bled out in Blood Square by lunch."

Tempus stayed an impulse to touch his old friend Theron's knee under the table.

But Brachis didn't rise to Theron's bait. Instead, the priest bowed his way out in a swish of copper-beaded robes.

"God's balls, Riddler," said the aging general to the ageless one, "do *you* think we've angered the gods? More to the point, do you think we've *got o*ne to anger?"

Theron's jaw jutted so that the pitting of age made it look like a pecan shell, or the snout of the moth-eaten geriatric lion he so much resembled from his thinning, unkempt mane to his scarred and twisted claws. He was a big man still, his power no mere memory, but fresh and flowing in corded veins and leathery sinews: big and powerful in his aged prime, except when seen in close proximity to Tempus, the avatar of storm gods on earth, whose yarrow-honey hair and high brow free from lines resembled so much the votive statues of Vashanka still worshiped in this land. Tempus' eyes were long and full of guile, his form heroic, his aspect one of a man on the joyous side of forty, though he'd seen empires rise and fall and fully expected to see the end of this one—to bury Theron as he had and would so many other men, with all their might ranged round them. And Theron knew the truth of it: he'd known Tempus since both were seemingly of an age, fighting the Defender on Wizardwall's skirts when the Rankan Empire was just a babe. The two were honest with one another when it was possible; they were careful when it was not.

"Got a god to anger? We've got *some*thing mad enough to spit, I'll own," Tempus replied. Now, Tempus knew, was not the time to raise false hopes of Vashanka the Missing God's return in a warrior who'd willingly and knowingly come to a throne whose weight would kill him. Kingship was the dirtiest of jobs, and Theron had become the man to do it by default. "If it's Vashanka, then it's a matter between Him and Enlil. Theomachy tends to kill more men than gods. Don't be too anxious to get the armies' hopes up. The war with Mygdonia won't end by gods' wills, any more than it will by Nisibisi magic."

"That's what you think this infernal darkness is, then—magic? Your nemesis, perhaps… the Nisibisi witch?"

"Or yours: the Nisibisi warlocks. What matter, gods or magic? If I thought he had the power, I'd pick Brachis as the culprit. He'd do without both of us well enough."

"We'd do without all of his well enough. But we're stuck with one another, for the nonce. Unless, of course, you've a suggestion… some way to rid me, as the saying has gone since time immemorial, of all turbulent priests?"

The two were fencing with words, neither addressing the real problem: in the Rankan capital, the storm was being taken as an omen, and a bad one, on the nature of Theron's rule.

The aging general fingered a jeweled goblet whose bowl was balanced upon a winged lion and sighed deeply at almost the same time that Tempus' rattling chuckle sounded: "An omen, is it, old lion? Is that what you *really* want? An omen to make this storm a mandate from the gods, not a critique?"

"What *I* want?" Theron thundered in response, suddenly sweeping up the artsy, jewel-encrusted goblet of state and throwing it so hard against the farther wall that it bounced back to land among the dregs spilled from it and roll eerily, back and forth in a circle, in the middle of the floor.

To and fro it rolled, first one way and then the other, making a sound like chariot wheels upon the stone floor, a sound which grew louder and melded with the thunder outside and the renewed clatter of hailstones which resembled horses' hooves, as if a team from heaven was thundering down the blackened sky.

Now Tempus found the hair on his arms raising up and the skin under his beard crawling as the wine dregs spattered on the floor began to smoke and steam and the dented goblet to shimmer and gleam and, inside his head, a rustle—familiar and unfamiliar—began to sound as a god came to visit there.

Tempus really hated it when gods intruded inside his skull. He managed to mutter "Crap! Get thee hence!" before he realized that it was neither the deep and primal breathing of Father Enlil (Lord Storm) nor the passionate and demanding boom of Vashanka the Pillager which he was hearing so loud that the shimmer and thunder and smoke issuing from the goblet and dregs before him diminished to insignificance. This was neither voice from either god; it was comprised of both.

Both! This was too much. His own fury roused. He detested being invaded; he hated being an instrument, a pawn, the butler of one murder god, the batman of another.

He fought the heaviness in his limbs which demanded that he sit, still and popeyed, like Theron across the table from him, and meekly submit to whatever manifestation was in the process of coalescing before him. He snarled and cursed the very existence of godhead and managed to get his hands on the stout edge of the plank table.

He squeezed the wood so hard that it dented and formed round his fingers like clay, but he could not rise nor could he banish the babble of divine infringement from his head.

And before him, where a cup had rolled, wheels spun—golden-rimmed wheels of a war chariot drawn by smoke-colored Trôs horses whose shod hooves struck sparks from the stones of the palace floor. Out of a maelstrom of swirling smoke it came, and Tempus was so mesmerized by the squealing of the horses and the screech of unearthly stresses around the rent in time and space through which the chariot approached that he only barely noticed that Theron had thrown up both hands to shield his face and was cowering like an aged child at his own table.

These horses were harnessed in red leather that was shiny, as if wet. Beyond the blood-red reins were hands, and the arms attached were well-formed and strong, brown and smooth, without hair or scar above graven gauntlets. The driver's torso was covered by a cuirass of enameled metal, cast to the physique beneath it, jointed and gilded in the fashion chosen by the Sacred Band at its inception.

Tempus did not need to see the face, by then, to know that he was not being visited by a god, nor an archmage, nor even a demon, but by a creature more strange: as the chariot emerged fully from the miasma around it and the horses snorted and plunged, dancing in place, and the wheels screeched to a halt, Tempus saw a hand raise to a brow in a greeting of equals.

This greeting was for him, not for Theron, who cowered with wide eyes. The face of the man in the chariot smiled softly. The eyes resting upon Tempus so fondly were as pale and pure as cool water. And as the vision opened its mouth to speak, the god-din in Tempus' ears subsided to a rustle, then to whispers, then to contented sighs that faded entirely away when Abarsis, dead Slaughter Priest and patron shade of the Sacred Band, wrapped his blood-red reins casually around the chariot's brake and stepped down from his car, arms wide to embrace Tempus, whom Abarsis had loved better than life when the ghost had been a man.

There was nothing for it, Tempus realized, but to make the best of the situation, though seeing the materialization of a boy who had sought an honorable death in Tempus' service wrenched his heart.

The boy was now a power on his own—a power from beyond Death's Gate, true, but a power all the same.

"Commander," said the velvet-voiced shade, "I see from your face that you still have it in your heart to love me. That's good. This was not an easy journey to arrange."

The two embraced, and Abarsis' upswept eyes and high curved cheeks, his young bull's neck and his glossy black hair, felt all too real—as substantial as the splinters that had somehow gotten under Tempus' fingernails.

And the boy was yet strong—that is, the shade was. Tempus, stepping back, started to speak but found his voice choking with melancholy. What did one say to the dead? Not "How's life?" surely. Certainly not the Sacred Band greeting…

But Abarsis spoke it to Tempus, as he had said it so long ago in Sanctuary, where he'd gone to die: "Life to you, Riddler, and everlasting glory. And to your friend… to *our* friend… Theron of Ranke, salutations."

Hearing his name shook Theron from his funk. Still the old fighter was nearly speechless, quaking visibly.

Seeing this, Tempus recovered himself: "You scared us half to death. Is this *your* darkness, then?" Tempus stepped back and waved a hand toward the sky beyond the corbeled ceiling overhead. "If so, we could do without it. Scares the locals. We're trying to settle in a military rule here, not start a civil war."

A shadow passed quickly over the beautiful face of the Slaughter Priest and Tempus, seeing it, wanted to ask, *'Are you real? Are you reborn? Have you come to stay?'*

The shade looked him hard in the eye and that glance struck his soul and shocked it. "No. None of that, Riddler. I am here to bring a message and ask a favor—for favors done and yet to be done."

"A*hem.* Tempus, will you introduce me? It's my palace, after all," the emperor growled, bluffing annoyance, straining for composure, and casting covetous glances at the horses (if such they were) which stood at parade rest in their traces, ears pricked forward, just a bit of steam issuing from their nostrils.

"Favors," Theron murmured, "done and yet to be done…"

"Theron, Emperor of Ranke, Supreme General of the Armies and so forth, meet Abarsis, Slaughter Priest, former High Priest of Vashanka, former—"

"Former living ally," Abarsis cut in, smooth as a whetted blade, "and ally still, Theron. We've a problem, and it lies in Sanctuary. Speaking through priests is a matter for gods; my mandate is different. Tempus, whom we both love, must listen to gods, not priests." His grin flashed as it had once in life: "But on this occasion, I am… well-equipped… to interpret." Then he shifted and his gaze caught Tempus' and held: "The message is: 'the globes of Nisibisi power must be destroyed; all the gods will rejoice when it is done. Destroyed in Sanctuary, where there are tortured souls of yours and mine to be released.' The favor is: 'grant Niko's wish in a matter of children… yours and Ours.'"

Ours? There was no mistaking the emphatic tone Abarsis had used—a tone reserved for deific matters and one word spoken by the dead High Priest of Vashanka who had come so far to utter it. Liking the smell of things less and less, Tempus took a step backward and sat upon the table's edge, thinking, *For this, he comes to me. Wonderful. Now what?*

For Tempus, who could refuse a god and obstruct an archmage, knew, looking at this shade who was once Stepson, called Abarsis, that he could refuse this one nothing. It was an old debt, a mutual responsibility stretching far beyond such trifles as life and death. This was a matter of souls, and Tempus' soul was very old. So old that, seeing Abarsis yet young, yet beautiful in his spirit and his honor in a way Tempus no longer could be, the man called the Riddler felt suddenly very tired.

And Tempus, who never slept—who had not slept since he had been cursed by an archmage and taken solace in the protection of a god three centuries past—began to feel drowsy. His eyelids grew heavy and Abarsis' words grew loud, echoing unintelligibly so that it seemed as if Theron and Abarsis spoke together in some room far away.

Just before he collapsed on the table, snoring deeply in a sleep that would last until the weather broke the following day, Tempus heard Abarsis say clearly, "And for you, Tempus, whom I love above all men, I have this special gift… not much, just a token: on this one evening, my lord, I have haggled from the gods for you a good night's rest. So now, sleep and dream of me."

Thus Tempus slept. And when he woke, Abarsis was long gone and preparations for Theron, Tempus, and a hand-picked contingent to depart for Sanctuary were well under way.

*

Trouble was coming to Sanctuary: Roxane could feel it in her bones. The premonition cut like a knife to the very quick of the Nisibisi witch, once called Death's Queen, who now huddled in her shrouded hovel on Sanctuary's White Foal River, beset from within and without.

Once she had been nearly all-powerful; once she had been a perpetrator, not a victim; once she had decreed Suffering and marshaled Woe upon human cattle from Sanctuary's sorry spit to Wizardwall's wildest peaks.

But that was before she'd fallen in love with a mortal and paid the ancient price. Perhaps if that mortal had not been Stealth, called Nikodemos, Sacred Bander and member in good standing of Tempus' blood-drenched cadre of Stepsons, it would not seem so foolish now to have traded in immortality for the ability to shed a woman's tears and feel a woman's fleeting joy.

But Niko had betrayed her. She should have known; if she'd been a human woman she would have: No man, and most especially no thrice-paired fighter who'd taken the Sacred Band oath, would feel loyalty or honor toward a woman when it conflicted with his bond with men.

She should have known but she hadn't even guessed. For Niko was the tenderest of souls where women were concerned; he loved them as a class, as he loved fine horses and young children—not lasciviously, but honestly and freely.

Now that she understood, it was an insult. She was no waif, no fuddle-headed twat, no inconsequential piece of fluff. And there was injury to add to insult's sting: Roxane had given up immortality to love a mortal who wasn't capable of appreciating such a gift.

She had been betrayed by her "beloved" over a matter that should have been towering only in its insignificance: the "life" of a petty mageling, a would-be wizard called Randal, a flop-eared, freckled fool who fooled now with forces beyond his ability to control.

Yes, Niko had dared to trick Roxane, to distract her with his charms while this posturing prestidigitator, whom she'd thought to have for dinner, got away.

And now Niko lurked in priest-holes, palaces, and princely bedrooms, protected by Randal (who had a Globe of Power similar to Roxane's own, and more powerful) and the counter-magical armor given Niko by the entelechy of dreams.

Not once did sweet Stealth venture riverward, though his de facto commander, Straton of the Stepsons, rode this way on evenings to visit another witch.

This other witch, too, was an enemy of hers: Ischade the necromant, whom by rights the Stepsons should have hated more than they did Roxane, vilified in their prayers as they nightly did Death's Queen.

There was some irony to that: Ischade, a tawdry soul-sucker with limited power and unlimited lust, was a friend of the Stepsons, ally of the mercenary army which was all that stood between Sanctuary and total chaos now that the town was divided into blood feuds and factions while the Rankan Empire's grasp grew weak and the Rankan prince, Kadakithis, was barricaded in his palace with some salmon-eyed Beysib slut from a fishy foreign land.

And Roxane, who'd been Death's Queen on Wizardwall and flown high, ruler of all she once surveyed, was shunned by Stepsons and even by lesser factions in the town. Shunned by all but her own death squads, some truly dead and raised from crypts to do her bidding, some only a hair's-breadth away from mossy graves like One-Thumb, the Vulgar Unicorn's proprietor, alias Lastel, and Zip, guttersnipe leader of the PFLS (Popular Front for the Liberation of Sanctuary) rebels who couldn't get along without her help.

She had Snapper Jo, of course, her single remaining fiend—a warty, gray-skinned, wall-eyed beast, snaggle-toothed and orange-haired, whom she'd summoned from a nearby hell to serve her. Yes, she still had Snapper, though lately he'd been taking his spy's job of day-barkeep at the Vulgar Unicorn too much to heart, thinking silly thoughts of camaraderie with humans (who'd no more accept a fiend as one of them than the Stepsons had accepted Roxane).

And she had her snakes, of course, a fresh supply, whom she could witch into human form for intervals (though Sanctuary's snakes weren't bred for masquerading and turned out small, sleepy in cold weather, and even more dull-witted than the northern kind).

Still, it was a pair of snakes (a butler-snake and a bodyguard) whom she called to build a fire in her witching room, to bring her chalcedony water bowl and place it on a column of porphyry near the hearth, to stay and watch and wait with her while she poured salt into the water and words came from her mouth to make the salt into her will and the water bowl into the open wounds of Sanctuary. Not wounds of flesh, but wounds of spirit: the arrogance of loyalty given and withheld; the gall of greed; the acne of innocence; the lacerations of love; the pustules of passion which prickled such hearts as Straton's, as Randal's; as those of the prince/governor and his flounder-faced consort, Shupansea (fool enough to keep snakes herself, thinking that Beysib snakes might be immune to Nisibisi snake magic); and even as Niko's own consuming compassion for a pair of children he wet-nursed like some useless Rankan matron.

The water in her bowl took chop as the salt hit it, then began to cloud and then to bubble as if salt had turned to acid in hearts all around the town. The color of the water grew grayer, more opaque, and outside her skin-covered window, snow began to fall in giant flakes.

"Go, snakes," she crooned, "go meet your brothers in the palace of the prince. Meet and eat them, then defeat the peace between the Beysib and her Rankan host. And find those children, both, and bite them with the poison of your fangs, so that death beats down on midnight wings and Niko will be forced to come to me... to me to save them." Almost, she didn't get those last words out, because a chuckle rose to block her curse's end—especially the word "save."

For as she'd looked into the bowl she'd seen a vision, then another. First she'd seen riders, and a boat with a lion rampant on its prow: one rider was her ancient enemy, Tempus, called the Sleepless One, avatar of godly mischief; another was Jihan, a more potent enemy, Froth Daughter, princess of the endless sea, a copper-colored nymph of matchless passion, a sprite with all the strength of moon and tides between her knees; another was Critias, Strat's partner and better half, the coldest and boldest of the Stepsons, and the only man among the lot of them who didn't need more-than-mortal help to do his job. And on the ship, now seeming like a wedding gift, all wrapped in gilt and gloriously colored sails as it drew nearer, was a man she'd helped become a king, one who owed an unequivocal debt to Death's Queen: Theron, Emperor of Ranke, who was so anxious to pay Roxane's price he was trekking to the empire's anus to bow his knee.

Oh, yes, she thought then. *Trouble, let it come.* For Roxane, once the visions were cleared from the salted water of her bowl by an impatient, dusky hand, had an idea—an epiphany, an inspiration for a vengeful task to undertake, fitting to all the harm that past and present denizens of Sanctuary had done her. She'd seen the error of her ways, and now she'd seen a new solution. She'd given up too much for Nikodemos, who'd turned on her and spurned her. She'd trade this batch of hapless souls to get back what she'd so foolishly bargained away.

And then it was left to her only to dismiss the snakes, drink the water in the bowl, and settle down spread-legged in the middle of her summoning room floor, awaiting the Devils of Demonic Deals, the Negotiators of Necromancy, the Underworld's Underwriters, to appear, to take the bait a witch could offer and then, when sated, be tricked into giving Roxane back immortality in exchange for the deaths of a pair of children (who might be gods if ever they grew up), and that of Nikodemos, who deserved no better if he'd thought to spurn the witch who loved him and survive it. Of course, she'd throw in Tempus, too, for fun. He'd make an undead of choice to send raping and pillaging up and down the streets of Sanctuary of an evening, streets so thick with hatred and slick with blood no one would even think to worry about what kind of death they got.

For Sanctuarites cared only for this life, not the next. They were ignorant of choices made beyond the grave, or given up today for trifles. They didn't know or care that an eternity of hell could be had for cheap, or that the gods offered out another way.

This was why she liked it here, did Roxane. Even once she'd sacrificed Niko and his ilk—the entire Sacred Band and unpaired Stepsons, if she got lucky—she'd stay around. Once there was no more Ischade to interfere, no silly priests like Molin Torchholder to try to resurrect a dead god's cult, the place would let her have her way.

And so, decided, Roxane crooked a finger and, from nowhere visible, a sound like hellish hinges squeaking reverberated through her chamber, a non-door swung down, and a Globe of Power could be glimpsed, spinning gently on its axis of golden glyphs, its stones beginning to glow as its song of sorcery spun louder and, from hells Sanctuary wasn't used to accommodating, a demon choir began to chant.

It was the old way, the only way: evil for evil, tenfold. And she'd promised hell to pay, visited upon this town for its offenses and its slights. There remained only to touch flesh and nail to the globe spinning larger, closer, right before her eyes.

She reached out and braced herself, for a demon lover would come with contact: one did need to pay as one went, even if one was Nisibisi's finest witch.

Her nail screeched into the high peaks' clay, and a demon screeched into existence between her knees, and a hellish gale whose like was known as wizard weather up and down the land stretched from Sanctuary's southernmost tip up along the Rankan seaboard where the imperial ship was under way.

And everywhere men remarked that, even for wizard weather, the gale was fierce and loud, and full of sounds the like of a goddess being raped in some forgotten passion play.

*

Sanctuary promised nothing of the sort to Critias, who'd ridden down country at an ungodly rate with Tempus and his inhuman consort, Jihan, daughter of the primal power men called Stormbringer (when they were so unlucky as to have to call Him anything at all).

The ride—across No Man's Land, a shortcut full of shades and mirages through a desert the party shouldn't have been able to cross in twice the time—hadn't been the kind of trip Crit liked. It was too fast, too easy, too full of magic—or whatever the equivalent was when power was fielded not by a human mage, but by Jihan, daughter of Stormbringer, lord of wind and wave.

Now that they'd nearly reached the town, it was too late for Crit to ask his commander questions—whether, as rumor had it, Abarsis had really appeared to the Riddler in Theron's palace; why, even if that were true, Tempus had seen fit to split his forces: the three of them were worth more than the score of fighters accompanying Theron on his ocean voyage.

But straight answers were lacking in the Rankan Empire this season and Tempus, with Jihan around, was more obscure than usual.

So it came to pass that Tempus said to Crit as they rode down the General's Road to the ford at the White Foal River: "Make your own way henceforth, Stepson, among the pigs in their mire. Find Straton and reconvene your covert actors: I want the whereabouts of Roxane and her power globe by midnight."

"Is that all?" Crit asked, sarcasm finding its way into his tone. No disrespect, but gods whispered in the Riddler's ears and never spoke to Critias at all, so that orders like these always seemed impossible, issuing from nowhere, although he'd hardly ever failed to carry through a task, however vague, that the Riddler set him.

But this time, as his sorrel stallion pawed the White Foal's mud and lewdly eyed the blue roan Jihan rode, Crit was more than usually defensive: Down in Sanctuary, across the White Foal somewhere, was Kama, Tempus' daughter, whom Crit had got with child. It had been in the Wizard Wars, against the Riddler's orders, and ill had come of it for everyone involved. He'd not thought of her (an act of will, not fortune) until this moment, but looking out across the Foal where the lights of Sanctuary's whorehold, the Street of Red Lanterns, were twinkling in the dusk, suddenly the mercenary fighter could think of nothing else.

And Tempus, who understood too much too often, who healed from every mortal cut he took, who buried everyone he loved in time and enjoyed the confidence of gods and shades, said softly in a voice like a river coursing gravel, "No, not *all.* A start. Take a unit of your choosing, find Straton, use what he has, destroy Roxane's power globe by dawn, then seek me in the palace."

"And is *that* the whole of it, Commander?" Crit asked laconically, as if the task were simple, not a death sentence or an invitation to mutiny.

Crit saw Jihan's feral eyes go wide. The Froth Daughter, achingly attractive to a fighter with her form clothed in scale armor shining like the dusk, looked between the two men and whispered something to the Riddler, then looked back at Crit.

The long-eyed Riddler just stroked his gray's arched neck. "It's enough," replied the man Crit served and often had thought he'd die to please.

Later that evening, riding alone through the Common Gate in search of Straton, Critias was no longer so sure that an honorable death would be a privilege—not when it was here.

Sanctuary hadn't changed. Or if it had, the change was for the worse. There were checkpoints everywhere. Crit had to bully his way through two of them before finding a soldier he knew—someone who had an armband he could commandeer.

By then he'd skirted the palace (green-walled because some sort of fungus or moss was growing there), and entered the Bazaar where illicit drugs, girls and boys, and even lives were hawked openly in twisting streets.

His back unguarded, his sorrel spooked and dancing, he was heading for the Maze, a deeper slum than this one, against his better judgment because he didn't want to look for Strat where his erstwhile partner probably could be found: lying in with the vampire woman who held sway in Shambles Cross and used the White Foal to dispose of victims.

From between two produce stalls Critias heard a hiss and a low whistle: old northern recognition signs. Adjusting the armband (a dirty rainbow of cloth specked with long-dried blood), he looked about: to his right was a fortune teller's tent. A S'danzo girl, Illyra, worked there. He saw her standing in the doorway.

They'd never met, yet she waved—a hesitant gesture, part warding sign, part blessing.

The last thing Crit wanted was his fortune told: he could feel his fate in his pouch, where amulets grew heavy; on his neck, where hairs stood on end; in his gut, which had frozen solid when Tempus had calmly ordered him to his death on a flimsy pretext. Crit had never thought the Riddler held a grudge about his daughter and her miscarried child. But there was no other reason to send Stepsons up against a witch like Roxane.

Was that, then, what Abarsis came to Theron's palace to tell Tempus? That it was time a few more Sacred Banders made their way to heaven? Was Abarsis lonely for his boys? Before Tempus had led the Band, Crit had fought for the Slaughter Priest. But in those days Abarsis had been flesh and blood, even if obsessed with tasks done for the gods.

"Psst! Crit! *Here*!"

Between the stalls, opposite the fortuneteller's tent, were too many shadows.

Crit sat his horse, arm crooked over his pommel, and waited, watching where his mount's ears pricked like dowsing rods.

Out from the gloom came a hand, white and long—a woman's, despite the leather bracer.

Crit squeezed with his right knee and the sorrel ambled forward: one pace; two. Then he said, "Hello, Kama. What's that you've got there, friend or captive?" Beside the woman half in shadow was a waif—a flat-faced boy with almond eyes and scruffy beard who wore a black rag bound across his brow.

The boy didn't matter. The woman, crossbow pointed half to port so that its flight would skewer Crit's belly if she pulled its trigger mechanism back, mattered more than Crit liked.

Tempus' daughter laughed her throaty laugh that had gotten Crit in trouble long ago. "Looking for someone?" Kama never answered stupid questions. She was as sharp as her father, in her way. But not as ethical.

"Strat," he said simply, to make things clear.

"Our 'acting' military governor, now that Kadakithis lies abed with Beysibs? The leader of the militias and their councils? The vampire's fancy man? You know the way: down on the White Foal. But do take an unfortunate or two to appease her hunger—for old time's sake, I'll warn you."

Crit didn't react to Kama's acid comments on Strat's faring. For all he knew, it might be true; and he'd never show her she could still reach him, let alone hurt him. He said, "How about this pud you've got here? Will he do?" For the signs of something intimate between the woman and the street tough were clear to see: hips brushed, though Kama held the crossbow; whispers went back and forth through motionless lips.

And the youth was armed—slingshot on one wrist, dagger at his hip. The slingshot was arrogantly aimed at Crit's eyes by the time Kama said, "Don't make the mistake of thinking you understand what you're seeing, fighter. You'll need help. If you're smart, you'll remember where and how to get it. Strat's part of Sanctuary's problem, not its solution."

Everyone found comfort where they could in wartime, and Sanctuary was war's womb, a microcosm of every horror man could foist upon his brother—worse now with factions holding checkpoints and militias ruling blocks whose inhabitants were never certain. The idea of Strat being a part of Sanctuary's problem nearly made him draw his own bow. Crit knew Kama well enough to know, if quarrels were loosed, his would find its mark first: her womanly hesitation would be her last.

And he might have, right then, no matter what her provenance, but for the pud who didn't know him and didn't like any northern rider, especially one talking to *his* girlfriend. The sling-shot grew taut, the boy's eyes steady as his stance widened.

So there was that: a deadly interval of stalemate broken only when a drunk caromed off a nearby doorway and knelt down, retching in the street.

Then Crit cleared his throat and said, "If you're still a member of our Sacred Band, woman, I'll want you at the White Foal bridge two hours before dawn. Spread the word among the Third Commando, too. I'll need some backup on this. *If* the Third's still led by Sync, and *if* he's not succumbed to Sanctuary's blight, I should be able to expect it."

"Old debts? Words of honor?" Kama rejoined. "Honor's cheap in Sanctuary. Cheapest this season, when everyone has a power play to field."

"Will you take my message, soldier?" He gave her what she wanted—recognition, though he'd rather call her whore and take her over bended knee.

"For you, Crit? Anything." Teeth flashed, a chuckle sounded, and he heard her mutter, "Zip, relax; he's one of us," and the youth behind her grumbled a reply before he slouched against a daub-and-wattle wall.

"Before the break of day we'll be there… How many would that be you'll need?"

And Crit realized he didn't know. He hadn't a plan or a glimmer. What would it take to wrest the Globe of Power from Roxane, the Nisibisi witch? "Randal will know—if he's still our warrior mage. Don't ask questions woman, not here. You know better. And Niko, find him—"

"*Seh,*" the young tough behind her swore. "This one's walking wounded, Kama. *Niko?* Why not ask the—"

"Zip. Hush." The woman stepped out a pace from shadows, smiling like her father—a show of teeth with no humor in it. "Critias… friend, you've been away too long, doing what high-born officers do in Rankan cities. If not for… past mistakes… I'd ride with you and explain. But you'll find out enough, soon enough, from your beloved partner. As for Niko, if you want him, he's in the palace these days, playing nursemaid to kids the priesthood loves."

Before he could escalate from shock to anger, before he thought to move his horse in tight and take her by the throat and shake her for playing women's games when so much was on the line, she melted back into her shadows. Then there was a grating sound, followed by scrabbling. A square of light came and went. And when his horse danced forward, both Kama and the boy called Zip were gone—if they'd ever been there.

Riding Mazeward on a horse suddenly and unreasonably skittish, Crit cursed himself for a fool. No proof that it *was* Kama. What he'd seen could have been some apparition, even the witch Roxane in disguise. He'd touched nothing; only seen something he *thought* was Kama. There were undeads in Sanctuary who resembled the forms they'd had in life. And some of those were Roxane's slaves. Though if any such had happened to Kama, he told himself, Strat would have sent word to him.

At least, the Strat he *used* to know would have. Right then, Critias could count the things he knew for certain on the fingers of one hand.

But he knew he was going to the vampire woman's house to find his partner. It was just a matter of time: Kama's allegations were already eating at his soul.

He had to learn the truth.

*

Kadakithis' palace was full of fish-eyed Beysibs: Beysib men with more jewelry on their persons than Rankan women from uptown or Ilsigi whores; Beysib women—female shock troops with bared and painted breasts and poison snakes wound about their necks or arms—who seemed never to blink and gave Tempus gooseflesh.

Kadakithis wanted to introduce Tempus and Jihan to his Beysib flounder, Shupansea. Before Tempus could protest, in the prince/governor's velvet-hung chamber, that he needed no more women in his life, the Rankan prince had called the Beysib matriarch forth.

Jihan, beside him, took Tempus' arm and squeezed, sensing what passed on first glance between her beloved Riddler and the lady ruler of the Beysib people.

For Tempus, noises lessened, the world grew dim; and in his heart a passion rose, while in his head a god's voice he'd not heard clear for years urged: *Take her. For Me. Ravage the slut upon this spot!*

The woman's fish-eyes widened; a snake slithered on her arm. Her breasts were fair and gilded; they stared at him with come-hither charms and it was only Jihan who restrained him, prince or no, from doing what Vashanka wanted then and there.

What *Vashanka* wanted? Tempus, who never backed away from any fight, took three retreating steps as Jihan whispered, "Riddler, my lord? What is it? Has she witched you? I will tear her legs off one by—"

"No, Jihan," he muttered through clenched teeth in Nisi, a tongue neither prince nor foreign matriarch understood. He shook Jihan's grasp from his arm and rubbed the depressions her fingers had made: the Froth Daughter's strength nearly equaled his own. But neither of them was a match for Vashanka who, Tempus was now certain, in some way had come again. He was here—more infantile, more tempestuous than ever; but here.

And what that meant to a man who'd forsaken the Pillager and taken up with Enlil to balance a curse (no longer so sure upon his head), Tempus couldn't say. But there was no doubt in him that soon he'd take some woman—this one if Vashanka had His way of it—and consecrate whatever wench into the service of the god.

He simply stepped forward, on his best behavior where the prince could see, one palm sweating on the hilt of the sharkskin-pommeled sword, and took her hand.

"My lady, Shupansea, men call me Tempus—"

She interrupted: "The Riddler. We have heard tales of thee."

And then from behind a curtain came Isambard, acolyte and priestly apprentice to Molin Torchholder, running without regard to his priestly dignity, calling out: "Quickly! My lady! My lord! There are dead snakes in the palace! There are *more* snakes than there ought to be! And in the children's rooms, where Nikodemos is... he's cut one of the sacred snake's heads off!

Tempus unsheathed his sword, and Jihan did, a *Snakes?*

Isambard skidded to a stop an arm's length from Tempus' chest and lapsed into panicked silence until his master entered the chamber. Molin Torchholder, ever mindful of his position and demeanor, did not immediately clarify his acolyte's exclamations. Instead, the high priest appraised the assembly as if they, not he, were the breathless intruders.

"Ah, Tempus. Back in town at last?" Sanctuary's hierarch inquired, his voice carefully modulated to conceal the manifold anxieties Tempus' unexpected presence caused him.

"That I am." Tempus detested priests, especially this one. And so he grinned, thinking that Brachis, when he arrived with Theron's sailing party, would put this foul, dark-skinned priest in his proper place. "Well, Torch, your minion seemed to have a problem moments ago. Surely you've got it as well?"

Kadakithis was scratching his golden curls, his handsome but vacant face petulant: "What's this, Molin? Dead snakes? Is your state-cult out of hand again? I told you Nikodemos was no fit guardian for those children. I—"

The Beysib monarch interjected smoothly, "Let me see these dead snakes, priest. And mind you, I'm never sure that these troubles aren't made by the Rankans who announce them."

By then Tempus and Jihan were running down the hall, toward secret passages Tempus knew like the back of his sword-hand or Jihan's female mysteries, which led to the lower chambers where, near the dungeons, Niko and the children (whom some said were more than that) were being kept.

*

Ischade's Foalside house was more home than haunt, less forbidding than Roxane's to the south, but hardly an inviting place to visit.

Unless, of course, one was Straton, her lover whom she'd guided to de facto power in Sanctuary's factionalized streets; or an undead such as Janni or Stilcho (both of whom had once been Stepsons); or a mageling such as Haught, who learned what he could from the witches and sought to wake the power in his Nisibisi blood.

Strat had been with Ischade hardly long enough for a candle to burn low when Haught, whom Straton hated, came gusting in the door.

The place was softly lit and full of colors; precious gems and silks and metals strewed the floor.

Straton was, by then, the finest thing she had, though: a human man, with all his prowess, not an animated corpse or witchling.

She could love him, could Ischade, with a finer passion than the rest. But she could feel in him a struggle, one that made shoulders sweat and muscles twitch.

She'd known that, hold him though she would, the day must come when holding Straton would be hard.

His narrow Rankan eyes were haunted, deep-set, his jaw squared with indecision lately when he came. And now, rolling off her at the sight of Haught (a hated, half-understood rival; a symptom of all about Ischade Strat couldn't justify or wish away), he reached for a robe she'd found him, shrugged it on and, with just his sword belt, stalked outside.

"When you're done with… it, him, whatever… I'll be seeing to my horse." Strat still grieved for his lost bay warhorse; its death was something she could and would undo, if only she thought Straton could handle the revelation that death was no barrier to Ischade.

Oh, he'd seen Janni, seen Niko embrace an undead partner. And Strat had not reacted well.

"What is it, Haught?" she asked, impatient. She didn't like the hubris growing in this Nisi child. He was difficult, growing stronger, growing bold. And she wanted to get back to Straton, who served her ends, who worked her will and excused her wiles and helped her hold her interests in the town. Ischade's interests were important. And they were too tied up with Strat now to let Haught get in the way.

So she thought to dance around the Nisi ex-slave, freed by her but not free of her. She'd only started her mesmerizing when a sanguine hand reached out and grasped her wrist.

Impertinent. This one soon would need an object lesson. She swallowed his will with a stare and let him see he couldn't even blink without her say-so. She whispered, "Yes? Your business, please."

And Haught, so pretty, so fiery underneath his slave's face, said, "I thought you'd want a warning. His boyfriend's coming." Haught's chin jutted Mazeward. "What use he'll be once Crit's come hence, you might not like. So if you want, I could—"

There was murder in the slave-bait's eyes. Murder sure of itself and offered teasingly, a sexual ploy, a sensuous violence.

She denied it, not telling Haught that Strat was so much hers that Crit couldn't get between them… because she wasn't sure. But she was sure that Straton's left-side leader, Critias, could not be murdered by one of hers. Not ever. Not and allow Ischade to keep what she had now: subtle power over more factions than anyone else had, more even than those who dwelt in the winter palace and looked to gods to aid them.

The dusky wraith who was Ischade said a second time, "I don't *want,* Haught. I *never* want. *You* want. I *have.* And I have need of both Stepsons—of Straton and his… friend. Go back uptown, see Moria, talk to Vis; we'll have a party for returning heroes tomorrow evening in the uptown house. Wherever Crit is, Tempus is as well. Find the Band's best and invite them all. We'll play a different game this season. You tread carefully, do you hear?"

Haught, motionless and unblinking till she loosed him, sought the door with the slightest inclination of his head and the most refined swirl of his cloak.

Trouble, that one, by-and-by.

But in the meantime, if she must fight for Straton, would she? She didn't know. She had a horse to raise, now, to see for certain what would happen. Strat would have more decisions to make tonight than one.

*

Niko was holding one child under either arm when Tempus and Jihan came upon them in the nursery.

One babe, Arton, had thumb in mouth; the other, Gyskouras, gave a single cry on seeing the interlopers.

Then Gyskouras—god-child, Niko was certain—held out his tiny hands and Jihan, mayhem forgotten, stepped over a decapitated snake oozing ichor, her arms outstretched and the red fires of Stormbringer's passion in her eyes.

"Give him to me, Stealth," Jihan crooned, calling Niko by his war-name. "My comfort's what he seeks."

Niko's gaze flickered questioningly to Tempus, who made a sour face and shrugged, sheathing his sword and squatting down to examine the snake.

Niko gave the first child to Jihan and shifted Arton, who immediately began to wail. "Me, too! Me, too! Take Arton, or tears come! Take Arton!"

In moments, Jihan held both children, the dark-haired and the fair, and Niko was kneeling opposite Tempus, the snake between them.

"Greetings, Commander. Life to you."

"And to you, Stepson. And everlasting glory." The words were only formula tonight, an afterthought from Tempus, who had a dagger out and with it turned the snake's head toward him.

"How did you kill this thing, Stealth?" asked the Riddler.

"How? With my sword…" Niko's brows knit. His canny grin came and went and his hazel eyes grew bleak as he slipped his weapon from its sheath and laid it across his knee. "With this sword, the one the dream lord gave me. You mean it's not an ordinary snake?"

"That's what I mean. Not a Beysib snake, anyway. Look here." Tempus turned the snake and Niko could see tiny hands and feet, as if the snake had been starting to turn into a man when Niko's stroke had killed it.

And the ichor, now, was steaming, eating like acid into the stone of the palace floor. "Why did you kill it?" said the Riddler gently. "What made you think it would attack you? Did it threaten? Did it rear up? What?"

"Because…" Niko sighed and tossed back ashen hair grown long enough to flop into his eyes. He'd shaved his beard and looked too young for what he was and what he'd been through; his scars were pale and the haunted look he bore made Tempus glance away. These two were each other's misery: Niko loved the Riddler and feared the consequences; Tempus saw in the youthful fighter the curse of a man the gods desire.

"Because," Niko said again, voice low and heavy with words he didn't want to say, "Arton told me to. Arton—the dark-haired—he's the prescient one. He knows the future. He protects the god-child. I'm glad you're here, Commander. It's hard trying to—"

Tempus got abruptly to his feet. "Don't say that. You can't know it, not for sure."

"I *know* it. My Bandaran… my *maat* knows what it sees. *Maat*—my balance, my perception—shows me too much, Commander. We have things to talk over; decisions must be made. These children must go to the western isles, else there'll be havoc. I don't want the blame of it. Gyskouras, he's yours... your son—or your god's. I prayed.... Did the gods inform you?"

"You could say that." Tempus turned away from Niko and the words came back over his shoulder to the young Stepson and hit as hard as a blow from the Riddler's hand. "Abarsis. He came and told me. Now we're all down here. Why in any god's name didn't you just take them and go, if that's the answer? Theron will be here presently." He turned on his heel and faced Nikodemos. "You're sequestered here like a babysitter while Sanctuary is torn by the wolves of civil war? Are you no longer a Sacred Bander? Do you command some regiment, a cadre of your own? Or did Strat give you leave to—"

"It was by *my* order, Sleepless One," came an unctuous voice from behind: Molin Torchholder. The priest was accompanied by Kadakithis and at the prince's side was the Beysib woman, streaming tears, holding a dead and definitely Beysib snake in her arms and weeping over it as if over a stricken child.

"*Your* order, Molin?" Tempus said and shook his head. "I own I didn't think you'd have the nerve."

"He's trying to help, Tempus," said Kadakithis, looking worried and drawn, trying to comfort the weeping Beysib monarch and keep peace as best he could. "You've been away too long to judge this at face value. Nikodemos has been of exceptional help to the State and we thank you for his loan." The prince's eyes strayed to Jihan, a child on each hip and a beatific gleam in her inhuman eyes.

"Let's go to the great hall and talk about this over food and drink. I warrant you're all tired from your long journey. We have much to decide and little time. Did I hear that Theron is coming? Tempus," Kadakithis' princely smile was strained, "I hope you've told him good things of me. I hope, in fact, that you'll remember your oath. I wouldn't want to end up like my relatives in Ranke—spitted and bled out like pigs in the town square."

If the curse—or its ghost—was still in effect, it would mean that all whom the Riddler loved were bound to spurn him and those who loved him doomed to perish.

It was this that bothered Tempus as he put a hand on Kadakithis' shoulder and assured the prince that Theron would look with kindness on Kadakithis' particular problems here in Sanctuary, that "he's coming because the Slaughter Priest manifested in the Rankan palace and told us Theron and me look to the souls of our soldiers. That's why we're all here, Prince—and lady."

He didn't tell them not to fear. Both the prince/governor and the Bey matriarch were too familiar with statecraft to have believed him if he had.

It wasn't until after dinner that everyone realized there were too many dead Beysib snakes in the palace for Niko—or the single strange snake he'd killed—to be responsible. And by then, it was nearly too late.

*

Strat's horse was at the gate. The bay horse he'd loved so well, who'd carried him through so many campaigns. And Ischade was standing in her doorway, where night blossoms bloomed, watching with that look she had which cut through the shadows of her hood.

She'd healed the horse, obviously. She had the healing touch, when she wanted to, had Ischade. He was so glad to see the bay, who nuzzled in his pockets for a carrot or the odd sweetmeat, that it took him a while to clear his throat and make sure his eyes were dry before he turned to thank her: "It's wonderful having him back. There's not another in my string to equal him—not his size, his stamina, his conformation. But why didn't you tell me? I'd not have believed he could be…" His words slowed. He looked harder at her. "… healed. That's what you did, isn't it? Spirited him away somewhere after I had to leave him for dead, and nursed him back to health?" The horse's teeth felt real enough, nipping his arm for attention. "Ischade, tell me that's what you did."

Her words were wispy as the wind. "I saved him for you, Straton. A parting gift, if this visitor of yours…" She pointed up the road, where a figure could be seen if one looked hard through the moonlight—a rider so far away the sounds of his horse's hooves were yet masked by the breathing of the bay. "…if this visitor makes an end to what is—was—between us. It's yours to say."

With that, she turned and went into her house and the door closed, of its own accord, with an all-too-final sound.

He'd never heard it close that way before.

He examined the bay from head to tail, from poll to fetlock, waiting for whomever it was Ischade said was coming, but he couldn't find a scar. It was bothering him more and more. He'd seen Janni, once a Stepson, now a decomposing thing motivated by revenge upon its Nisibisi murderers; he'd seen Stilcho, in better shape, yet still not one to be mistaken for a living man. But the bay was just exactly what he'd been: all horse, all muscular quarters and deep-hearted chest.

The bay couldn't be a zombie horse. At least he didn't think it could.

He was just thinking to mount up and see how it went when the approaching rider drew close enough to halloo: "Ho! Strat, is that you?"

And that voice froze Straton like a witch's curse: it was Critias. Critias, his left-side leader; Crit, to whom he'd sworn his Sacred Band oath. "Crit! Crit, why didn't you tell me you were coming?"

Crit just kept riding toward him, inexorable on a big sorrel. Crit, seeking him here. That meant that Crit had heard. That he knew, or thought he knew, the hows and whys of something Straton barely understood himself.

They'd come together to Ischade's house the first time—met her together. Then, Crit had tried to "protect" Straton from the necromant. Now, if damage there was, it was done.

Crit said, "Am I too late?" crooking one leg over his saddle and fishing in his pouch for the makings of a smoke. In Ischade's garden there was always a weird light and it underlit the line officer's face so that Strat couldn't tell what Crit was thinking. Not that he ever could.

Something inside him tensed. He said, because there had been no Sacred Band greeting between them, "Look, Crit, I don't know what you've heard or what you think, but she's not like that…"

"Isn't she? Still got your soul, Ace? Or wouldn't you know?" Crit's eyes were slitted and he fingered the crossbow hanging from his saddle.

Strat noticed that there was an arrow nocked, and that the bow would fire, from that position, straight into him at the click of a safety and the touch of a trigger. He tried to shrug away the suspicion he felt, but he couldn't. "You're here to save me from myself? She's the only reason we've survived here—the Band, the real Stepsons—while you and the Riddler have been up-country playing your palace games. I'm not asking you where you've been. Don't ask me how I've spent my time. Unless, that is, you're ready to be reasonable."

"I can't. I haven't time. Riddler wants us to roust Roxane, get the Globe of Power and destroy it by sunup. Maybe your soul-sucking friend will have a few ideas as to how to help us, if she likes you so well. If she does, maybe I'll let her live until you can explain. Otherwise…" Crit lit the smoke he'd rolled and the spark illumined a carefully-arranged face that Straton knew wasn't one to argue with. "Otherwise, I'm going to burn her ass to a crisp and then do what I can to beat some sense back into you… partner. Before it's too late. So, you want to call her out? Or just come with me and we'll die like we're supposed to, shoulder to shoulder, fighting the Nisibisi witch."

Strat didn't have to call Ischade; she was suddenly beside him, somehow, though he hadn't heard the door open or seen light spill out and he didn't think Crit had, either.

She was so tiny in her cowl and long black cloak. He wanted to put an arm around her shoulder, dared not; then dared. "She's on our side, Crit. You've got to—"

"The hell I do," Crit said, and shifted his gaze to her. "I bet I don't have to explain one whit to you, honey. I just hope you're not too hungry to wait awhile. We've got something on that's just your style."

"Critias," said Ischade with more dignity than Strat would ever have, "we should talk. No one has been hurt; no one has to be. You come—"

"—to get my partner. We can leave it at that."

"And if he is unwilling to leave?"

"Doesn't have squat to do with it. I've got responsibilities. So does he, even if he's forgotten them. I'm here to remind him. As for you, we can use you. Come help out, and I'll let you have your say—later. Right now, I've got orders. So does he." Critias gestured to Strat, who looked at Ischade and could not, in front of Critias, plead with her for patience, for help, or even for his partner's life.

But Ischade didn't strike Crit dead, or mesmerize him. She nodded primly and said, "As you wish. Straton, take the bay horse. He'll serve you well in this. I'll ride your dun. And we'll give Critias what he wants. Or what he thinks he wants." She turned then to Crit: "And you, afterwards, will give me the courtesy of a hearing."

"Lady, if any of us can hear anything after sunrise, I'll be more than willing to listen," said Crit as Ischade raised a hand and Strat's dun trotted toward her.

*

Roxane had been waked abruptly from exhausted sleep when Niko lopped the head from her finest minion: she would miss the bodyguard snake. And Stealth would regret what he had done.

She'd paid a heavy price this evening; her thighs ached and her buttocks smarted as she got out of her bed and felt her way through the dark.

Her Foalside home was small at some times, large at others. Tonight, it was cavernous with all the forces she'd disturbed.

She found her witching room and sluiced the sweat from her body as she filled her scrying bowl herself.

Then, trembling with pain and fury, she spoke the spell to open the well that held the power globe, and another to summon a fiend of hers: the slave named Snapper Jo who spied for her in the Vulgar Unicorn where he tended bar.

Before the fiend arrived, she spoke her spell of utmost power and in the bowl she saw a fate she didn't understand.

Men were there; and the cursed Beysa; and a goddess called Mother Bey, locked in love or hate with Jihan's terrible father, Stormbringer. And these two deities straddled the winter palace while, inside, Niko played with children and Tempus with the fates of men.

She trembled, seeing Tempus and Niko in one place—that very place where her surviving snake (more talented than most) slithered corridors in Beysib-snake disguise, biting and killing where he could.

Good. Good, she thought, and brought back Niko's face to the surface of her bowl. But this time, the vision was not of him alone. Over one of Niko's shoulders she could see the Riddler (or the Rankan storm god, whose aspect was the same); over the other, a woman's face. And that face, comely in an awful way, was her own.

The meaning of it, remaining hidden, chilled her.

She could do only so much; she had certain words to say.

She said them and the dark witching room was lit with balefire. Its light touched the globe in its hidey-hole of nothingness and the globe began to spin.

If there was some bond of fate between her and egregious Tempus, the thread must be cut. Even if it were Niko's life, she must do the deed. And the baby god could not be suffered to survive. Both children's lives and souls were promised to a certain demon of her recent, intimate acquaintance.

And the cold she felt, which raised the hair on sanguine Nisi skin as smooth as velvet, which drew back lips as beautiful as any that had ever spoken death for men: that cold had to do with failing and winning; with perishing and surviving.

As the door to her outer chamber shivered from something scratching on its farther side, she decided.

She let the globe spin faster, let the colors from its stones bathe her in their light.

A rushing wind filled the scrying room and in its midst was a woman's form, changing shape.

Black mist spun around the comeliest of female guises. Black wizard hair grew long and covered limbs cut clean and meant to hypnotize any man. Her fine long nose grew chitinous, then hooked; her firm flesh sprouted feathers.

By the time Snapper Jo, still wiping his claws on his barman's apron, thought he'd better open up the door himself, an eagle with a wingspan ten feet wide stood where Roxane was before.

And Snapper, her spy among the Sanctuary denizens, who tended bar at the Vulgar Unicorn, clacked prognathic jaws together and wrung his clawed and warty hands.

"Mistress," he gurgled in his fiendish, grating voice, "is that you?" His eyes that looked every which way squinted at the eagle swathed in dusky light. He squatted down, gray gangly limbs limp in submission. "Roxane?" said the fiend again. "Call Snapper, did you? Here I be, for what? Some murder? Murder do, tonight?"

The eagle cocked its head at him and let out a screech no fiend could misconstrue, then took wing and flapped by him, out the door, leaving him bleeding from a flesh wound made by claws much sharper than his own.

Muttering, "Damn and damn and murder damned," the fiend scuttled after her.

Looking askance at her black shadow in the moonless sky, Snapper Jo chewed a long orange lock of hair in dark frustration. To be human was his wish; to be free of Roxane his hidden dream. But sometimes he thought he never would be quit of her.

And the trouble was, at times like these, he didn't care. He was hungry as the night for blood; just the thought of carnage made him giddy.

So he scuttled on, following the eagle in the night, cackling wordlessly under his breath as Roxane, in eagle's guise, led him toward the winter palace, then lost him in Shambles Cross when he came across a fresh and bleeding morsel of a corpse.

*

Jihan was alone with the two children, her scale-armor discarded, cuddling one to either breast on Niko's bed in the nursery when the snake, man-sized but silent, slithered in.

The Froth Daughter was not human, but she was lonely. Tempus was no man for progeny. He considered nothing but himself.

Jihan had wanted children of her own and been refused by him. Now, thanks to her father, fate, and Niko, she had two fine boys to care for, one of them Tempus' own.

She would never give them up. She was ecstatic in her joy. And drowsy.

Thus she didn't see the snake until it reared, fangs bared, and struck like lightning, biting Arton on the arm.

Then, wide awake with two terrified babes to hold (one wounded and screaming, the other howling just as loudly), she cowered.

To reach her sword or freeze the snake, arching high above the bed and glaring fire-eyed down at her, she'd have to put down one or both children—or risk slicing or freezing the babes.

This the frustrated 'mother' could not, would not, do. She tried to shield Gyskouras with her body, interpose her own arm, even force it like a gag into the snake's gaping jaws.

But the snake was wise and quick and its jaws unhinged, so that it bit right through Jihan's arm and punctured the god-child's flesh and shook the Froth Daughter and the child, stapled together by its fangs.

Jihan wailed in rage and agony, a sound not heard in Sanctuary since Vashanka battled Stormbringer in the sky at the Mageguild's fête.

And that brought help, though she barely knew it as her body fought the poison and her arms, about the snake's neck, grew weaker as she wrestled it. Even Tempus and Niko paused in horror at the sight of Jihan locked in bodily combat with the viper, the god-child being crushed in between.

Beside Tempus, Niko drew a breath and then reached out: "Riddler! Quickly! Take this dagger."

The dagger, like Niko's sword, was dream-forged and it felt hot in the Riddler's hand.

He raced his Stepson, on his right, to reach the snake and the two of them began to hack away.

With every stroke acid ichor spouted, so that Tempus' skin sizzled, blistered, and peeled.

There was no time to fear for Niko, beside him as if they were once more a bonded pair.

Jihan was wound in coils, protecting one child who was absolutely silent. The other, Arton, was curled up moaning, forgotten on the floor except when ichor struck him and he squealed in pain.

The snake didn't flail or shrink from the damage Niko's sword did, though Tempus' deeper cuts could give it pause.

The Riddler realized barely in time what must be wrong: just as the snake was tensing and Jihan, mouth open and eyes bulging as the breath was squeezed from her, called his name and the viper fixed Niko with a gaze that pushed Stealth backward and made him drop his sword.

For no snake, not even a Nisibisi snake, should be growing larger and bolder as it fought and bled.

Tempus looked up and around and saw the source of the snake's supernatural power: an eagle perched, bating, in the bolt-hole of the palace wall.

Beside him, Niko faltered, his face blistered, his ankles entangled in the ever growing coils of the snake.

Tempus knew he risked Stealth's life as he stepped out of striking range and raised his knife-hand.

His eyes met the eagle's and it called softly, a cry like a baby's; it raised its head and clacked its beak.

Then the dagger Stealth had loaned him flew through the air and struck the eagle's breast.

A screech like a witch burning at a stake resounded, so that Niko lost his footing, hands clapped to either ear, and fell among the deadly coils.

But it was a chance Tempus had had to take.

As he strode forward, faster than anything else within that room because, at last, his wrath had brought the gods awake and power rose within him, the eagle overhead burst into flame.

The flames began around the dagger in its breast and licked hot and higher as the bird took wing.

But Tempus had no more time for watching birds or taking chances; he heard a dagger fall from the bolt-hole's height as he waded amid the coils—first to Stealth, who still fought gamely though ichor had burned one eye shut and his limbs were bound round with writhing reptile.

Pitting all his strength against the failing power of the snake (now shrinking but perhaps not fast enough), the Riddler struggled.

Vaguely he heard voices behind him as palace guards gathered. "Stay back!" he shouted without looking.

He was watching Jihan's eyes pop, her more-than-mortal hands clutching the noose of serpent still at her throat.

The damned thing was dying and as it did it was whipping back and forth, tossing Niko like a hook on a fishing line, crushing Jihan. And somewhere, in that thrashing mess of green slime and human limbs, a child was lost.

Tempus' child, Niko had said. But that wasn't why the Riddler hacked as if splitting cordwood with Niko's dream-forged sword. He'd never fought harder than he did then to free Stealth; if there was kinship between him and any here, it was strongest for his partner.

Admitting this, while all around pieces of snake flew like steaks from the block of a master butcher and smoke rose as ichor ate at stone, Tempus found reserves of strength in anger.

This youth, foolish Stealth, was not going to die on his account and leave the Riddler with yet more weight to bear eternally. Jihan and the god-child (born of a ceremonial rape) were both more than mortal; those two would survive. But Arton, the second child, could die here. And Niko's foolishness was mortal foolishness, risking all to save one child. Yet the ideals of sacrifice for honor, valor, and love defined the Sacred Band ethos: *Life to you, and everlasting glory.* So he and Abarsis had taught them, and so it would be today.

Tempus didn't notice when Beysib and human help pitched in beside him: his god-given speed made them seem too slow and the task too great to make their efforts matter.

But Jihan, once he'd cut through the widest coil at her throat, was help worth having.

Once she was free, and it was clear that she'd saved the children from immediate death, the Beysibs, the Rankan priest and Kadakithis crowded around the Froth Daughter and her charges.

Which suited Tempus, who finished cutting the yet-quivering coils from the Stepson who'd fought beside him and helped Niko to his feet.

Only when the young fighter, squinting through his one undamaged eye, put a hand on Tempus' shoulder and said, "Life to you, Commander—and thanks," and collapsed into his arms, did Tempus have a thought for the snake-bitten children or Jihan.

For he'd found out, there among the butchered chunks of snake and royal ranks of confusion, that the bond Niko and he once shared was stronger than ever.

Jihan limped over to him, where he lay Stealth down, and frowned at the burns on Niko's face and his ichor-eaten eye. "The placenta of a black cat, powdered at midnight, Riddler, will heal his eye. The rest, I can do."

The Froth Daughter's hand was gentle on Tempus' face, turning it away from his injured Stepson. "We have children who are worse hurt," Jihan said. "Both are poisoned by snake-bite." Her chest was heaving, her muscles torn; flaps of skin hung loose from her thighs as if a man-wide rope had burned her.

But the children, Arton, and Gyskouras—who might be his or perhaps the offspring of the god—had crowds to care for them and all of Sanctuary's priesthood to pray for them, while Stealth had only what a Stepson could expect.

Tempus sat flat on the floor, knees crossed under him, ignoring ichor slick which smarted and caused his skin to hiss and curl. "Get me what medicine you can, Jihan. You and I must heal this one. He wouldn't want life returned by magic."

They exchanged glances: one immortal and mortally tired; one feral and full of the fire of fierce and forgotten gods.

Then Jihan nodded, rose up, and said, "Your dagger skewered the eagle-witch. I saw it. She's wounded, maybe gone for good."

But it didn't please him, not at the price Niko always seemed to pay for others' follies.

Sometime in that interval, because Niko was conscious and could hear, Tempus affirmed and renewed their pairbond so that he had a right-side partner once again. And so that Niko, should it matter, would know that he was not alone.

*

Down by the White Foal Bridge, the gathered Stepsons waited: Kama was there, with a dozen hand-picked fighters from Sync's 3rd Commando.

It made Crit uncomfortable to command the Riddler's daughter's unit, so he gave them the periphery, made them stand the watch, kept what distance from her he could.

Strat, on the other hand, was comfortable with everything coming out of the dark that evening: with his bay horse, with paired Stepsons riding up holding torches, with Ischade's whispered council; with men who once were Stepsons and now were no longer men—who stayed in shadows when Crit looked at them straight on.

Strat had "explained" about Stilcho and Janni and Ischade's talent for raising uneasy dead. Strat said it was a favor she did them, a gift to those who'd died with their honor blighted.

Crit hadn't argued—there wasn't time. Strat was addled, bewitched, and if Crit got through this he was going to beat some sense into the big fool as soon as possible, do something final about Ischade or make her loose her hold on Strat.

If.

Something puffed and popped and Crit's horse shivered. Looking to his right, Crit saw Randal, the Stepsons' warrior mage, decked out in Niko's armor.

"Greetings, Crit. I heard you'd like some help." The flop-eared mage looked older, more fearsome tonight in dream-forged battle gear. He caught Crit staring at his cuirass. "This?" Randal touched his chest. "It's Niko's, still. Just a loan. We… have an understanding, but no pairbond." The freckled face aped a smile that was wan in torchlight as his horse reared and Crit realized it wasn't quite a horse at all: it was definitely transparent, though horse-like in every other respect.

"Help. Right. Well, Randal, you know the Riddler's orders, if you're here. Any advice? Or should we ride right in there, storm the place, burn it to the ground?"

At his knee came a touch as soft as a butterfly landing. "I told you, Critias, just walk right in and take it. Walk in by my side, if you will.… She's not at home and, if my guess is right, quite indisposed."

Crit looked from Ischade to Randal for confirmation. Randal nodded. "That's my best guess as well." The mage scratched one ear. "Only, I'll go in with Ischade. Roxane's my enemy, not yours. At least, not so much so. And you don't trust Ischade… no offense, dear lady."

"None taken. Yet," said the woman on foot whose head reached only to Crit's knee, but who seemed taller than anyone else about.

Strat rode up, concerned, looking at Crit as if to say, 'You'd better not start trouble now, partner or not. Don't push your luck.'

"I'm going," Crit said. "I have my orders."

"Into a witch's house?" Strat shook his head. "You may be my partner, but these are my men, until we've worked things out. We needn't risk them, or you. We've got friends to deal with magic who deal with it routinely. Ischade. Randal. Please be our guests—" As he spoke, Strat bowed in his saddle and, one hand outstretched in a sweeping gesture, motioned the mage and the necromant to precede the fighters up the cart-track to Roxane's house.

And as his gesturing hand neared Crit's horse, his fingers snatched Crit's rein, and held it.

"Strat," Crit warned. "You're pushing matters."

"Me? I thought it was you, mixing in what you don't yet understand."

"Let go of my horse."

"When you let go of your anger."

"Fine," Crit sighed, holding up empty hands and feigning a smile. "Done."

Strat stared a moment at him, then nodded and freed the horse. "Let's go, then… partner?"

"After you, Strat. As you say, you're in command— at least till morning."

*

Inside Roxane's Foalside home was a smell like burning feathers and a glow as if the whole place smoldered.

Ischade was well aware that, any instant, the premises might burst into flame. She said so to Randal.

They'd never worked this close, the Tysian Hazard and the necromant.

It was an eerie feeling, especially when Randal drew his kris, a recurved blade, and said, "It directs fire. Don't worry, Ischade. I didn't fight the Wizard Wars for nothing," in his tenor voice.

They walked over boards that creaked as if the place had been abandoned for eternity and Ischade's neck grew cold with trespass.

Randal said, waxing more the fighter with a woman watching, more the expert First Hazard of the Mageguild with a famous witch pacing by his side, "I'll open the rent where she keeps the globe, get it out for you. But you'll have to destroy it. I can't."

"Can't?" she said, disbelieving.

"Shouldn't, really. You see, I've got one of my own. I wouldn't want it to think I'd turned hostile. You should understand."

She did.

Odd to work so closely with a rival mage of rival power. She wondered if there would be a price.

And there was, of sorts, though it did not fall on them directly.

When Randal had made the requisite passes with his hands and a flap in space fell down and the globe lay revealed, Ischade's soul wrenched: she loved beauty, baubles, precious trinkets, and the power globe was all of those and more. It was the most beautiful, potent piece she'd ever seen. If not for Randal, here and witness, even despite Strat she would have claimed it for her own.

When he got it out, the floorboards creaked and the roof above began to smoke.

She could see that it singed him and how he'd expected that, now with the timbers above flaring like tarred torches.

In the ruddy light, Randal knelt down, and she did also, and he told her what words to speak.

Then he said, "Reach out and set it spinning—just a push with your palm will do."

As she touched the globe, Ischade felt a shock more intense than any she'd known for ages. This was not a matter of raising dead or ordering the lives of lesser mortals. This was a matter of power great enough to flout the gods.

And there was a bite to all Nisibisi magic, a corrosion different from her own. She rocked back upon her heels, nearly mesmerized herself though nothing less could have done it to her.

Randal pulled unceremoniously at her elbow. "Up, my brave lady. Up and out before the beams fall down and roast us or she… comes back… somehow."

Then Ischade realized that her sense of Roxane's presence might be more than just echoes from the globe.

Quick as smoke she got her feet under her and ran, Randal beside her, toward an open window.

Once they'd scrambled through, there was a roar as deep as any dragon's and the whole house burst apart in flames.

In the middle of the blaze Ischade could see the globe, still spinning, spitting colored fire of its own and spouting tongues of purer fire that licked up toward the heavens.

Horses thundered, coming near.

Strat was there, lifting her up onto the bay's rump as if she were a child, and Crit did the same for Randal.

Neither asked if the task was done. All could see the globe, spinning brighter, whirling larger, consuming the lesser flame of burning wood and stone and thatch and blazing like a star.

The horses were glad to be reined back; the heat was singeing. You couldn't hear a word or even the trumpets of mounts who hated fire as they reared and walked backwards on hind legs.

For it seemed, as the house collapsed, that the sky itself caught fire. Demons of colored light slunk through that wider blaze and slipped away.

Wings of lightning beat against the firmament where a rising sun was dwarfed to dullness by their light.

And down from purple lightning and clouds that came together, combusting to form a great cat-thing with hell-red eyes who swiped at it as it came, flew an eagle.

A flaming eagle, descending from the sky, chased by a giant cat of roiling cloud so black it swallowed all the heat, as if a house cat chased a sparrow in the dwelling of the gods.

The bird plummeted, wings bent. The cat struck, sent it spinning, struck again.

A scream like heaven rending issued from one, a growl like hell's bowels settling came from the other.

Then the bird tumbled, then righted, then darkened and streaked, shrinking, into the lessening flame that had been the witch's house.

Ischade saw that bird dive among the timbers where a Globe of Power was now melted, fragments of white hot clay and parboiled jewels, and take a fragment in its beak and speed away.

When she looked away, she saw that Randal, face beaded with sweat and freckles standing out black as soot, had seen it too.

The mage gave an uneasy shrug and smiled bleakly. "Let's not tell them," he whispered, leaning close. "Maybe it's not… *her.*"

"Perhaps not," Ischade replied, looking up at the smoldering sky.

*

The morning after the sky caught fire, Tempus was sitting by Niko's sickbed when Randal came to call.

"I'll see to him, Commander," said the mage, who touched his kris, from which healing water could issue.

Jihan had applied the powdered placenta of some unlucky cat, and Niko's eye was healing.

But these wounds would take a while, even with magic to help them.

In the nursery-turned-hospital, beside the stricken fighter, two children lay in sleep from which no one had yet managed to rouse them.

This, Tempus knew, was really what Randal must do here. But he had to say, "Stealth and I have reaffirmed our pair-bond. Can you tend him in good conscience, with a minimum of magic?"

Randal himself had once been paired with Stealth, at the Riddler's order, and loved the western fighter still.

The mage looked down, then up, then squared his shoulders. "Of course. And the children, too… if I have their father's permission?"

"Ask the god about his offspring. He's the stud, not me," Tempus snapped and stormed out.

He had a woman to ravish to placate the god within him, a necromant to thank in person, and a welcome to prepare for Theron, emperor of Ranke.

But Jihan found him before he found a likely wench on the Street of Red Lanterns.

Her eyes were glowing. She squeezed his arm and wanted to know, "Just what kind of houses are these?"

He had half a mind to show her, but not the time: she'd come to get him to mediate between Crit and Strat in matters of command and to ask whether they could all attend a "fête for returning heroes" being given by friends of Ischade's who lived uptown, and whether he'd noticed anything strange about Strat's bay horse.

And since he had troubles enough of his own, and Jihan was one, he agreed to go with her, gave permission for the Band and Stepsons to attend the fête, and lied about the horse, saying he hadn't noticed anything strange about it at all.

Chapter 7: Strangers in the Night

That evening, Tempus paid no heed to the story that Critias told. Instead he stood guard with his partner, Niko, all night long in Thrax's cave. Tempus never slept and Niko seldom did, since the goddess Harmony had graced him with her favor. But both grew drowsy, itself a troubling sign—and saw things in the night. Or thought they saw things.

Did they truly see black *erinyes* and *nereids* and all manner of nymphs and naiads come sneaking from the deeper cave to entice and seduce his sleeping soldiers? slide among them? whisper in their ears of love and comfort? kneel before them? bestride them and kiss them all over?

If they did, there were too many for Tempus and Niko alone to fend off. As dawn broke, they woke the Sacred Band and Niko told them then: "If some creatures came to you in dreams, we need to know."

No one admitted to being kissed or fondled, or to having riddles whispered in their ears. By morning, the storm had not abated. His Sacred Band had not slept well; eyes were red and tempers short and, pent up in the cave, none loved his fellow quite so well as they had the day before.

"Riddler," Niko said. "Let's go back in there, confront those two. This storm is unnatural, Randal swears."

"What storm isn't unnatural, when it travels with us?"

"Then, Commander, let's make our way onward: I'd prefer the rain to being trapped here with Thrax and that breasted lion." Niko was chary of sorcery: he'd been too long possessed by a witch of fearsome power, years before. He'd dressed for war this morning: *linothorax,* armbands, sword-belt girded on. Weapon of the god, child of *maat*, he watched everything with a mystic calm belied only by lips drawn white.

"Randal, Critias, Straton." Tempus called them close, looking hard to see if any of the three seemed different, ensorcelled, entranced. Everyone looked up when the senior staff convened. "Niko wants to go before the storm stops . We met a local godling called Thrax and Arton's sphinx, deep in the cave, and I said we'd stay the night and leave when the weather broke."

Straton squinted over his shoulder, at the driving rain beyond the cave's mouth. "Looks clear to me out there, Commander. Just a drizzle, nothing we can't handle."

Crit said, "And the horses would be happier, outside and moving, where forage and water is better."

Randal said, "I'll do whatever pleases you, Commander; you know that. But…"

"'But,' Randal?" Niko's hand went to his hip where his short sword hung.

"But I wish you'd told me sooner. Leaving here won't leave behind problems more than mortal. And…"

"And?" Niko and Tempus and Crit said together, while Straton shook his head and muttered, "Witchy-ears, the Riddler wants to leave. So we leave. Now."

"And," said the mage, standing taller, "we have our main force to consider, on their way to join us. Another night here won't make—"

"The greater Band will find us," said Tempus, decided, "when the god decrees."

The relief among his senior Stepsons was palpable. Niko flexed his hands and sought Lysis and Arton, his trainees. Crit and Straton gave orders.

And all the while, Tempus waited for the god to make some sign. But here in the cave belonging to Thrax, son of Ares, ancient giant, and his inscrutable sphinx, Enlil did nothing, said nothing.

Unless it was that, once they formed up and exited the cave and turned their horses north, the sky began to clear—over Niko's head, at least, and wherever Tempus' partner rode. The rain let up. The wind stopped keening and pushed thunderheads round the heavens, leaving silver mare's tails and mackerel sky behind.

Had he seen Sacred Banders seduced by ghostly creatures of ancient myth? Tempus wasn't certain. He gave commands and each was followed without delay. His Trôs horse had its ears up, not flattened, as they rode the hilly ground into sunlight.

Perchance the Theban goddess, Harmony rode with them, bringing sunshine and balance with her, keeping watch upon her Thebans and her lover, Nikodemos.

What difference, if Enlil was silent? More and more the storm god lodged within him, where a spear had touched his heart, not apart from him. Another squall darkened the northern horizon; rain pelting down in sheets ahead, dividing up the sky: comment enough from the storm god of the armies.

So when they rode unchallenged toward yet higher ground (and down again, and up, until they encamped by a spring that Straton liked despite the bugs drawn by its water) and no Sacred Bander dropped off his horse or went berserk or behaved in any way strangely, Tempus was willing to believe that they'd left Thrax and his oracle behind.

That night, when they'd lit their fire and hunted well, and were feasting on partridge and fresh-killed pig, Randal offered to tell the evening tale, saying, "Brothers and sisters, sometimes love and passion and ensorcellment wear one another's masks. I'll recount deeds few men know, of how the Sacred Band put one of its own to rest, an undead soul much beloved and much tormented."

"I'm not staying here for this," Niko said to Tempus, very low, when he realized what story Randal proposed to tell. Then, louder: "Critias, I'll relieve Arton; take this watch." Niko settled his shortsword in his scabbard, raising it slightly and letting it fall back, then stood and left the firelight abruptly.

Crit stared after him knowingly but said nothing.

As Tempus went after his rightman, he heard Randal saying, "Now this tale shows how a town lost its magical manna, and what happens when too many see sorcery and pretend not to, and feel they're safe when they are not. So once you've heard it, you might think twice if there's something you're holding back that your officers should know, or if you've recently encountered strangers in the night—or if you find yourself in the arms of someone new for reasons you've forgot..."

Chapter 8: Pillar of Fire

Death was riding the feral wind that blew in off Sanctuary's harbor—even Tempus' Trôs horse could smell it on the sooty breeze as horse and rider picked their way down Wideway to the wharf and the emperor's barge made fast there.

The Trôs danced and snorted, its hooves sending up sparks from ancient cobbles that seemed, in the dusky air, to have lives of their own. The sparks whirled round the Trôs' legs like insects swarming. They darted hither and thither on smoky gusts drawn seaward from the pillar of fire blazing between the heavens and the Peres house uptown. They skittered along Tempus' clothing like dust motes from hell, stinging when they touched his bare arms and legs. They alighted upon the Trôs' distended nostrils and that horse, wiser than many human inhabitants of this accursed thieves' world, blew bellowing breaths to keep from inhaling whatever dust it was that glowed like fire and burned like hot needles when it landed on the stallion's dappled hide.

The hellish dust was the least of Tempus' troubles on this morning that had lost its light, as if the sun had slunk away to hide from the battle under way beneath the sky. Oh, the sun had risen, brazen and bold, illuminating the flaming pillar raging up to heaven and the storm clouds with their lightning ranged round it. But it had been eaten by the storm clouds and the soot of the fire and the lightning spewing up from the grounds around the uptown Peres house and down from the furious heavens of the gods, who smote at witches' work and cheeky demons with equal force.

And it was this absence of the morning, this vanquishing of natural light, that bothered Tempus (accustomed to analyzing omens and all too familiar with godsign) as he rode down to greet Theron, the man he'd helped bring to Ranke's teetering throne, and Brachis, High Priest of Vashanka, while around the town civil war and infamy reigned, unabated.

If the chaos around him (which he'd once been sent here to banish) weren't enough of an indictment of his performance, then the skittishness of the Trôs horse made it certain: he was failing ignominiously to bring order—even for a day—to Sanctuary.

And though some men would not have taken the responsibility and clasped the fault for all Sanctuary's catalogue of evils to his bosom, Tempus would and almost gladly did. The state of town and loved ones fulfilled his own dire prophecy.

Only the Trôs horse's distress truly touched him now: animals were pure and honest, not dour and divisive like the race of men. It might not be his fault that Straton lay, somewhere, in the clutches of the revolution (Crit was sure), dead or held for ransom. It might not be because of Tempus, called the Riddler, that Niko was the perennial pawn of demons and foul witches. It might not be directly attributable to him that his daughter, Kama, was now sought as an assassin and revolutionary by his own Stepsons and the palace guard, thus creating a rift between her unit, the Rankan 3rd Commando, and the other militias in the town that no amount of diplomacy would ever bridge if she were executed. It might not be on his account that Randal, once a Stepson and the single "white" magician Tempus had ever trusted, was a burned-out husk. Or that Niko stared sightlessly at the pillar of flame uptown in which Janni, (Niko's onetime partner and a Stepson who'd sworn Tempus a solemn oath of fealty) burned eternally. Or that Jihan had been stripped of her Froth Daughter's attributes, humbled to the lowly estate of womankind. Or that the god-child Gyskouras looked at him with fear and loathing (even trying to shield the other boy, Arton, from Tempus whenever the children saw him coming).

But it probably was. He was the root and cause of all this slaughter: it was his curse, habitual (as Molin Torchholder, a Nisi-blooded slime in Rankan clothing, maintained) or invoked by jealous gods or hostile magic. He didn't know or care which force now drove him: he'd lost interest in which was right and which was wrong.

Like the day around him, black and white and good and evil had lost their character, merging with the sullen dusky noon into an unsavory amalgam to match his mood. But it bothered him that the Trôs was nervous, sweating, and distressed. He reined it down a side street, hoping to avoid the greater gusts of dust. For he knew that dust as he knew the voices of the gods who plagued him: each particle was a remnant of pulverized globes of Nisi power, magical talismans reduced to pinprick size and myriad in number.

If Sanctuary needed anything less than a dusty cloak of Nisi magic wafting where it willed, he couldn't think what it might be.

And then he realized what lay ahead, down a shadowed alleyway, and drew his sword. A little honest swordplay might cheer him up and ahead, where PFLS rebels in rags and sweatbands fought Rankan regulars in the street, he knew he'd find it.

Though he was overqualified for street brawls (a man who couldn't die and had to heal, whose horse shared his more-than-human speed and more-than-mortal constitution), this enemy's numbers made the odds more even: four Rankan soldiers, against a mob of thirty, were trying to shield some woman with a child from whatever the mob had in mind.

He heard shouts over the Trôs' hoofbeats. It lifted into a lope and trumpeted its war cry, speeding gladly toward the fray.

"Give her up, the slut—it's all her doing!" cried one hoarse voice from the mob.

"That's right!" A shrill, woman's voice seconded the rebel's demand: "S'danzo slut! She bore the accursed god-child's playmate! S'danzo wickedness has taken away the sun and turned the gods' ire upon us!"

And a third voice, streetwise and dark, a man's voice Tempus thought he ought to recognize, put in, "Come on, Walegrin, give her up and you go free—you and yours. We're only killing witches and their children today!"

"Screw yourself, Zip," one of the Rankans called back. "You'll have to take her from us. And we'll have a couple lives in exchange—yours for certain. That's a promise."

Tempus had only an instant to realize that Walegrin, the garrison commander, was one of the Rankans under siege, and to add up all he'd heard and realize that the blond soldier's sister-of-record, Illyra, must be the woman whose life was the subject of a traditional Sanctuary street corner debate. Then the Trôs was sighted by the rebels at the rear of the crowd, which began to part but not disperse.

Missiles pelted Tempus, some barbed, some jagged, some meant for rolling bread or holding wine, and some designed for war. He ducked an arrow hurtling toward him from a crossbow, his senses so much faster that he could see the helically-fletched blue feathers on its tail as it sped toward his heart.

The Trôs was hit between the eyes with a tomato: it had seen the missile coming, but never flinched or ducked. Its ears pricked like a sighting mechanism aligned upon the crowd: it was a warhorse, after all.

Tempus found this affront unacceptable, and took exception to the brashness of the crowd. Reaching up with his left hand while still holding his reins, he plucked the arrow from the air when it was inches from his heart and, as he seldom did, flaunted his supernatural attributes before the crowd, holding the arrow high and breaking it between his fingers like a piece of straw while bellowing in his most commanding voice, "Zip and all you rebels, disperse or face my personal wrath—a retribution that will haunt you till you die, and then some: you'll leave my fury to your descendants as a bequest."

Zip's voice called back from a gloom in which all white faces looked alike and darker Wriggly skins faded to invisibility: "Come get me, Riddler. Your daughter did!"

He set about just that, but not before the crowd surged inward as one body, pinning the four Rankans, and the girl they'd thought to shield, against the wall.

Tempus kneed the Trôs in among confusion, took blows, and swung back and down with his sharkskin-hilted sword, inured to the death he dealt. His conscience was salved before the fact by giving warning. His blood-lust now reigned unimpeded. Rebels fell like wheat before a scythe under his blade, a sword the god of war had sanctified in countless bodies just like these, across more battlefields than Tempus cared to count.

But when, finally, the crowd broke to run and none clawed at his saddle or bit at his ankle or tried to blind the Trôs horse with their sharpened sticks or hamstring it with their bread knives, he realized he'd been too late to save the day.

Walegrin, his bloody face pummeled beyond recognition so that Tempus could only recognize him by his braided blond locks and the tears streaming from his blackened sockets unheeded, would live to fight another day: he'd been innermost, protecting Illyra (the S'danzo seeress who should have foreseen all this) with his own big body. But of the other three soldiers, the first one's gullet was split the way a fisherman cleans his catch; the second one's neck was hanging by a flap of skin; and the third one was hacked apart, limb from limb, his trunk still twitching weakly.

However, it was not the soldiers who drew Tempus' attention. Rather, it was the woman they'd tried to shield, who in turn had been protecting her child. Illyra's S'danzo skirts were heavy with blood. Cradling a young girl's body in her arms, she wept so silently that only Walegrin's grief let Tempus know that the child was surely dead.

"Lillis," Walegrin sobbed, manliness forgotten because his niece was slain. "Lillis, dear gods, no… she's alive, 'Lyra, alive, I tell you." But all the desperate wishes in the world would not make it so.

The S'danzo woman's eyes were wise and face was tired beyond her years. Her own belly bled profusely where the axe had hewn her daughter and gone through child, into mother. Illyra met Tempus' eyes before she turned to her brother, who could no longer command so much as his grief:

"Tempus, isn't it? And your marvelous horse?" Illyra's voice had the sough of the sea wind in it and her eyes were bleak and full of the witch-dust settling all about. "Shall I foretell your future, lord of blood, or would you rather not read the writing on the wall?"

"No, my lady," he said before he looked above her head and beyond, to where graffiti scribed in blood defaced the mudbrick. "Tell me no tales of power. If doom could be avoided, you'd have a live child in your arms."

Then he reined the Trôs around, setting off again toward Wideway and the dockside, forcing his thoughts to collect and focus on the audience with Theron soon to come, and away from the writing on the wall behind the woman: "The plague is in our souls, not in our destiny. Ilsig rules. Kill the witches and the priests or perish!"

It sounded like a good idea to him, but he couldn't throw in his lot with the rebels: he'd made a truce with magic for the sake of his soldiers; he'd made a truce with gods for the sake of his soul.

Perishing wasn't an option for Tempus. Sometimes he wondered if he might manage it by getting himself eaten by fishes or chopped into tiny pieces, but the chances were good that his parts would reassemble or—worse—that each morsel of him would reconstitute an entire being.

It was difficult enough existing in one discrete form; he couldn't bear to be replicated countless times. So he smothered the rebellious impulse to join the rebels and see if it was true that any army he led could not lose its battles.

He was bound by oath to Theron; to the necromant Ischade in solemn pact; to Stormbringer in another; and to Enlil, patron god of the armies now that Vashanka was metamorphosing into something else within the body of Gyskouras, the storm god's son. And he'd spent an interval with the Mother Goddess of the fish-faces in which he'd learned that Mother Bey had lusts as great as any northern deity.

So he alone, acquainted with so many of the players intimately and capable of standing up to more-than-human actors, was competent to negotiate a settlement among the heavens through supernal avatars and earthly rulers, the representatives of their respective gods.

This task was complicated, not helped, by Kadakithis' impending marriage to the Beysib ruler. Success was further obstructed, not advanced, by Theron's arrival here and now, when all was far from well and men had brought their hells to life by meddling with powers they did not understand.

So he didn't care, he decided, what happened here, beyond his personal goals: to protect the souls of his Stepsons and those who loved him; to reward constancy where it had been demonstrated (even by mages and necromants); to clear his conscience so far as possible before he trekked back north, where the horses still grazed in Free Nisibis and the Successors on Wizardwall would welcome him to what had become the closest thing to home he could remember. But to do that, he must see Niko on the mend and on his way to Bandara; he must do what Abarsis had counseled. And more:

He must douse that thrice-cursed pillar of fire burning with renewed fervor uptown, and spewing fireballs and attracting lightning and spitting bolts into the sea, before a storm blew up from the disturbance.

For if a storm came riding the wake of all this chaos, then Jihan's powers would be restored, and Tempus would be saddled with the Froth Daughter for eternity. Now he had a chance to slip away without her and let her father, the mighty Stormbringer, keep His word: find Jihan some other lover.

So he was hurrying, as he reined the Trôs toward dockside where the Rankan lion blazon flapped in a sea-wind too strong not to be promising wild weather. And the Trôs, scenting the sea and his mood, snorted happily, as if in agreement: the Trôs would as soon be quit of Jihan, who curried him to within an inch of his life daily.

And if a storm would bring the dust to ground, and all the magic of Nisi antiquity with it, then that was not his problem—not if he played his cards right.

*

For once, Crit was grateful for the witchy weather that plagued Sanctuary worse than all the factions fighting here.

"Getting Strat" was not going to be the easiest thing Crit had ever done, but he wasn't denying that the job was his to do. Straton, called Ace, was his partner. Their souls were too bound up to chance letting Strat die with any strings on him, no matter which witch was holding the end of them.

And Strat couldn't be allowed to die in flames, not in some burning house that wouldn't burn down but only burned on and on like no natural fire.

Not that common sense was saying otherwise as Crit crouched at the heat's end, where waves of burning air licked his face despite the water he was palming over it intermittently. Staring at the flaming funnel, waiting for a plan to come clear, Crit reflected that his Sacred Band oath made no distinction between natural and unnatural peril. He hadn't sworn to stand by Strat, shoulder to shoulder, until death separated them if it must, only in cases where it was convenient, or magic wasn't involved, or Strat was behaving as a rightman ought, or the problem didn't involve an urban war zone and the possibility of being roasted alive.

The oath was binding, under any circumstances.

Watching the fiery tornado, like nothing he'd ever seen but the waterspouts of wizard weather or the cyclone that had manifested in the last battle on Wizardwall, he was trying to determine whether there was a pattern to its burning and its wriggling, whether the lightning spewing from the cloud above was predictably seeking targets, or random; and in general just how the hell he was going to get in there.

Because Strat *was* in there. Everything pointed to it; Randal was sure of it; no ransom demands had come forth from the PFLS. Crit's orders were to fetch Strat and Kama.

Kama could wait until all the hells froze over and Sanctuary sank into the sea, for all he cared. He'd had an affair with Tempus' daughter, true: he was willing to pay for his indiscretion, not complaining. But Strat was his partner. Strat came first.

If they'd had arguments, then that was normal. They'd have them again… over women especially. Disputes went with pairbond and he'd beat Strat silly if he had to, to win his point. As soon as he had the porking bastard back where he could pull rank, they'd settle things.

But you couldn't settle anything with a dead man, unless he became *un*dead like the freakish bay horse who was partially present, trotting around the Peres house on ghostly hooves, its coat looking as if it reflected the flaming whirlwind around which it circled—or was a part of it. The horse was insubstantial, sort of. Yet if he could catch it, maybe he could ride it up the back stairs.

Strat had ridden it. And the horse and Crit were both here for the same reason: Strat. He decided to follow the horse on its rounds and forsook the cover of jumbled stone, remnants of the Peres' garden wall, behind which he'd been crouching. The heat waves emanating from that spinning horror of flame struck him with force; he could feel his eyelashes singe and his lips start to blister. Head down, following echoing hoofbeats as much as the flickering glimpses he could get of this 'horse,' he edged along in its wake.

If the fire in the house would just burn *down,* like any normal fire did once a fire had consumed its fuel, things would be so simple: he could begin mourning. He'd thought of just considering the whole unsightly and unnatural mess as a funeral pyre, calling for reinforcements, and making the Peres estate Strat's bier. They'd say the rites, hold some funerary games. Crit would put everything he owned up as prize or sacrifice.

But he couldn't do that, not until he knew for certain that Strat really was dead and wholly dead: not likely to be resurrected by Ischade.

For that was what he feared most: that the necromant wouldn't be content to let Ace stay dead; that she'd pine for her lover and eventually call him up from ashes, make him an undead like poor Janni, who was somewhere in the cone of the fire. Crit couldn't imagine how or why, but he could see, if he squinted, the dead Stepson Janni, fully formed and unconsumed, doing something that looked like bathing under a waterfall, but doing it in a heat that would melt bone in seconds.

Crit had learned, fighting magic and sometimes fighting it with magic, not to ask questions if he didn't want to know the answers. So he left the matter of Janni to those who ought to tend it: to Ischade, who'd raised Janni's shade after a proper Sacred Band funeral; to Abarsis, who'd come down from heaven and escorted Janni's spirit on high, and done it where the whole Band could see. If there was an argument about propriety here, it was between the necromant and the ghost of the Slaughter Priest. It wasn't a matter for a decidedly unmagical fighter like himself. If Janni hadn't once been Niko's partner and a Sacred Bander, what Ischade had done wouldn't have been the business of any Stepson. As things stood, all you could do, if you were so inclined, was pray for Janni's soul. But it bothered Crit intensely because the same thing could happen to Strat. Ischade could make it happen.

He wondered idly, trailing the ghost horse on its rounds about the Peres estate, how you went about killing a necromant. If Strat didn't come through this intact, he was going to find out. Maybe Randal would know—if Randal ever again was capable of doing more than swallowing when you put a spoon of gruel in his mouth.

There had been a few minutes, he'd been told, when it seemed that Randal and Niko had come through their battle with Roxane and the demon in good shape. But physical flesh—even mage flesh and Bandaran adept's flesh—could take only so much. The two were alive; they'd live on. Whether they'd ever be as hale or as smart as they once were, only time would tell.

Rounding a burned-out wall, the heat lessened perceptibly and Crit could stop squinting and raise his head.

The ghost horse was still right in front of him. In fact, when Crit stopped, it stopped. When he took a linen rag and wetted it from the water skin dangling from his belt, the specter craned its neck to look back at him, ears pricked, as if to ask what he was doing.

What he was doing was anybody's guess, but he didn't try to tell the ghost horse that. The bay horse was still bay. It had a black mane and tail (although when the hot wind ruffled them they streamed out like charred cinders, not horse-hair). It had a red-gold hair coat (now flame red and flickery as the patterns from the fire chased each other along its flanks). It had black stockings (which resembled burnt timbers). But now the ghost horse was more substantial than it had been around front, where the fire was brighter.

Then it pawed the ground and whickered, still fixing him with a firelight-centered gaze from liquid horse eyes.

The come-hither look and the forefoot pawing the ground were unmistakable to any horseman: the bay wanted Crit to hurry up, climb aboard: it wanted to go for a ride.

"Oh no, horse," he said out loud to it. "I came by myself—no reinforcements, no backup. I did that because nobody else ought to risk his life. Or sacrifice it, if that's what's going to happen here… because this is a matter between pair-bonded partners."

The horse snorted disapprovingly, as if to remind Crit that it knew he was trying to cover his own fear. Then it slowly turned around, so that its rump was no longer facing him, and ambled toward him.

The big, liquid, oblong-centered eyes said: *Strat is mine, too; horses and men are partners; mount up and let's stop playing games. He's waiting.*

"Strat, damn you to hell," Crit whispered, shaking his head to clear it of horse-thoughts and horse-needs and horse-loyalties. This wasn't even a living horse, just a shade, something Ischade had conjured from a dead animal. But the thing kept coming, head high, feet carefully placed to avoid stepping on its dangling bridle reins.

Bridle reins? Had the reins been there before? He didn't think so.

The horse, now an arm's-length away, stopped still. It whickered softly and the whicker said, *I love him too.* The forefoot, pawing the ground impatiently, added: *We don't have much time.* And then the horse, in the manner of high-schooled horses like Tempus' Trôs, bent one foreleg at the knee, curling it and lowering his forequarters, the other front leg outstretched, while it arched its neck in a bow meant to enable a wounded man or a high-born lady to mount it without difficulty.

"Crap. All right," Crit said through clenched teeth and strode resolutely toward the bowing ghost horse, trying hard not to think too much about what he was doing, or whether he might be imagining the whole thing. Maybe a piece of timber had fallen on him, a piece of masonry collapsed so fast he hadn't had time to realize it. Maybe he was dead too: dead but denied a peaceful rest; trapped in some netherworld with the ghost horse on which he'd wander forever, seeking his lost right-side partner.

But no: The sky was full of lightning, there were shouts and mutters on the breeze from somewhere nearby where factions fought. There was a plague in Sanctuary, all right, but not some ordinary one that turned your lips blue and made your armpits sore: it was a plague of human failing, of confusion, of greed and desire and endless power plays.

As he mounted the bay (which felt surprisingly substantial for a ghost horse), he admitted to himself that it wasn't the magic or the gods which made Sanctuary such a foul pit, but human excess. Magic was no more to blame than sword or spear or rock. There were enough rocks on the earth to eradicate the race; magic couldn't do a better job, only a more colorful one. Rock or spear or wand or Nisi globe didn't murder on their own, nor enslave. Weapons must be wielded. The true culprit was human greed and human will. And the killing never stopped. In the name of magic or the name of god or the name of honor or nationalism or progress or liberation, it was just killing.

And because this had always been so, and would always be so, Critias had come to the profession of arms himself: the only protection he could see was to be a perpetrator, not a victim.

That was why Strat had made him so angry when he'd become entangled with Ischade: Strat had become a victim, and Crit had a horror of helplessness. Even if Strat were just a lovesick fool, Crit still thought he'd been right when he had shot past his friend that night on the balcony. If the shot had served to bring Straton to his senses, then Crit wouldn't be here, pulling himself up into the sometimes-saddle of Strat's sort-of-corporeal bay. Riding into he-didn't-know-what for abstracts of honor and duty. Abstracts weren't going to keep him alive if the steaming stable toward which the bay was ineluctably heading crashed down upon his head.

The stables weren't exactly ablaze, but they had corn magazines and straw and hay in them and sparks smoldered on the roof.

Crit reached forward to grab the bay's reins, but the beast had had a mouth like iron in life and it was no better in afterlife.

He sawed on the reins to no avail, then quit trying in time to duck as the horse trotted determinedly through the open stable doors and headed for wide stairs which must lead to the stable's loft.

Crit shifted his weight, thinking to throw one leg over the saddle and check out the stable loft on foot, when the horse started climbing.

"Vashanka's balls," the task force leader swore, flattening himself to the horse's neck as it climbed a flight never meant for anything of its size and boards creaked and groaned. "Horse, you'd better be right."

It was: at the stair's head was a landing, and as the bay's bulk appeared there, a woman stifled a scream.

Crit struggled to see shapes in the dark. The climb up the stairs had been too fast. Everything was still milky green to Crit's fire-dazzled vision. He heard voices and slipped from the bay's back, his sword in hand. Together, man and ghost horse ventured into the dimness, horse's head snaked low, man's sword paralleling its questing muzzle.

"Dear gods, what's that smell?" Crit muttered to himself.

Someone answered: "Strat. Or me, Critias. Which smell do you mean?" And the voice of Stilcho was familiar to Critias, who had once thought him the best of his kind of Stepson. Blinking, Crit strained to see the ruined visage of the undead soldier. Stilcho was one of Ischade's minions. He should have known the witch would still have her talons in Strat, one way or another.

Crit was going to swing his sword up, cut the one-eyed, ghoulish head from Stilcho's torso and hope decapitation would provide the poor soul what rest Ischade had denied—not because he expected his poor quotidian blade to do the job against magic, but because he was a soldier and he could only do what he was trained to do. When his vision cleared enough to see, Stilcho's face was neither so ruined nor so hostile as it ought to be.

And a hand touched his right shoulder, squeezed, and rested there: Stilcho's hand, warm and with the pulse of mortal blood in it so strong Crit fancied he could feel it coursing.

"That's right," said Stilcho softly through a mouth hardly scarred, "I'm alive again. Don't ask—"

Crit's question, "*How*?" hung in the air until Stilcho volunteered, "It's just too complicated, Stepson. Ask about Strat, that's what you're here for… or at least that's what *he's* here for." Stilcho jerked a thumb toward the bay horse, head low, snuffling, taking slow, careful steps toward a shadow that might be a prostrate man with a woman crouched by his side.

"That's right, Stilcho—Strat. That's all I want. Not you or your witch woman." Was it Ischade there, bending over Strat? It must be: Ischade's ghost man and ghost horse, and the necromant herself, ringing Strat round with magic. Crit considered seriously for the first time the possibility that he was going to die here. He didn't believe for a moment that Stilcho was "alive" in the way that Crit—or Strat, please gods—was alive.

He said to Stilcho, "That's him, then? He's alive, if he can't control his bowels. I'll just take him and be—"

A voice from the loft's shadows said, "Shit, Stilcho, he'll kill me," as Strat's hand reached up feebly to stroke the ghost horse's questing muzzle.

The horse started to bow down again, not realizing that Strat was too badly wounded to mount, no matter how easy the ghost horse tried to make it.

Crit found that he was blinking back tears. Unreasonably, he wanted to sit down cross-legged where he was, let things take their course… even if it meant burning to death in this damned loft with a partner too sick to be moved but well enough to remember that Crit had shot at him.

Crit said, "I wouldn't—couldn't. I busted my butt getting here, Strat," but it came out hoarse and low and he said it to the straw scattered on the loft's floor at his feet.

The woman was trying to help Straton, who didn't realize he couldn't get on that horse by himself.

Crit sheathed his sword and put his hands in the air, then walked over to the place where the ghost horse nuzzled its master encouragingly. Strat, half-prone, was staring at him. The big fighter's hand was clutched to his chest or belly—Crit couldn't tell which, from all the blood in the way. "Strat… Ace, for pity's sake, let me help you," Crit said, bending down on one knee, empty hands outstretched.

The ghost horse neighed impatiently and butted Straton's shoulder. Behind Straton, the woman stood up: this was not Ischade; this was the woman named Moria from the Peres estate, dressed in street rags so that he hardly recognized her.

Stilcho said, "Strat, maybe you'd better… it's not going to be safe here much longer. They can take better care of you than we—"

"Stilcho," Moria hissed, "come away. It's for them to talk out."

"Talk?" Strat laughed and the laugh choked him, so that he gurgled and wiped his mouth with a hand that came away bloody. "We just did."

The wounded fighter reached with his bloody hand to take one of Crit's. "Well, Crit, you going to watch, or you going to give me some help?"

"Strat…" Crit embraced his partner, oblivious of might-be enemies about him, searching for harm, testing strength, mouthing harsh words that covered too much emotion; "You stupid bastard, when I get you fixed up I'm going to beat some sense into you."

And Strat said, "You do that," just about the time the bay horse trumpeted joyously as he felt Strat's weight on his back and Crit began the arduous process of leading the mounted, wounded man out of the stable's attic to safety—at least of the sort a Sacred Band partner could provide.

*

Fire raged inside Ischade, now that she had quenched it in her clothing and her hair. It might have been her very wrath that caused the houses across the alleys on either side of her to flame up as she passed—uptown alleys she'd traveled before and now again on her way to Tasfalen's velvet stronghold.

An ache and a fury was in Ischade and perhaps it spread around her. But perhaps it was simply the pillar of flame and the young fires it set, so that better uptown streets (where

Sanctuary's troubles never spread and rebels never sped) were a smoking labyrinth like some upscale version of the Maze.

Rebels skulked here now, and peasants, looting: Wrigglies, arms laden with pilfered, sooty treasure, jostled her, saw whom they bumped, and slunk away. She spied rape and nearly stopped to feed: these mortal murderers wasted the best part of their victims, let the manna go, let the essence, precious soul and energy, escape. Ischade was weakened by the struggle in Peres', somewhat. Somewhat. But not too much.

She moved on, through a day mercifully veiled in clouds and soot and a storm now rising off the sea. She wondered, as the sky blackened with thunderheads boiling up, if the storm was natural or summoned, then thought it didn't matter: the storm was convenient, either way.

She saw an enclosed Beysib wagon, overturned by brigands. Bald heads of Beysib males littered the environs like play balls from some devil's game, their accustomed torsos near but not attached. She saw what fate was dealt a pair of Beysib women and wondered what the rebels thought to gain. If they kept their war to downtown, they might win it. Up here, they asked for retribution that would last for generations.

Amid pathetic cries, she stopped awhile, and closed her eyes—trusting to a cloaking spell to hide her. When she moved on, she was emboldened, strengthened, but sick at heart: for her to be reduced to scavenging was demeaning. But war did what it willed.

Thunder wracked the streets and she looked upward, grateful for the lowering, gusty dark but wary: she'd finish what she started, unless the storm gods intervened. She owed Tempus something. And she owed Haught a different thing. She had her word to make good. She had her interests to secure. She had work to do before retiring to the White Foal's edge.

It was not painless for Ischade, this sneaking to Tasfalen's in the daylight. Janni, one of hers, was still trapped in the cone of flame where Stormbringer and demons argued, where Roxane had been and now was not.

What would Tempus, who wanted the souls of his soldiers freed of strings and tortures, make of Janni's plight? Hardly an honorable rest, in the Riddler's terms. But a piece of bravery, in hers, the like of which she'd never seen.

All for Niko, or for something more abstract? she wondered as she found Tasfalen's gate and then climbed his stoop. There her thoughts turned to Haught and Roxane and what lay ahead, as she dealt with locks of natural—and other—kinds and doors likewise doubled. And, as the last portal opened to her will, a raindrop struck her cheek, and then another, and thunder rolled.

The storm would ground the dust and douse the fires and she knew it was too great a luck for Sanctuary, the most luckless town she'd ever seen. She knew also that, inside the flaming pillar back at the Peres house, evil was held at bay by one whose name could not be spoken but could be approximated: Stormbringer, the weather gods' father—Stormbringer, whose daughter Jihan was close at hand. And then there was no time to put it all together: there was a ring on the finger of the mageling Haught which she could see with her inner eye.

This she stroked and called home to her. Its spell, still strong, would bring the scheming apprentice—if he was not already here. She stepped inside.

In the ground hall full of shadows she paused. The door behind her closed at a gust's whim. The slam it made was daunting.

Her hackles rose. She hadn't thought of the ring Haught had until she'd entered. Was it her will, or only her perception, that saw him here? Why had she come here? Suddenly, she wasn't sure. On the ground-floor landing, she shook her head and touched her brow with her palm. She owed Tempus none of this… not this much. Tasfalen was dead, a minion to be summoned to the river house. Why, then, had she risked the streets and come up here? *Why?* She couldn't fathom it.

And then she did, when Haught's silken voice oozed down the stairs from a shadow at their head.

"Ah, Mistress, how kind of you to visit sickbeds with so much at stake."

She reached out for the ring he wore, but the apprentice was reaching on his own: grown desperate, he was full of pain, and wanted to make her a gift of it. Suddenly (more because she underestimated what lay behind him and what hid within him than because of Haught himself) she was dizzy, spinning in another place, a place of blood and murky water—of ice and great gates whose bars were rent as if a giant had bent them out of its way.

Niko's rest-place! How had she come here? Not by Haught's strength. And a laugh tinkled—a laugh with razor edges that cut her soul: Roxane. Yes, Roxane. But something less and something more hobbled through that gate, misshapen and huge, and shrunk until Tasfalen's beauty masked it.

Then the thing… for it was part Tasfalen, highborn mortal lord; part witch; and part Haught… held out its hand to take her arm as if to escort her to some formal fête.

She met its eyes and gripped her own ribs with both her hands: to touch it might imprison her here. This was where Janni had lost those last shreds of self-concern that made him act predictably in the interest of what life he still led. The eyes that bored into hers were gold and slitted; deep behind them glowed a purple fire she knew wasn't right.

She forced her leaden limbs to work and retreated a step, watching first her feet and then scanning the horizon, while she wound wards that worked in Sanctuary but which were much weaker here.

Niko's star-shaped meadow, once ever green and pastoral, the very essence of spirit peace, was frostbitten, brown and gray and riddled with ice like arrows. Where trees had spread rustling leaves, their boughs now held shards of flesh and writhing things resembling tiny men who cried like kittens being drowned. Here that stream which was the ebb and flow of Niko's life ran with swirls of red and blue and pink and gold: blood shed and to be shed; magic winding it round and chasing it; Niko's faith and the love of gods bringing up behind.

The Tasfalen beast was cajoling: "Come, my love. My beauteous one. We'll feast." He flicked a glance toward the trees hung with anguished, living things. "The boughs are ripe for picking, the fruit is sweet."

And she knew then the only salvation here, for her, was in the stream. She didn't know the consequence if she should do what her wisdom told her: take a drink.

Before she could lose her nerve or be mesmerized, she whirled about and jumped knee-deep into running water.

And bent. And drank.

Then saw Niko, when she raised her dripping lips, sitting on the stream's far side, his face calm, unravaged. His quick, canny smile came and went and she noticed he wore his panoply: the enameled cuirass, sword and dirk forged by the entelechy of dreams.

"It's a dream, then?" she said, feeling the icy water with its four distinct and different tastes run down her chin and hearing a lumbering behind her much louder, and a rasping breath much deeper, than Tasfalen's form could make.

"Don't turn around," Niko advised as if he were training a student in the martial arts; "don't look at it; don't listen. This is my rest-place, after all—not theirs."

"And me? It's not mine, fighter. Nor are you."

"And they are. I know." There was no abhorrence in the Bandaran fighter's glance, just infinite patience. And as Ischade looked, his visage changed, contorting through a metamorphosis that seemed to include all the tortures of his recent past: eyes rolled up, cheeks split over bone, lips purpled and torn, teeth cracked and crumbled, bruises filled with blood.

Then the entire process reversed itself, and a handsome man still in the last bloom of youth regarded Ischade once more.

"You're very beautiful, you know… in your soul," Niko said. "It shows here. In spite of everything."

Behind her, the Tasfalen-thing was shambling closer. She could hear it splash into the stream. She almost whirled to fight it. Her fingers spread into a shape suitable for throwing counterspells.

Niko shook his head chidingly: "Trust me. This is my place. As for your welcome here—when I needed help, you came here, where risk is greater than mortals know, and tried to aid me. I haven't forgotten."

"Are you dead?" she asked flatly, though it was impolite.

His smooth brow furrowed. "No, I'm sure not. I'm reclaiming what's mine… with a little help." Behind the fighter, a semblance of the pillar of fire came to be.

He knew it was there without looking. He said, "See, you must trust. We're giving Janni his proper funeral, you and I. At last. And you, who kept him from worse and soothed his conscience, ought to be here."

"And… *that*?" Ischade meant what was behind her. All her hackles risen, she found her mouth dry and eyes aching—if she had a mouth here, or eyes. It seemed she did.

"We'll put them back where they belong—not here. They're yours to deal with, in the World."

He must have seen her frown, for he leaned forward on one straight and unscarred arm that might never have been shattered when a demon raged inside him: "Roxane is… special. Different. Lessened. I'm free of all but my own feelings. For that I don't apologize. Like you, I deal in more than one reality. But I ask you for mercy on her behalf…"

"*Mercy*!" Incredulous, Ischade nearly burst out laughing. The thing that was part Haught, part Tasfalen (who was dead and had housed Roxane once and now did again, if Ischade understood the rules by which Niko's magic games were played) was shuffling close behind now, intent on biting off her head or munching on her soul. This thing had been one with a demon. It had merged with devils. It had taken fire out of the hands of archmages such as Randal and used it even against her. All of this, Ischade was sure, was Roxane's twisted evil come to ground. And Niko wanted mercy for the witch who had made his life a living hell and wouldn't offer him so much mercy as clean death would bring.

"That's right—mercy. I'm not like you, but we've helped each other. Tolerance, balance—good and evil: each resides within the other, part and parcel."

Ischade, who'd seen too much evil, shook her head. "You *must* be dead, or still possessed."

"Look." Niko's speech slipped into mercenary argot. "It's all the same—no good without evil, no balance… no *maat.* If we lose one, we lose the other. It's just life, that's all. And as for death—we get what we expect."

"And you *expect* what?" Now she realized that Niko himself was not naive, or helpless, or entirely benign. "From me, I mean?"

"Mercy, I already told you." The fire-well behind him began to shimmer and to dance, swinging its hips like a temple girl. "To your kind; for the record. For the balance of the thing. Janni we will take now."

"We?" It was one of the hardest things Ischade had ever done to engage in philosophical discussion with Nikodemos while, behind, the shambling thing had come so close she could feel its fetid breath upon her neck, and fancied that breath moist and felt, she thought, a strand of drool land in her hair. *Don't look at it; don't turn around—it's Niko's rest-place and his rules, not mine, apply.*

"We," Niko said as if teaching a simple lesson any child should understand. And then she did: behind him, a ghost appeared.

She knew ghosts when she saw them: this one was a spirit of supernal power, a fabled strength, a glossy being of such beauty that tears came to Ischade's eyes when it sat down beside Niko, ruffling his hair with a fawn-colored hand.

"I am Abarsis," it smiled in introduction, and she saw the wizard blood there, ancient lineage, and love so strong it made her heart hurt: she'd given up such options as this ghost had thrived on, long ago.

"We need Janni's soul in heaven; it's earned its peace. Give it that, and we will restore you totally: all you were; all you had… including this northern pair of witches… even this amalgam behind you of all their hate. If, as Niko asks, you show them mercy, then the gods will be well pleased."

"And if not?" This was no place for Ischade—she had no truck with gods or ghosts of dead priests. *Damn Tempus, who muddled all the sides and made ridiculous demands.*

"That's done long since," said the ghost, unabashedly reading her mind. "We're here for Janni only, and to give a gift for your safekeeping him until we could take him home. Now name it, Ischade of Downwind. Choose well."

She wanted only to get out of there, to be whole and well and fighting on her own terms, dealing with her own kind. And before she could say that, or think of something better, Abarsis, one arm around Niko, raised his other hand to her, saying: "It is done. Go with strength and purpose. Life to you, Sister, and everlasting glory."

And the rest-place went out like a light. The icy stream of colored water, the pillar of fire which aped reality, the snuffling horror at her back which she'd never truly glimpsed but only felt—and the two fighters, one spirit, one man of balance: all were gone as if they'd never been.

She was standing on the dry floor of Tasfalen's house and Haught was taunting her to come up the stairs.

Mercy, Niko had asked of her. She wondered if she knew, still, what it was and how to show it to creatures like these.

"Ischade… Mistress, aren't you curious?" Haught was rubbing the ring and she could feel the feedback of magic twisted, a deadly loop fashioned by a brash and foolish child.

Temptation made her shift from foot to foot. She was stronger, she could feel it: Niko and his guardian spirit had given her that. She could end them, here and now—Haught and whatever animated Tasfalen. For although she hadn't seen *him* yet, she knew he must be here: the rest-place revelation was like a map, a schematic, a design which fit over human ones. So Tasfalen was here, reborn, animated by some power. And Niko had wanted mercy for Roxane…

Two and two fit together with a snap: it was Roxane, *inside* Tasfalen, animating him.

Ischade whirled on her heel and fled toward the door. For a moment it resisted, but her strength prevailed.

Haught, behind her, came running down the stairs with a shout.

But she was faster: she wrenched the door open, slipped through, and bolted it with magic from the farther side.

Then, stepping back, Ischade considered mercy in all its meanings: if Tasfalen and Roxane were with Haught, in any state of being whatsoever, mercy could only take one form.

And with strength loaned her from the rest-place of a mystery she didn't understand and under the benediction of the high priest of a god in whom she had no faith, Ischade began to weave a spell so strong and fast she had no doubt about it holding.

All about Tasfalen's house she wove the ward—a special one, one that would keep the house sealed and keep those within locked up until they learned what mercy meant.

When it was over, she realized she had worked her spells in the midst of a downpour which had soaked her to the skin.

Picking up her heavy robes, she headed homeward. Perhaps she should have found the Riddler and told him what she'd done. But there were Crit and Strat to think of, and she didn't want to think of Strat—who was with Tempus by now, alive or dead.

She wanted to think only of herself for now. She wanted things to be just as they always had been before. And she wanted to think about mercy, a quality quite strained and strange, but strengthening, in its way.

*

In Tasfalen's house, what had been Roxane lay abed in Tasfalen's body, half-conscious, rent in memory and power, a mere fragment knowing only that it wanted to survive.

"Duuu," it mumbled, and tried again to move the lips of a corpse twice resurrected. "Duuussss." And: "Duuussss. Hau-uugh … duuusss."

The ex-slave was rattling windows barred by magic, cursing horrid spells that couldn't get outside, but bounced around the corners of the house and back upon him like ricochets, so that each one was more trouble than it was worth. Eventually Haught's panic ebbed and he stalked over to the bedside, looking down at the fish-white pallor of the man who'd brought him here.

Snatched him from somewhere—from *else*where… perchance from oblivion. Someone else might have been grateful, but Haught was too wise, too angry: he knew that all witches took their price.

He'd thought to win. He'd lost. He was captive now, captive in a mansion with fine things around him, true. But he was caged like an animal by his former mistress. And he was here only because of Tasfalen.

Nothing else could have done this. So he crouched down, thinking of ways to kill the already-dead; ways to get the Roxane out of Tasfalen, where it was bodiless and weak.

But then he began to listen, to try to understand what the thing on the bed was saying: "Duuusss, duuusss, duuusssttt …"

"Dust?" he guessed. "Do you mean dust?"

The eyes of the revivified corpse blinked open, startling him so that he fell back and caught himself on his hands.

"Duuussss," the blue lips said, "onn tonnnn."

"Dust. On your… tongue?" Of course. That was it. The dust. It wanted the dust. Not ordinary dust, Haught realized: the hot dust, the bright dust, the fragments of the Nisi globes of power. And the corpse was right: the dust was their only hope—his as well as… hers.

For the first time, Haught thought about what it meant, being caged with Roxane, the Nisibisi witch-in-man's-body. Or with what was left of her. If she perished, those who held her soul would come for her. And Haught might be embroiled. Entangled. Taken. Swallowed. Absorbed like interest payments.

His skin horripilated: there was enough intelligence in that twice-resurrected body to have seen the answer before he did.

What else was there, he was in no hurry to find out. And he had a long, trying task ahead of him: the dust in question must be collected, mote by mote. It was going to be arduous: the place was full of dust, most of it non-magical. It might take days, or weeks, or years, to gather enough—especially when Haught had no idea how much *was* enough.

When he had it, what would he do with it? Give it to the invalid ex-corpse? Or find a way to make use of it himself? He didn't know, but he knew he had plenty of time to decide.

And, since he had nothing better to do, he thought, he might as well start collecting what dust he could, mote by mote by mote…

*

The storm pelted Sanctuary with all the fury of affronted gods. Rain sheeted so hard that it punctured skin windows in the Maze; ran so thick and wild in the gutters that the tunnels filled up and sewers overflowed in the better streets while, in the palace, servitors ran with buckets and barrels to place under leaks that were veritable waterfalls.

On the dockside, everything was awash in tide and downpour, which gave Tempus the perfect opportunity to suggest that Theron, Emperor of Ranke; Brachis, High Priest; and all the functionaries forget protocol and begin their procession now, to higher ground and drier quarters.

By the time the Rankan entourage reached the palace gates, Molin Torchholder had already arrived, Kama in tow.

In the palace temple's quiet, Torchholder was giving grateful thanks for the storm which had come to quench the fires (that, unattended by gods, threatened to burn the whole town down) while, at the casement, Kama stared out over smoking rooftops toward uptown, where the pillar of fire spat and wriggled.

She had sidled into the alcove, away from priestly ritual, and she couldn't have said what made her hair stand on end: whether it was the cold storm winds with their blinding sheets of rain (so fierce that she could see it bounce knee-high when it struck the palace roof), or the demonic twistings of the fiery cone which resisted quenching.

She was more conscious of Molin than she should have been. Perhaps that was the reason for the superstitious chill she felt: she was about to be indicted for attempted assassination and sedition, and she was worried about what the priest really felt in his heart… about how she looked and whether he believed her and what he thought of her; about whether anyone of her lineage ought to be thinking infatuated thoughts about anyone of his.

It wouldn't work; he was a worse choice for her than Critias. But, like Critias, it was impossible to convince Molin of that.

This sad truth was evident in nothing he'd said—yet it was plain to see in everything he did; in the way their bodies reacted when their flesh touched. And this frightened Kama beyond measure: she'd need all her wits now just to stay alive. Her father would take Crit's word over hers without hesitation; oath-bond and honor outweighed any influence she had on the Riddler.

If she'd been born a man-child, things might have been otherwise. But things were as they were, and Torchholder was her only hope of reprieve.

He'd said so. He knew it for a fact. She didn't like feeling weak, being perceived as vulnerable. And yet, she admitted, she'd spread her legs on the god's altar for the priest now coming up behind her, who slid his arm around her shivering shoulders and kissed her ear.

"It's wonderful, the timely workings of the gods," Molin Torchholder said in an intimate undertone. "And it's a good omen—our good omen. You must… Kama, you're shaking."

"I'm cold, wet, and bedraggled," she protested as he turned her gently to face him. Then she added: "While you were communing with your Rankan storm god, my father and Theron's party came through the palace gates. My time is at hand, Molin. Don't hold out false hope to me, or gods' gifts. The gods of the armies won't overlook the fact that I'm a woman—they never have."

"Thanks to all the weather gods that you *are*," said the priest feelingly and, after peering into her eyes for an uncomfortably long instant, pulled Kama against him. "I'll take care of you, as I have taken care of this town and its gods and even Kadakithis. Put your faith in me."

Had anyone else said that to her, Kama would have laughed. But from Molin Torchholder it sounded believable.

Or she wanted so to believe it that she didn't care how it sounded.

They were standing thus, arms locked about one another, when a commotion of feet and then a discreet "Hrrmph" sounded.

Both turned, but it was Kama who whooped a short bark of disbelieving laughter before she thought to choke it off: before them were Jihan and Randal, the Tysian Hazard, arms around each other.

Or, more exactly, Jihan's arms were around Randal's slight and battered frame. She was holding the mage easily, so that his feet hardly touched the floor. Randal's gaze roamed a little bit but he was conscious: his quizzical, all-suffering look confirmed it.

Jihan's eyes were full of red flames and Kama heard Molin exclaim under his breath, "The storm—of course… The storm has brought back her powers."

"Powers?" Kama whispered through unmoving lips. "Were they gone? Back from where?" and Molin answered, just as low, "Never mind. I'll tell you later, beloved." Then he said, in his most ringing priestly voice, "Jihan, my lady, what brings you to our storm god's demesne? Are the children well? Is something amiss with Niko?"

"Priest," Jihan stamped her foot, "isn't it obvious? Randal and I are in love and we wish to be married by the tenets of your… faith… god, whatever. Now!"

Randal hiccoughed in surprise and his eyes widened. Kama would have been more concerned with the exhausted little wizard if she wasn't still reeling from shock: *Beloved*, Molin had called her.

Randal raised a feeble hand to his brow and Kama wondered whether the casualty was capable of standing under his own power, let alone making any decision about marriage.

So Kama said, "Randal? *Seh,* Witchy-ears, are you awake? My father isn't going to like you marrying his girl ranger, not considering the use he tends to make of her. I'd…"

Jihan's free hand outstretched, pointing, and Kama's flesh began to chill.

Molin stepped in front of Kama. "Jihan, Kama meant no slight. She's in dire straits herself. With our help, Froth Daughter, you shall be able to wed your chosen mage before…" He craned his neck to peer out the window, where no sun could be seen, just the demonic pillar of fire and the lightning of Stormbringer. "…before sundown, if that's your desire, and I will wed mine. If you aid me, my gratitude and that of my tutelary god will be inscribed in the heavens forever and—"

"You're marrying a mage?" Jihan's wing-like brows knitted but her pointing finger, with its deadly cold, wavered, and her hand came to rest on her own hip.

"Not a mage. Kama, here. I can divest myself of Rosanda easily enough: she's abandoned me. But I'll need your help in securing Tempus' permission… He's your guardian as well as Kama's."

"Guardian?" both snapped in unison as two feminine spines stiffened and two wily women considered alternatives.

"Someone," Torchholder intoned through the objections of the two females, "must set the seal on the betrothal pacts," thinking that he'd found a way to free Tempus from Jihan and, for that boon alone, Tempus owed him any favor he cared to ask.

For Kama's hand, Kama's freedom, and Kama's honor, he'd be glad to call their debt even. But for Kama's willing love he needed more. Standing behind her, his arms circling her in the proper pose of the protective husband, he whispered, "Trust me in this. Accept a formal betrothal. I am sacerdote of Mother Bey, Vashanka, and Stormbringer. It will take a month to untangle the necessary rituals. It will take longer—if you desire."

The tension along Kama's spine eased. She let out her breath with a careful sigh.

Once more, Molin Torchholder gave fervid thanks to the stormgod, who had seen fit to visit rain upon this paltry thieves' world in all His bounty, to quench the fires of chaos, and even to restore Jihan's powers.

Over Kama's head, as he looked out the window, it seemed to him that even the demonic pillar of fire was shrinking under the onslaught of the god's blessed rain.

*

Tempus was still trying to explain to Theron (who'd come down here to the empire's nether-parts because of that black, ominous rain falling in the capital of Ranke, and because of Abarsis' visit, and because it was the tendency of omens to make or break a regent's rule) that the plague had been specious. He assured Theron that the fake plague was a handy way to keep Brachis under wraps. He averred that the storm was merely natural and that the fires and the looting were simply consequences of the demonic pillar of flame (which had much to do with Nikodemos and nothing at all to do with Theron's arrival).

Tempus had just finished counseling the new Rankan emperor that "No one will construe it otherwise, my friend, unless we show weakness," when they came upon Molin Torchholder in Kadakithis' palace hall.

"My lord and emperor," Molin purred to Theron, and bowed.

Tempus stifled an urge to let Theron know that Sanctuary's architect/priest was a Nisi wizardling in disguise, a pretender and defiler, and a loudmouthed meddler to boot.

Theron, who didn't quite remember Molin but recognized the ornate robes of office, said sharply, "Priest, what's wrong with your acolytes that this place is cursed by weather, witch, and demon? If you can't restore order to your little backwater of the heavens, I'll replace you with someone who can. You've till New Year's day to set things right here—and no argument." Theron's leonine visage reddened: he'd found someone to blame for at least part of what was wrong here.

Only Tempus noticed the amusement nestled in the shadows around the emperor's mouth as the Lion of Ranke bawled, "Go to see Brachis. This is his mess as well. Tell him my decree: either Sanctuary is made pleasing in the sight of gods and their chosen representative—*me*—or you and Brachis will be looking for new jobs come year's end."

Molin Torchholder was too smart to wince or bridle. He stood stolidly, eyes fixed on Theron's hairy left ear until he was certain that the emperor was finished.

Then he responded, "Very good, my lord Emperor. I'll see to it. But while I have your ear—and Tempus'—some news: Last night Prince/Governor Kadakithis pledged his troth to the Beysib queen, Shupansea… an alliance is ours now for the asking."

"Really?" Theron's manner mellowed; he rubbed his hands. "That's the sort of omen worth retelling."

Tempus found his dagger in his fingers; he cleaned dirt from its chased hilt absently, waiting for Molin's other shoe to drop.

And drop it did: "Moreover … if I have leave to continue, sire? Many thanks." Then: "The esteemed Froth Daughter, spawn of Stormbringer who is father of all the weather gods, will marry our own archmage, the Hazard Randal. This alliance, too, is fortuitous for—"

"*What*?" Tempus could scarcely believe his ears, or his good fortune.

Stormbringer, at least, kept His word.

Molin continued, not deigning to notice the Riddler's outburst: "—for us all. And to make a threesome of favorable omens, I myself propose to marry—with all suitable ceremony and with Tempus' permission, of course—the lady Kama of the Third Commando, daughter of the Riddler. Thus the armies and the priesthood will be wed as well, and internal strife ended…"

"You're going to *what?* You're mad. Crit says she tried to mur—" Tempus bit off words of accusation, thinking matters through as quickly as he fought in battle. Torchholder was canny: the move was one sure to bring him power, consolidate his position, put him beyond Tempus' retribution and above reproach. But it would also save Tempus' daughter from a lengthy inquisition: even Crit would admit that, since Strat was alive and would recover, Kama was more useful to them living than dead, if she shared Torchholder's bed.

And Crit had sent word to him that there was some evidence that PFLS members had used the blue-fletched arrows against Straton. Crit had warned Tempus against hasty action, using all his operator's wiles to posit misdirection, to give Tempus an honorable way out of accusing his own daughter of an attempt at murder.

"So you'll make an honest woman of my… daughter. Just don't expect a dowry, congratulations, or any leniency on my part if you later wish you hadn't: a divorce will get you killed. So will infidelity, or perfidy of any sort." This was the least he could do for his daughter. And, said before the emperor, Tempus' conditions bound like law. It was a good thing that a priest of Vashanka could have more than one wife, though Tempus wouldn't have wanted to be Molin when that one's first wife heard this news.

Torchholder blanched, but smiled and said, "I'm off to tell her, then. And you'll take care of the other matter… the little misunderstanding she had with certain troops of yours?"

"That goes without saying," Tempus growled while Theron looked back and forth between the two, uncomprehending.

When Molin had hurried away in a swish of robes, Theron elbowed Tempus and said, light eyes sparkling, "Don't suppose you'd tell an old warhorse what all that was about?"

"Petty squabbles, unimportant. Now tell me about this expedition you want to mount—the one to the uncharted east, beyond the sea. It interests me; I'm restless. My men need some mortal enemies to fight. This going up against magics and the gods tends to dull an army's spirit. They want a battle they can win upon their own.

And Theron was glad to do that. They worked out their terms on the way down to see Nikodemos and the so-called god-children in their nursery: Tempus would take his forces, Stepsons and 3rd Commando and whomever else he chose from the empire's legions, and strike east. He'd ship the horses such cavalry must have, and weapons and provisions; he'd bring back intelligence and rare goods, if there were any; he'd set up embassies for trade and size up weak principalities for conquest. And he'd do it without any help from witch or god—taking just Jihan (and Randal) and his fighters.

The two old friends shook hands as they came down a flight of stairs and headed for the nursery, with Theron sighing wistfully, "I only wish that I could join you, Riddler. This kinging is even less than it's cracked up to be. But it makes me feel less trapped, setting you free, even for a few months…"

Tempus pushed the door inward and Theron fell silent.

The Rankan emperor remembered Nikodemos from the battle for the throne at the Festival of Man. He'd been with Tempus once when the Riddler had had to bail his Stepson out of a Rankan jail.

The ashen-haired youth sitting with a babe on either knee looked tired, wan, and somehow much too gentle to be the same much-lauded fighter. But when Niko raised his head and wished them life and glory, this was clearly the youngster whose fate was dogged by a Nisibisi witch.

Tempus left Theron's side and strode to where Niko sat.

As he did, Gyskouras buried his young head in Niko's *chiton* and began to weep at the sight of his supposed father, and Arton, understanding more than children should, shook his dark-haired head and told his blond companion: "Kouras, be brave. Don't cry."

"Let him. They're clear tears, and that's a blessing," Niko said softly to the children, then looked up at Tempus and beyond, to Theron: "You'll excuse me for not rising, lords. They're tired. They're undisciplined. They've had too many adventures for boys so young."

"So have you, we've heard, Stealth," Theron said kindly, remembering all that went on upcountry to win him the throne from Abakithis, and how much Niko had sacrificed to that end.

"You're still taking these boys to Bandara, Niko?" Tempus asked offhandedly.

"If you still agree, Commander. If you'll give me leave."

Tempus almost said that Abarsis had usurped command from him in the matter, but he was too pleased with the outcome of his talk with Theron. "Leave you have, and leave to meet us in three months back in the capital. We're mounting an expedition and I want you along."

Something changed in Niko's face, as if a tension had been released. "You are? You do?" Niko let the children slide off his lap and got slowly, carefully, to his feet. The signs of all he'd been through then showed clearly: bruises, favored muscles, a stiffness time would have to heal. "I'm glad… I mean… you might have thought me too much trouble—all I bring with me, wherever… my witch-curse and my ghosts and all."

"You're the best I've got, Niko," said Tempus levelly. "And the only man I've called partner in a century. Some things can't be changed."

And although Theron might not have understood the last bit, Niko did, and moved painfully to embrace Tempus, stepped back, bowed as best he could to Theron, and then, with a blush of humility, mumbled that he'd best begin preparations to take the boys and make away.

Tempus took Theron out of there, then, and on the way back upstairs they chanced to glimpse the skyline out the palace window, where a hair-thin column of fire, a weakened pillar of flame, blew far right, then left, and then winked out.

Chapter 9: Joining Forces

Each day thereafter, when they camped, they camped near a spring. Springs spawn naiads, creatures of love and vengeance, so said every local legend Tempus knew. Straton routinely chose their campsites. Strat had spent that night in Thrax's cave; so had Critias; so had they all. Straton might be the most susceptible, however, to sorcery: he still rode a ghost horse given him by a witch.

Tempus voiced no concern to anyone, even Niko. Instead he watched Crit and Straton and the others closely while they slept each night, but saw no naiads come creeping—in itself no proof that none had visited among these fighters.

On the blustery eve when thirty-six more Sacred Banders crested the hill behind the one where they'd encamped, Lysis was the first to spot the force come riding: "Commander, Niko, they're here! They've got wagons, extra horses… I saw Charon, my father, I'm sure of it. And Kouras. But not Cassander or Sync…"

By then Straton and Critias, watering their horses at the spring near this evening's campsite, had seen their brothers approaching, four across, over stony ground. Strat's wolf-call rang-out: *all's well; come ahead.*

Charon's Thebans yowled back as if they'd always known the Stepson call-and-answer. Armored up, the approaching unit wore the green wool and gray linen of the Unified Sacred Band. At the fore, one rider carried a battle standard: gold sword and black feather crossed on a field of green.

Soon enough the thirty-six, a mixed Stepson and Theban contingent, were all accounted for, with their wagons, weapons, extra horses and provisions.

Charon went first to Critias, then came to Tempus to report. Behind him, Arton and Lysis and young Kouras, the storm god's son, were clustered on the slope. Beyond, Straton was assigning space to incoming warriors and horses and weapons and supplies.

Charon was heavyset, rough-hewn and tired, with graying hair long enough to curl around his ears. "Life to you, and everlasting glory, Commander: I return your Band to you in good order," said the Theban warrior-priest formally, helmet in hand. "All these are well enough, and the last group's not far behind us. No trouble found us on the journey…"

"And before?"

Charon inclined his head. "You'll want to talk to Kouras. My young partner has had a shock. His pregnant priestess miscarried and died, so he's sure his god deserted him." Charon's lips pursed. "About the will of heaven, I can counsel only Thebans—not a boy like Kouras, who thinks a god's blood runs in his veins."

"Understood. He may have truly been deserted, Charon—may still be: we're far from where his godly father can help him; local gods have local powers. But since you took Kouras as your rightman at my request, do you want to stay while I speak with him? And… were they singing, when the priestess lost the child and died, do you know? Hymns or paeans?"

Wrong song sung?

"Singing? I don't know. I wasn't there when the girl Seriti died; perhaps I should have been—for the sake of Kouras. Commander, I've done all I can do—I don't know Kouras' mind, his god, or his culture. Perhaps you can do better, since he believes you helped beget him."

So Charon went to get Kouras where he and Arton and Lysis stood in a huddle, to bring the son of Vashanka up to Tempus.

Far to the south, thunder rolled and lightning pierced the sky.

When Kouras had climbed the hill, Tempus no longer cared whether there had been singing when Seriti died.

Kouras was white-faced, cold and hostile. Red-haired, green-eyed, and made for war: this boy named Gyskouras was beautiful and deadly, with all the fury of Vashanka, god of sack and pillage, blazing in his flesh. Of the three youngsters Niko had trained on Bandara and sponsored as Stepsons, Kouras was the most talented; but his berserker god had marked him, every inch and sinew.

"She's dead. Seriti's dead," Kouras said without preamble or honorific. "Bled out while the priests in the palace watched. Died in a pool of her own blood. My baby boy she carried was stillborn." Kouras stabbed him with accusing eyes. "Nothing availed to save her. Not your Band's healer, Cassander. Not the high priest of Vashanka. Not your fish or magic jars or potions. Nothing." Kouras spread big hands; his swordsman's shoulders taut: looking for a fight; full of the anger of a man betrayed by all he's loved.

"It's not my Band more than it's yours, Kouras. Nor my healer, nor my fish or jars. What belongs to the Band belongs to us all: joy and sorrow included. Death comes; all things pass away. If Vashanka saw fit to take the child, then that's beyond you—or me—to fight. Accept it. There will be other girls, other children, other gods. And other deaths. Because you are a storm god's son, did you fancy yourself protected from mortal grief? It's not been that way for me."

"My god should have saved her. Saved the child. Could have."

"But didn't. And now you're far beyond the realm where your father, a local deity, has power. You may not be so favored here."

Kouras' head jerked up, as if Tempus had slapped him. "*Why*? Why did this happen? The god made me. He's a real god, Vashanka… I have godspeed… or I did. I heal like you and Nikodemos… or I did."

Behind the youth, Niko was approaching, eyes armored, concern obvious. Tempus stopped Niko in his tracks with the slightest shake of head: *Stay back.*

In a voice like gravel shifting underfoot, Tempus said: "Kouras, life tempers all. The storm god Vashanka brought life to you, as he has to so many others. As gods do, dallying with mortal women. So what? Vashanka is a berserker god. Love is no part of his vocabulary. Paternity isn't fealty. What you do with your god-given life is your choice. Be strong. Don't look to place blame on others: it's unseemly. You have a partner and, Theban or no, Charon is as good a mentor as you could hope for. Is it written that life is easier for the god-born? That heaven will clear your way forever? That nothing will ever harm you or those you love? Not if you're a storm god's son. Now we'll see what you really are, a world away from where your sire can help you. What we hope you'll be is a Stepson, and make us proud of the warrior you become."

"I'm—" Kouras' chin was trembling, eyes too bright. He paused, unable to speak.

If Kouras had expected Tempus to comfort him, reassure him, embrace him or commiserate with him, he'd been wrong. But letting the boy break down in tears with half the Band watching would do no good, only harden Kouras' dismay as he realized that all men face death and grief and fate alone.

"You're still a member in good standing of the Sacred Band of Stepsons. You have your duty, your comrades, your life unfolding. Thank Charon for putting up with your youth and inexperience. And take out this misfortune on no one else: if that girl's dead, you're the reason for it: character is destiny. Now go make yourself useful, Stepson."

Tempus motioned Niko forth. The audience was over.

Kouras looked over his shoulder, saw Niko, and stomped down the hill, bumping Niko's shoulder with his as he passed, rather than make way.

Niko's gaze followed the Pillager's son. "Charon told me," Niko said. "Vengeance? Or bad luck?"

"It's long since Kouras' sire shared my thoughts. Probably godly pique: where Kouras is now, Vashanka cannot follow. So, slate wiped clean. Entanglement left behind. We'll see what the boy can be, without his overweening, murderous god hovering over him." Tempus had good reason to despise Vashanka: when he and the Pillager had been joined, blood ran like rivers and empires fell for no better reason than deific hubris. "We'll watch him."

Niko nodded, attentive: waiting. Behind Niko, down below, Tempus could see first Kouras, then Randal, approach Lysis and Arton. Perhaps the mage could heal a broken heart.

"What else, Niko?"

"Charon says the rest of ours are several days behind him: going slower because of the wounded. Do you want to stay here and wait? Or push on?"

"We'll camp here tonight, go north tomorrow. Debrief Charon more. And keep watch over the Stepsons who slept in the cave."

As they came down from the hillock, the sun was setting, firing the heavens gold and red and bronze. Men were pitching tents and building bonfires, horses greeting one another shrilly. With forty-eight encamped here, they were better prepared for whatever they'd encounter, Tempus thought.

Just then some Thebans began to sing, as Thebans will, and pipes began to play. Tempus nearly ran then, and Niko raced ahead of him, but others were quicker. The pipes stopped playing. The songs broke off, unfinished.

All the hairs on Tempus' body raised and settled back. Thrax and his oracle were far behind. The sphinx's warning echoed in his head as he caught up to Niko, trying to explain to Charon that "we're not singing on this sortie, nor playing pipes," without seeming a fool.

After they ate, Niko came to him: "Should we let them have their fireside stories, Commander? I need some time with Charon and with you to go over details for tomorrow."

"Let them have stories, but no singing or flutes. Ask our mage to tell them a cautionary tale about mortals mixing with powers above their stations—the story of how we got Randal unbetrothed will do. Meanwhile, I want Crit and Strat with us. We need privacy to tell Charon what to look for, in case there's Thracian mischief in the air, or strangers in the night: nymphs or naiads from the spring—and warn him to watch his fighters while they sleep. This is mythic country we're traveling."

Thus they left Randal to tell all assembled a tale of how he'd gotten free of his promise to marry a Froth Daughter, a primal power of wind and wave…

Chapter 10: Sanctuary is For Lovers

Down on Wideway by the docks, a warehouse destroyed by fire was being rebuilt by fish-eyed Beysibs to house a glass-making enterprise as alien as the fish-folk who funded it. Nearby, a big man named Tempus sat alone in tattered trail gear on a mud colored horse as a storm rolled in from the sea.

Thunderstorms in Sanctuary during summer weren't uncommon. This one, loud as a wounded bear and dark as a witch's eye, cleared the dockside of folk while Tempus watched from shadows thrown by two overhanging roofs. These days in a revolution-wracked thieves' world suddenly bereft of the magic that had driven it, such storms meant that a new and feral god called Stormbringer was abroad.

Tempus, on a horse whose muddy disguise did nothing to hide its extraordinary girth or the intelligence in its eyes, cared not at all for the god behind the storm—if indeed the chaotic principle named Stormbringer could rightfully be called one.

He cared more than he wished to admit for that god's daughter: for Jihan, called Froth Daughter, primal expression of Stormbringer's lust for wind and wave, who was betrothed to Randal, the Tysian wizard, and trapped here until the marriage either was consummated or renounced. He'd cared enough to return to Sanctuary, though it was doomed by imperial decree and the folly of its own selfish inhabitants. Doomed to eradication at New Year's, when the grace period the new Rankan Emperor, Theron, had given Prince/Governor Kadakithis would elapse without order being restored here.

Then the Emperor's troops would come in a multitude—"Even though it be a soldier for every tramp, an arrow for every rebel, a legion if necessary," in Theron's words—and this thieves' world would be a fools' paradise no longer. Pacifying refractory towns was a passion of Theron's.

Pacifying wizard-ridden Sanctuary might once have been an impossibility, but not now: The feuding witches and the greedy priests had, between them, managed to destroy both Nisibisi Globes of Power before spring had sprung, leaving Sanctuary's magical fabric rent and its wards weakened.

At long last, Sanctuary had become what Tempus' fighters of the Sacred Band had always called it: well and truly damned. That this damnation had come from the greedy power plays of its lowlifes, rather than from the pillar of fire which had sprung from an uptown house to affront the heavens, didn't surprise Tempus.

The fact that no one in town save the weakened wizards and a handful of impotent priests knew the truth of it—how Sanctuary had destroyed its own manna and been deserted by the more prudent of its pantheon of gods—*did* surprise even the unflappable Tempus, called the Riddler, who now headed his horse into the storm and northeast toward the Maze.

He felt no twinge of nostalgia for the old days, when he'd ridden these streets alone as a palace Hell Hound in Kadakithis' employ, testing the prince's mettle for the Rankan interests who eventually chose Theron in Kadakithis' stead. But he felt a spark of regret when he passed the docks from which

Nikodemos, his favorite among the mercenary fighters who followed him, had departed seaward, bound for the Bandaran isles with two children who might have been Sanctuary's only hope.

As Niko might have been the only hope of a man who'd taken the name Tempus when he realized that his curse caused time itself to pass him by. But hopes were for Sanctuarites, the children of the damned, the dark Ilsigi whom Rankan and Beysib oppressors alike called Wrigglies; and for women touched with Nisibisi wizard blood who sucked purer blood in Sanctuary's steamy summer nights—for anyone but him.

Tempus was relieved of duty here, of all responsibility save what his conscience might impose. Conscience had brought him back here to complete preparations under way since winter's end, now that Theron had offered him a commission to explore the unknown east and immunity from prosecution for any mercenaries he chose to hire for the venture.

So once again, he would have his Stepsons, the Sacred Band of paired fighters and certain single mercenaries, and the 3rd Commando, Ranke's most infamous cadre, for company in the east during the trek to come.

And if his forces' imminent withdrawal from Sanctuary didn't signal and seal the town's doom, then Tempus hadn't out-lived a hundred enemies and their legions.

Though that wasn't what made him hesitate, brought him down from the capital to ride once more through garbage-heaped streets where the lawless fought each other block by block in open revolt and man by man over matters of eye color and skin hue and heavenly affiliation.

He didn't care about Sanctuary's survival. The town itself was his enemy. Those who did not fear him for good reason, hated him on principle; those who neither feared nor hated him had fled this dunghill long ago.

He could have left the withdrawal to Critias, the Stepsons' first officer, and to Sync, the 3rd Commando's line commander. He could have waited in imperial Ranke's palace with Theron, interviewing chart makers and seamen who told of dragons in the eastern sea with emerald eyes and of treasures in shoreline caves the likes of which the Rankan Empire had never seen.

Neither Jihan nor her intended, Randal, understood that their betrothal was the result of a deal Tempus had made with Stormbringer, the Froth Daughter's father—a deal he'd struck in expediency and haste with a god known as a master trickster. Though deal it was, Tempus was no longer certain it was prudent. He wanted both Jihan and Randal, the Stepsons' warrior-mage, for the eastward trek and neither one could leave until the matter of this pending marriage was decided.

So he was here, to yea or nay the wedding. To make sure that Randal (a Sacred Band partner and one of his men) was not trapped in hell's own bowels against his will. And to see that Jihan's father blew no storms of confusion in his daughter's eyes to keep her where He had chosen to abide.

Tempus had come in disguise, as best he was able. His form was heroic in proportion and his face resembled that of a god once known in Sanctuary, but banished now: High-browed and honey-bearded, that face looked upon the gutted ways of the warehouse district with all the disdain three centuries and more of life could impart.

It was the face of Vashanka, now called the Hidden God, that Tempus wore tonight. Selfish and proud, full of war and death, it was the face of Sanctuary itself.

That face made him feel at home here, as did the storm descending. In Sanctuary, self-interest never flagged; his presence here upon pressing, private business, was proof of that.

Turning up Shadow Street toward the Maze, he saw deserted checkpoints of some faction who claimed everything from Lizard's Way to the governor's warehouses as its own. That faction was said to be Zip's 'Popular Front for the Liberation of Sanctuary' (PFLS), as unpopular now as was Zip himself.

Tempus reined his horse left on Red Clay Street to reconnoiter, despite the gusts and darkening sky and thunderous promise of rain that made the Trôs horse under him shiver and throw its muzzle skyward.

He'd never exchanged a civil word with Zip, whom some said had caused far too much of the springtime carnage—whom Crit said had attempted murder and tried to blame the crime on Tempus' own daughter, Kama.

And since the target of the murderous attack had been Straton, Critias' Sacred Band partner, the pair had teams out night and day, even in the midst of the Stepsons' preparations to withdraw—teams seeking to even the score by taking Zip's eyes and tongue: an old Band prescription for curing traitors.

Lightning flared, a sheet sky-wide that banished darkness even on Shadow Street, so that Tempus saw backlit figures skulking from garbage heap to doorway in his wake.

This was PFLS territory all right.

The rain accompanying a peal of thunder, so loud it made the Trôs horse flatten its ears and lower its head, cared nothing for whom it wet; as the lightning cared not whom it unmasked.

Both Tempus and his horse were only cursorily disguised, the horse with berry juice and trail mud, and its rider with dyes no better. The rain bounced fetlock high on cobbles and ran down the Riddler's oilskin mantle to his sharkskin-hilted sword, where it formed rivulets like spilled blood and just as red from the dye it washed away.

Both man and horse were too large and too well-muscled for Sanctuary's own; both streamed water red as blood and splashed it behind them as Tempus loped his mount, oblivious to the torrent and the spray the horse's hooves kicked up, down the center of Red Clay Street. And that specter was one to stop a superstitious heart and make a criminal seek cover.

Yet at the corner of West Gate Street (where the sudden downpour swept seaward to the wharves down the slope so deep and fast that rats and cats and pieces of less recognizable flesh were carried along in its currents as if the White Foal River had changed its course) three men stepped out from cover, barring his path, knee deep in water, crossbows cranked and blades unsheathed.

Perfect.

In a rising wind so fierce it blotted out the Trôs' snorts of warning, and in a rain so dense no cat-gut or woman's-hair bowstring could be dry, any crossbow would shoot awry.

Tempus knew it. So did the three who stood there daring him to ride them down.

He considered it, though he'd not sought a confrontation, annoyed by the boys with sweatbands around their foreheads and weapons better than street toughs ought to have.

The Trôs (having more sense and being a larger target) stopped still and turned its head toward him, imploring him with liquid eye to remember why he'd come here, not merely take an opportunity luck offered and waste it to vent some spleen and make their presence known.

Still, this sort should have enough sense to fear him.

That none did, that one stepped forward and said in a thick voice with a trace of gutter accent, "Looking for me, big fella? All your bugger boys are," gave the Riddler time enough to realize that, while he'd been looking for the rebel called Zip, Zip had also been looking for him.

A noise behind, and then more sounds of moving men, gave Tempus and his horse a good estimate of the odds without their turning to see the dozen rebels climbing down from roof-tops and up from tunnels and out of cellar windows.

Tempus' skin crawled. Pain wasn't something he sought and, with no death at the end of it, he could suffer infinitely more than other men. But it was his pride that lent him pause: the last thing he needed was to be taken hostage by the PFLS and held for ransom. Crit would never let him forget it.

And the result for the PFLS would then be eradication—total and complete, not the minor harassment Crit had time to field while busy with a hundred other tasks as he got two fighting units ready to depart a town that had precious little else between it and total anarchy.

So Tempus said to the foremost fighter, "If you're Zip, I *am* looking for you," and slid off his horse, looping its reins loosely on his saddle's pommel. Whatever Tempus was worth, the Trôs was irreplaceable, and would make for the Stepsons' barracks on a whistled command.

But should the Trôs, with teeth and hooves and blood-lust strewing carnage in its wake, make for the barracks beyond the Swamp of Night Secrets, then the die for each and every rebel child was cast.

And children these were, the Riddler realized as he stepped closer: the boy out in front of his compatriots was well under thirty.

This youth held his ground, flashing a hand-signal that brought his troops in closer and made Tempus reassess the discipline and training of the rabble closing on him.

Then the Riddler remembered that this Zip had had some little congress with Kama, Tempus' daughter, a woman who was as good a covert actor as Critias and as good a soldier as Sync.

The boy nodded a crisp assent, then added, "That's me, old man: Zip. What's this about? You didn't 'accidentally' cross our lines. We won't make peace with Jubal's bluemasks—or with that Bey-licking Kadakithis, who's sold the Ilsigs out twice over."

The youth widened his stance and Tempus remembered what Sync had said of him: "The boy's got nearly enough balls, but they override his brains."

So Tempus responded, "No, not accidentally. I want to talk to you… alone."

"This is as 'alone' as I'm likely to get with you—you're not half so fetching as your daughter."

Tempus locked his fingers firmly on his sword belt, lest they cause trouble on their own, seeking a neck to wring. Then he said, "Zip… as in zero; nothing; zilch… right? Well, despite that, I'll give you a piece of wisdom, and a chance—because my daughter thinks you're worth it." That wasn't true—or at least he didn't think so. He'd never spoken to Kama about Zip. She'd earned the right to choose her own bed-partners, and more.

The flat-faced youth, standing in the rain, barked a laugh. "Your daughter lies in with Nisibisi wizards—or at least with Molin Torchholder, who's tainted with Nisi blood. Her idea of who's worth what ain't mine."

The rabble behind and around laughed, but uneasily. The Trôs at Tempus' side pawed the ground and pulled upon its reins to loosen them. He put out a hand to soothe the horse.

A dozen blades or more cleared their scabbards with a *snick* audible even through the pelting rain, while the three crossbows he could see were centered on his chest.

"The wisdom is: Sanctuary is for lovers, not fighters, this season," Tempus told the rebel leader. "Make peace among you, or the Empire will grind the lot into dust, and bury your flesh with corn to make it grow tall."

"Crap, old man. I'd heard you were tough—not like the rest." Zip spat. "But it's the same garbage I hear from them. Tell it to your troops—to the Whoresons and the Turd Commando. They're the ones causing all the grief."

Tempus' patience was near an end. "Boy, mark me: I'll call them off you for a week—seven days. In it, you meet with the other factions and hammer out some agreement, or by New Year's Day, the PFLS won't be even a memory. Nor will you live even that long, to verify it."

There was a silence, and in it someone muttered, "Let's kill the bastard," and someone else whispered back, "We *can't*—don't you know who that *is?*"

Tempus peered through the downpour and watched the flat face before him, emotionless and cold with rain streaking down it. There was strength in the youth, like the Enlibar steel some had thought would make a difference here—but, like the steel, Zip's strength was too little and too late.

Ageless eyes shocked against mortal eyes too sure of their doom and unwilling to seek favor. But another thing passed between them: the weariness of the young fighter, hunted by too many and willing to die against sheer numbers and superior force of arms, had turned to hopelessness; Zip's despair met its echo in the gaze of the fabled immortal who went from war to war and empire to empire, taking life and teaching the wisest something about the spirit's triumph over death.

Tempus, who had created, trained, and fielded the Stepsons, was offering a moratorium, some forgotten hope, where an ultimatum had been expected.

Zip's tone was skeptical when the boy answered: "Yeah, a week. All right. All I can say is the PFLS will try. I can't speak for the other factions. It's got to be enough that we try. Or—"

Tempus had to interrupt. A threat uttered in front of the youth's followers would be binding. "Enough, for you and yours. What they sow, they'll reap. You can come out of this with more than you expect, Zip—an imperial pardon, maybe a profession, and license to do what you do best for the good of the town you say you love."

"The town I'll die for, one way or the other," Zip murmured, because he'd understood what Tempus was saying and what had been unsaid in their met glance, and wanted the Riddler to know it, before he waved his men back without another word from Tempus.

It took only moments for the intersection where Red Clay Street met West Gate to seem deserted once again. It took no longer to mount the Trôs and head it toward Lizard's Way.

Tempus was thinking, as he rode the Trôs past a pile of refuse undoubtedly hiding at least one hostile youngster, that what Zip might gain, could he do the impossible and show progress toward peace (a coalition of rebel forces, a cease-fire committee, or even a pacification program) was more than the boy's wildest dream: a home.

There were no forces to replace the Stepsons and the 3rd . The Rankan army garrison was just that: Rankan. The Stepsons' barracks, won at so great a cost in life and love five years past, would be deserted; the job the Sacred Band did, undone. There would be only a handful of Hell Hounds to stand against Theron's battalions, Beysib oppressors, and the crime-lords of the town.

If Zip would only let him, Tempus was going to solve a number of problems that had seemed insoluble only minutes before, and do the youth the only favor one man can do another: give him a start on solving his own problems, a place to stand, a world to win—a fresh start.

If Tempus could keep his own people from killing the charismatic young rebel leader in the meantime. And *if* Zip knew a last chance when he saw one.

And *if*, in Sanctuary, where hate and fear passed for respect, Zip hadn't made so many enemies that, no matter what Tempus did, the boy's assassination wasn't as sure as the next thunderclap of Stormbringer's welcome-weather.

When that thunderclap did come, Tempus was already cantering the Trôs down Lizard's Way, headed for the Vulgar Unicorn, where a fiend named Snapper Jo tended bar and word could be spread fast, when a man had rumors he wanted on the wing.

*

Snapper Jo was a fiend of the gray-and-warty-skinned, snaggle-toothed variety.

His shock of orange hair stood out every which way from his head and his eyes looked in both directions at once, causing distress to certain patrons who wondered which orb to fix on when they earnestly begged for credit or leave to pass upstairs, where drugs and women could be had.

Snapper's job of bartending in the day at the Vulgar Unicorn was his most prized accomplishment—save the winning of his freedom.

Until recently he'd been the summoned minion of Roxane, the Nisibisi witch called Death's Queen. Then his mistress had freed him, after her fashion… or at least, she'd not come around lately to order him to this or that foul depredation.

The fact that Snapper thought of his former existence as a witch's servant as depredacious was central to the fiend's new outlook on life. Here among the Wrigglies and the mendicants and the whores, he was trying desperately for acceptance.

And he was managing. No one teased him about his looks or shrank from him in fear. They were civil, in the manner of humans; and they treated him as an equal, to the extent that anyone here ever treated anyone else so.

And in his fiendish heart of hearts, Snapper Jo wanted above all to be accepted by the humans—perhaps, someday, *as* a human. For was not humanity something in the heart, not on the surface?

Snapper Jo wanted to believe it so, in this weird inn where pop-eyed Beysibs were hated marginally more than blond and handsome Rankans; where dark skin and uneven limbs and snaggle teeth weren't disfigurements; where everyone was equally oppressed by the wizards from the Mageguild and the priests from uptown.

*

So when the tall, heroic man with the fearsome countenance—who seemed to be seeping blood (or bloody rain) from every pore—came in and spoke familiarly in a gravelly voice, saying, "Snapper, I need a favor," the day bartender drew himself up to his full height (almost equal to the stranger's), puffed out his spoon-chest and replied, "Anything, my lord… except credit, of course: house rules."

This, too, was part of being human: caring about little stamped circles of copper, gold, or silver, even though their value was only as great as the demand of the humans who fought and died over them.

But this big human wanted only information: he'd come to Snapper to consult.

The stranger said, while around him the bar cleared for a man's length on either side and behind him certain patrons skulked out into the storm and two serving wenches tiptoed into the back room, "I need to know of your former mistress—did Roxane ever find her way out of Tasfalen's house uptown? Has anyone seen her? You, of all… persons… would know if she's about."

"No, friend," said Snapper, who used the word 'friend' too much because he'd just recently learned its meaning, "she's not been seen or heard from since the pillar of fire was doused."

The big man nodded and leaned close across the bar.

Snapper leaned in to meet him, feeling somehow special and very favored to be having this conversation with so formidable a human before all the patrons in the Unicorn. Nearly nose to nose, Snapper began to notice, through his right-looking eye, some things about the man which were naggingly familiar: the hooded, narrow eyes which watched him with hot intensity; the thin slash of a mouth whose lips twisted with some private humor.

Then the man said, "And Ischade, the vampire woman? Is she well? Down at Shambles Cross? Holding court among her shades?"

"She…" Then memory jogged memory, and Snapper Jo raised a crop of goose bumps to complement his warts: this was the Riddler, the Sleepless One, the legendary fighter his former mistress had fought so long. "She… is, sire. Ischade… *is*. And will be, always…"

Snapper Jo had friends among the not-really-human, the once-dead, the straddlers of the void. Ischade was not one of them; but neither was this man, whom he now knew.

As he knew why the crowd had drawn back, this rabble who knew the players in a game they joined only as pawns and never of their own accord.

Snapper tried not to cringe, but his lips formed words involuntarily, words that whistled out sing-song, "Mur-der, mur-der; oh there'll be mur-der everywhere and Snapper's so happy without it..."

"When next a Stepson or Commando comes in, instruct him to seek me at the mercenaries' hostel. And don't fail." The man called Tempus lay coins upon the bar.

Snapper could see them glitter with his left-looking eye, although he didn't pick them up until the big man had gone, leaving behind only creaking floorboards stained ruddy to prove he'd been there at all.

Then the fiend called one of the serving wenches from the kitchen and gave the girl, whom he loved (to the extent that a fiend can love) all the money the Riddler had left him, saying, "See? Fear not. Snapper protect you. Snapper take care you. You take care Snapper, too, yes, later?" And the fiend gave a broad and lascivious grin to the woman he favored, who hid her shudder as she pocketed the equivalent of a week's wages and promised the fiend she'd warm his lonely night.

Things were tough enough, these days in Sanctuary, that you took what you could get.

*

"You want us to *what?*" Crit's disbelieving snort made Tempus frown.

For Tempus, the mercenaries' hostel north of town evoked memories and ghosts as bloody as the rufous walls here, hung with weapons which had won so many days. Here, Tempus and Crit had plotted to flush a witch without thought to the consequences; here, before Crit's recruitment, Tempus had put together the core of the Stepsons and taken command of Abarsis the Slaughter Priest's Sacred Band.

Here, even farther in the past, Tempus had burned a scarf belonging to a woman who was his most foul curse—a scarf that had been returned to him, magically whole and full of portent; a scarf he wore again around his waist, under his armor and his *chiton*, as if all between his first days in Sanctuary and the present were but a bad dream.

"I want you to protect, not hunt, this Zip, for one week," Tempus repeated, then added: "If, at the end of that week, there's no cease-fire coalition, no improvement, you can go back to collecting blood-debts."

Crit was the brightest of the Stepsons, a Syrese fighter who'd taken the Sacred Band oath more than once and was now paired with Straton, who in turn was entangled with Ischade, the vampire woman who lived down by Shambles Cross.

No one wanted the Sacred Band out of Sanctuary more than Crit. And no one knew Tempus' heart better, or more specifics of what had transpired while the Emperor was in Sanctuary.

Crit pulled on his long nose and stirred his posset with a finger, staring into it as if it were a witch's scrying bowl. "You're not…" he said to the bowl, then looked up at Tempus. "You're not thinking about using that bunch of Zip's as some sort of Sanctuary defense force? Tell me you're not."

"I can't tell you that. Why should I? They're trained, gods know—well enough for this town, anyway. And they're tough—as tough as any we trained ought to be, which most of them are. Niko himself spent some time working with the PFLS leader. And it shouldn't matter to you whom we leave in the barracks, as long as it's not Jubal. We can't have crimelords running things—Theron was very explicit. It'll take locals to police this place, or us."

"That's what I mean: none of us will want to stay to oversee that bunch of murderers—not me, not any of mine. Promise me you won't do that to me again, leave me with an impossible job and an intractable lot of disappointed fighters. The Band wants to go *with* you. I won't be able to hold them here. And Sync's commandos won't take my orders."

It wasn't like Crit to make excuses, so these weren't excuses: these were points the Sacred Bander urgently wanted Tempus to consider.

"Fine. I agree. I just want to make sure that you understand that Zip is more useful alive than dead… for one week. And that whatever is between you and my daughter—or not," Tempus held up his hand to forestall Crit's denial, "she's entangled with Torchholder, who's Black Nisibisi—an enemy. We leave her here. We take Jihan and Randal if we have to drug them senseless to do it, and we get our tails out of here—yours, mine, Strat's, the Stepsons', the Third's—and that's that. We're clear of a degenerating situation. If we can leave some force or other to help Kadakithis, then we're lily-white."

"That's why you came here in person, Commander? To cobble together some stopgap that won't hold because Theron doesn't want it to? You know what he wants: he wants a tractable, stable Empire's anus. And with the magic screwed up, or downgraded, or whatever it is Randal's been trying to explain to me, he can get it by force of arms. I don't see a winning side for us in that kind of fight, and neither do you… I hope."

Tempus grinned fondly at his second-in-command: "Get Straton disentangled, both from the witch and from his local responsibilities, and—on my explicit order—the two of you personally see that Zip manages to make his contacts. And that none of ours, the Third included, obstructs him. Then we're out of here, back to the capital with the best possible report under the circumstances. And, no, I didn't come down country for this. I came down for Jihan's wedding: to stop it."

*

Randal was in the Mageguild, consorting with the nameless First Hazard, trying to make some headway casting a simple manipulative spell to turn the swampy ground between the complex's outer and inner walls to gardens, when Tempus came to call.

The First Hazard was harried, a Rankan of Randal's age who'd assumed the dignity just when it no longer was one. The Mageguild had held the populace in thrall by fear and power for time uncounted. Now that the Nisibisi power globes' destruction had made simple spells uncastable and love potions useless, now that sympathetic magic was no longer so, the Mageguild adepts feared not merely for their income:

Once Sanctuary's denizens realized that no wards protected the haughty sorcerers, that spells paid for and tendered wouldn't work, that the Mageguild's collective foot had been lifted from Ilsig and Rankan neck alike, the Hazards' lives would be at risk.

So finding a way to render the grounds and walls malleable to magic was not simply an exercise: the Hazards might need an unbreachable fortress in which to hide from angry clients.

And Randal, whose magic was less affected than the local mages', who had a dream-forged *kris* at his hip and the protection of the very lord of dreams, had been called upon to aid his guild's relatives—although when the guild had been all-powerful, they had not liked the Stepsons' wizard nearly so well as now.

"It's not me, you know," Randal was trying to explain to the First Hazard, whose war name was Cat and who looked more like a Rankan noble than a practiced adept who'd earned such a title. "My magic, such as it is," Randal went on modestly, "is part curse and part dream-spawned… not dependent on whatever forces have been weakened in the south."

The Rankan adept looked at the Tysian wizard narrowly, then wondered aloud, "It's not some power play of Nisibisi origin, then? Nothing Torchholder, Roxane, and the rest of you northern wizards have dreamed up?"

Randal sneezed and wiped his freckled nose on his sleeve, ears reddening in embarrassment: "If I were so powerful as that, couldn't I rid myself of these damnable allergies?" His affliction was back, the one concomitant he was experiencing of the local adepts' distress: pollen, birds, and especially furred creatures could bring him to a paroxysm of distress. Once he'd had a handkerchief which quelled them; then he'd had a power which suppressed them: Now he had neither.

The First Hazard's impolitic retort was interrupted by an apprentice who burst in, saying: "My lords Hazard, a man has breached our wards, a stranger—that is, we think so, but he's coming—up the stairs. Now. And he's got his horse *with* him…"

The handsome First Hazard hung his head, staring at his twisting fingers in his lap, and lied to the wide-eyed apprentice: "It's a summoning. We were expecting him. Go back to your work… What is it, for dinner? We'll have guests, of course—man and… horse."

"Dinner? It's…" The apprentice was a witchling girl, thick-haired, short and comely, with a small waist that accentuated breast and hips despite her shapeless beginner's robe. Her face was rosy-cheeked and round, and Randal wondered why he'd never noticed her, then banished the thought: He was betrothed, soon to be wed to Jihan, a source of power he never mentioned in this afflicted Mageguild.

The girl, composing herself with obvious effort, said, "Parrots, fleas, and squirrel bunions, m'lords Hazard—a stew, if it pleases."

"What?" snapped the harried First Hazard. Then, when the girl covered her mouth under widening eyes, continued: "Never mind the accursed menu, get out of here. And keep everyone else away until the dinner bell. Go on, girl, *go*!"

As she scurried backwards, a clomping of hoofbeats could be heard, followed by a sound like porcelain crashing on a marble floor.

Then, through the great double doors whence the girl had just fled, a horse and rider came.

The horseman hadn't dismounted; the horse had eyes of fiery intelligence. It pricked its ears at Randal and whickered once. Its coat was mottled, red and black and gray, but there was no mistaking it: It was the Trôs horse of his commander.

Through a fit of sneezing he miserably endured, Randal hurried forward, saying, "My lord commander, welcome." Snort. Sneeze. Sniffle. "Welcome."

Behind Randal, Cat the First Hazard uttered a curse which bounced around the room in a gray and sickly pall until, once Tempus had dismounted, the Trôs horse flattened its ears at the half-manifested ectoplasm and kicked it to pieces.

"Hazard," said the Riddler to Randal. "And Hazard," to Cat. "Would you leave us, First Hazard? My wizard and I need to talk."

"*Your* wizard," said Cat, still reflexively acting as powerful as he'd once been. Then his color drained as he remembered his circumstances and put two and two together. "Oh, yes. *Your* wizard. I see, my lord Tempus. Dinner will be at sundown, if you'd grace us. I'm sure we can find some… carrots… for your… mount."

Not a word about the desecration of the Mageguild by a horse, not a single additional attempt to regain control where all attempts were useless: Cat just chewed his lip.

Even though Randal's eyes were already watering, he felt a deep and abiding sadness for the handsome young First Hazard, although in former times he had wished, more than anything, to be possessed of so fine a form and face and bloodline as the Rankan who scurried out of his own sanctum so that Randal and his commander could confer in private.

What you were, not how you looked, mattered most these days in Sanctuary. And Randal was the only warrior-wizard in a town that soon would value warriors much more than wizards.

"You need me, commander?" Randal said, trying to speak clearly despite the clogging of his nose which proximity to the Trôs horse was causing.

"Yes, I do, Randal." Tempus dropped the Trôs' reins and it stood, ground-tied, while the big fighter approached the small, slight wizard, put an arm across his narrow shoulders, and walked with him toward the First Hazard's empty purple alcove.

"I need your help. I need your presence. I need your whole attention—now and always."

Randal felt pride course through him, felt himself grow inches taller, felt his neck flush with joy. "You have it, Riddler, now and always—you know that. I took the Sacred Band oath. I have not forgotten."

Niko had forgotten, seemingly, but not even that cloud could block out the light of Tempus' favor—not, at any rate, completely, Randal told himself.

"Nor have we. The Band sets out for Ranke soon, there to meet with Niko and trek east. We want you on that journey, Randal—as a Sacred Bander, purely."

"Purely? I don't understand. It was Niko who broke the pairbond, not I."

"This is not about Niko. It's about Jihan."

"Oh. *Oh.*" Randal slipped out from under the Riddler's arm, its weight suddenly unbearable. "That. The Froth Daughter. She… well, it wasn't my idea, the marriage. You must know that. I'm not even—good—with women. And she's… demanding." The words came out in a rush, now that there was finally someone to tell who would understand the problem. "I've put her off so far, explaining that I can't… you know… until we're wed. But I'll lose so much… power, and there's precious little of that around, these days. She says she'll make up for it, through her father, but I'm not god-bound, I'm bound in—"

"Other ways. I know. Randal, I think I've a solution that might serve to get you off the hook, if you'll help me."

"Oh, Riddler, I'd be *so* grateful. She's—no offense—more your sort of problem than mine. If you could just get me away from her, as long as it's not taken ill by the Band. I'll sneak away, I'll meet you in Ranke, I'll—"

"No sneaking away, Randal," said Tempus through lips that had parted to bare his teeth.

That smile was one all Stepsons knew. Randal said dumbly, "We can't… hurt her, sir. No sneaking away? Then how…?"

"With your permission, Randal, I'm going to woo her away from you—steal your bride from under your very nose."

"Per*mission!*" Oh, Tempus, I'd be so grateful—so everlastingly and abidingly grateful…"

"I have it, then?"

"What? Permission? By the Writ and the devils who love me, yes! Woo away! And may the—"

"Just your permission will be enough, Randal. Let's not bring any powers into this whose responses we can't foresee, let alone control."

*

The woman was walking alone in the garden while, within the manse beyond, a civilized uptown party was under way. Her hair was blond and curly, bound up in the fashion noblewomen in the capital had adopted this season: held in place with little golden pins hafted with likenesses of Rankan gods.

He came upon her from behind and had his left arm crooked around her neck in seconds, saying only, "Hold, I'm not here to hurt you," while within him a god who shouldn't have been there stirred to wakefulness, stretched, and urged otherwise.

Ignoring the obscene and increasingly attractive suggestions the war-god in his head was making, he gave the woman time to realize who held her.

It didn't take long: She wasn't a typical Rankan woman of blood; no man without Tempus' supernal speed and talent could have caught her unaware.

She stiffened and, every muscle tensed so that his body began taking the god's suggestions literally, pressed back against him—the first move toward putting him off balance, ready to use her own arena-training in weight, feint, and misdirection of attention to try to escape.

"Hold," he said again. "Or suffer the consequences, Chenaya."

"Pork you, Tempus," she gritted in a surprisingly ladylike voice unsuited to the content of her words. He could feel her hands ball into fists, then relax.

Behind him, people indoors chatted and clinked their goblets.

"We haven't time for that, unless you're ready." He put his free hand on her hip and spread it, moving it forward to press against her belly and slip downward, putting her in a hold she'd never come up against in a Rankan arena.

"Gods, you haven't changed, you bastard. If it's not my body—for which you'll pay more than it's worth, I assure you—what do you *want*?"

"I thought you'd never ask. It's a little matter of an attempt on Theron's life: yours, I believe—something about boarding the barge. Not a smart move for a member of a decidedly *ex*-royal family: not for you, not for Kadakithis, who'll share Theron's wrath if it's revealed who tried to feed him to the sharks, not for any of what's left of your line."

"Again, halfling, what do you want?"

Tempus had two answers on the tip of his tongue at that point in time, one of which had to do with the god in his head, who was whispering, *She is a woman, and women only understand one thing. She is a fighter. It's long since We've had a fighter. Give her to Us, and We'll be very grateful—and she will be Our willing servant. Otherwise, you cannot trust her.*

To the god in his head, he responded, *I can't trust You, never mind her.* To the woman, he said, "Chenaya, beyond the obvious, which we'll see about"—still holding her tightly enough with his elbow that a slight jerk would break her neck, he began to raise her voluminous white skirt from behind—"I want you to do something for me. There's a faction here that needs a woman whom the gods decree cannot be defeated. What I ask, I ask for Kadakithis, for the continuance of your bloodline, and for the good of Sanctuary. What the god asks, I'm afraid, is another matter." His voice was deepening, and into him was pouring all the long held passion of Sanctuary's Lord of Sack and Pillage, Blood and Death.

Chenaya was a fighter, and god-bound. He hoped, as he began to explain the business which had brought him here and the god in him got out of hand, that she'd understand.

*

The sentry at the tunnel entrance to Ratfall, Zip's base camp in Downwind, was gagged and flopping in a pool of his own blood.

Zip had slipped in it, then stumbled over the body in the dusk before he realized what he'd stumbled on: Sync's calling card—the sentry's hands and feet had been lopped off.

He thanked the god whose swampy altar he still frequented that he'd come home alone as he raised up on hands and knees and, with his belt dagger, made an end to the quivering sentry's agony.

3rd Commando tactics were meant to terrify; knowing this didn't make it any easier to keep from retching. Knowing that it wouldn't have taken more than a few minutes for the sentry to have completely bled out didn't help Zip's frame of mind: Sync's people were probably watching him from the adjacent ramshackle buildings Zip called his stronghold.

The 3rd Commando leader, Sync, said quietly from behind him: "Got a minute, sonny? Some people here want to talk with you."

The words weighed on Zip like burial stones and his own pulse threatened to choke him. Through the entire winter, Sync's rangers had never rousted him. The 3rd's leader had professed autonomy, pretended friendship, left Zip's PFLS to its own devices—as long as they followed an occasional suggestion from the 3rd's cold-blooded leader.

But there had been talk of an alliance then: before Theron had visited Ranke; before Zip's faction had recruited too many and developed factions within its own ranks; before some fools among them had captured Illyra, the S'danzo, and killed a S'danzo child; before an arrow aimed at Straton had been laid at Zip's doorstep; before Kama had left Zip's bed and taken up with Torchholder, the palace priest; before a falling out with Jubal over a slave girl Zip had liberated... Before things had gotten too damned complicated, because Zip couldn't hold the territory he'd gained across the White Foal, territory he'd never wanted, like he'd never wanted to be so damned visible (and thus targeted) as Sync's behind-the-scenes maneuvering had made him.

"*Talk* with me? You call this talk?" Zip's voice was shaking, but Sync wouldn't be able to tell whether it was with rage or fear. At that moment, Zip himself couldn't have said which. Blood was all around him, sticky and warm and smelling all too human: the corpse beside him had farted, and worse, once death loosed its bowels.

On his hands and knees in blood and shit, Zip was thinking that this was probably it—the death he'd earned, in circumstances he'd dreamed too often. He waited to see if it was Sync's blade from behind that would do the talking.

A sandal splashed in the blood by his hand. Sync's Rankan-accented voice said, "That's right, talk. If your man here had talked before he acted, he'd be alive now." A gloved hand reached down for him; above it, a bracer with the 3rd's unit device of a rearing horse with arrows in its mouth gleamed—silver, polished, spotless, and whispering of a cruelty so legendary that even the Rankans were afraid to use the 3rd Commando.

Even Theron, who'd come to the throne by way of their swords, if rumor was truth, wanted the 3rd disbanded or under a tight rein. That was why, some said, Tempus, who had created them, had got them back: No one else could control them. Left to their own, the 3rd would slaughter Rankan emperors one by one and auction the throne to the highest bidder: Zip had heard Sync and Kama joke about it when the three were drunk. Zip let Sync help him up, busy trying to wipe the sticky blood from his palms.

Zip didn't argue about the dead sentry. You didn't argue with Sync, not over something as immutable as the already dead. You saved it for the plans that could get you killed.

The rest of Sync's unit were emerging now: at least twenty fighters—the 3rd never traveled light.

The sight of Kama in her battle dress, with the 3rd's red insignia burned into hardened leather above her right breast and campaign designators scratched below it, made his stomach lurch.

Kama was unfinished business, would always be. Zip said, "So, here I am. Talk," and found his tongue unwieldy.

Around her, he realized (as his eyes accustomed themselves to something other than the dead man, handless and footless, who still flopped helplessly in his inner sight), were others from the uptown gangs who masqueraded as authority in Sanctuary: Critias, a covert actionist from the Sacred Band who seldom ventured forth in uniform and never in daylight; Straton, his wide-shouldered, witch-ridden partner; Jubal, black as Ischade's cloak and with a look on his face much blacker; Walegrin, the regular army's garrison commander and brother of the S'danzo whose child Zip's men had killed; and a blond woman he didn't know, who wore arena leathers and had a bird perched on her shoulder.

He ought to be wary, he realized. This sort of crowd hadn't gathered for something as mundane as his execution. But his eyes kept sliding back to Kama and trying to fit the persona of her father over the woman who'd taught him things about lovemaking he'd never dreamed were possible.

And then he realized why these uptown hotshots were down in Ratfall: Kama's father. Tempus' minions, all of these were, some by choice, some by duty, some by coercion. And none of them with a good word to say of Zip, except perhaps for the Riddler's daughter.

Fear sharpening his eyesight, Zip looked beyond the gathered luminaries to their troops, and farther: to where his rebels skulked. None of them would move to save him—the odds weren't good enough.

And neither Ratfall nor Zip were worth saving, not at the kind of price the 3rd Commando would exact, if the dead sentry was a good example.

And he was. They'd made sure of that, had his visitors.

As he took deep breaths and resolved to tell nothing to this corps of fancy fighters (including the Stepsons' chief interrogator, Strat), Zip realized that something was indeed worth saving here: Behind the men, in the long shed against which 3rd Commando regulars leaned with studied insolence, was a store of incendiaries purchased from the Beysib glassmakers: bottles in which were alchemical concoctions that, once their wicks were lit and the bottles thrown, exploded with such force that the shards and flame and concussion from even one such bottle could clear a street—or a palace hall.

With or without him, the revolution could continue, as long as the Beysib glassblowers took the PFLS's money and Ilsig will-to-fight held out.

So, having determined that he had something to lose, Zip said again, "Talk, I said. What do you think this is, an uptown dinner party?"

"No," said the woman he didn't know, the one with the hawkish bird upon her shoulder, "it's a revolutionary council… a trial, actually: yours."

*

When Kama came back from Ratfall, her eyes were red-rimmed and she was so disarrayed that she ran up Molin's back stairs, hoping to have the girls draw her a bath so she could get the Zip-smell off her and the straw out of her hair before Torchholder saw her.

But Molin was home: She could hear Torchholder's voice, and that of another Rankan, coming from the front rooms.

She froze in horror, realizing suddenly that she couldn't face him—not now, with her thighs sticky and her blood up; and all her father's heritage aroused in her so that she wanted nothing to do with the half-Rankan, half-Nisi who had saved her life, and whom she owed so much.

But was debt the same as love? Zip's faked and fated "trial" had broken her heart thrice over.

The outcome (the verdict of conditional acquittal) was assured, by Tempus' decree. Zip was the only one who hadn't known it.

It was the crudest thing she'd ever seen men do to another man. And she'd been a willing part of it, the operator in her fascinated by all she saw: by human emotion and its interplay; by the passions of those who'd lost loved ones, and face, trying to justify the one and regain the other—all because Kama's father, the great Riddler, had ridden down from Ranke, looked upon the doings of Sanctuary's puny mortals, and not been pleased.

Sometimes she hated Tempus more even than she hated the gods.

And so she'd stayed with Zip, after the others had left, to lick the nervous sweat from his fine young body and to wipe the confusion from his heart in the only way she knew.

Zip was… Zip, her aberration: a physical match such as Molin could never be. But that was all. She could never make it more, or let it make itself more, or let Zip convince her it could be more.

Zip needed help, that was all. And everyone was using him, dangling him this way and that. She felt sorry for him.

So she gave him comfort in the night. It was nothing.

Yet the memory sent her bolting from Molin's doorstep because Torchholder was too intelligent to be fooled by mumbled excuses or headaches; because Kama just couldn't fake it tonight.

She roamed night-hot streets, though she knew better, almost hoping that some pickpocket or zombie or Beysib would accost her. Like her father, when pushed too hard, Kama craved only open violence. She'd have killed a Stepson or a 3rd Commando ranger, one of her own, if any dared cross her this evening.

She stopped in at the Unicorn, half-hoping for a fight, but no one paid attention to her there.

She wandered back streets on a borrowed horse, letting it drift barracksward, until she realized that her mount had brought her to the White Foal Bridge.

Then, as she gave the mare its head and it crossed the river bridge, she began in earnest to weep.

It was Crit she wanted now—whether to hold him or kill him, she couldn't have said if her life depended on it. But Crit was, as Zip would say, 'old business,' and Crit had noticed that she'd stayed with Zip.

Maybe she'd stayed with Zip *because* of Crit, brushing hips with his partner; and because even that partner, Strat, had sought warmer company than Critias': Ischade, for warmth that Crit reserved to formed ranks and duty squadrons and the next covert operation on his docket.

So when the sorrel string-horse ambled toward Ischade's funny little gate, as if by habit, Kama brushed her eyes angrily with her forearm and blinked away her tears.

In her nostrils was the rank smell of the White Foal in summer, carrying its carrion to the sea, and the perfume of night-blooming flowers of the occult sort that Ischade grew here.

And the smell of heated horse: Two were stamping, reins tied to Ischade's gate, and one of those was Crit's big black. She recognized it by the star and snip as it turned its head to whicker softly to the mount she rode.

The mare under her gave a belly-shaking acknowledgment and she realized that the horse she rode, and his, were lovers.

Hating herself for resenting even that, for her confusion and her doubts, she dismounted, trying not to think at all.

And walked up to the vampire-woman's gate, and pushed it with a sweaty palm.

Perhaps she was meeting her doom here: Ischade had no reason to cut Kama the kind of slack she allowed Straton, and Crit because of their pairbond, and Kama's father because of some bargain whose specifics Tempus had never revealed.

If Crit was in there, Kama wanted to see him. She focused on that and nothing else.

Love sucks, she told herself, and wondered what he'd say.

She knocked upon Ischade's door, which was lit somehow, though no torch gleamed or candle flickered in its lamp, before she'd thought of an excuse to give. She could always say she needed to debrief.

If Crit was there. If it wasn't a trap. If the necromant wasn't into women this summer.

The door opened and a small and dusky figure stepped out, closing it behind her so that Kama was forced to retreat a pace, then take a step down the stoop's stairs.

That put them eye to eye. The eyes of Ischade were deeper than Kama's hidden grief for a child lost long ago on the battlefield and the man who'd refused to give her another chance.

"Yes?" said the velvet-voiced woman who held Strat in thrall.

Kama, who was more woman than she'd have chosen, looked deep into the eyes of the woman who was all any man who'd seen her had ever dreamed of wanting, and felt rough, unkempt, foolish.

"Crit's horse… Is it…? Is he…?"

"Here? The both. Kama, isn't it?" Ischade's dark eyes delved, narrowed just a fraction, then widened.

"It… I—I shouldn't have come. I'm sorry. I'll just go and…"

"There's no harm. And no peace, either," said the vampire-woman who seemed suddenly sad. "Not if your father has the say of it. You want him—Crit? Take care for what you want, little one."

And Kama (who had never known her mother and thought of other women as if she herself were a man) found her arms outstretched to Ischade for comfort, weeping freely, sobbing so deeply that nothing she tried to say came out in words.

But the necromant drew back with a hiss and a warding motion, a shake of her head and a blink that broke some spell or other.

Then Ischade whirled and was gone inside, though Kama hadn't seen the door open to admit her.

Suddenly alone with her tears on the doorstep of one of the most feared powers in Sanctuary, Kama heard words within: low words, some spoken by men.

Before the door could reopen, before Crit could see her weeping like a baby, she had to get out of here. She didn't mean to come here: she shouldn't have. She needed nobody: not her father; not his fighters; not Zip or Torchholder; and, most especially, not the Sacred Bander called Crit.

She'd run down the path and thrown herself up on her saddle before the door opened again.

Anything the man in the doorway might have shouted was drowned out by the mare's thundering hooves as Kama slapped her unmercifully with the reins, heading toward the Stepsons' barracks at a dead run.

There was nothing Crit could tell her that she wanted to hear—except perhaps why she could forgive Zip, who had betrayed her and tried to pin Strat's attempted murder on her, when she couldn't forgive Crit, who had wanted to marry her and have a child with her.

*

Tasfalen's uptown estate had once been luxurious and fine, the centerpiece of one of Sanctuary's most exclusive neighborhoods.

Now it stood alone, blackened and charred but whole, while all around it skeletal remains of burned-out homes teetered for blocks, frameworks leaning on lumps of fused brick, so that occasionally a charcoaled timber snapped of its own weight and came crashing down to break an eerie silence that spread from here to the uptown house where a sorcerous pillar of fire had once raged, and beyond.

Not even rats ran these streets at night, since the pillar of flame had cleansed an uptown house and all the witchery that once had centered in its velvet-hung bedroom.

Tempus had called a meeting here, across the street from Tasfalen's front door, in the dead of night—a meeting of those concerned, once all his preparations had been made.

The sleepless veteran called the Riddler was the only one unaffected by the hours he and his had kept this week in Sanctuary.

Critias, who'd borne the brunt of delegated tasks, weaved on his feet with exhaustion as he set torches in the rubble of the house across from Tasfalen's. Had the light been better, the black circles under his eyes would have told a clearer tale of what he'd been through and what it cost him to petition Ischade for leave to do what tonight must be done here.

Straton, Crit's partner, worked silently beside him, unloading ox thighs rich with fat from a snorting chestnut who didn't like its burden, and oil in child-sized stoneware *rhytons*, and placing all on a makeshift plinth exactly opposite Tasfalen's door.

Tempus watched his Stepsons work without a word, waiting for the witch to show. Ischade had decreed this meeting be at midnight: necromants will be necromants. She was crucial to this undertaking, so Randal said.

Tempus hardly cared. The god was in him fierce and strong, making everything seem fire-limned and slow: his task force leader; the witch-ridden Stepson, Strat; the horses bearing sacrificial burdens. If he hadn't remembered that he'd thought it mattered, that he'd felt need to leave here owing nothing, he'd have left this stone unturned.

But Ischade owed him this favor—if it really was one. And Tempus, in turn, owed a debt he was loath to carry: a debt to the Nisibisi witch last seen behind that ward-locked door across the street.

Tasfalen's door. It had not opened since the pillar of flame had scoured the neighborhood about it. What might come out of there, not even Ischade was certain. Powers had convened to cleanse the ground here, but stopped just short of the house. Powers that no one thought would ever work together had taken a hand to bar that door—Ischade's sort of powers, and others from deeper hells; Stormbringer's primal fury, and thus those from the sort of heaven Jihan's father ruled.

Or thus, at any rate, Tempus understood it. The god in him understood something different—something of passion inbound and lust unreleased.

There was a *something* in there all right, the god was telling him: something very hungry and very angry.

Whatever it was—Nisibisi witch, a ravening ghost thereof, a demon entrapped, a shard of Nisi power globe—it hadn't survived in there since winter's end on stored foodstuffs and the occasional mouse.

If it was Roxane, behind Ischade's iron wards that not even the rip in magic's fabric could weaken, then the Unbinding would have to be carefully done. If it was Something Else, Tempus was prepared to give it battle: he'd once fought Jihan's own storm-cold father to a draw over matters in which he had less stake.

Snapper Jo scuttled up to the Trôs horse by which Tempus stood, the fiend's knuckles nearly dragging on the ground, its snaggle teeth gleaming in the torchlight: "Sire," it grunted. "See her? Snapper can't tell." In its distress, the fiend ramped like a bear: side to side, side to side. "Mistress won't like, won't like… Snapper go now?"

"Did you place the stone, Snapper?" The stone in question was a bluish gem, crazed and fractured, that Ischade had given Crit. For what payment, when the stone would help release the enemy witch (and perhaps release Straton, too, for duty to the east), Tempus hadn't asked.

And Crit never made excuses. But there'd been no soldierly cursing, no banter between the Stepsons here this evening. When Randal had come by briefly, to say Jihan would attend, there had been none of the usual teasing of the mage that passed for fellowship: Strat hadn't even called Randal 'Witchy-ears.'

Tempus knew he was pushing matters, but he had his reasons. And the god, risen in him, was all the sign he needed that his instinct wasn't wrong.

A part of this outrageous enterprise (the freeing of whatever lurked behind Tasfalen's doors) Tempus undertook to right a balance out of whack. This was something none of those about him sensed, but Niko, the absent Stepson, would have understood: Tempus labored now for *maat,* for equilibrium in a town that teetered toward anarchy; and for the Stepsons, who soon might go where Nisibisi magic was still strong and had better not, with a debt outstanding to a witch of Nisi blood.

But the greatest part of this seemingly evil deed—that Randal had begged him not to undertake and that had troubled Ischade enough to bring her here—Tempus did because of Jihan, and her father, Stormbringer; and a marriage that, if consummated, would bind a weather god to Sanctuary that no little thieves' world could or should contain.

Three hundred years and more of kicking around this world of god-inspired battlefields and wizard-won wars had taught Tempus that instinct was his only guide, that any man's sacrifice went unappreciated unless it was to propitiate a god, and that the only satisfaction worth having was wrested from the deed itself—was in the process of accomplishment, never in the result.

So the sacrifice he was about to make (not the sacrifice of laying the ox thighs on the oil and sending smoke up to heaven, but the sacrifice of his own peace of mind) would go unremarked by men. But he would know. And the god would know. And the powers who tended the balance which expressed itself in fate and weather would know.

How Stormbringer, Jihan's father, would react, only Jihan would know.

A movement caught his eye, and the god's eye within him knew it female. His scrotum drew up, ready to face Jihan in all her insatiable glory.

But it was Ischade, not Jihan, who came.

Tempus felt a twinge of distress, of uncertainty—something he'd rarely felt in all these years. Could Jihan ignore his invitation? His challenge? The power in the game he played? Could Stormbringer have gotten wind of Tempus' intention and mixed in? Tricking a god wasn't easy. But then, neither was tricking the Riddler.

Randal had assured him Jihan had said she'd be here. Tempus knew she thought she was involved with Randal to make him jealous, to make him fey, to make him come to heel. The question was, however, whether Jihan herself understood what she did and why: that Stormbringer had turned his daughter's eyes toward Randal.

Tempus wondered suddenly whether it would matter to Jihan if she did know. She wasn't human, any more than Ischade, so slight and yet so full of menace, or Roxane.

Jihan was still learning how to be alive; womanhood lay heavy and confusing on her, as it didn't on the witches and the accursed women who fought the witches of blood.

Ischade, no bigger than a child to Tempus, came striding up swathed in black, her face like a magical moon on midsummer's eve, her eyes wide as the hells she guarded.

"Riddler," she breathed, "are you sure?"

"Never," he chuckled. "Not about anything."

And he saw the necromant draw back, sensing the god co-habiting with him, a god the fighters called Lord Storm, whose name had been translated into more languages than the thieves' world knew, but always meant the same: the nature of man to fight and kill for lust and territory. On bad days, Tempus thought that the god who dogged him, chameleon-like, adapting by syncretism to different wars in different lands, was merely an excuse his mind made up—a way to hang his excesses and his sins on others, a faceless repository for all the blame for every death he'd caused.

But seeing Ischade's reaction to the god high in him made him realize it wasn't so.

The necromant took a step forward resolutely, cocked her head, licked her lips, and said, "You jest with me? When He is here?" Then, when Tempus didn't respond, she made a warding sign, withdrawing with a mutter: "Have your witch loosed, then. There's less trouble over there than is right here, with you."

And my fighter, Strat? he or the god wanted to ask, but did not. You didn't *ask* Ischade, you negotiated. Tempus wasn't in a position to negotiate, right now.

Unless…

"Ischade, wait," he called. Or the god did. And when she came close, he leaned down and let Enlil, the storm god of the armies, whisper in the ear of the necromant who commanded all the partly dead and restless dead who never went to Sanctuary's gods.

He tried not to listen to what the god said or what the necromant replied, but it was a bargain they made which concerned him—concerned the flesh of his flesh and the soul of his Stepson, Strat.

When he straightened up, the frail, pale creature touched his forearm and looked into his eyes. For a moment he thought he saw a tear there, but then decided it was the brightness that passion lent to necromants and their kind.

He could survive what the god had promised Ischade—or at least he thought he could.

It might be interesting to find out… if, of course, Stormbringer didn't kick his ass from one dimension to another for meddling in the Froth Daughter's affairs before he had time to make good on Enlil's promise to spend a night with the necromant.

Disconcerted, as Ischade disappeared—literally—into shadows, he mounted the Trôs and stroked its neck for comfort: his comfort, not its.

Up north at the Hidden Valley stud farm, a calmer life still beckoned. If he could only be content to do it, he could raise horses and a new generation of fighters to hold the line against the northern wizards with his friend Bashir.

But no matter how he craved a different life at times like these, when battle lines of uncertain composition were drawn, with stakes not so simple as life or death, and opponents whose strength was not corporeal, the god would never let him rest.

Torchholder, the half-Nisi priest, had told him all his curse and god-bond were merely habit. It might have been true on the day the priest said it, or true to a priestly eye; but it wasn't true here and now.

And here and now was always where Tempus was, not off somewhere in the realm of Greater Good or Mortal Soul or Eternal Consequence. He'd lost the ability to determine greater good, if there was one; his mortal soul he'd given up on long ago. And as for eternal consequence—he was its embodiment.

So when Jihan finally made her entrance, glowing softly to his god-shared eye (her muscular, lithe form still more feminine than any mortal girl's; her waist too small and breasts too pert and thighs too sleek below scale-armor no human hand had forged), he was more than ready to be just what he was, to lay upon her the consequence of her dalliance, of her games, and of her fate.

She came up to within an arm's length of the Trôs and it backed a pace: It remembered the way she used to curry it until its hide showed bare of hair.

He slipped off its back as her throaty voice, arch and full of childish vanity, said, "You wished to see me, Tempus? I can't imagine why. I did not invite *you* to my wedding."

"Because," he said, reaching out for her with a quick grab and a step forward, "there isn't going to be one."

His hand closed on her arm as hers grabbed for his belt.

They struggled there, and he dropped her by thrusting a leg between her thighs and kicking her balance out from under her.

It was a signal.

As Jihan cursed and raged and kicked beneath him among the charcoal and the bricks, Critias and Strat and Randal began the sacrifice of ox and oil, to pacify the god, while Ischade did whatever Ischade must do to release her wards.

Ravishing the Froth Daughter wasn't easy: She was as strong as he and just as agile.

He had counted on the lust they shared and the play-rapes in their past to turn her pique into passion and her body into an instrument he could play for best result.

And something of the sort transpired. Although who raped whom, he wasn't certain, when they rolled half-naked in the ruins, unconcerned with anything about them, while a witch cast spells and soldiers spoke ancient rituals and Randal, the Tysian wizard, presided over a fiery sacrifice meant to set whatever lurked in Tasfalen's free at last.

Since Tempus was, in his way, that self-same sacrifice to Stormbringer, father of Jihan; and since Jihan's legs were around him and her teeth sunk firmly in his neck; and since the god within him loved the rape-game and Jihan as well—and since Jihan was by then wreaking enough havoc upon his flesh to make him glad the god was in him to bear the brunt of it, he missed the spectacle taking place across the street at Tasfalen's.

As a matter of fact, the fireworks inside his head as the god and he and Jihan and her father came together blotted out the simulacrum of last winter's pillar of fire rising up to heaven from Tasfalen's home, which had been left unscathed then.

Later he was told that, as the pillar rose, the doors and windows of Tasfalen's flew open of their own accord and something fiery—something with huge bird's wings—flew out. And flapped and circled high above the place where Tasfalen lived.

And disappeared into the smoke which billowed everywhere: too much smoke to credit to burned ox thighs and jugs of oil; smoke that went up from, or down to, the chimney of Tasfalen's house, as if the light spewing from every window was the light of something burning bright within.

What burned in Tempus was a light unto itself.

Jihan was his match in all things physical. When they lay quiet, able to hear more than their own breathing and see more than their own souls, she whispered to him, with her head buried in his neck, "Oh, Riddler, what took you so long to come and reclaim me? How could you do this to me? And to Randal?"

"I'll take care of Randal. He'll understand. I want you, Jihan—I want you with me. I…" This was hard to say but he had to say it; not just for Randal's sake, but for the sakes of all who put their faith in him. "I… need you, Jihan. We all do. Come north and east and everywhere with me—see this world, not just its armpit."

"But my father…" The Froth Daughter's eyes glowed as red as the light he was just beginning to notice from across the street.

"Will he not honor his daughter's wish?"

Jihan's arms locked around his neck in a grip not Tempus nor death itself could break, and she pulled him down to her. "Then, Riddler, let us show Him that it *is* my wish."

He wasn't sure that, even with the war-god to help, he could manage to prove himself again so soon. But the god was, thanks be to Him, as insatiable as she and, though Stormbringer began to rumble and to shake the ground in pique (so that soon they thrashed and rolled in a downpour that quenched the fire on the altar and the fire in Tasfalen's house), it was too late for Jihan's father to intervene.

Tempus had wooed Jihan, and won her, and there was nothing even Stormbringer could do to change the Froth Daughter's mind once it was made up.

*

Zip couldn't believe the trouble he was in, forced into an alliance with so many who had good reason to wish him dead.

Jubal's hawkmasks escorted him out to the Stepsons' barracks to show him around. At least he didn't have to live there—yet.

The deal was, as he understood it, that he spearhead some addled alliance made up of all his known enemies and some he hadn't known he had: One, a blue-blooded bitch named Chenaya, had more balls than half the mercenaries lounging on the whitewashed parade grounds and she'd made it clear that she didn't expect the pecking order to hold for long unless she was at the head of it.

Heads tended to get lopped off in Sanctuary, he'd told her, with an exaggerated bow and outstretched hand meant to indicate that she could precede him into any grave, anytime, anyplace.

But Chenaya was some sort of Rankan noble, and didn't realize Zip was being snide. She'd just assumed he habitually bowed and scraped like any other Wriggly, and let him hand her up into her fancy wagon, telling him she'd see him later.

He would have felt better about all the changes if Jubal had said one word to him about settling matters, man to man; or if the Rankan Walegrin hadn't looked at him as if Zip were a goat staked out to lure a wolf; or if Straton wasn't twice his weight and conspicuously absent when Zip was shown the ropes at the barracks.

Yeah, he could hold out in the one-time slaver's estate-turned-fortress. Yeah, it beat the offal out of Ratfall. But somehow, he didn't think he was going to live to move his rabble in here.

And he didn't think the 3rd Commando was going to quit this town, where it was the most powerful single element save gods, wizardry, and Tempus, once the Stepsons were packed off to the capital.

Sync, the 3rd's line commander, was nobody's fool. And Sync was looking at him funny while whistling up a mount for Zip from the string herd and showing him how to put a war-horse through its paces.

The day was bright, and the horse was sweating, and Zip was riding around the training ring with Sync like some Rankan kid with his daddy when an arrow whizzed by his head close enough to nick his ear.

He cursed, dove off the horse's wrong side, and rolled toward the fence while Sync bawled orders and men went running about in a fine display of concern.

Zip went after the arrow and found it.

If it wasn't the same one that had been aimed at Straton from a rooftop last winter, it was a perfect copy.

"Zip, that arrow doesn't prove Strat—or any of the Stepsons—are behind this," Sync said, a stalk of hay between his teeth, an hour later as they walked their horses while men came in, sweating and dirty, giving desultory reports of no progress and grinning at Zip (the only Ilsig in the camp) with cold amusement in their eyes.

"Sure. I know. Probably somebody wants me to think they are. No sweat." And he half-believed what he was saying. If Strat wanted a piece of Zip, the Sacred Bander would take it with show and ceremony, lots of ritual, the whole exotic Band code enforced so that murder wouldn't be murder once it had been sanctified by the handy murderer's god.

The Sacred Band had an altar dedicated to that purpose, out in back of the training arena.

Arrow in hand, Zip walked over the altar with his new mount, thinking about making some kind of statement by kicking the piled stones apart.

Then he changed his mind, swung up on the horse, and loped it out of there.

He didn't really care who'd tried to kill him. From the talk he'd heard while in the barracks, neither did the Stepsons: they were more concerned over their walls and the weather.

He'd known that this whole business of putting him at the head of some cease-fire coalition was just a roundabout way of executing him.

Ritual execution, political style, wasn't a nice way to die. But then, Zip had killed enough to know there wasn't one.

He rode all day, through the Swamp of Night Secrets, thinking about his chances (slim) and his alternatives (none).

He was dead the minute he announced he wouldn't play the game; if he was dead a week or two later by pretending to play along, it was a week or two of living he wouldn't have otherwise.

Not a great shot, but it was the only one he had. He didn't have anywhere to run. He had too many enemies without adding Tempus to the list. If he diverged from the "arrangement," he'd have no chance at all of surviving. It would be open season on Zip—for professionals.

He had one hole card, maybe, in Kama. He couldn't imagine she'd have gotten intimate with him for any kind of revenge.

He wanted to see her; but by the time he got out of the swamp, the sun was going down and he knew he'd better head for Ratfall.

Although Sync had proved Zip wasn't safe in Downwind, *somebody* had proved he wasn't safe out at the barracks—and he'd known for a long time that he wasn't safer anywhere than his own abilities could make him.

So he went to ground in Ratfall, detouring only long enough to lay the arrow that had nicked his ear on a little pile of stones down at the White Foal River's edge.

He used to bring blood sacrifices here—to something. He wasn't sure what. But it liked the offerings. He thought maybe, if it liked him enough for bringing it presents, it might take offense at whoever had shot the arrow (which still had his own blood on it) and do its servant a favor.

Because without some god's help, a piece of alley-grime like Zip didn't have a whore's chance of making it through another Sanctuary night unmolested.

Tempus had been right: Sanctuary was for lovers, not fighters, this season.

Chapter 11: Lemnian Deed

Rainbows sparkled and doubled, then faded as clouds beset the sun. A light drizzle fell on the swampy plain as the Sacred Band of Stepsons struck for higher ground. Cavalry two by two and wagons single file, they picked their way with care through axle-high yellow grass hiding soggy turf.

The Trôs horse between Tempus' legs was in fine fettle, jigging and snorting his primacy to the black stud Niko rode at his right. A marsh wind blew salty and sharp. Late swarms of insects rose in clouds, swirling round the horses, then blew away like milkweed on the breeze. Niko waved them away from his face.

A river must be near, perhaps the Strymon—or should be, if they were skirting the plains of Therma. But geography changes as harbors silt up, and Tempus had never come this way in former times, when Thrace ruled here.

They didn't find the river that day, and pushed onward to a likely camp in the hills, away from marsh grass and insects and bog, where they could drink fresh water and see anything approaching. Or anyone.

Forty-eight men and laden wagons take time to settle in: find firewood, pitch tents, start cook-fires, light torches and see to the horses.

Alone, Tempus rode the Trôs up to the highest vantage point and looked north. He thought he saw a town or city: Possibly Chaetae, or maybe Physca, gleaming in the sunset, still days away. By now they should have passed a town or two, met Mygdones, Thracians, Macedonians, perhaps even Pelasgians… depending on who controlled this land these days.

Randal had said they were still south of Chaetae and Tempus had no reason to doubt the mage. So he turned his horse to ride back down and then he saw them: far to the south, riders in strict formation, coming across the marshy flats.

Tempus sought out Niko, who had Randal and the youngest Stepsons with him. Niko's face was grim. Randal's bony shoulders were hunched. Arton held Kouras by the arm and Kouras had blood smeared across his fuzzy upper lip, more blood dripping from his nose. The Theban Lysis stood with legs widespread, his hand on his short sword's pommel, looking behind the little group, toward the encampment.

"What happened here, Niko?" Tempus asked.

"Kouras offended the big Lemnian straggler, Dikti. She hit him. Arton grabbed Kouras before he countered. Randal stepped between Dikti and Kouras. Breisis came for Dikti. Lysis came for me." Niko shrugged, his voice barely audible.

From the tents Critias and Straton were approaching rapidly, Charon between them, gesticulating. No straggler women were with them.

"And this requires the entire senior staff? Why did Dikti hit him? Did she have cause?" With Kouras in the mix, anything was possible.

Yanking on Kouras' arm, Arton said apologetically, "Commander, it's easy to offend Dikti, everyone knows that. Kouras just asked her—"

"—to give me a toss." Kouras shook off Arton's grip. "What's wrong with that? She's a woman. I'm a man. I was done with my work…" Kouras fought a grin.

"She's a paired fighter, Kouras," Niko said, deadly cold. "What would she want with you?"

"Niko, Commander…" Randal raised both hands, signaling for room to speak. "I really think Kouras meant no harm. I saw the whole thing. This Dikti overreacted."

Only Lysis kept silent; the Theban was watching his father come their way with Strat and Critias.

"Lysis," Tempus said, "perhaps you'll explain to Kouras about 'Lemnian Deeds.'"

"Me? I was… Yes, Commander." Flushing, the Theban youth turned to face Kouras. "Kouras, the women of the isle of Lemnos found that their men were sneaking off to lie with Thracians on the mainland, so they killed their Lemnian men and lived on their island manless until Jason and his crew came visiting, or so the story goes."

Niko said, "Dikti might kill you too, Kouras, if you bother her again. And she'll be justified. Stay away from her. Stay out of trouble with her—and with the others. Your god can't protect you here."

"Niko," Tempus said, "Charon will handle this. I need you with me."

Far off, thunder growled, then abated; southern wall-clouds flickered weakly.

When Charon reached them, the Theban warrior-priest took stiff-backed Kouras off to one side.

"Lysis, bring my black," Niko told the young Theban as Critias and Straton came up, determinedly straight-faced and solemn.

"Creon? He's just been fed—"

"*Creon*?" Niko echoed.

"The black stud." Lysis blushed, chagrined. "*Hipparch,* sir, that's what we all call your horse. He's a gift from Harmony, our goddess. Creon was a king of Thebes … It seemed fitting." Lysis was taking backward steps: he knew Niko's temper, that soft voice, the distant eyes.

"Don't name the warhorses, henceforth. But yes, then, bring 'Creon.'"

"Come on, Arton. Help me." Lysis went running, Arton by his side.

Critias watched them go, while Straton palmed his smirk. Crit said, "Commander, Niko, Randal: life and glory. Anything we can do?"

"About Kouras? No. About Dikti?" Tempus didn't care. "That's up to you, Critias; you recruited her."

"Dikti," Straton said, "takes offense if the wind blows wrong."

Randal offered, "Arton and Lysis and Kouras… those boys all trained under me. I might be able to help… if you wish."

"That's right, they did. I'd forgot." Straton scratched his beard. "By Enlil's longest leg then, Randal, *do* something about Kouras. Cast a spell on him and strike him humble. Can you do that, mageling? before I geld him myself?"

Randal flushed and promised what aid he could.

The five of them waited there for Niko's horse as dusk came on, trying to make light of Kouras and his problems, talking of billeting Stepsons and the order of the watch; looking on as Charon worked his Theban wiles on his young rightman and Tempus' Trôs horse pawed the ground.

Finally Tempus said, "There's a force approaching from the south. About the right size to be ours. But not necessarily ours. I saw them from the hilltop, where the spring is, before the sun set."

"Where's that horse of mine?" Niko wondered.

"About time the rest of us showed up," Straton said.

"I'll send out scouts at dawn, to make sure those coming *are* ours," Crit said.

"By the Writ, that's good news," Randal said. "I mean… if it's them. I could fly over, under cover of darkness, Riddler, to see what's to be seen…"

So Tempus sent Randal on eagles wings to learn what force approached. Charon, and then Lysis with Niko's stallion, arrived from two different directions. Arton veered off to join Kouras.

As Niko swung up on his horse, he said, "Crit, you tell the Band their story tonight. One in which I have no part. Tell them about that gutter-snipe Zip, and the Riddler's daughter, and that witch of Straton's. Make these young lions think twice about the consequences of their behavior, about Sacred Band ethos, and what goes wrong when a Stepson starts breaking rules…"

Chapter 12: Wake of the Riddler

Tempus was gone from Sanctuary, taking his Stepsons and the Rankan 3rd Commando with him, leaving only outcasts and dross behind.

In the wake of the Riddler's departure, the town seemed more changed than it should have been because one man (called variously Tempus, the Riddler, the Black, and more scatological appellations) had gathered his private army of less than a hundred and ridden north. Sanctuary seemed emptied, drained, frightened, and confused.

It cowered like a snow rabbit run to barren ground and surrounded by wolves. It shivered and sniffed the breeze, as if undecided which way to run. It hunkered down in desperate paralysis, seeming to dream of better days while the cold spring wind blew wet promises of life inland from the sea and the wolves skulked closer, red tongues lolling from slavering jaws.

Among fetid streets on this spring evening in question, militias are keeping order, stamping around corners with deliberate tread. Whores whisper rather than croon in their doorways. Drunks stumble along whitewashed walls, afraid to stagger boldly in gutters where beggars lurk with ready blades. And the wind comes in off the uneasy ocean with a chuckle on its breath: Tempus, his Stepsons, and the 3rd Commando have left the town to its fate, ridden off in disgust to new adventures capable of resolution, wars winnable, and glory attainable. Sanctuary is not only doomed but shunned by its last best hope, the Riddler and his fighters.

The wind thinks nothing of whipping the town vacant, of chilling its nobles to the bone, of locking the neutered sorcerers in their Mageguild and the impotent soldiers in their barracks. The wind is Sanctuary's own, wind of chaos, gale of gloom.

Spring has never felt so ominous in the Maze as it does this season, where the first rough gusts blow detritus worse than rotting rinds and discarded rags through the streets. The sea wind rattles against the plate armor of the Rankan army regulars, clustered in fours as they police what can't be policed. It flaps the dark cloaks of Jubal the slaver's beggars, his private corps of cold enforcers who sell protection now at stalls and bars where Stepsons used to trade. It keens toward uptown and beats on the barred windows of the Mageguild where necromancers fear the unleashing of their dead now that magic has lost its power, more even than they fear the wrath of whores whose youth-and-beauty spells have worn away.

And the wind sneaks uptown, where what is left in Sanctuary that is noble tries to carry on, have its parties amidst the rubble left by warring factions of the various militias, by witches and warlocks, vampires and zombies, ghosts and demons, worshipers and gods.

This wind is of the sort you may remember, coming out of a gray wet sky which makes an end to boundaries and hides horizons. Sounds seem to come from nowhere, go nowhere. There is no distance and no proximity, no future and no past. There is no warmth, even from the one beside you.

When you reach out to take a hand for comfort, that hand is clammy as the grave. On such a day, the stirring of life these gusts portend is only legend, as if the wind itself is here to reconnoiter the very earth and then decide if the world deserves another spring.

Or not.

Down by the docks, alone, Critias ponders that question. Do the beggar armies deserve the warm sun on their face? Do the vampire's undead, over in Shambles Cross, need the kiss of sunlight? Can there be a bright morning for the mages, barricaded inside their fortress where dusk always reigns? Will Zip and his night-crawlers among the Peoples Front for the Liberation of Sanctuary tip the balance for or against the seasons' change? And does it matter if spring ever comes to this blighted thieves' world again?

For Tempus has gone, turned his back on everything and everyone. No more eloquent an omen could be taken from a dozen slaughtered lambs with jaundiced livers or the birth of twins joined at the lips.

Gone and left… what? Left Crit, is what. Left Crit in putative charge of the ungovernable, so that Crit's partner, Straton, had turned and walked away without a word. Gone somewhere was Strat—and not to the departed armies, either. No, Strat hadn't gone upcountry with the Riddler or west to meet Niko and thence embark on a secret sortie for Theron, emperor of Ranke. Strat, Crit was sure, had gone another way: down to embrace the darkness that was his lover, Ischade, the vampire who held sway in Shambles Cross; down to the White Foal River where corpses floated till they waked. Down into hell and this time it wasn't Crit's fault, but Tempus', who usually had more concern for the faring of his men.

But there'd been no reasoning with Tempus, who'd pulled the Stepsons out en masse, and the 3rd Commando with them, leaving the town to its own devices.

Leaving Crit to take responsibility for fair and all. For *un*-fair and all. So there was a new pecking order in beleaguered Sanctuary, and one which was 'fair' only to the extent that it insulted and imperiled everyone, while satisfying no one.

Put it down, Crit told himself, to the foul humor that caused Tempus to be called "the Black." Crit had the rest of the year to meet Theron's decree of a unified, pacified Sanctuary. If he couldn't manage it, Theron had promised to send the Rankan army here in force: a soldier in every hut and a fist in every face.

Not that Crit cared about the town per se. No, he didn't. But he cared about his reputation, about not failing, about always doing what he was charged to do.

Even though for the first time in his life he'd truly argued, threatened to quit, to mutiny, to bolt, when Tempus had charged him with imposing order where order had never been, Critias couldn't turn away from a job unfinished. No matter what it cost.

In short order it had cost him his only friends here: Straton, his right-side partner and Sacred Band brother; Kama, the Riddler's daughter, abandoned in Sanctuary along with those others who had most displeased her father; Marc, the weapon-smith who'd been his liaison with townies such as Zip; and Zip himself, leader of the Popular Front for the Liberation of Sanctuary (PFLS) and third-shift commander, who now looked upon Crit as the enemy because Crit was at the top of Sanctuary's military reporting chain.

Where he'd never craved to be, and where Strat had struggled so hard to land.

Shaking his head, Crit started as moisture that had condensed on his unkempt hair spattered his brow and cheeks. In nondescript dockside garb, he was waiting for a contact. Doing what he knew how to do because Crit was a shadow mover, not an empire shaker. Tempus had left him with a shattered infra-structure he needed to fuse, somehow, into a working whole. Or lose. Fail. Crit knew how to do everything required of a soldier but that—he didn't know how to fail. He'd never learned. Was constitutionally incapable of learning, Strat used to say. Crit missed Strat like food and water. He missed Kama less, but still loved her. And still hated the hierarch she'd taken up with: Molin Torchholder, the politicized priest of a pantheon alien to this Ilsig soil.

All the Rankan conquerors of this Ilsigi town of Sanctuary, and the Beysib invaders who had come after (and made an uneasy alliance by marriage with the Rankan governor, Prince Kadakithis), mistook the townspeople here for the sort that were governable. And Crit was now responsible to see that at least the appearance of governance was instituted and maintained here, where the balance between gods and magic had suddenly crumbled and all that remained to do was rule Sanctuary by force of arms.

As commander-in-chief of the policing forces, Critias was responsible to the prince/governor Kadakithis (who was answerable to Theron and might lose more than his palace if the emperor's demands weren't met); responsible to Kadakithis' Beysib consort, Shupansea (who wasn't even human, but some sort of fish-woman from across a forbidden a sea); responsible to Kama (because she was the Riddler's daughter and, by all the gods that loved the armies, Crit's woman more than Molin's).

Kama had conceived a child with Critias and they'd lost it on a battlefield. Since then, she'd found whatever man she could bed whose identity would be most hurtful to Crit when he found out. Which he always did, because she was her father's daughter and thought that women's ways were for lesser creatures, the way her father thought that men's limits applied only to his enemies.

Crit wanted more than anything to find Strat and simply leave, go up to Ranke and plead his case to Theron, get a new commission from the emperor. He was wasted here. Only Tempus knew what Critias had done to deserve this fate.

But here he was, with the rest of the unloved, unvalued, and unwanted: with Strat; with Kama; with Randal, a warrior-mage who was the lesser half of a broken Sacred Band pair; with Gayle, the only 3rd Commando whom Tempus had told to tarry.

And with those they'd hoped to leave behind: Ischade, the vampire; Janni the Stepson's half-reconstituted ghost; Snapper Jo, the fiend who had tended bar at the Vulgar Unicorn; and (uptown somewhere among the hellish ruins of last winter's incomprehensible war of magic) whatever was left of Haught, the Nisibisi mageling, and of Roxane, the Nisibisi witch.

Strat had said—the only thing Crit's partner *had* said about the matter—that Tempus had flat run out of nerve, turned tail and fled, leaving Critias holding the bag. The very bag that Strat wanted so badly in his grip, Crit had thought but hadn't said.

Waiting alone, with no backup (because with Strat gone to Ischade there wasn't a single man he'd trust at his back), down on the slippery dockside hoping his contact would show soon, Crit had had far too much time to brood.

He knew it: he knew himself. For the kind of subterranean work Crit was trained to do, self-knowledge was a prerequisite. If it weren't, his distress over Strat and the horrid triangle of the two of them and the vampire might well have killed him before this. Might kill him yet, if he became too distracted by it.

Crit had a job to do. Lots of jobs. He'd made sure of that. He couldn't afford too much time for reflection. This task before him wasn't going to be simple, but he needed to occupy his mind with something besides the conundrum of his partner. Tonight, he would concentrate on finding and restoring Tasfalen, whose entire noble family was missing and had been missing far too long. Torchholder wanted the popinjay found. Or wanted Crit killed in the finding, so that there'd be no rival of consequence for Kama's affections by the time Molin did whatever he was planning about his current wife.

Critias wasn't mistaking Molin Torchholder: in the priest's mind, this was a suicide mission he'd forced on Crit, knowing Crit wouldn't delegate this sort of task to what men he had available. Zip's half-tame militia wasn't good for much but swaggering and street fights on their night shift; Walegrin's barracks of day-soldiers soldiered well enough, but knew nothing of covert means; and Crit wouldn't ask at the Mageguild—even with the Stepsons' mage, Randal, in there, the price of magical aid in Sanctuary was always far too high.

So that left only Jubal's thugs, one of whom Crit awaited. Jubal's faceless horde of enforcers would spit out one with a face tonight, and that one would lead Crit to Tasfalen.

Once Crit had verified the continued existence of the noble (or lack of it—a corpse would do), he could get Torchholder off his back. And see Kama.

For Crit was about ready to force an end to that particular problem: either bring Kama back with him from the palace, to take up her rightful place in what was left of the Stepsons' barracks, or use her affair with Molin to blackmail the priest.

He wasn't sure which he liked better, but he liked both alternatives enough to bare his teeth in a humorless grin as he waited. And waited. And waited. He stood. He sat. He paced. He leaned. He heard his horse nickering, then pawing the cobbles. He checked its tack, stroked its nose. Strat's bay horse would have evoked the nicker he'd heard, but Crit didn't see the bay horse anywhere.

Just as well: Strat's bay mount made him nervous. Made everybody nervous who didn't like reincarnated horses with spots on their withers through which a man could glimpse hell itself if the light was right.

Because of the nicker, Crit realized he didn't want to see Strat right now. Not until he'd solved the problem of Kama and Torchholder. Not now, when the gray sky and the gray buildings and the gray dockside melded with the gray horse Tempus had left him, to take the sting out of deserting him.

The gray Trôs horse was a prize, one of the best from the Stepsons' stock farm up at Wizardwall. Worth more than a block of the Maze, contents included. Worth more than the whole town, to some men's way of thinking.

But Crit would have given the gray to Strat gladly if Strat would only renounce the ghost horse and the vampire woman who'd conjured it for him…

"*Psst,*" said a voice from behind him.

Crit refused to flinch or jump or betray the heart-stopping urgency within him that counseled a dive for cover, a drawn sword.

He turned slowly and said, "You're late, Hawkmask."

"We aren't hawkmasks any longer," said an oddly accented voice from under a shadowing hood. "And *I* never was. We're just freelancing, we are. Just working for pay. You like mercenaries, being you was one." A languorous, professional lilt in a northern-accented voice that nevertheless had a threatening, nervous edge to it.

Crit squinted into the gloom but the only thing he saw better for his trouble was the rigging of a small fishing boat bobbing behind the stranger, much farther down the quayside than the cloaked man.

Was it his cloak or a masking spell or a trick of the light that veiled this face in gloom? The fellow was out of reach, but just barely. And familiar, but so was half of Sanctuary. Someone he'd rousted long ago, Crit's mind said, and started spinning through the years, seeking to match a face to the voice he recognized.

Crit asked, to hear the voice again, "What do you want, honest work? There isn't any, not here. Prefer my service to Jubal's? Is that what you're getting at?"

"*Yours?* You've got a service, now? *That's* how come the black man sent me to help you out?" The hooded man's words were sibilantly northern and the tension underlying his words was laced with satisfaction.

Somebody they'd once done something to, for sure. Somebody the Sacred Band hadn't treated with kid gloves. Somebody who was enjoying this more than he ought, because he feared Crit and his kind more than he'd admit.

"Got a name, friend?" Crit said easily, shifting enough that he could slide his hand onto his belt and his fingers toward his knife's hilt without being either too obvious or too surreptitious. It wasn't a threat so much as a punctuation mark.

The contact saw, and tossed his head. "Vis. Ring a bell, Commander?"

Commander. Crit still couldn't get used to it, not in Sanctuary, not in this context, not with all the term's current connotations. Did Tempus still hold Crit's affair with Kama against him so venomously that he'd sentence him to years of hard labor here with violent death at the end of it?

For Crit remembered this "Vis" now, and what he recalled didn't put him at ease. Mradhon Vis, a northerner: thief; malefactor; one-time partner-in-crime of the Nisibisi mageling, Haught. And gods knew of whom or what else. They'd beaten information out of Vis more than once, when the Stepsons were fighting the Nisibisi witch here. Straton, the Stepsons' chief interrogator, had. Crit had been in command of the intelligence unit then. They'd brought this fool up to the Shambles safe house, drawn the iron shutters, and taught him the sort of respect that turns to hatred if left untended.

There were dozens, perhaps scores, of Vises that Crit and Strat had made in Sanctuary. If Crit lived long enough, one of them was going to try to kill him. Perhaps this one. Perhaps tonight.

"Vis," he repeated, his voice low. "Right, I remember. Well, let's go, Vis. Let's see what you've got."

"My pleasure, Commander," said the mercenary with a nasty chuckle. "If you'll follow me into those shadows there, the worst is yet to come."

*

"I'm telling you," whispered Kama intently to Straton over her beer, "Zip's moving the altar stones uptown to the Street of Temples—moving them *and* what they housed. Or house. Or will house again."

Finished, she sat back, surreptitiously eyeing the other patrons of the Vulgar Unicorn. No one had heard, she was certain. Still, she'd been careful of her volume, added a drunken slur to her voice.

No one human had heard, that is…

The fiend who was tending bar late tonight had great gray ears and eyes that looked every whichway. His warty countenance was averted, but that meant nothing. In the bronze mirror behind the bar he could be watching them…

"So what?" Strat growled, truculent, right hand absently rubbing his damaged shoulder. Perhaps once the best man with weapons among the Stepsons, Strat was doubly wounded now: Ischade either couldn't, or wouldn't, heal his shoulder; and there were no Stepsons here for him to be among.

"So, we've got to stop it," she said. Her heart ached for Strat, and for them all, left here where nothing of consequence remained in the wake of her father's leave-taking. She and Strat had something in common now—something more than Critias. They must shore up the sagging bulwark of command because Tempus might be testing them. None of the others realized it, but Kama did. If her father rode into town of a morning, ready to welcome them back into the fold if only they'd put the town to rights, Kama hoped not be found wanting.

But the big Stepson was too drunk, or too deeply hurt, to understand what she meant. "Stop it? Why? So Zip's found some sort of pet demon or minor deity—some Ilsig spirit to worship. What difference does it make? The gods fare no better here than magic—or fighters."

Straton believed only in the magic of Ischade, Kama knew. He'd seen too much: too many dead reborn, too many undead abroad in the streets at night. Strat had seen his doom here in Sanctuary and embraced it: he was as much the vampire's creature as any of her slaves.

"C'mon, Straton," she insisted blearily, tugging on the Stepson's sleeve. "Come with me. I'll show you."

"You and your lovers." Strat grumbled over the screech of his stool's legs on sawdusted board. "What the frog you wanna do about it if you find him lickin' his demon's feet?"

"Ssh," Kama warned, putting her small hand to the flat of Strat's back and pushing him toward the door like a wife who'd made her nightly trip to the Unicorn to bring her drunken husband home to bed.

From behind the bar, Snapper Jo saluted her with his raffish inhuman grin, dipping his bristly chin in a gesture of respect.

Great. Homage from a fiend; friends in high places; estranged from her real friends because of that: because of Molin, who had another wife, Crit and Gayle and Randal avoided Kama like the plague. Only Straton, in similar circumstances, of all the men she'd campaigned with during the Wizard Wars, acknowledged her. And Zip…

As Strat had jibed, Zip was another of Kama's lovers. Men used their muscle and their sex for intimidation, and no one thought ill of them for it. Kama was a different sort of operator, but used what she had, however she must. Whatever worked to do the job. It stung her to the quick the way the men she'd fought beside treated her now, simply because she'd let the high priest wield his influence to help her.

If her father had had a dozen lovers, or a hundred victims of his holy raping member, no Stepsons would have blinked, no Sanctuarite would have snickered or presumed to criticize. Maybe she should strip her next bed partner at knifepoint, proving herself her father's daughter to one and all. Maybe then Crit would stop looking past her whenever they met…

Strat stumbled in the doorway, belched, and staggered down the stairs to the street. Straton's bay horse whickered, its ears pricked in its master's direction.

Kama shivered. The damned ghost horse was dead as a doornail, just didn't know it.

Strat didn't seem to know it either: the Stepson fumbled in his pouch, came up with a chunk of sugar beet, and held it out to the ghost horse on an open palm.

The velvet lips of the bay ghost horse delicately snatched the treat, and it snorted in pleasure.

Well, maybe not quite as dead as a doornail. But unnatural as hell. Unnatural as Sanctuary, a place Kama was determined to leave completely out of the history she was writing of her father's exploits. Sanctuary deserved no chronicler, as it deserved nothing more than the obliteration it was so obviously seeking.

The town had its own genius, Kama was sure, an Ilsig spirit that had finally had its fill of interlopers and was nudging the place itself toward oblivion's precipice. She wanted only to be quit of this scrofulous town before Sanctuary was razed to the ground by Rankans, gutted and left to rot by Beysibs, or torn stone from off of stone by internal strife.

A historian, Kama knew all the signs of a town dying. Sanctuary didn't lack a one: its gods were impotent; its magic had lost its power; its populace was polarized by generations of hatred; its children wanted only to destroy.

"What, Strat?" she said, startled by words undecipherable but still ringing in her ears. She looked up.

The big Stepson was already mounted, reins in his right hand, his left forearm carefully resting on one thigh. "I said, finding Zip should be easy—it's his shift, the dead of night. You want him, let's go up to the command guard-post."

Kama shook her head. "Told you: he's moving those damned stones. And the porking whatever that lives in 'em—tonight. Heard it from a reliable source."

The guard-post was safe for Strat, this time of night: Crit had the day shift; Strat's erstwhile partner spent his evenings in an old safe house in Shambles Cross that the Stepsons used to run.

“So where, Kama?” Strat’s voice was suddenly uneasy.

“Down to the river, soldier. If you can handle it—the White Foal’s banks, I mean—so close to Ischade’s.”

“Pork what I can handle, woman,” said Strat, the ale getting to his tongue. “I’ve picked up that snipe Zip by his collar more than he’s picked up your skirts. You wanted help. You’ve got it. If you’ve changed your mind, that’s fine, too. But we can’t just sit here.”

She got her horse, her neck hot though the night was chill with the bone-deep cold of a recalcitrant spring. Her fingers were numb on her slick reins; the roan she rode bucked and jittered under her. The wrong horse for this job: too skittish, too green. But the Stepsons had taken their string, leaving only what wasn’t held in common. Except, of course, for the single Trôs-bred that should have been hers, but had gone to Critias because Tempus wasn’t above that sort of insult.

It wasn’t fair, but then her father had never been.

Tempus didn’t want a daughter, didn’t care, however much Kama tried to make him. A woman wasn’t consequential, not to him. And her affair with Torchholder had made things worse, not better.

Was Tempus trying to tell her, by giving Crit the horse and forcing Crit to stay on along with her here, that if she went back with Crit, he’d forgive them both? Was Crit being singled out as an acceptable choice? Or did Tempus simply not give a pig’s fart?

The latter, most likely. She was going to try to do the same: try not to care. Try to understand and overcome the trial that was Sanctuary, the punishment of being stationed here. But because she *was* stationed here, assigned like any of Tempus’ men to onerous duty, she hadn’t had the heart to refuse the posting. That would have been playing on her blood relationship, asking special favors; admitting that she, a woman, couldn't handle hard duty like the men.

Help the garrison commander and the hierarchy restore some order here, that's your job. You're a good intelligence collector. Collect, her father had said to her, but nothing more. Nothing personal, and nothing beyond what was said in that meeting where the rear guard was singled out.

Meanwhile, Crit had stared boldly at her across the table in the safe house, knowing already whom Tempus was intending to name as commander-in-chief of Sanctuary's disparate armed forces. Knowing she'd have to come to him, serve under Crit's command.

It stank. She kicked her roan and slapped its poll and, under diverse and punitive instruction, it settled down. Jogging beside the half-drunken Straton toward the river, she wished she was anywhere else, doing anything else. Trying to keep Zip from making this sort of mistake wasn't her job, but Crit's.

Straton knew that, too, but hadn't voiced it. Critias was head of the combined militias, including the fifty grunts that made up Walegrin's regular army barracks, but Zip was an undercommander, responsible for the second and third shifts each day.

No one but Crit, or someone from the palace hierarchy, could tell Zip to leave the riverside altar undisturbed and make it stick.

Kama would die before she went to Critias and asked him to solve a problem she couldn't. Bringing Straton into it made the message she was sending the more clear: *We who love you won't be treated this way. You've snubbed us both for your precious command, now live with it. But don't expect us to bow and scrape.*

Strat had wanted the Sanctuary command billet, *should* have had it. Crit couldn't have wanted it less, so he got it. And that kept the vampire with her hidden agenda out of things, but at a personal cost only Tempus could have decreed. Only Tempus, who had no conscience, could split a Sacred Band pair as he'd split the love-match that once had been Kama and Critias.

Suddenly, Kama found her eyes blurry. She swiped impatiently at them with the back of her forearm. She couldn't afford emotion now; feelings clouded her judgment. Her anticipation of men was generally good; of Critias, it was woefully inadequate.

Of Strat, her forewarning was little better. Or maybe it was just the fact that Crit was Straton's partner, or the fact that Strat was drunk and his horse a numinous creature that caused them to take a shortcut over the White Foal Bridge and down a road leading right past Ischade's Foalside home.

*

Zip was laboring in an altered state where every night noise was new and hostile, down by the White Foal's edge where he could barely see the eerie lights from Ischade's house up the bank. He had a wheelbarrow and, at the bank's crest, a wagon. He had three of his militia guarding the wagon, but he'd per-mitted none to come down here. Not to the shrine.

No one should touch the piled stones but Zip himself, the thing he served had told him. As it had told him to bring it blood (and worse), it had decreed the time and manner of its uptown move. It wanted to live on the Street of Temples, with the gods. Zip had found it a place, an alley behind the Rankan storm god's temple, and there it swore it would be content to stay.

And he'd found it a new sacrifice, a special gift that one of his girls had brought him. This girl, Shawme, wanted a job on the Street of Lanterns and deliverance from Ratfall. In exchange for what Shawme had found on the Downwind beach, Zip was happy to oblige. The red-eyed thing that lived inside the stones would like its new gift, Zip was sure.

He hunkered down beside the knee-high pile of rocks and said, "Look here, Lord, I've got a present for you, when we're moved. But now I've got to start on the stones, by myself… if you won't let my boys help."

He waited for a reply, but only a glimpse of a burning red eye and a sound like shifting weight came to him in response.

What *was* it he served here? Most times, it didn't speak; it prompted Zip without words to do this or that. He'd get a feeling of a presence, and the gifts he brought it—pieces of human flesh, wineskins of warm blood, precious baubles—would disappear. Was it inimical only to Rankans? or to everyone? Zip wanted it to be his friend. He wanted it to be the Ilsigs' friend, guardian of the revolution, since he was bound to have one.

He wanted it to show itself, magnificent and powerful, and help bring down Zip's enemies. So far, all it had done was take the sacrifices, give him bad dreams, and let him know it wanted to move uptown.

So did they all. So did every last one of Zip's Ratfall movers, everyone trapped in the Maze and policed to wits' end. So did the twelve-year-old mothers and one-legged fathers of Zip's revolution, which he'd never wanted. He might have disavowed the struggle if Tempus hadn't tagged him. But Tempus had.

Zip didn't understand why the Rankan power players wanted Zip's help, or the PFLS on their side. The Rankans wouldn't believe that there really *wasn't* a PFLS when he tried to explain that a score of gang members with lamb's blood and paintbrushes didn't make a political movement.

But since his thieves and mendicants would receive the protection of what police Crit controlled in Sanctuary if they took the night shift, and Zip took responsibility, his entry into the power structure and polite… society… had just *happened.*

Being co-opted by the enemy wasn't what bothered Zip the most. What bothered him the most was that his bad boys and girls were doing exactly what they'd done before—extort, blackmail, roust and roughhouse, burn and plunder—and doing it now with the protection and for the benefit of the state.

None of this made any sense, until it made all the sense in the world. When Zip realized what Tempus had done to him, it had been too late. Zip was already part of the establishment: a hated enforcer; a dog with a Rankan collar; and his militia no better than any of the cannon fodder in Walegrin's demoralized army. They hadn't triumphed over the opposition, they had become it.

They were no longer the revolution. They were now the sustaining force behind the injustice that had created them and their revolution.

When he'd said as much (shouted it, actually) to Crit in fury, the cynical Stepson had flashed white teeth and said, "What's your problem? Not having fun now that you're legal? Preying on the hapless is all your type knows how to do, and this way you won't turn up handless or headless because of it. You're the talent, and we're the talent scouts. Thank your slime gods you've been discovered and put to work before you ended up greasing some slaver's wagon wheels."

That was another thing that bothered Zip: Critias seemed to know more about Zip's affairs than anybody could. "Slime gods" was an obvious reference to the Foalside altar. And as for the slavers… Zip had sold more than one soul down that river of sighs, to finance the revolution. But then it had been a matter of conscience. Now it was a gods damned state *business,* for pork's sake.

Gayle, the 3rd Commando liaison, had told Zip not to mind it, just make his list of expendables. Zip hated himself these days, as much as he hated Kama, the twit who had gotten him mixed up in all this, and her damned 3rd Commando ethos that excused the foulest misdeeds as exigencies.

'*Whatever works*' might work for the Riddler's daughter and her lot of death dealers, but it didn't work for Zip.

Especially when, if he wasn't careful, he was going to become just like them.

So here Zip had this altar, this god or whatever it was, this eater of sacrifices that never exactly said it could expiate his sins, wipe him clean, but surely must mean it. It was this thing in the altar with its red eyes that was making him believe there was some method to all his madness. It had a plan. It wanted Zip to infiltrate the Rankans and the Beysibs, to learn how to command and study the weaknesses of their joint enemies. It was a living thing in there—or at least a *real* thing (which other gods weren't, so far as Zip could tell). It had wants and needs.

It wanted flesh and it needed blood and it wanted to move uptown and it needed Zip to be the militia commander to serve it. He had to serve something. He couldn't justify what he and his little band of rebels were doing otherwise. He had to have a Cause and the red eyes in the altar, the slurping sound of fresh blood being drunk and the godlike belches afterwards—these were his Cause.

And only the river god knew what it wanted of Zip, but it *did* want him. Nobody had ever wanted him before. Then came, all at once, Kama and the Riddler and the river god and… No, Kama had come before the god, but that didn't matter.

It mattered that he got the stones uptown. With a quill he marked each stone as he lifted it from the pile into his wheelbarrow. When the barrow was full, he could almost see into the heart of the altar.

But then he had to wheel the barrow up the slope (no easy task) and when he'd done that and given the stones to his boys to load on their ass-drawn wagon, someone came out of the gloom and hailed him.

"Yo," he called back, while motioning his boys to cover the stones in the wagon. "Who comes?"

One horse, out of the gloom: a single rider. He walked toward it, hand on his belt knife, his neck aprickle, back stiff.

Finally the rider answered, "Zip, it's me."

Zip cursed under his breath. "Kama, stay there. The footing's tricky. I'll come up." He turned his head and said to his rebels, "Get down there. Load the rest of the stones. Take 'em where I told you. Careful to mark them and put them back just like they were. I'll catch up."

Truth be told, Zip knew he wouldn't. And he knew the god was going to be angry, although he didn't know what form the river god's wrath might take.

Then he thought he did: Kama was beautiful, sliding off her horse in the diffuse light of a cloud-banked moon. She always hit him that way, no matter how he told himself he didn't need the kind of trouble she represented.

And Kama was trouble, in doeskin boots and leggings, smelling like new-mown hay with trail dust in her hair. All about her person, as clear in her velvet thighs and firm breasts as in her face or her sweet breath, were the indications of her class: her speech, her bearing, the gulf that was between them and never could be bridged, no matter how Zip tried.

Notwithstanding, he tried then again, wordlessly and desperately, as if laying her on her back in the mud was somehow going to do it. But it didn't. It never had, never would.

She laughed softly and accommodated him until urgency overtook her, but it was always the high-born girl with the silky skin who was slumming, who found him exciting for all the wrong reasons, who played with him casually although touching her was probably worth Zip's life if Critias or Molin found them.

So when she said, as she quivered, her mouth to his ear, "Strat's here with me, somewhere back there. Don't panic, just be quick," all his passion threatened to ebb, then exploded while her nails ran down his back.

"Damn you," he said, rolling over and off her, the best rejection he could manage and far too late.

"Stand in line for that," she chuckled, her fingers reaching for him, trailing along him, tapping him intrusively with unspeakable truths. "It's been too long since we've done this."

He was staring up at the clouds which hid the moon like a translucent city wall. "Not long enough by half. Not when you're sleeping in with priests and commanders-in-chief. I'm a lowly watch officer, remember? I'm gettin' over you. Got something of my own now."

Like he hadn't, before. He bit his lip and almost looked away from her. But he couldn't. It was her damned body that did this to them both, every time: Riddler's daughter, enemy of the blood, twice his experience and probably twice his brains. What did he think he was doing?

Then he thought he knew what she was doing: "Zip," she said in a seductive tone he wished he'd heard long minutes earlier, "don't move that pile of stones. You don't know what you're disturbing. None of us do."

He sat bolt upright. "Now I get it. You ask nice, and Strat's along to ask nasty if I don't agree, right? Well, it's none of your business, Rankan whore."

He jerked to his feet, fumbling with his pants. He couldn't see his fingers clearly and blinked fiercely, trying to lace himself together. "Don't come around me no more, hear? Not on your father's business or because one of your boyfriends thinks I need it. I don't. And I never will. Not this way."

She was up too, calling his name. He couldn't run from her, not from a woman where some of his boys might see. He remembered the time she'd nursed him back from the grave's edge; and the way she'd started all this, kissing him when he was too weak to do the sensible thing and bolt.

She liked 'em helpless, hurt, battle-scarred and war-weary, he knew. He couldn't figure what Molin had, but power was a legendary aphrodisiac. And like her father, she spread her favors around.

He couldn't handle her. He kept wanting to treat her like a Ratfall girl: claim her, claim exclusivity with her. He had a comical vision of himself sitting at some strategy table with her, all oiled and leathered and shiny brass-plated in Ranke where her kind moved jade pieces representing armies around marble map-boards. And jammed his hands in his pockets, walking hurriedly away.

"Zip," she called, catching up, reaching out (and he couldn't seem to jerk his elbow loose from her grasp). "We need you. *I* need you. And you owe me—"

He stopped. He should have known it would come to this. "Right, we're all working together now and, anyway, one time you saved my ass so I'm yours to command? No chance, lady. These are Ilsig matters, and you aren't one. Understand? Or do I have to say it in Rankene?"

"I understand that you found some sort of talisman on the beach and that if you give it to that… thing… you've been feeding on human flesh, you might not be able to finish what you start. If you've got to move the stones, I'll make a deal with you."

Zip crossed his arms and looked down at her. At least he had that advantage: he was taller. He said; "Go on, let's hear it."

"I won't tell anyone about the altar, or what's in it, as long as no perceptible trouble comes from it, *if* you'll give me the talisman you were going to give to it."

"How do you find out this crap?" he blurted. "Is it Randal, your pet mage? You been following me? What?"

She merely gazed up at him, her eyes full of a surety and power that her little, female body shouldn't have been able to contain, let alone radiate. It was Tempus' blood in her, some more-than-human attribute, he was certain.

He said then, "No. I'm not doing anything like that. Why should I?" and turned to go back down the hill.

But Straton was there, on that freakish bay horse everybody knew about, come from nowhere, out of nothing, leaning on his saddle horn, cleaning his thumbnail with a glittering blade. There, right between Zip and the path down to the riverbank.

"Going somewhere, pud?" asked Strat.

"Strat," Kama said, "I can handle this."

"I was just leaving," Zip replied to Straton.

"No, you can't," said Strat to both of them. Then: "Zip, what she wants, you give her. What she ordered, you do. Or deal with me. Kama, there's something more important than 'piffles' going on out there. Finish with your boy toy and let's get going."

Kama winced but held out her hand steadily, saying to Zip, "Either give me the talisman, or Strat and I are going down there and crush five or six of those stones. Do you want to risk that, and what will follow if the three of us have a falling-out?"

Zip looked from the big fighter to the slight woman and saw a shared purpose there; an implacable, uncaring deadliness common among those sure that their Cause was worth serving. He had to learn to match their spirit. Until then, he'd never win against them.

He reached into his belt pouch and handed Kama the object that a girl named Shawme had found in the sea wrack. A talisman, Kama had called it. The object hardly glittered; it wasn't even gold, just bronze. "Here, take it. And take out your lust somewhere else, from now on. I don't want to mess with you no more."

Strat's raw guffaw rang out as Zip stalked away; its sound scratched blood from his soul. Zip wondered if the thing in the altar would consider the extenuating circumstances under which he'd lost its gift.

And what would happen if it did not.

*

Ischade's Foalside home was dimly lit, numinous. When they got there, Kama recognized Crit's gray horse and squeezed her eyes shut. No wonder Strat had come running to get her: Crit closeted with Ischade was naphtha too close to a torch.

"Gods, Strat, we both still love him, you know?"

"I figure," Strat agreed in an odd tone. "But he doesn't love us. Get him out of there, Kama. If I go in, it's just more trouble. *She* won't have taken kindly to him sticking his nose in where it doesn't belong."

Kama was already off her horse, handing Strat its reins. "I know. You stay mounted then: there's no use of you two getting into a brawl over this." Poised to sprint for the door, she turned back: "Strat, we have to get used to things the way my father left them, even though it hurts all of us. Crit didn't want this command. Not this way."

"That and a silver coin will still get you laid at Myrtis'."

Bitterness unanswerable. Kama sprinted for the door she'd always shunned, behind which was something she didn't want anything to do with: Ischade.

Through the gate, up the steps, and stop; hearing your own breathing, wondering what you'll do if she's hurt him, ensorcelled him, gotten her claws into him as she had gotten them into Strat and Janni and Stilcho and the rest…

Knocking with your heart pounding louder, suddenly aware that there was more than one male in there behind that forbidding door, and hoping those other voices aren't undead voices. You've only seen the undeads at a distance, and even the memory raises gooseflesh…

Ischade's door doesn't open, so much as disappear, cease to be.

"Ah, Madame Ischade, I'm here for Crit." Blurted like a fool in a voice higher than you've heard yourself use since school days.

Inky eyes deeper than any uncursed well, a pale face whose features are somehow indiscernible, and a hand cold as anything Kama could remember touching.

"Good," nodded the creature in her cowl. Behind her were colors, rioting jewel tones, but Ischade was all white and black. Black. "Come in." Black eyes, so deep you could sleep in them.

Don't fall into any trap. Don't look at her too long. "Crit?" On tiptoes. "Crit?" The swathed shape moves away. *"Critias?"*

There he is, with two men she recognizes: Vis, and a beggar with a stutter, a creature called Mor-am. *Wrong company, wrong place, wrong something going on here.*

Kama shivered and felt the jab of throwing stars nestled in her belt. She'd gotten those stars from Niko and they were poison-tipped, deadly. Yet… Could you kill anything here, in the lair of the necromant, Ischade? Would anybody killed here—or any*thing*—stay dead? Could Kama take out the beggar, the mercenary—*and* Ischade—if Crit needed that much help?

She could try, couldn't do less.

Then Crit came slowly to the door, his gait telegraphing annoyance, but nothing worse. "Good evening," he said and Kama couldn't figure where the vampire woman had disappeared to. "What brings you here, Kama?" Taciturn, emotionless, controlled.

He somehow shouldered her outside. Through a door that at first wasn't a door and then was a door, slamming shut. Crit's hands were on her shoulders, tight and hard, digging: "Fool," Crit whispered, "don't mix in this. I've got enough troubles." His lips hardly moved when he spoke; the hollows under his cheeks were too deep; his whole bearing was wrong and Kama was terrified.

"Crit, gods, whatever it is, you can't do it alone. Strat's with me. We're here to help—"

"Strat? With you? He bunks here, Kama. Sleeps here. Does whatever he does here. For her. Not for us. Go away. I'm finding someone for Torchholder. Special orders."

Kama tried to shake off his grip. It wouldn't shake. She said defiantly, "Whatever you're doing, I'm doing. Special orders."

He couldn't verify that, not without going to Randal. And Randal might lie for Kama, might say Tempus had sent a message. The touch of him made her ache and she wondered whether if, for just one night, every lover in Sanctuary could be in the right bed, things might straighten out.

Critias' usually handsome Syrese countenance had none of its gentility tonight; it was a fright mask: just shields for eyes and a slash where his mouth should be. He tucked in his chin, bent to stare into her face, then shook his head infinitesimally: "You want in? Fine. We're going uptown to the ruined blocks, to see if we can't find Tasfalen in one of the houses left standing there. That's where *she* says to look. Me, the two back-streeters she owns… and you. But no Strat."

"Crit, he… Strat—"

"Can't be trusted. Too much *her* creature, these days. Tell him to back off, out of sight till I leave. Tell him if he wants to talk to me, get rid of the undead horse as a sign of good faith. Or of returning sanity. I don't need a ghost horse—or a ghost rider, which is what he's becoming. Go on. Tell him. Then meet me at the gate."

He gave her a little push and she wished he felt so strongly about her, even if those feelings were as hard and fierce as what he felt for Strat.

Like a page in court, she ran back to Strat's horse and said, "'He says he's going uptown to find Tasfalen for Torchholder. Doesn't want you involved. We'll talk to you later. You stay with Ischade. If this goes wrong, we need someone on the outside who knows where we went and what happened. And we may need Ischade's—*your* help."

"He didn't say that."

"No, he didn't. I'm going with him, and I'm saying it."

"I'll come."

"He *did* say that, Strat: you're not to come along. Crit wants you here, just in case…" It sounded like what it was: a whitewash.

Strat's horse backed a few steps and from there she heard Straton say, "Go on, then. Ischade's warned him off, told him something. I'll find out what. You need help, you'll get it." His voice was thick.

She was glad she couldn't see Strat's face. She ran blindly to her horse, grabbed a handful of mane, vaulted onto its back, and urged the skittish roan toward the iron gate where weird flowers bloomed. In her belt, next to the poisoned stars, the talisman she'd taken from Zip seemed hot against her leathers, hot enough to make her perspire.

It was the proximity to Ischade's wards making her sweat, she told herself. Nothing to fret over. She had plenty to worry about without adding the talisman into the bargain.

*

Crit crossed one leg over his saddle's pommel and lit a smoke, staring at the building across the street.

No sign remained, not on its steps or to either side of the rubble they'd passed getting here, of the whirlwinds and firestorm of destruction that had ravaged Tasfalen's ancestral home.

This building was intact, its shutters drawn. The vampire woman had been certain of where to look, but uncertain that looking was wise.

"She said," Crit told Kama, "that Tasfalen's in there with Haught. You remember Haught."

"I remember," Kama said through clenched teeth.

Mor-am and Vis stood off to one side, ordered to accompany them by Ischade, who evidently was in charge of more than her Foalside cottage. *Damn* Tempus, for putting Crit between sorcerous rocks and political hard places. Vis had brought Crit to Mor-am, who'd grinned and brought him to Ischade with more satisfaction than Crit liked.

And the vampire had been civil. Both of them had kept Strat's name out of the conversation. "Our mutual friend" was what they called Straton, and because of that friend, Ischade was willing to tell Crit where to look.

And to warn him: "There is more, Critias, in that home than just two men in a house. Do not go inside, but merely open the doors—if you can."

This was said for Strat's sake, Crit knew, not his own. He unclenched a fist with difficulty and found he'd dug his nails into his palm, that his fingers were stiff from the clench. "She said," he told Kama, "you'd have the right key for this lock."

"Excuse me?" Kama kneed her mount closer to his: Tempus' daughter; once Crit's lover and now Torchholder's whore.

"You heard me, Kama. Got anything on you that might do the trick?"

"You're sure Ischade didn't mean that metaphorically?"

Crit knew what Kama was alluding to: Tempus and an inhuman sprite had coupled before a magically-locked door uptown, and strange things had happened.

"I don't care what the vampire meant; we're not trying anything like that. What have you got that might work?"

"Keys," said Kama with maddening common sense. "Lots of keys. To my place, the guardhouse, the Shambles safe house, Molin's—"

"Spare me the list. Let's try some." He swung one leg over his gray's withers, reaching for his crossbow as soon as his feet hit the ground. A bolt might smash the lock, even if it was a stout one.

They drop-tied their horses without a word, a sign both of them were thinking this might not be survivable. Critias cast a look at Kama, wondering how she'd managed to insinuate herself into this mission so fast, so deftly. And admitting he was glad to have someone there. He was a Sacred Bander, trained to depend on a partner. He wouldn't have tried this alone, and Vis wasn't the sort of man you could trust on your right side.

Not that Kama was any sort of man at all.

Having crossed the street, Crit looked back once because he'd heard Vis' voice: not words, just a tone.

And saw a wave of farewell so eloquently hostile and so gloating that he almost shot the mercenary there and then.

Kama read his mind; she touched his arm: "There Ischade's. They'll wait. They'll run back with word if we don't come out. We need them."

"Crap," Crit said.

"Agreed," Kama said with a ghost of her father's smile.

Then they climbed the steps and Crit put his back against the stone, crossbow ready, attempting to cover every avenue of attack while Kama tried key after key and cursed like a Nisibisi freeman.

Finally she said, "No luck. Nothing works." She slumped against the doorjamb.

They looked at each other too long, until Crit had to look away. In that lengthy silence they heard something move inside, behind the stout wood of the door.

Then they looked at each other again.

"Want to knock?" Kama said lightly.

"I don't think so," Crit replied in the same tone. "We could start digging at the wood with—"

"Wait," said Kama, simultaneously digging in her belt. "This, maybe." She held out a piece of bronze about half the length of her hand and shaped like a knobbed bar or rod.

"Never fit," he said critically, still holding his crossbow at the ready, still glancing from shadow to shadow down the quiet street. Still watching Vis and Mor-am as best he could.

"Might not need to. It washed up on the beach. I heard about it from some of my… people. This 'talisman' turned a gold coin to lead, and copper to clay, in the finder's purse."

"So?"

"So, let's see if it'll do something to that lock's metal."

"We're here." Crit shrugged, trying to ignore the implications—for the moment: Kama wasn't the finder; Kama had appropriated this talisman from someone, for her own purposes. And she'd heard about it through some informant of whom Crit was totally ignorant. Nothing was going to work right in Sanctuary unless they all started pulling together. But what he wanted to do to Kama right then wouldn't facilitate anything of the sort.

Kama shrugged too, added a sour twist of her thin lips, and bent to the door. Crit didn't dare look away to watch, but he heard her tap bronze against bronze. And curse. And tap again, and chortle.

"So?" he said when she stood up and carefully put the talisman back in her belt.

"So, do we want to be polite now that the lock's no problem?"

He took one hand away from his crossbow and, balancing the bow on his hip, felt for the lock: it was gooey.

Crit brought his fingers to his lips and smelled White Foal mud, rank with rot. He swore and told Kama to explain herself.

"I heard," she said, "it might do something like this. That's all."

"Great." He spat over his shoulder. "Next time you 'hear' of something like this, you come to me with it."

"I did."

"Beforehand," Crit said, just as there was a scuffling sound and then a dragging noise behind the door and he and Kama jumped back in unison.

The door opened like a casket's top. And there, behind it, stood something very much like Tasfalen, the popinjay noble who'd been missing so long. "Yes*sss,*" said the noble in an entirely horrible voice, a voice that seemed not to have been used for a thousand years.

Behind this manlike shape, Crit could see another: Haught.

Over those two images, he saw superimposed the glowing countenance of Ischade, a slight crease between her eyes. Ischade was shaking her head, her lips forming a word.

And that word was *"Run."* In his inner ear, he heard it again: *Run, if you value your soul.*

"Come on, Kama. Sorry to disturb you, Tasfalen," said Crit as he retreated rapidly down the stairs, Kama's arm in a death-grip and still holding the loaded crossbow one-handed. "We just needed to verify your whereabouts. Stop by the palace when you can: Molin Torchholder wants to see you."

By the time he'd finished saying all of that, Crit had dragged Kama halfway to the street and she was whispering urgently, "What's the matter with you? Lost your mind? Your nerve?"

"Finished, that's all. We're finished here. I have no reason to arrest that man. I only had to find him." His voice was shaking and Kama heard it.

He didn't look at her as they made for their horses. He couldn't stand to see scorn in her eyes. But he saw it in the eyes of Ischade's two waiting minions, and it burned like hellfire.

"What's the matter, Stepson, Tempus take your balls up-country?" Vis shouted from a safe distance as Crit mounted up.

He got off one quarrel, but his aim was half-hearted. It smashed harmlessly against the brick beside Vis' head.

And then there was Kama to deal with, slouched in her saddle, frowning.

Crit said, "We have to report this to Torchholder. I need you. Let's go."

Kama reined her horse after his, either unwilling to dispute his statement or unable.

One way or the other, he'd let the matter of the talisman go if she'd just give him a chance. How he was going to keep Kama with him tonight, Crit couldn't fathom, but he'd give it a try. Torchholder would have to make do with a written report. It was simply too damned cold in Sanctuary to sleep alone tonight.

*

The sky was beginning to lighten, turning regal above the temple tops. Zip's black sweatband was sopping although the waning night lay as chill on the Street of Temples as it had at the White Foal's edge.

Hand to the small of his back, Zip straightened up from the piled stones in the alleyway. He was alone now. He'd sent his boys scurrying with a flurry of invective when he realized what they'd done.

Or what he'd let them do. They'd touched the stones, because of Kama and Strat. Worse, they'd mismarked the stones they'd touched.

Zip had spent the rest of the night trying to sort out the mess. Now all he had to show for his labors was an empty pile of stones that wouldn't sit exactly right, wouldn't form the beehive shape they'd had down at the riverbank.

One more time, Zip put the stones he was sure of—the top three—in place. One more time they fell inward, toppled others, and tumbled in a jumble in the alley beside the Storm God of Ranke's temple.

And again, as the last stones rolled and finally came to rest, the ground beneath Zip's feet seemed to tremble.

This time he hardly noticed the earth's tremors over his own.

The river god wasn't pleased, Zip knew that much. Maybe it was gone, or hadn't ever come here; *wouldn't* come here because Zip had disobeyed its wishes by letting his boys move the stones, and botched its relocation. Zip had an awful feeling that the red-eyed thing was more than a little vexed about the disarrayed condition of its home. Worse, he wasn't sure any more whether this site was truly good enough, being not quite *on* the Street of Temples, but somewhat off the thoroughfare.

If only his boys had marked the stones properly. If only Kama and Strat hadn't interfered. If only the day would stay its coming a little while longer. Zip had been in tight spots before. Given time and calm, he could sort the matter out.

There were thirty-three stones in all. Some of them had Zip's careful marks. It couldn't be impossible to figure out which stones must comprise the bottom row.

Yet it was. He couldn't do it. He'd tried four times. And now the dawn was threatening to break. First the sky would regain its power, eating up the stars. Then royal purple would creep along the temples' walls, then gouts of red and orange flame would eat the darkness. When the celadon and rose of true dawn came, with them would come the priests and acolytes, padding toward their morning duties.

Zip would be discovered where Ilsigs feared to tread: in the hallowed reaches of a Rankan temple. Then the river god would have its revenge.

He knew it was coming. He was shaking all over, anguished; too weak to run, too tired to hide. He felt as if all his spirit was leeching away with the darkness, as if his soul was as dismantled as the home of stone he couldn't rebuild.

He squatted down beside the tumbled blocks of half-dressed limestone, nearly in tears. He wanted to make amends. He hadn't meant to let the unclean hands of his rebels desecrate the river god's temple.

He'd tried to do the right thing…

And *in extremis* (like so many men before him over thousands of years), Zip began to pray: *Lord,* he asked soundlessly, eyes closed, hands upon the stone he'd marked himself, the capstone of this puzzle he couldn't solve, *0 Lord, forgive Thy servant. Evildoing has befallen me. In my foolishness, I have sinned against Thee. Forgive Thy servant and help me to make things right. Help Thy servant to make Thy temple and I will bring the blood of a virgin under twelve, the eyes of an ox, the penis of a Rankan noble—whatever Thy desire is, just make it known to me and I will do that thing. But help me not fail in the making of Thy temple, and give me a sign that this place is acceptable to Thee. Before I get my ass hauled off to jail in the bargain,* he added, still silent, eyes yet closed.

For he'd heard a sound that stiffened him as if he were turned to stone unyielding as the blocks over which he labored:

the click of a horse's hoof against a pebble; the scrape of an iron shoe on cobble.

Holding his breath, he heard more: the swish of a long tail, the creak of leather, the jingle of harness.

Frog, I'm porked for good and all.

Obviously, he told himself, this was the river-god's wrath come upon him. He was going to open his eyes, turn around, and there would be some palace hotshot, some regular-army mover, some Beysib lady fighter, waiting to take him off to the Hall of Justice for screwing around on the grounds of the Rankan storm god's temple. Not even his commission as watch officer could save him now. Not from the penalty for profaning holy ground when that ground was holy to Rankans.

He opened his eyes and looked straight ahead, at the jumble of altar stones. Well, he'd tried. He wondered what was going to happen to the altar stones, to the river-god's home, and to the god himself—if the god was indeed inside that pile of stones. Would the river god magically get itself and its stones back to the river where it was safe? And if it couldn't, what would then befall poor Zip, who'd managed to pork up a god's life as well as his own?

He bit his lip and then, decided, turned from the waist to face his fate.

There, behind him, was a single horseman. The horse loomed in the gloom, its huge chest seeming to stare at Zip with a panther's eyes and a panther's gaping, toothsome jaws.

Zip blinked. What faced him was no creature half cat, half horse, but a warhorse wearing a panther-skin *shabraque*. And the panther who had given its skin to blanket this horse had been large, with glowing eyes, and so magnificent that its head had been not merely skinned, but stuffed so that glassy eyes stared at Zip as angrily as its living eyes might have.

The horse was the color of White Foal clay, its mane and tail and stockings black. Its bridle and reins were of woven stuff like swamp grass, and from it wafted a marshy odor. It pawed the ground, neck arched, and only then was Zip's attention drawn to the rider now dismounting.

Zip never remembered scrambling to his feet, only the swing of the rider from his saddle, the cloak as dark as the pre-dawn sky, and the feathered helm that inclined toward him as the rider said, "What have we here?"

"Uh, I'm just trying to put this back like it ought to be." Zip waved vaguely behind him, toward the altar stones tumbled there, trying to protect the unassembled shrine with his body.

The rider's helmet turned slowly. He was armored in browns: bronze or hardened leather or some combination: Zip couldn't tell. But armored in the way of well-to-do professionals: arms free and bare but for bands and wrist braces; cuirass and loin guard; greaves below his knees; and all of it fitted custom to his body. Slung at his hip was a cavalryman' s sword and equipment belt. Behind, on the saddle, Zip could see two shields, long and short, and a bow and quiver; but in the rider's hand was only a spear.

Coming toward him without another word, the man used the spear as a staff, digging the ground with its butt-spike. When this faceless apparition was nearly upon him and Zip was beginning to wonder if there really were eyes inside that frightful helmet, the armored man finally spoke again: "I see your problem."

And he walked right past Zip, whose nose was wrinkling at the salty smell of marsh emanating from him, and on toward the pile of stones.

"No, don't! Please! Nobody's supposed to touch—" Zip lunged unthinkingly toward the armored man whose horse, behind Zip, screamed and reared, hooves flailing.

Zip threw up his arms and dived to the dirt as the horse stalked upright toward him.

At the same time, the armored man turned slowly and held up his spear. The horse came down on all fours and bowed its head, snorting.

Zip scrambled to his feet. "Look, like I said, nobody's supposed to touch—"

The armored man's head swiveled toward him. "This one first." His spear pointed to a certain stone, then jabbed toward it commandingly when Zip only stared. "*This* one. Now."

Zip found his hands on the stone. And then on another, the one that the spear touched next. And another, and another. Zip labored there, under the direction of that spear, until the sky was red and gold and he held the final stone in both his hands, chest heaving.

Poised over the pile, afraid that attempting to place this last stone would tumble all the others, Zip blurted breathlessly, "You're sure?"

The helmeted head nodded once, up and down, and the spear jabbed forward commandingly.

Zip placed the stone atop all the other stones and a spark seemed to jump from the rocks. It bit his hand, crawled up his wrist. It hurt like fire.

He staggered back, squinting at the stones suddenly too bright, as if they'd ignited. He shielded his eyes from the glare. A trick of the dawn light, he told himself when he opened his eyes again and the pile was still there, neither burning nor singed, not even smudged, but squat and sturdy.

Squat! Sturdy! A rough beehive of stones, solid as the temple wall in whose shadow it rested. Success! Relief flooded

Zip. Before he knew it, he was on his knees at the low opening, peering inward, trying to see if the river god was there.

And he saw something… red and glowing, restless in its appointed dark. And reached out to touch the stones, which were cool and real and snug in place.

He pushed on one. It didn't shift. He pushed on two. They didn't budge. He chuckled and then he grinned. He put his cheek to the cool stone, knowing now that the spark that had seemed to bite him was just some phosphorescent insect and the rest had been illusion, a moment of waking dream.

Because the river god was not angry at him—it had come to abide in the temple he had built it!

Zip gave a wordless shout and then remembered the armored man. He got up from the altar, hand already outstretched to thank the stranger, but there was no one there. No man in fighter's garb. No horse in panther-skin *shabraque* with panther feet dangling from its back.

Nothing but increasing daylight in an alley where no Ilsig dared be caught, not even Zip, the third shift watch officer of Sanctuary.

"Got to go, but I'll be back, Lord," Zip muttered, giving the shrine a final pat before he fled. "I'll be back."

*

Kama's roan had bolted during the night, found some way to slip its halter and make away. "She does it all the time," Kama said to Crit, who was sure someone had gotten into the barn and stolen the mare. "There's no door that beast can't open, no knot she can't chew through. She'll be out at the Stepsons' barracks, mark my words."

This stopped all conjecture about the horse, and Kama's attempt to lighten Crit's mood. It wasn't the Stepsons' barracks any longer, not with so few Stepsons left. Nobody stayed there now. It was too lonely. The place was used for storage of gear and extra horses. These days, Crit stayed here, at the Shambles safe house. Strat stayed… wherever Strat stayed. Randal, who could have claimed the right to stay at the barracks, was sleeping in the Mageguild. And Kama herself preferred any number of beds with men in them to a solitary one full of unhappy memories.

"I'll take a string horse out there and check," she said lamely. "You've got to go to work, anyway. See you… later?"

"Tonight's fine with me," said Crit gently, and then with more fire in him: "If you want to join me over at Ischade's… I can't let this thing with her and Strat go on like this. I've got to get him out of there, away from that witch."

"Why?" Strat had been there for them, in his way. When they'd come back to the guard post to write their report he'd been waiting, full of Ischade's warnings and a more honest concern. But Crit couldn't unbend, wouldn't let Strat have an opening so that amends could be made.

"She says," Strat had offered, using the unadorned pronoun, as they always did, to represent the fearsome necromant, Ischade; "that 'there's more trouble coming out of that Tasfalen house uptown than you or yours can handle.' Leave it to me and Ischade, all right?"

Crit hadn't said a word to that at first. Just stared at Strat in that way he had, which made you want to sink into the earth right there and then. After too long a pause, he'd said what Kama had hoped he wouldn't:

"Us, is it? You and her, you mean? Or some of your soulless zombies under mutual command?" Strat had been braced for it, by then. Kama wanted to crawl under the table, pretend she didn't understand what was happening and suggest they

all go to breakfast—anything but sit there, a mute witness to the rending of a Sacred Band oath.

Strat had said only, "Crit, I signed off on your paperwork, what more do you want? You can't handle this. We won't tell anyone if you don't. Tasfalen's... *our* business. So's Haught. Keep your people away from them, that's all I'm saying." And with that, Strat had left.

There was a time Kama would have taken Crit to her bosom on this sort of rebound and felt as if she'd won something. But the comfort he needed wasn't hers, and all the acrobatics he'd put both of them through that evening so he could finally fall into an exhausted sleep didn't help what was ailing Critias.

Or didn't help enough. Still, she said, "Wait for me tonight," and left him, thinking that, if things were going from bad to worse with Strat, Crit might really need her help. He needed someone's. And Kama knew that, no matter what trouble it caused with Molin or anybody else, whatever Crit needed, she had to try to give him.

Love tends to be like that, even in Sanctuary.

*

Alone in his office, Critias pretended to work on the duty roster until his eyes started to sting. Then he gave it up, having made little progress, and began to put his papers away, thinking that he'd go down to Caravan Square and see if he could find Kama another horse.

But as he was leaving, Gayle came in, muttering that there was "some porker outside you'd better take a look at, sir—personally."

"I'm not in the mood," Crit snapped, then said: "Sorry, Gayle, it's not you. It's that damned Zip. Anybody report anything odd last night?"

The dead of night was Zip's shift, so as to whatever had happened about the stone shrine, Crit didn't expect anything like an honest report from the watch officer. Wouldn't have, even if Zip could write more than his name.

"That's what I'm saying, Commander: you'd better come have a look at this guy, blew in to the mercenaries' hostel last night, claiming all sorts of privilege. Now he's looking for Tempus." Gayle shrugged and grimaced, anticipating Crit's next question. "Didn't tell him anything, either way."

"Just where 'outside' is this fellow?"

"Down at the storm god's temple, like he owned it. Nice horse, nice gear, lots of loose change."

"Right. I'm on my way." They all knew the type—they *were* the type, before Tempus had welded them into something more usable by Empire.

Gayle was still hovering and Crit understood why: "Somebody's got to watch the shop, friend."

Gayle screwed up his face. "Porking waste, all this porked-up paper work's something any porking fool can do."

"Not when it's mine, it isn't. If Molin comes by, keep him here; tell him we're making copies and need his signature on something—anything. Try to find out what he's up to on this Tasfalen matter. And let him know that, far a as we're concerned, it's closed: we found the man in question; he's not accused of anything; there's nothing more we can do."

Gayle was nodding intently, trying to memorize all of that, as Crit left.

His gray horse was still where Crit had tethered it, Enlil be praised. If that one disappeared, then it was going to become Stepson business, and fast. But it hadn't. He rubbed its nose and it whickered softly as he mounted up and headed off into the early morning sunlight.

The worst thing about this new duty was getting accustomed to sleeping at night, working in the daytime. For Crit's money, sunlight was something you left to the cattle. In Sanctuary, like most other venues he'd worked, what was worth doing got done at night.

But command made its demands, and when he got to the storm god's temple he wished he'd commanded his mage, Randal, to come to the Street of Temples with him.

The horse that was tied in front of the temple screamed money and power from every trapping and the panther-skin *shabraque* it wore was of a style and quality Crit had never seen before.

"Where's the owner of this horse?" he demanded of the temple acolyte who'd obviously been paid to watch over it and was doing that from a distance: the *shabraque* wasn't the only part of this beast with teeth.

"In back, Commander, down that alley." The acolyte rolled its eunuch's eyes heavenward as if to say, 'Don't ask me why these warriors do what they do.'

Crit looked at the tethered warhorse, whose saddle had hung on it both a large and small shield as well as other implements of close and regimented fighting, and blew out a long, slow breath.

Crit's dues to the mercenaries' guild were still paid up. He rode, rather than walked, down the alley on the southwest side of the storm god's temple until he came to a man eating a skewer of lamb and drinking from a wineskin, leaning up against the temple wall near a pile of stones.

"Life to you," Crit said cautiously, keeping rein contact with his horse's mouth with one hand and his other on the crossbow he could shoot without disengaging from its saddle hook.

"And the rest, as follows," said the other man whose helmet, on the pile of stones, was of an ancient style from far to the west. "I'm looking for Tempus."

"You've found his first officer." Old habits died hard. "I'm holding the bag here till he returns."

Everything about this fighter screamed trouble; the fact that he was looking for the Riddler didn't mitigate that: whomever Tempus wanted for his next sortie, he'd already contacted.

"You'll do, then."

"Thanks. Do for what?"

"I'm offering my services. Tempus needs a little help here, I was told." The man was Crit's height but somewhat heavier, in his middle years, scarred enough by war and wind and sun to suggest he was mortal. His head was broad and large and resembled, more than anything else, a human version of the helmet he'd set on the piled stones. The red-brown eyes in that face held Crit's implacably, and the Stepson had the unmistakable impression that he was being judged.

"He's not here, I said."

"But the problems are, and you're short-handed, so they say up at the guild hostel."

"Who sent you?" Bluntly put. If this fighter was a mercenary, as he implied, the guild records could tell him something about the man he was looking at—if Crit needed to know any more.

A quirked smile flashed white teeth. "Your need, for certain—and the Riddler's. The storm god, if you like."

Critias hated this sort of innuendo. The man before him was of a fighting class not usually under his command; and if the newcomer was staying in Sanctuary, some accommodation between them must be made. The last thing Crit needed was a man like this working against him. And if the stranger was what he seemed—an acquaintance of Tempus—then he might represent a light at the end of Crit's personal tunnel.

The man leaning against the wall merely chewed on his stick of lamb chunks and eyed Crit and the gray horse until Critias knew he must dismount or create an enemy. When he'd done that, the newcomer threw away his stick of lamb and came toward him. When the warrior reached the pile of stones, he put one foot up on it and retrieved his helmet. "I'm known as Shepherd," he said, and held out his hand.

"I bet you are," Crit replied, grasping it. Between them was the pile of stones and, somehow, Crit didn't want to touch it. He remembered what Kama had said about Zip and the stones, but it didn't seem anywhere near as important as the man before him. "Well, Shepherd, I'm not using my war name here these days, so it's just 'Critias.'" He disengaged his hand and unconsciously wiped it against his hip.

Behind Crit, his horse snorted. Duly prompted, the Stepson said, "We've got plenty of work for the right sort of man, but what kind depends on how long you're staying. And what sort of references you can produce. More, I hope, than just evidence of a storm god's favor."

"More than the gods' favor, yes," said Shepherd, tapping his foot on the pile of stones. "Gods: can't live with 'em, can't kill 'em." He shook his head in mock disgust, to make it clear that the remark was a joke, but it seemed strange to Crit, as strange as this Shepherd come to Sanctuary in the wake of the Riddler.

Chapter 13: Ravener, Where Art Thou?

During third watch, Tempus thought he saw a movement in the moonlight on the hillside. He and Niko scrambled up the rocky slope but found nothing, so they backtracked to walk the campsite, among sleeping soldiers, searching for anything untoward.

"There, Riddler," Niko whispered and drew his short-sword, pointing with it. "By Straton's tent."

Movement: a flicker in moonlight, a curve of hip, a flash of breast. When they got there, they found nothing but Critias and Straton, snoring. Then thrice more they saw movements, scattered among the troop tents: naked and graceful, unearthly lovers in the night. Male? Female? Both? Neither?

Whenever Niko and Tempus approach, they scatter or dissolve into wisp and mist and softest night. "At least they aren't erinyes." Erinyes, hideous supernatural avengers, suckers of blood and life, are winged and clawed; they fall upon mortals and make undeads out of the unsuspecting. Niko has had his brushes with undeads…

"Maybe naiads. Maybe nothing—trick of the moonlight." Tempus grunted, craning his neck toward the hilltop spring.

"If we didn't need the water, we could block the spring, fill it with rocks…" Niko's eye-whites gleamed.

"*If* we saw naiads and *if* they're from that spring. To kill a naiad, we must destroy the spring that spawned it. How many springs have we camped by, marching here?"

They searched all night but saw no more, just shadows in the chancy light of moonset.

With the dawn, a handful of Charon's fighters woke chilled, fevered, sweating; some coughed and retched.

Tempus didn't like it.

Worse, he found that none could wake his Sacred Banders who'd slept in Thrax's cave: not Critias nor Straton nor Lysis nor Arton; not Perses nor Simias nor Dikti nor Breisis; not the two Stepsons who'd been with Niko when they'd confronted Thrax and his sphinx there. Night by night since then, naiads might have been at work…

"Of all your personal guard, only I'm still standing. What now?" Niko asked Tempus.

Stepsons who could not be roused from slumber. Naiads in the night. Fever and fatigue among the Sacred Banders newly arrived: "We stay here awhile. We'll not try to move our squadron till the sleepers wake. I won't put them in wagons; we'd need to leave weapons and supplies behind if we did. This sleep's unnatural."

Enlil, show Thyself, Ravener. Protect those who fight in Thy name. Will You let these minor powers play You foul? The Stepsons now sleeping are Your most loyal warriors, who've risked life and limb for You a hundred times.

Enlil shifted and thrummed inside him, but said no word, gave no sign—unless it was that Randal came gliding overhead soon after, back from his reconnaissance: an eagle's shadow, right to left over this unconsecrated ground.

Niko looked up: bird omina mattered to his rightman; right-to-left was the best of omens.

"Get Randal, Niko. Bring him to me. And Charon: too many of his are sick."

The new sun touched Niko's cheek. "And if Charon's ill?"

Most of Tempus' senior staff yet slumbered. "You think Charon will spread this plague? Not to me, he won't. Not to you, I'd wager. Bring him if he can walk. If he can't, bring whomever *maat* allows."

When Niko returned, he brought both Randal and Charon with him. Randal was waving his arms at Charon in animated debate; the mage dropped them to his sides when he saw Tempus. Charon's skin was waxy, his brow moist and furrowed.

About how to meet this plague and the sleeping curse, Randal and Charon disagreed: Randal wanted to try magic spells; Charon wanted to sing and play pipes and sacrifice a fresh-caught bird to Harmony, his Theban goddess.

"Let's wait," said Niko. "Not all of Charon's contingent is ill—Kouras isn't. Not all who slept in the cave are asleep today: I was in that cave; you were, Riddler. We're wide awake."

"Commander," Charon pleaded, "remove the prohibition against the flute, at least. Flutes are dear to our goddess. Harmony can heal us all, like *that,* if we but ask her fervently."

At Charon's words, Niko looked away from Tempus and down at his empty hands, unspeaking: the Theban goddess had brought him back from death. He knew her power. But it was Thebans who sang and played their hymns, the first night they were in camp. And Harmony hadn't saved all her Sacred Banders, at Chaeronea or Meridian—just some.

"My order stands, Charon," Tempus said. Not even Niko argued, whatever he felt: Tempus' rightman hated sorcery and loved the Theban goddess, but wouldn't ask him to favor one course of action above another with so much at stake. "No singing, no pipes or flutes."

"Charon," Randal chided, "you can play flutes all day long but flutes won't wake Critias and Straton and the rest. My way is best. I'll need to start right now…"

Round and round they went and, in the end, Tempus allowed Randal to work his sorcery and Charon to convene his Thebans and pray to Harmony for aid, but with no hymns going up to heaven.

All day, Charon and Randal labored but naught availed them, not the prayers of Charon's fevered flock nor Randal's incantations among the tents of Tempus' personal guard.

When the afternoon sun began looking toward its bed Tempus got Niko and together they found the mage, scratching signs upon Crit and Straton's tent-flaps.

"Randal, we sent you to learn who approaches with so many cavalry. Now who is it?" Niko said.

"What?" Randal wipes his nose on his wrist and rises, a pot of bird blood and a quill in his left hand. "Oh, I forgot, with all this turmoil… It's Sync headed here, as the Riddler thought: the last forty-eight of ours, plus their wagons and their horses. Some wounded men yet in wagons; some horses ponied behind: that's why they're going slow, I'd say; they're bringing those still recovering from the dream lord's war."

"Why didn't you report this right away? If it hadn't been them, we'd be in greater trouble now and should have been preparing."

"If it weren't them, I would have. I've been a little busy. You collared me to attend to this new crisis as soon as I became a man once more. Don't upbraid me, Stealth… You or the Riddler could have asked before…"

"Leave it, Niko," Tempus says. "We know who's coming; that's enough."

In former times, Enlil, You'd tell me what I needed to know. Why not today?

Still no answer from the storm god, just a soughing in his ears. So was there something here that intimidated even gods? Some deep, ancient belligerence, freed by the war's disturbance of a more fundamental order? Some revolt beyond place and time, where Meridian once held sway?

Here and now, he had Nikodemos beside him, his Trôs horse between his legs, and nearly a hundred fighters pledged to him: the core of his Sacred Band of Stepsons—better than any force ever under his command. And Lemuria awaited… if he could only get them safely there.

He'd chosen to journey north first by cloud and then by land (rather than by his sister's mystic power) to bond his force and weigh the instabilities filling the vacuum left by the Great War. With none ruling in Meridian, the realm of dreams, a new imbalance could become profound. Or so his sister Cime said.

"Niko, let's ride out, meet Sync's unit. There's nothing here for us to do." *Before the sun sets. Before the naiads creep…*

So they rode southwest. Astride his Trôs, with Niko on his right, he felt better, away from sleeping Stepsons and sweating Thebans and the distress among his tents that could not be bested with spear or sword.

The moon was high, and bright enough to ride by, when Niko said, "Commander, Straton asked his necromant about you and she told him: 'Vies with gods, he does. Your commander reaches for yonder stars and gods do eye him.' Is that what we're doing: reaching too high? Vying with gods?" Niko's voice came from deep in his chest. "Are the gods humbling us? Making Critias and Straton and the rest pay for our pride?"

This one was like no other, had always been, even before a goddess touched him. "You think we're prideful, Niko?

Compared to overweening gods? 'Gods have intentions,' as Thrax's oracle said. So do we. You've billeted in Lemuria, walked Meridian's streets: is heaven any closer or farther than it has ever been? Now you're listening to sphinxes and witches? Better, listen to your *maat.*"

Niko's goddess-given black stud shied at a furry carcass in their path, bumping the Trôs and jamming Niko's left knee against Tempus' right. The two stallions fussed and squealed, then steadied. "I think I'm where I should be—on your right, Riddler, for as long as you'll have me. With the Band, wherever you lead us. And my *maat* agrees."

But Niko didn't say whether Harmony agreed. "And your goddess?"

"Keeps her silence here."

"As does Enlil. So this place may be godforsaken. We'll forsake it ourselves, soon enough, now this last unit's come."

When they found Sync, dark and lanky on a big blue roan, at the head of forty-eight fighters riding four abreast through the moonlight, Niko hailed the 3rd Commando veteran.

Sync's wolf call answered; then the task force leader rode up:

"Commander, herewith, I return your Band to you as I received them." Sync spoke the ancient formula used when some are dead and wounded. "Riddler, Stealth, life to you and everlasting glory. All be well with you, and with your fighters."

Not well enough. Ravener, where art Thou? Or does it matter if You are here? Tempus had gone without gods and against gods and survived each time, his strength and speed and curse blending into some infernal mandate of their own.

As Sync and Niko traded questions and reports, Tempus rode down the line alone to find Cassander, sometime *hippiatros*—horse doctor; sometime *iatros*—doctor of men.

When he came to the shuttered medical wagon, Cassander was riding ahead of it. The Band's wide-eyed healer met his gaze and squared his bristly jaw as Tempus described the problems in the camp.

"Commander, were your horse long in the lowlands? Were Charon's? Did you ford rivers, streams? Sleep where the bugs were thick? I can treat fevers and chills if the cause is simply illness, not curses or spells. I have sweet wormwood tincture with me, and some bark that's worked before. As for the slumberers, I'll need to see them to give you an opinion. From what you say, I can't tell what's wrong."

Cassander halted his horse until his shuttered wagon came abreast, then leaned toward it, giving terse orders in Koine Greek to someone inside. The wagon creaked on its axles as if a person moved suddenly within. Cassander saw Tempus' face and said, "My assistant will prepare a compound as we travel."

"Good," he told the healer. This Sacred Bander had lost his elder partner in battle; if he'd found someone to help him, well and good. "When we reach the camp, examine the sick and sleeping, then come straight to me. Ten fighters in a slumber from which they will not wake, and a fever loose in camp: you'll be much in demand."

Then he loped his horse back up the line to rejoin Sync and Niko.

Late that night, when the last tent had been pitched and all fires were lit, too many were missing, too many voices silent. Cassander was busy with the ill and sleeping but Sync was there, with all his fighters, who'd bravely come to sit with the others and eat and talk, pretending all was well.

Niko and Tempus were mounted yet, waiting by the fire for Cassander to finish looking at his patients, when Randal said to the assembled soldiers (passing wineskins and greeting one another and whispering among themselves):

"We've been telling stories of the Band's history every night. For those of you who've just arrived, tonight you're in luck. This bit of Band history will show you magic in a different light. You'll learn how I came to possess the dart-tube which the commander used to help us win the Battle of Meridian…"

While Randal began his tale, Cassander appeared by Tempus' horse, his hair clubbed back, his demeanor grave, drying his hands on clean linen. "Commander, for the fevered and the retching, we'll use the woodworm formula; I've treated that malady before. We'll start tonight. As for the sleepers… I'll tell you in the morning. If you agree, my assistant and I have a remedy to try at sunrise."

"Try anything you think will wake them," Tempus said to Cassander. Critias, Straton, so many Stepsons… too many sleeping as if they'd never wake.

Above, a wet wind began to howl. Black clouds scudded in, blotting out the stars, assaulting the moon. And from one side of heaven to the other, lightning flashed and clashed while, in the far distance, thunder rumbled.

And Randal, after one look at the darkening sky, kept on with his tale from long ago and far away…

Chapter 14: Red Light, Love Light

Sunset gilded Sanctuary's domes and spires as Shawme, the new girl at Myrtis' Aphrodisia House, sat upright in her backroom bed. Fists clenched, she took deep breaths, shaking off her bad dream.

Her blue eyes wide, she stared hungrily out the window, at the sundown to which she woke, at the window frame itself, at the whitewashed walls of her little room. This room was plain by Aphrodisia House standards, but not by Shawme's. The room had a real window with glass panes; it had a feather bed and clean sheets; it had a writing desk-cum-dressing table on which were such luxuries as pots of body paint and makeup, kohl and powdered cowrie shell, even a hair brush made from boar bristles, and a bone comb; it had a closet with clothes in it—clean clothes, free from holes, dresses of fine sheer silk and even a coat to keep out the spring chill.

This was a room of unimaginable luxury, high above the street, not like the room in the dream from which Shawme had awakened to flee. In the dream, she'd been back in her old Ratfall burrow, shared with five other orphans, fighting over the raw and bony thigh of a dead cat they'd found in the street. In that dream, the other girls had teased her that all of *this* was a dream. They'd been sure there was no room for her in the

Aphrodisia House, no job among the perfumed women of the evening, no marvelous future unrolling day by day.

In the dream, Shawme had been back in Ratfall where no one had a future and no one had a past, not a chance or a hope. Except Zip. And Zip didn't pay any mind to the youngsters. You couldn't matter to Zip until you weren't a child anymore …until the PFLS found a use for you.

Shawme unballed her clenched fists and rubbed her eyes with her hands. As the dream's terror fled, joy filled her and crested into exultation. She was really here! She'd made it out of Ratfall!

So all of this was true and real: the down coverlet she pulled up against her naked shoulders; the lavender-scented oil lamp ready to light by her bed as night came on; the beautiful sunset—because even in Sanctuary, the night could be beautiful when you were safe within the walls of a fine house instead of lurking cold and vulnerable on the streets.

And all this was real because of Zip. Zip had noticed her, all right, when she'd come to him with the treasures she'd found on the Downwind beach. Zip had looked at her with focused eyes for the first time and Shawme's heart had skipped a beat. You couldn't do any better than Zip. Zip was the fantasy lover of all the young girls in Ratfall and half of Downwind. Zip's power could shield you. Zip's connections could get you anything—even *out.*

In front of Zip, Shawme had bitten her lip and pretended she wasn't about to swoon. For her plan to work, she must act like a grown up and impress the PFLS leader. The PFLS (Popular Front for the Liberation of Sanctuary, called 'pifles' on the streets) was working with uptowners now: Zip's connections were legend in the shanty towns. She'd smiled bravely and said, "I found something—things you'd want. I'll give them, for a price."

And he'd let her show him, let her tell him, what she'd found: a bronze rod that turned noble metal to dross; an amulet of uncertain value; a rusted knife whose edge could be coaxed to life. There'd been one other thing she hadn't shown him, but that was her secret still.

And the PFLS leader had seemed to be impressed, and said, "What's your name, girl, and what do you want for these?"

Shawme had replied, as cool as if she dealt with handsome rebel leaders every day, "I want out of Ratfall. I want a room in the Aphrodisia House. I want to be one of Lady Myrtis' girls and meet a noble lord and marry well." Her chin was high, to show she knew the ways of the world and the implications of what she was saying. While she spoke, she ran spread hands down her bodice and over her hips as she'd seen a whore do once, when she was uptown in the Maze where men could afford to buy a woman's favors and women sold themselves for money rather than having to give themselves for survival.

Zip's eyes had narrowed, his mouth had twitched. He'd stroked his stubbled chin and gazed ruminatively at the treasures she'd found. Then finally he looked up from under his black sweatband and said, "That's what you want, I'll see what I can do. But leave these with me, or somebody might take them from you and you'll have nothing to trade but what you started with."

She'd been suddenly uncomfortable under his stare, a different expression than he'd had before. It seemed to go right through her clothes and she thought, terrified for an instant so that she'd begun to shake, that he would ask her to demonstrate her expertise, such charms as could qualify a girl for Myrtis', the finest house in all of Sanctuary's red-light district.

If he had asked, all chance of Shawme's escape to luxury and bright tomorrows would have been dashed upon the spot, for Shawme had no idea what a man like Zip would want from a woman, let alone a professional woman.

In point of fact, Shawme had no idea what to do with men, except run from them and throw whatever you could at them if they got too close. If you didn't do that and they grabbed you, the next thing you knew you were battered, bleeding and pregnant.

But it wasn't that way for the uptown women of the Aphrodisia House, and ever since she'd found that out, Shawme had wanted to go there.

So when Zip's voice deepened, she was terrified. If he found out she knew nothing about the job she'd demanded in exchange for the treasures she had, he'd never help her. And if she ever was to let Zip do what men did to women, she'd need to know what she was doing. Or else he'd laugh.

Men always laughed at virgins.

Shawme's virginity was still a problem now, after a week at Myrtis'. She'd meant to tell Myrtis, when the time was right. But the time had never been right. Zip had gotten her the interview, and sent her uptown with an escort. She hadn't returned to Ratfall, not for the whole two weeks since then.

She'd been taught to bathe herself, to deal with her moon flow, to make herself soft and beautiful, to keep from getting pregnant. But she'd been taught nothing of how to rid herself of the awful curse of virginity.

Or of how to please a man.

All the other girls—older girls, poised girls, wise girls with gold rings in their ears and gemstones in their noses—assumed she knew her trade. They were arch and competitive, and their gossip had teeth. If they found out, she'd be driven from here, back down to Ratfall. As she'd been in her dream.

But no one had found out, and Shawme was going to go downstairs this evening, for the first time. Tonight, she would be among those in the great salon, posturing and fanning themselves, luring men upstairs.

Tonight, Shawme would become the woman she was pretending to be.

She'd lied about her age, said she was eighteen, when she was years younger. But no one had noticed. All the other girls were too busy counting conquests. W*ho* came to see you mattered most here: who came more than once, who became your regular, who your regular knew and what kind of gifts he brought you. It was a different world.

And she was on its threshold. Her heart calmed, she stretched in her bed, watching the sunset slink into dusk, the colors no more beautiful than the garments worn by the girls downstairs.

Myrtis had given her the smallest room, the plainest clothes, the lowest percentage, but only because Shawme was the 'new' girl.

"Except for Zip, you wouldn't have this bed at all," Myrtis had told her, not unkindly. "We've got a waiting list of girls that's long enough to stretch to the White Foal Bridge. You'll have to make your way here, make friends, develop regulars. Then you'll have your own money, and we'll settle up what I've advanced you against a piece of your gross."

Shawme hadn't even known what a "piece of your gross" was, until she'd gotten up yesterday early and snuck out of the house to meet Merricat at Promise Park.

Merricat was Shawme's only uptown friend, a girl apprenticing at the Mageguild because of her shadowy, powerful aunt up north. The two girls had met on the beach one day, and been fast friends ever since.

When they'd first met, Merricat had been crying as she beachcombed, and Shawme had drawn her knife, ready to protect the other girl if she could. Merricat's tears, it turned out, were tears of unrequited love for Randal, the powerful mage who served the Stepsons.

So they'd had something in common, both girls unnoticed by the men of their dreams. Merricat had confided all about Randal, and Shawme had told of her hopeless love for Zip.

Then together they'd concocted this scheme, that was supposed to make Zip notice Shawme, come to the Aphrodisia House someday and sweep her off her feet. "After," Merricat had said wisely, with a nod of her prim little chin, "you have mastered the womanly arts better than anyone else. To make Randal love *me, I* must become a wondrous adept."

Merricat had given Shawme a charm to veil virginity yesterday. "I've ensorcelled this mandrake, but I'm not very good at all this—yet," Merri had cautioned her with a frown. "So be careful." Merricat was shorter, rounder, and fairer than Shawme, with a plump face and button eyes and all the softness of good breeding. Yesterday when they met, Merricat had had her peregrine, Dika, with her, the gift her aunt had sent to qualify Merricat for Mageguild apprenticeship in the first place.

"I trust you, Merri!" Shawme had replied, rubbing her tanned arms because suddenly she didn't.

"Trust Dika, it's his doing. Lightning and thunder, I hope it works." Merricat was suddenly solemn. She leaned forward on the park bench: "And you'll tell me, promise. What it's like. Who it is… everything. Or I'll curse you. You wouldn't want that."

As long as Dika didn't curse her too, it probably wouldn't hurt worse than growing up in Ratfall, Shawme thought. Out loud she said, "Of course, as soon as… *it*… happens, I'll put my oil lamp on my window's ledge. But won't you know, by magical means?"

Merricat lived in constant fear of being found wanting, of failing in her apprenticeship. "I *should* know," she said, her full lower lip beginning to tremble, "but I probably won't. I'm not good enough, Shawme," she said, a whine edging her tone. "I'll never—"

"Shush, bitch," said Shawme sharply, and then regretted the gutter talk up here where words meant different things. Shawme took Merricat's fine, soft hand and squeezed it hard before letting go. "You're better than you think. Dika knows it. He's not flying away."

Merricat reached up, onto her shoulder to stroke the peregrine who perched there. The bird cocked its head at Shawme and opened and closed its beak once, as if in agreement.

"He's right, Merricat. Must go before I miss breakfast."

"And I miss bed check. Good luck with Zip."

"Good luck with Randal."

So the two friends had parted, Shawme armed with a root of dried mandrake on a thong that was supposed to keep her secret safe from discovery.

Keep it safe, tonight. Tonight she would lie abed with her first man. She rubbed her tawny arms, stroking the fine sun-paled hair on them. She hoped he would be beautiful, bold and not too old. She wanted him to be just like Zip, with a full head of hair and a lithe young body, with high cheekbones and the fire of revolution in his dark eyes...

But he could as easily be a fat, greasy-lipped merchant from the Street of Weavers, or a smelly drover from Caravan Square. If she'd had a god, Shawme could have prayed for a beautiful lover. But there were no gods left in the part of Rat-fall that had spawned Shawme from the chance meeting of an Ilsig matron and a soldier who, from Shawme's blue eyes, was probably Rankan.

No gods to pray to, but prayers aplenty. Shawme closed her eyes and chanted: "Red light, love light, first light I see tonight. Wish I may, wish I might, have the boy I love tonight."

Quick as a spooked cat, she opened her eyes and there, out the window, she saw the first lights flare along the town's skyline. Against the torpid blue of early evening, they seemed like an omen: Zip would come, she was sure of it. Come to make sure that Shawme had a customer on her first night in Myrtis' parlor. Come to make a woman of her.

Sliding out from under her coverlet, she clutched the mandrake root around her neck on its thong. Thanks be to Merricat's magic; everything would be all right… *if* she could just decide whether to wear her blue dress, or her red one.

For a girl who'd never before owned even one dress, but only cast-off shirts and skirts, beggar's rags, choosing between two new and filmy dresses with low cut bodices and gilded laces was no small challenge. When she'd donned the blue one and was gliding down the stairs of Aphrodisia House, male laughter was already rising over the raucous strains of music from the ground floor salon.

Tucked beneath that dress, tightly bound with a scarf to her thigh, was the other thing she'd found on the beach that night, the weapon she hadn't shown to Zip, the weird artifact from the sea that Merricat had squinted at, glowered over, and told Shawme to keep very close, very secret.

*

The guard was changing in Sanctuary, and nowhere were the winds of chaos more keenly felt than in the Mageguild.

Even Merricat, who hadn't been an apprentice very long before pillars of fire uptown had signaled the coming of the 'New Era,' knew that. Merri could see it in the faces of the adepts, in the hunched shoulders of the handsome, mysterious and nameless First Hazard.

She could feel it in her classroom sessions when a real mage was teaching, as Randal was this evening. Usually, when Randal taught the gathered apprentices, Merricat found herself daydreaming. She'd watch Randal's freckled face and envision it gazing fondly on her in some secluded bower to which he'd whisked her for private lessons. She'd stare at his prodigious ears and taste what it would be like to nibble them. She'd meditate on the strong arms of the warrior-mage in his adept's robes and wonder what it would be like to feel them around her.

But not tonight. Tonight even Randal—who always made Merricat feel calm and safe and from being exposed as an untalented imposter among the students—even Randal seemed tense and wan.

The lesson was in progress, though, and Merricat tried hard to concentrate.

"...go to your trances, and then we'll start adventuring up among the planes. On each plane we visit, you'll have time to look around, meet denizens. When you meet a denizen, be sure to remember its name. The eventual object of this lesson," Randal said in a commanding voice that forced Merricat's attention away from daydreams, away from schemes to get Randal alone on pretext of discussing Shawme's plight, away from everything else...

"...the object is, eventually, to reach the twelfth plane, where you will encounter a spirit guide, a connection to help you negotiate among netherworld powers. This is magic of the most potent sort, magic of the kind that will stay with you life-long and determine even your afterlife. It has nothing to do with mundane spells failing, with irate harridans complaining about inefficacious love potions—"

The score of students tittered.

Randal continued: "This is profound business. Some of you will make this journey slowly, in stages. Some will only partly complete it during this term. But to be truly an adept, you must in your lifetime journey to the twelfth plane, conquer all that stands in your way to do so, and there meet your guide face to face. Your guide is your representative where feet cannot tread. This guide is privy to knowledge you otherwise cannot tap, to power you'll never wield on your own."

A hush fell over the students. Randal's voice had deepened even further. In his fighter's tunic and dark pants, he was the picture of a field mage, so much more suited to giving this lesson than some soft adept in a festooned robe of power. When Randal leaned forward, his neck outthrust, his eyes raking their ranks, no one even shifted in surprise at the words he spoke next:

"Class," Randal said in a suddenly softened voice that signaled his most intense concern for their welfare. "This is a lesson not without its dangers. Afterwards, there will be no teasing among you, no bravado from those who proceed faster toward those who go slowly. All of you are about to risk your sanity and mortal persons among the planes. Go cautiously, go with determination, and go with my blessing." The warrior-mage straightened up.

A murmur ran through the students.

When it subsided, Randal said, "And now, if you'll all put your feet flat on the floor, hands flat on your thighs, I'm going to guide your trances."

As Randal intoned the relaxation litany, Merricat let his voice be her beacon. When he instructed her right hand to rise of its own accord from her lap and hover before her face, it seemed that her hand was indeed weightless. And when he told her to open her eyes and behold the manna of her person, she was unsurprised to see a green nimbus surrounding her fingers, to see the bones beneath the skin, and to see blue lightning spurting from her fingertips.

When she was instructed to close her eyes again, they closed without her volition. When she was told that her hand would now fall to her thigh and, when it did, she would open her eyes and see the first plane around her, she was not afraid.

Until her hand hit her thigh. Then Merricat was plunged into vertigo. If she could, she would have grabbed onto her chair. But she could not. Her body was under Randal's control, not her own. When the snap of his fingers caused her eyes to open, she beheld a landscape wind-whipped and strange, stretching forever in all directions, where hills had crests like frozen waves and trees were perfect spheres. Beneath those trees were others and she knew (without knowing how she knew) that some of those others were her fellow students.

She knew because she was under one such tree and beside her were creatures part human, part not. One creature came toward her in wide strides, staring at her through one burning round eye, cocking the head of a falcon and saying through the beak of a bird: "Welcome, Merricat, to the first plane. What is it you seek here?"

"Knowledge," said Merricat as she'd been coached in Randal's lesson. "Friends. Powers of mind."

The beak of the bird grew large and from it came the words, "There are no friends for you on the first plane, as there are no friends for you at Aphrodisia House. You must seek higher. Here, as there, you will find only tools."

"Give me one, then," she heard her own voice say, and was appalled at her temerity.

The bird head nodded and the bird beak came close.

She wanted to shy away from the sharp beak but she could not. Her palm extended and the beak neared the soft offering of her flesh. Then into her palm it dropped an insect, like a wasp. The insect tickled her palm and on her flesh, with many legs, it danced. And as it danced, a wasp's nest came into being and into it the wasp soon crawled.

Then Merricat's hand became very heavy and the next thing she knew, it had fallen to her lap, for Randal's voice was saying "…at the count of three, your spirit will return to your body and your eyes will open and you will be in your seat among your fellow students."

It was as if the adept spoke only to her. She listened only to his voice as dizziness again overcame her. She was flying through clouds of many colors, among ancient seas, and farther.

When she found her body, she felt absolutely sucked into it and her spirit came to rest in its prison with a thud that was her hand hitting her thigh.

Her eyes opened. She blinked. The students around her were all pale-faced, white-lipped, and silent. No one looked at anyone else. Merricat looked at her hand on her thigh.

In the palm of her hand was a red blotch about the diameter of the small wasp's nest. The hair rose all over her body. Surely this must mean something, or else she'd done it all wrong… What connection could the first plane have to Shawme's plight and the thing she'd told her friend to keep secret?

She was shaking, trembling all over. Her skin was blotchy, red and fishy white.

She didn't hear the rest of the lesson, she heard only Randal's voice, the sole comfort in her universe, which now was no comfort at all. She must tell the adept what she'd done, how she'd failed, and find out what the omen meant. She must.

When the class filed out, her throat constricted: what if Randal left before the last of the students were gone? She couldn't chase him down the halls, or sortie to his private chamber where real magic was always under way. She just couldn't.

Right now Randal was surrounded by other questioners, excited voices asking about what they'd seen on the first plane. Merricat waited until all but two of them were gone and then walked slowly up the row toward the front of the study hall.

As she approached, she felt the mage's eyes on her. And met them to see concern there, and recognition.

For what she was sure was the first time, Randal had noticed her—not simply because she was giving a dinner menu to the First Hazard and he happened to be in the room, either. But noticed her with his whole attention.

If she hadn't been so frightened, she'd have blushed red as a beet. As it was, her gait stiffened and her steps slowed.

Then Merricat stopped. She held back, watching, miserable. She didn't have the courage to walk brassily up to the mage, who was pestered with unending questions from other students. No matter the meaning of the wasp omen, she'd go to Shawme by herself. They'd figure it out together. She couldn't, just couldn't, bother Randal with her insignificant problems, not when the whole Mageguild was reeling from the magical recession taking place in Sanctuary; not while teaching a new generation must seem so futile…

Randal winked at her.

Her hand flew to her mouth. She must have imagined it. Two students were much closer than she, prattling away. She clutched her slate, on which she'd scratched not a single note tonight, to her bosom.

He winked again, and she heard him say to the two fawning apprentices, "You two compare experiences; it will do you both good. Right now, I have an appointment with this young lady, whom I can't keep waiting any longer. Go practice first-plane access. Tomorrow we do the second plane. Go on, now."

Both students looked over their shoulders at her with resentful, jealous eyes that widened visibly when they saw what "young lady" Randal meant. She glimpsed surprise and a new respect and something nastier in their backward glances as they left, whispering together.

With their departure, she and Randal were alone. She drew back a step. He didn't follow but stood unmoving, hands hooked in his fighter's belt, a slow smile spreading on his freckled face.

He was so bold, so handsome, so brave. He was the Stepsons' chosen mage, a fighting magician who'd battled in the Wizard Wars. He was the most romantic single figure in the beleaguered Sanctuary Mageguild and Merricat wished miserably that she could disappear, sink through the floorboards, and be gone.

What did he care of her troubles, her doubts, her questions? She wished Dika was here, a comforting weight on her shoulder. Sometimes Dika seemed to speak for her, lend her courage. But not tonight. Falcons weren't welcome in Mageguild study halls.

Neither was she. It was obvious that the keen eyes of Randal were reading her soul. She trembled, went up on tiptoes, and eyed the doors through which the others had gone. Still time to run.

"Well, Merricat, how was your trip to the first plane?" said Randal gently as at last he came toward her.

He knew her name! She could hardly believe it. She said hastily, "Well, it's fine, there was a blird who spook weirds to me, and round trees." Damned and tongue-tied, she wanted to die. She closed her eyes…

…and heard Randal's voice so close she nearly fainted, saying, "I saw something or other of that, I must admit. Would you like to talk about it over a drink?" and felt the mage touch her arm lightly, oh so lightly.

Saw something? What a mage he was! Talk about it over a drink? She took deep breaths and opened her eyes and said fervently, "Oh yes you, bless!" Mortified, Merri put her hand to her mouth again. If she could just calm down, her words wouldn't get scrambled. *Blird who spooked weirds.* She cringed inwardly.

The mage's fingers covered hers and drew her hand away from her lips. Then he was examining her palm, where the wasp-nest's mark still could be seen. When he looked up, his brow was furrowed. "What's here means more to me than you'd understand. It would be a favor if you'd share your experience with me, and anything else that might be relevant that's happened to you lately. Wasps and I have a… special understanding."

The hand that wasn't holding Merricat's went to his waist, where a wavy sword, short and foreign-looking, hung in a tooled scabbard.

Miserably, afraid to trust her traitorous voice, Merricat nodded. How to tell him about it all? About the wasp on the first plane, and the weapon her friend Shawme had found—that silver tube that shot tiny wasp-like pieces of metal when you blew through it: the weapon Merricat was certain that Dika had wanted Shawme to keep?

In fact, how to tell Randal anything at all, with her tongue tied in knots and her heart pounding? How indeed, while she was sure to the very depths of her soul that she'd done something wrong in helping Shawme, and in coming to the Mageguild, and in falling hopelessly in love with the famed and fearsome mage Randal in the first place?

*

Shawme was trembling uncontrollably and afraid someone would notice her, making herself small in a corner among the other girls in Myrtis' salon. And someone had. One of the musicians, a percussionist who pounded drums and shook bells and crashed cymbals, kept watching her as he played.

The attention of the musician made things worse. As did every man who came ducking in through Myrtis' beaded curtains; who stalked around the room, drink and smoke in hand, and touched this girl or that before making up his mind and escorting his chosen up the backstairs to some girl's room.

Worse, because none of them so much as ogled Shawme: she might as well have stayed upstairs. Worse too, because if a man did approach her, she was sure she'd break and run—unless, of course, that man was Zip.

After a while she closed her eyes, secure in her corner with stout red frescoed walls against her back, certain she'd get through this whole night unnoticed. As much trouble as that might cause with Myrtis, she knew she could handle that. Other girls must have failed to make conquests on their first night here. Most of those who'd gone upstairs already did so with men they obviously knew quite well, men who took them boldly in strong arms and crushed silken bodies against armored chests with no preamble.

Shawme didn't know anyone like those soldiers, anymore than she knew the sort of brocaded nobles who came in groups of twos and threes, smelling of perfume like the women, and gathered up giggling ladies by the armload.

The only man who noticed her was the musician, a youngster with barely a beard and naked, sweaty arms. Her sort. From undistinguished beginnings. Eking out a living among his betters and here to please. The more he watched her, the more Shawme felt a kinship. She began wondering if, when his music was done, the youth would come toward her.

But things didn't work out that way.

She was studying the frescoes in the salon through a growing fog of smoke, finally realizing how instructive they were to an ignorant girl. On them men were portrayed doing what she'd seen dogs do in the street. And women knelt before them, doing mysterious things that involved kissing. Shawme was trying to guess at what that would be like, feeling her mouth grow dry and her heart pound as each successive man took someone else and the crowd of women thinned... Meanwhile she tried not to notice and prayed that Myrtis wouldn't come down tonight to find Shawme the only unclaimed girl, the only one who hadn't made a copper's worth of profit for the house. So she didn't notice the newcomers until the beaded curtain rattled, and then she quickly lowered her eyes.

Three laughing men had come in together, arm in arm, with a fourth behind them, taciturn. The three were military men, highly ranked since they'd been allowed to wear their weapons in here. The fourth was armed as well, and unsmiling. His glance caught hers before she looked away.

In front of Shawme's corner was a couch on which three older girls reclined, each showing thigh or bare perfumed shoulder or a hint of rosy breast. The three jolly soldiers, unmistakably a little drunk, came their way. The tallest one was blond with braids in his hair and a goblet in his hand.

He stared directly at Shawme for three heartbeats, and on the fourth her heart threatened to stop entirely. That look was a look of recognition, but she couldn't remember ever meeting such a soldier. She was sure he was coming for her.

She shrank back in the corner, trying to push her way through the frescoed walls; trying to get breath into her lungs, enough breath for flight if he held out a hand to her as she'd seen men do here.

She would run right past him, duck under his arm and fly out through the curtained doorway, into the street, back to Ratfall. She'd run and run until her heart burst.

But the blond man looked away then, at the girls on the couch between Shawme and his soldier friends, and held out a hand to one of them, who squealed, "Oh, Walegrin, you're looking fit tonight," and giggled.

In relief, Shawme squeezed her eyes shut. In that solitary darkness, her relief was eaten up by chagrin. Then came embarrassment and mortification, shame and despair. No man was going to choose her. She was going to fail. All the other girls would laugh at her.

She thought to herself, Perhaps it's the mandrake. Perhaps it's ugly. Perhaps it's working too well and keeping the men away. So she reached up behind her neck, eyes still shut, and undid the thong that held the root there.

When the thong came undone, she opened her eyes and surreptitiously pulled the mandrake from between her breasts, hiding it behind her, under the cushions of her bench against the wall.

When she straightened up, a shadow fell on her. She looked up. And up.

Standing directly in front of her was the fourth man, the one who'd come in alone.

Shawme thought wildly: He's not here for me; he's going to ask one of the girls on the couch. But all of them were gone. While she'd had her eyes shut, they'd left with the blond soldier and his friends

There was no one else in this corner, darkened by the big man's shadow, but Shawme. She craned her neck, unable to rise as a girl should, her knees like water

He seemed gigantic, all dark cloth and leather. She looked up past his weapons belt at her eye level, and could hardly see his face, just the dark shadow of new beard and a hand that came suddenly toward her.

"Young lady," his deep voice said, "what's your name?"

"Shh—Shawme," she quavered and hated herself.

His hand was waiting.

Somehow, she lifted hers. Then, with his help, she was standing

"Your room, if you please," said the voice and still she had no clear impression of his face. Her gaze was now level with his broad chest, and his eyes beat down on her with such fire in them… as only the eyes of Dika the peregrine had ever done before

Too late to run, the deed all but done, she remembered her training: "A drink, kind sir, or something stronger?" Drugs were purveyed at Myrtis': drugs to embolden, drugs to give stamina, drugs to make up for whatever needed making up for, so Myrtis had told her.

"I'm known as Shepherd, little lamb," he said and she knew from his tone that he wanted no drink nor anything at all but her.

At the last minute, while his hand inexorably drew her from the corner toward the stairs, she remembered the charm that Merricat had given her—her mandrake root, without which this man was soon going to know she was a virgin.

Anguished, she halted. Their arms stretched out between them. She hadn't the strength to pull away.

His big head turned questioningly and she saw his profile for the first time: a grown man's profile, hard and seasoned; a bold nose and lips trying not to laugh above a stubbled chin. This was a stark man, a man from whom you ran on the streets because such men took what they wanted. There was no fooling such a man as he.

"I—I forgot something, left something on the bench."

"You don't need that, not with me," he said with such authority that Shawme could do nothing but obey the pressure of his tug, which pulled her in and under the circle of his arm.

Up the stairs they went, the big man's right arm crooked around her neck, her right hand pressed against her collarbone by his grip, his fingers against her throat.

Shawme hadn't remembered the stairs being so many, or the trek to her backroom bed so long. His breath in her hair was hot and the things he said were a matter of tone, not words.

His tone said, 'You're mine, I'm in control. Relax and you'll be fine.' His words said whatever Shepherd thought she should hear, but she heard only an end to her childhood in them.

It didn't matter what his words were; it didn't matter that she took moisture from his lips to wet her own. It didn't matter that he wasn't Zip, even.

It only mattered that she not fail, that this Shepherd not be angry when her virgin blood was spilled, when her l lack of expertise was on display.

When they got to her room, Shepherd wanted no help with his leathers or his weapons. Help with his boots was something any fool could give. And then he helped her, wordless and with a strange look on a face that seemed unaccustomed to humor or kindness but displayed both in red-brown, fiery eyes… eyes so much like Dika's…

When it became clear to him that she was unworthy of the job she held, ignorant and ill-prepared, an imposter, she was sure he'd leave her, go straight to Myrtis and complain.

But this Shepherd did none of those.

He treated her like fragile glass, like the musicians below in the salon treated their instruments. And soon enough she was learning, under his hands, why the other girls went to work smiling each evening.

She learned enough so that, when the moment came for her skirts to come off, she was forgetful of everything: what he must soon find out; how disappointment and disgust would oversweep him; even of what form his wrath might take.

And then it happened: Shepherd sat back on her bed, his diaphragm with its line of dark hair quivering, and said, "Take that off." His voice was very harsh "Put it on the table. Now!"

"It?" She was breathless, her voice a fear-constricted squeak. How could she take off her virginity? How could he even see it? He'd just this moment glimpsed her unclothed form.

Then she followed the big man's pointing finger, and relief flooded her. The silver tube was what he meant: the sea-gift, the one Merricat had advised her to keep. "This?" she asked with fake aplomb. "I always wear it"

"Not with me, you don't." He rose up, off the bed, and she saw his body start to change.

Chest heaving, she blurted, "Please, don't go. I'll take it off."

Hands on hips, he waited until she did. Then he took her in his arms and, his lips against her breast, said, "The rest of it, I can handle. Just trust me, lamb."

And somehow, she whispered to him, "But I don't know… I've never… I don't have anything to offer you, no tricks, no skill—"

"You have something none of those others could offer, lamb," he replied in a rumble that made her legs weak. "Something only you can give. And for it, I'm going to give you a lesson in love as has never been taught in Sanctuary."

Suddenly she knew that Shepherd knew, somehow, and that he wasn't going to be angry, no matter if she bled all night. What she didn't know, until he tapped her on the mouth with a reddened finger, was that it didn't have to hurt to become a woman.

Any more than she'd known anything about the joys of womanhood that lay beyond her body's barrier. All of those, this Shepherd showed her before, while she dozed, he slipped away, leaving a piece of gold upon her pillow.

*

"Wake up, wake up!" said Merricat, shaking Shawme's shoulder. Behind Merricat, Randal hovered in the doorway, with Myrtis beside him. And Myrtis was wringing her veiny hands, saying, "…this is highly irregular, Mage, and the least you can do for me, since I allowed it, is make our weather-control spell your first priority."

"Later, Madame," said Randal. "Now leave us, if you please."

Shawme was rubbing her eyes and stretching widely, unaware or unconcerned that there was a man in the open doorway behind Merricat.

"Merri!" Shawme smiled with delight. "What are you doing here? Never mind, I've got so much to tell—" Then Shawme noticed Randal and stopped speaking. She pulled her coverlet up around her neck and hunched in her bed.

"Shawme, this is important," Merricat said quickly in a low voice. "That's Randal, the mage… my instructor. He wants to talk to you. About *that.*" Merricat pointed to the silver tube on the table beside Shawme's bed.

"That?" Puzzlement crossed Shawme's face. "It doesn't matter. Thank you for the mandrake, Merricat. Thank Dika. I had the most wonderful—"

Randal crossed the room in quick strides. "Pardon the intrusion, miss, but did you—?" Randal stopped and looked at Merricat imploringly.

"Shawme," Merricat demanded, leaning over the other girl stiff-armed and reaching for something glinting gold on the pillow with her other hand. "Does this mean what I think?" Merri fingered the gold coin.

"Oh, yes, and it was wonderful! I can't tell you how wonder—"

Merricat's face fell; she blinked back tears. If it hadn't happened yet, Randal had promised that he'd sponsor Shawme for Mageguild apprenticeship, to get her out of Aphrodisia House. Now… Merricat turned an imploring face to Randal. "Too late," she whispered.

"I thought it might be," said Randal, and Merricat saw Shawme's eyes dart from face to face as the others spoke. "Shawme, if you will answer my questions and cede this instrument," he ignored the coin that Merricat held, and tapped the table on which the silver tube rested, "to the Mageguild, you'll have my undying gratitude and enough money to move out of here into your own house, and favors to be claimed from Merricat and myself whenever you need them. Such favors as a mage can grant."

"What? Why? I—"

Beaming, Merricat sat back, looking fondly upon her friend, who was saved after all by the generous auspices of Randal, the most wonderful mage who ever lived.

Randal replied, "It's too long to explain. This tube washed up on the beach, I was told?" The mage stood over Shawme and began to voice his questions.

Shawme nodded and answered every one while Merricat held her friend's hand, until Randal asked, "And will you tell me who you went with, tonight? Who came up here with you, and what happened then?"

Shawme's jaw set. Her eyes seemed to go cold. She said, "You want the pea-shooter, take it. My client didn't like it anyway."

"And your client...?" Randal blushed and Merricat thrilled with love. "Did he, ah, was there blood spilled here tonight?" Randal pressed.

"What *is* this?" Shawme demanded, bolt upright now. "You told him, Merricat! How could you? It was our secret. Get out of—"

"Shawme, I had to; it's important. Did it happen, the spilling of blood?" Merricat's grip tightened on Shawme as the other girl tried to shake it off.

"Of course it did, and it was wonderful!" Shawme's anger blazed. "Now get out of here, Merricat. I'm never going to forgive you for this. My business, bitch, is with this-here mage, not the likes of you."

Merricat stood up uncertainly, head hanging. Randal put a comforting hand on her arm, a reassuring touch that told Merricat she'd done the right thing, no matter what Shawme thought.

Randal stepped forward then, saying to both girls, "Shawme, Merricat, friends in life are too few to fall out over something like this. Shawme… Merricat was brave and tireless in your behalf. Merricat, your friend needs your understanding. Blood shed in this way, right now in Sanctuary, *is* important. All of what I've promised you, Shawme, is still yours—money, favors for the asking—even if you won't answer me. But as a favor to me, we need to know if the man who gave you this coin is anyone *we* know, whether he's friendly or inimical to us."

Shawme blinked like a startled alley cat. Merricat was afraid her friend would ask Randal just who the mage meant by "we," but Shawme didn't.

She didn't say anything at all. She threw back the coverlet hiding her nakedness and vaulted from the bed. There, on the linen, was proof of the act, and of Shawme's boldness.

Merricat's friend reached languorously for her robe, head high, a proud expression on her face.

Just when Merri was beginning to think it must have been Zip who'd come to Shawme and made her a woman, the Ratfall girl said, "He calls himself the Shepherd, or something like that." Shrugging into her robe, Shawme snatched the gold coin from Merricat's fingers. "He gave me this, and more." Her eyes burned.

Merricat scrambled off Shawme's bed and backed right into Randal, her own body feeling wooden and numb. Peering into the mage's face desperately, Merri strove for comfort and found none.

Randal shook his head infinitesimally as Shawme flounced by, announcing her intention of "going back downstairs, where there's food and drink for celebration."

Left alone in the courtesan's room, Randal said only, "*Shepherd,* by the Writ." He sighed deeply. "The only good in this came from you, Merricat. And will have to come from you, henceforth. You must help your friend, even if she doesn't understand anything about why you're doing it. And you'll need all your powers, as well as my help. Are you up to it?"

Powers? Merricat had no powers, but Randal did. And Shawme needed her. The blood spilled tonight was spilled in sacrifice, a ritual shaping the future; one that Shawme hadn't understood, but was now inextricably bound up in. And in a way, it was all Merricat's doing.

She saw Randal pick up the silver tube and fondle it, then look back at her and offer his arm.

She'd done something right. "Of course I'll help Shawme. Even if I didn't want to, an apprentice always obeys the adept who is her instructor. Have no fear, honored mage. I shall do whatever you advise."

Then Merricat took Randal's proffered arm and let him escort her out of the Aphrodisia House and back to the Mage-guild, where she belonged.

Chapter15: When the Right Song is Sung

Breathe out and remember, hero of my soul,
Recall your life and sing again.
Do not wander far from me among the wispy ghosts.
Wake to joy and smell the new day on the grass,
Breathe out life and call my name.
Then like horses grazing on sweet blossoms we shall be,
And the sun will shine your glories.
How fierce you were when first we met;
The heavens did rejoice in you.
Wake to me again;
Be all you were again.
So far from me you sleep.
Breathe out and call my name,
Recall my voice.
Do not die forgetting
How I love thee.
The wind already sings your praises.
Breathe out life again,
Taste my love again.
We have so much yet to do.
Breathe out death another day.

Near dawn, lightning struck so close to Tempus and his horse, waiting among the tents, that it raised the hair on his forearms; so bright it left its image long on the eye. Blue sparks danced between the Trôs' ears, but his was a seasoned warhorse: the stallion held its ground.

The sky split wide open and rain poured down. Then stopped, as abruptly as it came. Wind raced among the tents and blew away the clouds. The sun rose bold and crimson, then gold, then lit the sky cornflower blue as Niko rode up to meet him and together they sought the healer.

Then thunderbolts struck again, this time in the middle of camp while Cassander visited the slumbering Stepsons in their tents and his young assistant, always at his heels, chanted some ancient rhyme: medicine of incantation.

Is a chant a song?

"Come back to me unbroken, unharmed," went the verse. Smooth-cheeked, slight and small with short dark hair, this quick-eyed, beautiful youth followed the healer like a dog, a sack shouldered over a Stepson's green cloak so long it nearly dragged the ground. "Breathe out thine ills; wake with ease…"

Tent by tent, the healer and his helper ducked their heads and slipped in between the flaps.

Everyone watched, but pretended they did not as the healer and his assistant went about their duties, visiting every sleeper's side, slumberer by slumberer.

What they did there was between the *iatros* and the gods.

Sync came up, stubble-faced and bleary-eyed, hands on hips, but said nothing. Charon joined Sync, then Randal. Even Kouras, who should have been busy elsewhere, skulked behind the tent where Lysis and Arton lay sleeping.

"Breathe out thine ills, wake with ease," came the chant on a sudden gust that rattled the tent-flaps behind which Straton and Critias lay.

Now gathered from the Theban contingent were men whose fevers had broken; and all who had no pressing duties joined them. The Band's progress, the fates of many, hung on this, everyone knew. Tempus wouldn't leave his Stepsons senseless, nor cart them off like casualties of war. It would end here, one way or the other.

Randal caught Niko's eye but Stealth only shook his head, staring at the tents and beyond, miles away.

"Greet the day, and feel its might," came the verse from the tent.

Then silence reigned. Within and without, no one moved; no horse so much as stamped a foot; no Sacred Bander touched a whetstone to his blade.

Quiet within the tents, quiet without, until Tempus thought his ears would pop: No wind, suddenly; not a breeze disturbed them…

Till someone called, "Where is everyone?" and Arton tottered into daylight, then steadied himself against a tent pole.

Kouras whooped.

Lysis stumbled out of the tent next, doubled over, then straightened up, knuckling his eyes: "Kouras! What's—?"

Men elbowed one another, chuckling; a murmur arose. Randal hurried off toward Arton and Lysis just as fast as Charon did. The grin on Charon's face was wider than the sky.

Stepsons drifted that way, by twos and fours, not wanting to seem too anxious, not wanting to show surprise: Of course they'd believed—known Cassander could wake the sleepers. They'd seen stranger things in the Riddler's service, seen men plucked from the grip of certain death so many times…

Still Cassander the healer and his helper stayed within the tent of Critias and Straton. Chanting from that direction was barely audible now. Down the row between the tents, Tempus saw Simias and Perses come reeling into the sunshine, the grizzled leftman's arm over young Perses' shoulders for support. Next, Breisis and Dikti burst out of their tent, whispering to one another. And the paired Stepsons who'd come south so long ago with Abarsis, part of the Slaughter Priest's original Sacred Band, staggered into the sunlight, bemused and squinting.

Fighters began to greet their brothers with soft battle cries. All the fevered Sacred Banders who could walk were collecting; others stuck their heads out, trying to see.

When all but two slumberers had awakened, Niko said, "Should we go see to them: Crit, Strat?"

"We'll wait," said Tempus. Showing favor to Critias, his executive officer, or to Straton, the Band's chief interrogator, might be expected, but he knew those two: they abhorred any sign of weakness, and falling asleep on duty was a far cry from a war wound, no matter how deadly so much sleep might become…

Just then, Cassander shouldered his way out of Crit and Straton's tent, his assistant close behind. And Critias, fully dressed, came forth next as if nothing had ever been amiss, hair combed, beard trimmed, helmet in his hand. Behind him came Straton, so big he nearly crouched as he emerged; and he was armed and armored.

Now revelry overswept the camp. Wolf-calls rang loud; men shouted and ran to slap Cassander on the back. The *iatros'* little assistant, cloak snugged close, stayed behind the healer, hands tight around his sack of medicines.

Crit came straight for Tempus and Niko; Straton paced him on his right, taking strides nearly as wide as his shoulders.

Niko would have ridden that short distance to meet them, but Tempus stayed him with a sign.

"Commander," said Critias, standing tall. "Reporting fit for duty. Both of us."

Niko urged his horse one step forward, bent down and squeezed Straton's shoulder: Strat was Niko's dearest friend among the Stepsons. Then Niko backed his horse three paces, until it was once more abreast of Tempus' Trôs.

"We'll leave that determination to Cassander, Critias." Tempus beckoned to Cassander.

The healer saw, and left the admiring crowd around him, his young helper in tow.

"Commander?" Cassander, in quilted tunic and leggings, had a cloth bound round his head and a somber air he was struggling to sustain. His assistant, a youth too pretty by half, stared at Tempus from fey gray eyes.

"Strat and Crit think they're both fit for duty. Is that so, Cassander?"

"If they say they are, then they are," replied Cassander, always careful where Critias was concerned.

"Good. I need to wave my *kerkos* over some plants that need water," said Straton, and hustled Critias off by the arm.

"And these others?"

"The sleepers should be encouraged to move around, do normal tasks, eat and drink and raise a sweat," Cassander advised. "Some will need to drink a lot; some won't."

"What about the fever-stricken?" Niko was looking at Cassander's aide.

"If what you want to know is whether we can travel tomorrow, *Hipparch,* the answer is yes. Some of these will take days to heal, but I can put the weakest in my wagons. Different people react to these fevers differently. It's in the blood."

"Well fought, Cassander," said Tempus, who had not mistaken the meaning of the chants and the timing of Cassander's work among the tents. "Go back to your patients."

Now Sync stepped up to the healer and spoke in Cassander's ear; Charon bustled to and fro among his Thebans; horses neighed for their breakfasts; and the Stepson camp began to sound and look like a warfighters' bivouac, not a funerary convocation.

On his big black horse, Niko leaned toward Tempus. Above his rightman's head, bright clouds and dark swirled and barged, pushing at one another; the sky was clear to the north and east and bursting with storm to the south and west.

"Shall we stand watch for naiads again tonight, Commander? And oracles and Thracian gods?" A hint of Niko's canny grin from younger days played over his partner's face.

"Or whatever comes to meet us," said Tempus. "Critias and Straton may have rested easy, but you and I know better. Let's get these Stepsons fit to travel. It's a long march yet to where we're going."

And so it was. As it always would be.

When they set out the next morning, riding the sun up, Tempus might have seen a lioness' tawny shape, a flash of eagle's wing, pert breasts in the dapples of the copse. But he and his partner hadn't seen a naiad all night long. So if the sun shone down on them like the shield of Ares, Tempus could forgive such a brash display of power. Local gods were jealous of their might because they had so little of it.

With his Band behind him and Nikodemos beside him and a challenge such as none he'd faced before beckoning him onward, he could not resist thanking the storm god for making this glorious day, full of wild surmise and bold endeavor and the joy of life all around him as he led his cadre north.

And if Cassander had snuck a nymph in boy's clothing among them, or if Breisis and Dikti dissolved into the mists of Meridian from which they'd come, or if naiads kept his warriors company on cold and dreary nights, what difference did that really make?

Let his fighters take comfort where they might in the evenings. For in the mornings, they must fight for life and freedom of the human spirit, as he saw fit. He and he alone defined their missions. They would brave all with clear eyes and what equanimity they could summon, as they always had. And could. And must.

And remember.

www.ingramcontent.com/pod-product-compliance
Lightning Source LLC
Chambersburg PA
CBHW030539310726
48979CB00010B/1973/J

* 9 7 8 1 9 4 8 6 0 2 5 2 5 *